To Jordan,

   Life is meant to be enjoyed.
One of the best ways to enjoy
life is to pursue your dreams
and make them happen.

              Dan Pekarek

              12-24-04

DLPekarek@aol.Com

Alcent
Adventures

DANIEL L. PEKAREK

Seattle, Washington
Portland, Oregon
Denver, Colorado
Vancouver, B.C.
Scottsdale, Arizona
Minneapolis, Minnesota

Dedication

This story is dedicated to the Waldenbooks' Stores
in which most of it was written.

Acknowledgements

Production of this book was made possible through
the efforts of the following people:

Albert Bjorgen
Storyline and Engineering Consultant

Peter Fisher, M.D.
Medical Consultant

Daniel L Pekarek
Author and Editor

Joan Pekarek
Assistant Editor and Proofreader

Berk Brown
Assistant Editor and Proofreader

David Pekarek
Cover Image

David Marty
Cover Design

Amy Vaughn
Interior Design

Elliott Wolf
Publisher

Chapter One

TIME: Day 28, Early Afternoon

Captain Jerry Jerontis, Moose, Zeb, and two crew members were on the Challenger, which was orbiting Alcent (the third planet of Alpha Centauri A) at an altitude of 200 miles. They were on the starship to pick up a water glider, construction tools, and building materials for small homes. Also, they planned to search Alcent for evidence that Zeb's fiancee, Zonya, and her colleagues were still alive.

On Pioneer Island, the people who had arrived on Day 27 were on the beach of South Bay having a party to celebrate their completion of Earth's first manned interstellar journey. Having lived inside a starship for nearly seven years, they were ready to cut loose on a warm sandy beach.

Doctor Connie Nemard, wife of Captain Jerontis, had arrived on Pioneer Island on Day 1 with her husband. They were accompanied by their close friends, Moose and Dianne, and were the first humans to land on Alcent.

Connie was not at the beach party; instead, she was working in an experimental vegetable garden. She wondered if plants brought from Earth would do well on this alien planet. While inspecting a tomato plant, she noted that it was loaded with blossoms and small green fruit. It appeared to be healthy and free of parasites.

It was a peaceful, slow-paced afternoon, and the radiant energy pouring down on Connie from Alpha Centauri A made her feel warm and drowsy. The feeling was enhanced by the pleasant caress of a gentle breeze. Maybe I should go to South Bay and stretch out on the beach for a short nap, thought Connie.

Then, a shadow passed over her, and she felt the downdraft from large wings. Connie looked up and saw a huge pterodactyl glide over her and land barely ten yards away. Instantly startled out of her

1

drowsiness, she reached for her pistol and discovered that she was unarmed. How did I forget my gun, she wondered.

Connie was upset that she had carelessly forgotten her sidearm, but she did not panic, because she realized that if the pterodactyl had wanted to eat her, she would already be dead. Nevertheless, she felt endangered by the sudden appearance of the big predator. She hoped that it was one of the pterodactyls from Western Island. They had been friendly.

Intently focused on the huge creature, Connie attempted to identify it. Two things were immediately obvious. It had landed on one foot, and it appeared to be carrying something with its other foot. When the creature turned to face her, Connie saw that it was King, the big male from Western Island. Even though King had once saved her life, Connie still felt uncomfortable to be unarmed in the presence of a 400-pound raptor with awesome killing ability.

She wondered why King made her feel threatened by landing so close to her. He had never done anything threatening before this. Maybe he wasn't trying to be menacing. Connie looked at the big pterodactyl and wondered what was on his mind. She didn't have to wait long. King was still standing on one leg. He reached out with the other leg and gently placed on the ground what he was holding.

Connie immediately recognized the bundle as King's offspring and noted that it appeared lifeless. King looked at Connie, then at the still infant, then back at Connie. His eyes seemed to be pleading for assistance.

Just then, a second shadow passed over Connie. She looked up and saw Queen circling ever lower. When her altitude dropped below 50 feet, she banked into a tight turn and glided to a touchdown a few yards behind King.

Now, I am facing two of these creatures without a weapon, thought Connie. Fortunately, I don't think they mean me any harm. It looks like their infant is sick and that they've come to me for help. Maybe pterodactyls really are capable of thinking. Is it possible that they have the intelligence of prehistoric humans? If so, they might think I am a goddess who descended out of the heavens and that I can make their infant well.

Connie made eye contact with Queen. Her eyes seemed to be asking for medical aid while she shifted her gaze back and forth between

Connie and her baby. I wish they weren't standing so close to their youngster, thought Connie. I would like to examine it.

Maybe I should call Dianne and ask for help, thought Connie. She reached for her communicator, but she came up empty-handed and said, "I forgot my communicator and my gun. I am getting careless. I guess I'll have to do this alone."

Connie looked at King and Queen. She pointed at herself; then, she pointed at the infant while staring at it. She hoped the big pterodactyls would understand that she wanted to examine the youngster. She paused; then, while looking at the big birds, she made a pushing gesture toward them. Apparently, they understood, because they stepped backward a few yards.

"So far, so good," whispered Connie, as she slowly walked toward the infant. She noticed that the big predators were watching her closely, but they made no menacing moves. When she reached the baby, she noted that it looked as limp as a rag doll. I wonder if it's still alive, thought Connie, as she knelt beside it. Seeing no obvious injury, she reached out to turn it over. When her hands contacted the baby, she said to herself, "This poor thing is burning up with fever."

Connie gently turned the small pterodactyl over. The problem was immediately obvious. There was a small gash in the baby's right thigh. It was infected, swollen, and oozing smelly pus. This reminds me of the injury that almost killed Zeb, she thought. It even smells just as bad. I wonder if it's the same bacteria. I could quickly find out in the medical lab, if King and Queen will allow me to take the infant there. They were alertly watching, so Connie pointed at the infant, then at herself, then at the large habitation capsule, which contained the medical lab.

Connie wasn't sure if they understood, but they did step back a couple more yards. She looked at the big creatures and tried to read their minds. Then, she slowly and gently picked up the sick baby and started walking toward the medical lab. A brief glance over her left shoulder told Connie that King and Queen were following her, but they were keeping their distance.

After entering the capsule, Connie placed the sick infant on a table near one of the large windows. King and Queen stood outside the window and watched Connie take a blood sample and a pus sample. She entered them into the lab's automated analysis machine. It quickly identified the problem microbe as the same one that had almost killed Zeb.

Connie started an I.V. with the antibiotic that was so effective at treating Zeb. Then, she poured some of the antibiotic into the open wound to clean it. She hoped the infant wasn't allergic to it and that life threatening damage hadn't already occurred. When she was satisfied that the injury was clean, she closed it.

With the medical work done, Connie called Dianne to tell her about the presence of the pterodactyls and what she had just done. She finished with, "I think you should warn everyone to stay on the beach. Evidently, King and Queen have learned to trust you and me, but I don't know if that trust applies to the people who came down yesterday."

"I don't know either," replied Dianne, "but they can't stay here forever. How are you going to get King and Queen to leave without their infant? And if you convince them to leave, how are you going to tell them to come back for their baby when it's cured?"

"I don't know. Any suggestions?"

"They seem to have understood the hand gestures you've been using, so you might continue with the sign language."

"That does seem to be my only option," agreed Connie. "But there is one thing that worries me about this."

"What?"

"Suppose I am successful at getting them to leave now and return tomorrow at about this time, what will they do if I am unable to cure their infant and they come back to a dead baby?"

"That question is impossible to answer. We don't know how intelligent they are, and even more important, we don't know how emotional they are."

"They were smart enough to bring their sick baby to me for help."

"But that should've been an easy decision. We've helped them before, and they might think we are gods who can do anything."

"That's exactly what worries me. Suppose I fail to cure their infant, are they going to recognize that we have limitations? Or are they going to think that we are gods who let their baby die?"

"I see what you're getting at. In the first case, they might appreciate your effort. In the second case, they might become angry and attack you."

"If I fail, I'd better have my gun ready."

"Whether you succeed or fail, I will be with you," assured Dianne.

4

"I'm counting on that, but if I fail, I am willing to bet that they will still be grateful for my effort. Also, I believe that they have emotions, and that they will feel a sense of loss."

"Based on our experience with them, I agree. And I suspect they are every bit as intelligent as early humans."

"I am about to test their intelligence again," responded Connie. "With simple hand signals, I will see if I can get them to leave and come back tomorrow afternoon."

"You can do it, and I am going to put on a video headset and watch you with the camera on top the robot lab."

Connie checked the baby pterodactyl and noted that its condition had not deteriorated. She also noticed that King and Queen were still watching her through the large window. To assure them that she was trying, she carefully searched the infant for additional injuries but did not find any.

I guess it's time to test my sign language skills, Connie thought, as she cautiously stepped outside and faced the big raptors. Wanting them to leave, she pointed at them, then at Western Island. Next, she pointed at Alpha Centauri A, which was still high in the afternoon sky. With a large sweeping downward motion of her arm, Connie tried to indicate the sun setting. She turned to the east, pointed at the horizon, and tried to indicate a sunrise with a sweeping upward motion of her arm. She continued the upward motion until she was again pointing at Alpha Centauri A. Then, she pointed at Western Island and with an exaggerated motion, attempted to indicate to King and Queen that they should return.

Wondering if they understood, Connie shifted her gaze back and forth between them, awaiting their response. They turned to each other and did some soft back and forth squawking. Then, they looked at their infant for a few moments before returning their gaze to Connie. "I don't know what's going on in their minds, but their eyes seem filled with hope and trust," commented Connie. "I wonder if they understood my sign language."

The answer wasn't long in coming. King took one last look at his infant, then at Connie. He turned to the south and began running. He spread his wings to their full fifty-two-foot span, began flapping them, and quickly became airborne. Queen followed him, and together, they returned to Western Island.

After watching them fly away, Connie sat down on the front

porch, feeling drained of energy. Her communicator beeped. It was Dianne. "I knew you could do it," she said.

"I am glad that it's over for the time being," Connie responded. "I feel wiped out."

"You should feel that way. You just faced a pair of fierce wild creatures who are expecting you to work a miracle."

"I hope I don't disappoint them, but however this turns out, there's no longer any doubt in my mind that these birds are at least as intelligent as early humans. They might even be the smartest creatures on this planet."

"They sure didn't have any trouble understanding your hand signals," responded Dianne.

"We'll know that for sure if they come back tomorrow afternoon."

"Until we know them better, I think everyone except you and me should be off the plateau tomorrow afternoon."

"Good idea," replied Connie.

Meanwhile, on the Challenger, Jerry was unaware that his wife had once again had an encounter with pterodactyls during his absence. He was helping Zeb search for Zonya, while Moose and his crew were loading the cargo shuttle.

Zeb was not from Earth. He was a humanoid who had come to Alcent from B-2, the second planet of Alpha Centauri B. He had lived alone for thirty years, because he had been deserted and left to die by his colleagues, who turned out to be enemies. Even worse, they abducted Zonya.

When Zeb was found by the people from Earth, he was near death because of a serious infection. Even though he still wore an ankle cast, he was now healthy and wanted to find out if Zonya was still alive. To search for her, he used his ability to communicate telepathically, while Jerry used the Challenger's instruments to search for evidence indicating the presence of a colony of humanoids.

The Challenger had now been orbiting Alcent for 66 days, and its instruments had gathered a massive amount of data about the planet. Jerry wondered how best to wade through all of it looking for a humanoid encampment. It was like searching for a needle in a haystack. He decided that he needed to have the computer do the searching, but what would he tell it to look for.

Jerry needed to discuss the problem with Zeb, but he and Zeb could not speak directly to each other. Zeb had not yet learned English, and Jerry did not understand Zeb's language. However, Michelle, mission reporter, had learned the basics of Zeb's language and could carry on a conversation with him. Since she was on Pioneer Island, Jerry and Zeb had to speak to each other through Michelle using their communicators.

Jerry called Michelle. After exchanging greetings, he said, "Please ask Zeb if he's been able to telepathically detect anything that might narrow our search area."

Michelle did as requested; then, she reported: "Zeb has not found anything, but he believes that his enemies traveled far to the south along the ocean coast after deserting him."

"Why does he think that?"

"He said he helped them build a large, sturdy raft. It was equipped with sails and capable of ocean travel."

"I am aware of that, but why does he think they went south along the coast? They could just as easily have gone north."

"Zeb said he telepathically probed the mission leader's mind and discovered that his objective was located far to the south. He was unable to find out how far or even why this journey was so important. The mission leader was very good at guarding his mind against telepathic spying."

Jerry thanked Michelle for her assistance; then, he considered Zeb's comments. I wonder what that mission leader was searching for that was important enough for them to leave Clear Lake. Why would they undertake such a hazardous journey after landing in a superb area? What were they looking for? Now that 30 years have gone by, is Zonya still alive? What kind of camp would survivors be living in today? If they're living a primitive lifestyle, they might have daily campfires to cook food. Our infrared telescopes would see them.

Jerry asked the computer to find the infrared data for Pioneer Island. He browsed through it until he found the infrared signatures of their many campfires. He instructed the computer to use this data as a guide and search the database for the area along the seacoast south of Pioneer Island. He further instructed the computer to begin the search by looking at data from small islands isolated from the countryside by at least 100 yards of water. Even if these people came here well armed, they would've eventually run out of ammunition, thought Jerry. Then, they would've become easy prey for the big T-

Rexes, which means that they're probably living on a small island where there aren't any T-Rexes. Fortunately, these brutes aren't able to swim.

"What else can I look for?" Jerry asked himself. He thought about what Zeb had told him a few days after they had found him. The large Apollo-type capsule they had landed in was very rugged and provided a good shelter. Also, it contained their computers, research instruments, and communications equipment. For these reasons, it was incorporated into the raft design. If that raft still exists, that capsule would provide an easily recognizable radar signal. Even if the raft doesn't exist, they may have found a way to beach that capsule. Jerry thought about how heavy the capsule must have been and concluded, there is no way they could've moved it inland for any significant distance. Therefore, it would have to be on the ocean beach, a river beach, or an island beach.

Jerry used a computer to figure out what kind of radar return this kind of spacecraft would generate. Then, he asked the computer to search the radar data for evidence of the capsule's existence.

The Challenger's computers were the most advanced available in 2092, the year that it left Earth. They had enormous capability and were extremely fast. Even though Jerry had asked the surveillance computer to search a huge database for some small specific information, it only took it a few moments to fulfill both requests.

On the wall-sized video screen in front of Jerry, an outline of a small island appeared. There was a red dot near the center of it, indicating the presence of a campfire. While he was looking at the sketch, it began to take on a three-dimensional appearance as the computer processed radar data to do the island's topography. Then, a red "X" denoting the presence of the landing capsule appeared on the beach near the red dot. "I've found them!" Jerry exclaimed.

But no one heard Jerry, because he was alone on the flight deck. Zeb was on the observation deck, where he had to be to use his telepathic ability to communicate with someone on the surface of Alcent. His telepathic powers were dependent on energy waves created by his brain. These energy waves could not pass through the Challenger's metal hull, but they could pass through the transparent plastic hull of the observation deck. However, Zeb's telepathic search for Zonya had been fruitless. When his communicator beeped, he answered it.

It was Michelle. "I have good news for you. Jerry has found a campfire on a small island. The data revealing the campfire was taken three days ago. Your landing capsule is also there."

Zeb became electrified with excitement over the possibility that Zonya might be alive. But his emotions quickly cooled. Thirty years is a long time, he thought. Even if Zonya is alive, she may have fallen in love with one of her abductors. She may no longer be interested in me, but I would like to talk to her anyway.

"Are you still there?" asked Michelle.

"I didn't mean to give you the silent treatment, but what you just said had quite an impact on me. Tell Jerry I will join him on the flight deck, shortly."

By the time Zeb arrived, Jerry had displayed the island's location on a second video screen. Through Michelle, Jerry told Zeb, "It is 1600 miles south of Pioneer Island. That puts it at about ten degrees north latitude."

"That's pretty close to the equator," commented Zeb. "There must be a hot, humid climate in that region."

Jerry called up optical data for the area. The images showed very dense jungle. "I would sure hate to try to find someone in there," he said.

Turning his attention back to the island, Jerry noted that it was located in a fairly large river that flowed into the ocean. According to the computer, one had to sail 89 miles upriver from the ocean to get to the island. At the island's location, the river was 400 yards wide and slow moving. The island was nearly a half-mile long, but it was only 90 yards across at its widest point. Jerry asked the computer for detailed images of the island. It responded, "High-resolution images do not exist for this location."

Jerry checked the Challenger's orbital parameters. "It's going to be six hours before we pass over that island. By then, it's going to be dark. I would like to get some daylight pictures yet today."

"Zeb agrees with you," Michelle said.

Jerry looked at Zeb and noted his obvious eagerness. Then, he called Moose. "I need to change our orbit. Are you guys prepared for acceleration?"

"Give us a few minutes to secure the materials we just put on the shuttle."

"Okay."

Through Michelle, Jerry said to Zeb, "I am amazed that your enemies could sail 1600 miles on the ocean with nothing more than a raft equipped with sails. Then, there was the 89-mile journey upriver against whatever current was there."

"That must have taken a lot of determination," Zeb responded. "I wonder why the journey was made."

"I would sure like to find out," stated Jerry.

"Maybe Zonya can tell us," suggested Michelle.

"If she's alive," Zeb said, sounding hopeful.

"We'll soon find out," commented Jerry, after receiving a message from Moose that they were ready for ignition.

Jerry entered the parameters for the desired orbit into the flight control computer and directed it to begin the antimatter engine ignition sequence. While the computer did its job, Jerry monitored instrument readouts. The main engines hadn't been fired in more than three weeks, and even though he didn't expect any problems, he wanted to keep an eye on them.

However, they ignited on schedule and operated flawlessly for several minutes. After they were shut down, Jerry said, "In about 20 minutes, we'll pass over that island at an altitude of 135 miles, and I will get some detailed images of the area."

"I am going to the observation deck," Zeb said. "I will try to telepathically contact the people living down there."

When Zeb reached the observation deck, he looked down on the beautiful, life-filled planet far below and wondered: Is Zonya really down there? What about our mission leader? Is he down there and still alive? If he is, I will make him pay for what he did to Zonya and me. But how many enemies do I have down there? What if they have prospered and multiplied? What if Zonya decided long ago that I could not survive on my own? Would she have grudgingly embraced our enemies out of necessity? If so, she may have become fully interwoven into their community with children and grandchildren. If that has happened, it will be very difficult for her to leave and live with me. This will be true, even if she treasures the wonderful relationship we once had, Zeb thought, sadly.

If the mission leader is alive, what will he do to Zonya if he finds out that I am healthy, on this starship, and looking for her? I guess that would depend on the relationship between her and the rest of the group. But no matter what the relationship is, he might still use her as a hostage to prevent me from settling an old score with him. It looks like I could cause trouble for Zonya by alerting them to my presence on this starship. Surely, they've seen this ship. I spotted it moving across the nighttime sky a few days after it arrived. But what do they know about it?

Zeb thought about the question. What they know depends almost entirely on whether the mission leader is alive and well. His telepathic ability was so good that he could even covertly probe an unsuspecting mind. If he had done that to these humans, he would've learned that this starship is not from B-2. But since he doesn't understand English, there isn't much else that he could've learned; unless, he was able to get into their minds deep enough to have looked at some of the images stored in their memories. If so, he might already know that I am alive, because all of the humans saw pictures of me the day they found me. However, I don't think that he knows I am on this ship, and I don't think I should reveal my presence to him. That means I cannot telepathically probe the island in search of Zonya, at least, not yet.

I will learn what I can from the pictures that Jerry will be getting. While he's taking them, I will stay here on the observation deck and keep my mind open to the possibility of telepathic contact from someone on the island. No! I can't do that either. If the mission leader is alive and attempts telepathic contact with this ship, he will find me. He will recognize my mind and know I am here.

Zeb immediately left the observation deck and headed for the flight deck. There, the metal hull would block telepathic contact.

While on the way to the flight deck, he contacted Michelle and explained his thinking to her. He finished just as he arrived.

Jerry looked at Zeb and wondered why he had returned just as they were approaching the island. Jerry didn't have to wait for an explanation. Michelle provided one immediately.

"Tell Zeb I agree with his reasoning," responded Jerry.

Then, images of the small island started appearing on the wall-sized video screen. It was quite rocky, and even though it had a few trees and shrubs, it was free of the dense jungle that grew on both sides of the river.

Jerry asked the computer for close-ups of the campfire site and the landing capsule. The images appeared instantly. Even though the Challenger was still a few minutes away from closest approach, the images already had enough detail to confirm that the encampment had been found. A small log cabin, a rock fire pit, and the landing capsule were all visible.

Jerry searched the island for other cabins, but found none. "Apparently, this is a small community," he said.

As they neared closest approach, Jerry limited surveillance to the vicinity of the cabin, fire pit, and landing capsule. He asked the computer for maximum resolution images. These would show details down to a small fraction of an inch.

As the Challenger's powerful optical instruments surveyed the campsite, sharply detailed video appeared. The log cabin looked sturdy and well maintained. The area around it looked neat and orderly. There was even a garden nearby.

The fire pit was equipped with a structure to hang cooking pots on, and there was a neat pile of firewood. "The cut edges on the firewood make it obvious that they still have usable saws," commented Jerry.

Fifty feet from the water, the landing capsule rested on a gravel beach. Noticing that the beach was fairly flat, Jerry said, "They must have floated the capsule to its current resting spot when the river was a few feet higher than it is now."

At that moment, Zeb's heart skipped a beat when he saw a woman step out of the capsule and walk to a shady area next to a tall tree. She spread out a blanket and dropped a pillow on it. Stretching out on the blanket, she looked straight up into the cloudless sky for a few moments before closing her eyes. Then, a man lay down beside her. First, he looked closely at her; then, he let his eyes search the sky. Resting on the ground beside the man was a long bow and a quiver full of arrows. "It looks like he is wary of flying predators," Jerry said.

Michelle translated the comment to Zeb, but he ignored it, because he was staring at the man and the woman. He asked Jerry if he could get more detail in the image.

Jerry asked the computer for image enhancement, and the image became a bit sharper. "This is the best we can do from this altitude," he said.

Jerry turned to Zeb and saw that he looked very sad. "Want to share your feelings with me?" he asked, through Michelle.

"My worst fears have materialized. I am looking at Zonya, which makes me happy. However, the man she is with is the mission leader, the person who ordered that I be deserted and left to die, but they look so young."

"They might be much older than they look," commented Jerry. "Our optics are good, but at this distance, they are not good enough to show the facial lines that come with age."

At that moment, two children entered the scene. One of them knelt beside the woman and tugged at her left arm. The woman sat up and faced the child. They appeared to be talking.

"This is even worse," Zeb said. "It looks like my Zonya is not only married to my enemy, but it also looks like they have children."

Attempting to console Zeb, Michelle said, "Things aren't always the way they appear. There might be some other explanation."

"Thanks for saying that, but right now, it looks hopeless as far as getting Zonya back is concerned. And I cannot settle an old score with my enemy either, because that would hurt Zonya, if she is now in love with him."

"I think we should observe the campsite for a few days," Michelle suggested. "We need more information before you jump to conclusions."

Zeb silently stared at the image on the screen, attempting to glean more information from it, but it was starting to lose detail as the Challenger's orbital speed carried it farther away. "Ask Jerry if we can stay on the Challenger for another day or two."

Jerry discussed the request with Moose, who said, "The shuttle is full. There isn't room for everything we came up here to get. We need to go down, unload, and come back tomorrow for the rest of the stuff."

"Zeb and I are going to stay up here until tomorrow, maybe even longer."

"Want me to stay and help with the recon?"

"The two crew members who came up with us aren't pilots."

"That's true, but the shuttle is perfectly capable of going down under the direction of its flight control computer."

"Good point, but our shuttles are critical equipment. An onboard pilot is a good backup to the computer."

"Sounds like you want me to go down with the shuttle."

"You are an expert pilot."

"Thank you! We're going to button up this bird and begin the procedure for leaving the hangar deck. In less than two hours, we'll be back on Pioneer Island."

13

"Have a safe flight."

"Thanks!"

Jerry turned his attention back to Michelle. "It's going to be about an hour-and-a-half before we're back in position to take another look at that campsite. Until then, I'm going to take a second look at our video."

"What are you hoping to see that you haven't already seen?"

"I don't know, but when we saw them in real time, it was quite emotional up here, and I may have missed something important. Tell Zeb what I am planning and ask him to stop me if he sees anything he wants to study. I will freeze the image and try to extract some additional detail with the image-enhancement software."

"Okay and I will look at the images too. I might see something that you guys miss."

"Good."

A short time later, Zeb urgently held up his right hand and said, "Stop!"

Jerry froze the image. It was the picture of the woman sitting up in response to the child that had tugged at her left arm. The arm was outstretched.

"Can you increase the color contrast of her upper arm?" Zeb asked.

Michelle relayed the request to Jerry, who immediately circled the woman's upper arm on the video screen. He asked the computer for maximum color contrast.

Her skin tone was golden bronze. With color enhancement, the tone appeared richer, but there was very little color variation over the length of her upper arm.

"What are you looking for?" Michelle asked Zeb.

"Many of the women in my society had tattoos on their upper left arms. It was the custom at the time we left B-2. Zonya was a passionate, warmhearted woman. The tattoo she wore was a flaming red candle shaped like a heart. Its symbolic significance is something she was proud of."

"I don't see a tattoo," commented Michelle. "How big was it?"

"It was about two inches high and a little over an inch wide."

"Judging from the detail in this image, we should see a tattoo that large," Michelle said.

"You're right," agreed Jerry, who immediately asked the computer for a pixel-by-pixel color reading of the woman's upper arm.

Jerry studied the color report and said, "There are no shades of red on her arm. Is it possible that this woman isn't Zonya?"

"Please go back to the best image we have of her lying down and looking up," requested Zeb.

Jerry scanned back through the images until he found the sharpest one. He froze it and asked the computer for maximum detail.

Zeb intently studied the woman for a full two minutes while searching his memory for some little detail he may have forgotten. Finally, he said, "That woman looks enough like Zonya to be her twin sister."

"Or maybe her daughter," suggested Michelle.

Zeb became electrified with excitement as he considered the possibility. "Her apparent youth was the first thing that I noticed," he said. "Is it possible that I am looking at Zonya's daughter and grandchildren?"

"The feeling I get when I look at her is that she might be between 25 and 30," Michelle said. "The children look between five and ten. It all adds up."

"The man she's with also looks between 25 and 30," commented Zeb. "Is it possible that he might be the son of my enemy? Is it possible that all of my former colleagues are dead and that these four descendants are all that remain?"

"There is only one house on the island," commented Jerry.

"The landing capsule is also there," stated Zeb. "It isn't super big, but it is large enough to provide shelter for one or two people."

"Are you ready to assume the risks involved in attempting telepathic contact?" Jerry asked.

Zeb considered the question for a few moments before responding. "On our next orbit, it will be early evening on their island. They might have a campfire to cook dinner. It seems reasonable to assume that most of them will be present for their evening meal. Let's see how many there are before I decide on attempting contact."

"I like the plan, but our next pass over the island is 45 minutes away. Let's use that time to continue studying the video we already have."

Meanwhile, down on Pioneer Island, people were beginning to leave the beach party and return to Stellar Plateau, which was a large rock formation on the south lobe of the island. It rose 150 feet above the surrounding terrain, and measured 300 yards wide by 700 yards

15

long. The east, south, and west faces of the plateau were nearly vertical cliffs. The north side was a fairly steep rock slide.

The interstellar pioneers had only two ways to get on and off the plateau. On the south end, they had built a wooden cage, open-air elevator suspended on a rope. Swinging during ascent and descent was prevented by guide ropes. On the north end, they built a hiking trail down the rock slide. It had a grade of 15% to 20% and seven switchbacks.

The pioneers had chosen to live on Pioneer Island for many reasons. Chief among them was that it was located in the middle of Clear Lake, which was twenty miles wide and forty miles long. This large body of fresh water isolated them from the hostile, dinosaur-dominated countryside. On Pioneer Island, they sought additional safety by selecting the plateau as the site for their homes.

Dianne was the first one to return from South Bay. With her were Connie's daughter, Denise, and Michelle's son, Matthew. Denise was five years old with blonde hair and blue eyes. Matthew was six years old with hazel eyes and brown hair.

Dianne had already told the children that Connie had a baby pterodactyl in the medical lab. As the trio approached the lab, Connie stepped onto the front porch to greet them. Upon seeing her mother, Denise ran up to her and said, "I want to see the baby 'dactyl. Is it still sick?"

"Yes, but it's getting better."

"Can I see it?"

"I want to see it too," Matthew demanded.

"Okay, but I don't want either of you to touch it, just look at it. And speak softly, because it's sleeping, and we don't want to wake it."

The children agreed to Connie's conditions, so she took them into the medical lab. The children cautiously approached the chick and stared at it in total fascination.

"It looks dead," commented Matthew.

"I want it to live," Denise said. "Will it get well?" she asked.

"I don't know. It has a serious infection," Connie responded.

"But mom, you saved Zeb when he was infected."

Connie pointed at the I.V. and said, "I am giving it an antibiotic to kill the tiny bug that is making it so very sick."

"Is that how you made Zeb get well?" Denise asked.

"Yes!"

"Then, this baby 'dactyl will get well too."

Connie smiled at her daughter and appreciated the innocent confidence that she expressed in her medical ability. I wonder if King and Queen think on the same level as my daughter, she silently asked herself.

On the Challenger, Jerry and Zeb were approaching the island where Zeb's people had been discovered. The first images were starting to come in, but the island was still too distant to see fine detail.

"I see someone tending a fire," Jerry said, "but I don't know if it's one of the people we looked at earlier."

"I see a second individual entering the scene," added Michelle, who was down on Pioneer Island watching the images.

"This person appears to be hanging a cooking pot over the fire," commented Jerry.

A little later, when the Challenger was directly above the island, two children stepped out of the log cabin and headed for the campfire. "They look like the children we saw earlier," Zeb commented. "Also, the man and woman look the same. It's dinnertime, and there are only four people present. Maybe there really are only four of my people down there."

"I think there are at least five," argued Jerry.

"Why do you think that?" asked Zeb.

"There are five chairs around their outdoor table."

Zeb examined the chairs. "Three of them look like they're for adults," he said. "The other two appear to be for the children."

While the trio looked at the chairs, the children sat down at the table. "They're sitting on the tallest chairs," stated Zeb. "Now, the big question is: are there three adults living down there or are there two adults with an extra chair?"

"Let's stop watching them for a few moments," Jerry suggested. "I want to search their campsite for other tables and chairs."

Realizing that their speed was rapidly moving them away from the island, Jerry completed the search rather quickly. "I don't see any other tables, but there are three full-sized lounge chairs in front of the cabin."

Speaking to Michelle, Jerry said, "I think Zeb should attempt telepathic contact on our next pass."

"Why?"

"His only concern was that his enemy might still be alive, and that he might use Zonya as a hostage. We think there are only three adults down there. The woman looks like Zonya's daughter. The man looks like the son of Zeb's enemy. If the third adult is Zonya; then, Zeb's enemy is dead. If the third adult is Zeb's enemy; then, Zonya is dead. Either way, the hostage situation is impossible."

"There are a couple key words in your argument," responded Michelle.

"Which words are you referring to?"

"*Looks like*. The adult male *looks like* the son of Zeb's enemy. But that man could be Zeb's enemy. We cannot tell for certain from this distance. We know that the woman is not Zonya, because of the missing tattoo, unless she found a way to remove it here on this primitive planet, and that seems highly unlikely. Besides that, according to Zeb, she was proud of that tattoo."

"You're suggesting a bad set of circumstances for Zeb. You're saying that Zeb's enemy could be alive and that he might have both Zonya and her daughter to use as hostages to keep Zeb from settling an old score."

"It is possible."

"I can't deny that, but there may be a way that Zeb can find out without alerting them to his presence."

"How?"

"Ask Zeb if he can telepathically probe their minds while they're sleeping without waking them. If he can, find out if he can identify Zonya's mind and his enemy's mind."

"If he can do all of that, I'm not sure that I want him living with us on Pioneer Island."

"This is something we need to know about him, and this is a good time to find out, if he'll tell us."

"I'll talk to him and let you know."

A few minutes later, Michelle said, "Zeb told me that he can sense the presence of a sleeping brain, but he cannot identify it. However, if the sleeping person is dreaming, he can sense the energy field created by this kind of brain activity and identify the individual. If the dream is vivid enough, he can sometimes even see what the dream is all about."

"Can he do this without waking the individual?"

"Yes, unless he or she is sleeping very lightly and on the verge of waking up anyway."

18

"Does he want to telepathically search the island for Zonya and his enemy tonight?"

"Yes, but not on the next orbit. He will wait until the orbit after that."

After a few moments of silence, Michelle asked, "What are you thinking about?"

"I'm wondering if I'll have to learn how to guard my dreams after Zeb learns English."

"I don't think you need to worry about him. He's not the kind of person who will be snooping around in your mind."

"What about the people on that island. They might be tired of living in isolation, or their situation might be desperate. They might want to be rescued. They might want to live with us on Pioneer Island. Can we trust them to respect the privacy of our minds?"

"We don't know if everyone in Zeb's race has telepathic ability. That power might be limited to a few gifted individuals."

"That is one more thing that we need to find out."

"It's going to be well over three hours before Zeb puts his telepathic ability to use. What are you going to do with all that time?"

"I haven't been up here in four weeks, so I am going to roam around and get reacquainted with my starship. But before I do that, I'm going to the cafeteria to eat dinner. I am hungry."

"Zeb is probably hungry too, and he would definitely appreciate a guided tour of the ship."

"No doubt about that, but I will need you as an interpreter, so I can answer all of his questions."

"Be more than happy to help out."

More than three hours later, Zeb and Jerry were again approaching the island home of the humanoids from B-2. "It is really dark down there," observed Jerry. "This is one of those rare occasions when both of our suns have set and neither one of our moons has yet risen."

"Unless they're sitting around a campfire, they should all be in bed sleeping," stated Zeb.

"I don't see a campfire," commented Jerry. "But let's make sure that they aren't outside doing some star gazing on this rare dark night."

Jerry accessed the Challenger's nighttime reconnaissance capability. Its light intensifying software could turn a scene lit only by starlight into an image that looked almost like it was taken during daylight hours. After briefly searching the campsite, he said, "It looks deserted, and I don't see any light coming out of their windows. We can't be certain that they're indoors and asleep, but it looks that way."

"I am heading for the observation deck," stated Zeb.

Jerry looked into Zeb's eyes and noted the eagerness there. Then, he saw the anxiety. What can I say to him? Jerry silently asked himself. He has been alone for thirty years, and now it appears that all of his former colleagues are dead, except one. Which one? Will it be Zonya? If she is alive and well, will she welcome Zeb back into her life?

Zeb seemed to sense that Jerry knew what was going on in his mind, because he appeared reluctant to break eye contact. But he had to get to the observation deck, because they would soon be directly over the island.

"Good luck!" Jerry said. "Let us hope and pray for the best."

"Thank you," responded Zeb, as he turned and left.

When Zeb arrived on the observation deck, he put on his night-vision goggles and stared down at the island. He intently focused his mental energy and slipped into the trance that he needed to be in to telepathically search the campsite. He quickly detected the energy fields emanating from the brains of five sleeping individuals. Search as he might, he was unable to find more than five.

He shifted his focus from one to the next, hoping to catch one of them dreaming. The first dreamer he discovered was not familiar to him.

Zeb was able to identify the originator of a mental process in the same way that people identify a known person from the unique sound of his or her voice. When hearing a stranger speak, it can usually be determined whether the speaker is adult or child, male or female. Zeb was able to use his telepathic power to recognize the unique signature of each person's mental processes. He could easily identify known individuals. When tuning in to a stranger, he could usually determine whether the individual was adult or child, male or female.

Zeb focused his mind ever more intently on the dream he was watching and listening to. He thought it might be happening in the mind of the young girl. She was having a happy dream. It was about a special occasion, a party. She seemed to be the center of attention; perhaps, it was her birthday. There was singing. A pair of new, attractively decorated moccasins appeared. She tried them on, admired them, and walked around excitedly. Then, she gave an older woman a big hug and said, "Thank you grandma."

Zeb instantly became very excited, but the dream abruptly ended, and he never saw the face of the girl's grandmother. The young girl wasn't yet very tall, and Zeb only saw that part of her grandmother's body that she hugged.

He urgently contacted the minds of the others, but none of them were dreaming. The Challenger's orbital speed was rapidly carrying Zeb away from the island, and he was very tired from the intense mental effort required for telepathic communication. He came out of his trance and dozed for several minutes.

When he woke up, he thought, there is no doubt that it was the girl who was dreaming. Which grandmother gave her the moccasins? If it was her mother's mother, then Zonya is alive, or she at least was alive at the recent party. After all these years, I am so close to finding out, but I still don't know. There's no way I can sleep tonight. I have to talk Jerry into keeping the Challenger in an orbit that will bring us repeatedly over this island until I find out.

Zeb went to the flight deck. He called Michelle, so he could explain the situation to her and Jerry. After briefly pleading his case, Jerry agreed to the requested orbit.

Less than two hours later, they were again approaching the island. Zeb was on the observation deck intently focusing his mental energy. He dropped into a trance and began telepathically searching the island. Again, he found only five individuals. He switched his mental probe from one to the next hoping to find one of them dreaming.

In less than a minute, Zeb found a dreamer, and immediately recognized her. Even though in a deep mental trance, he cried out loudly, "I've found Zonya! She is alive!" Michelle heard the announcement and translated it to Jerry.

Zeb viewed the images in Zonya's dream and saw that it was about him when he was much younger. He saw himself asking her to marry him. Then, he saw and heard Zonya say yes. She kissed him, and they passionately embraced. What a happy moment that was, Zeb thought.

Zonya's dream continued and he saw her become very sad. He saw her bound hand and foot as she lay on a sturdy log raft. She was crying as the raft sailed away leaving him behind. Zeb thought, she still dreams about that dreadful event 30 years ago when she was abducted, and I was abandoned. I must end this sadness.

Hoping to overpower Zonya's dream, Zeb gathered every bit of mental energy that he possessed. Telepathically, he exclaimed to her, "I am alive! I am in the starship passing over your island!"

The strength of the message struck Zonya with such force that she was instantly shocked out of a sound sleep. She bolted into an upright position. Sitting on her bed, she supported her head with her hands while resting her elbows on her knees. That dream was so real, she thought. It almost seemed like Zeb was telling me that he's still alive. I wish that were true, but after all these years on a planet as savage as this one, it doesn't seem possible.

Still in telepathic contact with Zonya, Zeb listened to her thoughts. Then, he reaffirmed, "I've had some close calls, but I am alive."

"This is too good to be true," she replied. "I've missed you so much. I've been terribly lonely. I need to touch you, to feel your arms around me. Then, I will know that you really are alive and that my mind isn't playing tricks on me because of wishful thinking."

"You can rest assured that I am definitely alive. Like I said, I've had some close calls, but I've been lucky. During my darkest hour, I was rescued by some wonderful people from Earth. They saved my life. At this moment, I am in their starship. We've already passed over your island. In a couple minutes, we'll drop below the horizon, and I'll lose contact with you. I need some information before that happens. How many of you are there?"

"There are five of us."

"Who is the young woman that looks like you?"

"She is our daughter."

"Our daughter?"

"Yes! I was a few days pregnant at the time we were separated."

"I've missed her childhood, and I wasn't there to help you raise her. Now, I really have a score to settle with the man who separated us."

"He is already dead."

"Good! But who is the man I saw with our daughter?"

"He is the son of the man who caused us so much grief."

"Our daughter is married to the son of our enemy. I don't like that."

"It's OK! He is a wonderful young man. He's like a son to me."

"What do you mean?"

"His father was killed before he was born. His mother died two months after he was born. At that time, all of our colleagues were dead, and I was alone with two babies to care for. Our lives were filled with constant danger. Somehow, I managed to survive and protect the children, but I was very lonely. Back then, I was sure that you were alive. How I wished that I could've had you at my side. However, I knew how far apart we were and that you could not join me, because you were unarmed, had no boat-building tools, and didn't even know where I was. But now, you've come back. When will I see you?"

"I need to discuss that with Jerry, the Captain of this starship. It is getting late, and I can't ask him to stay up any longer. I will ask him to have us pass over you tomorrow morning. Then, we can discuss getting together."

"I can't wait," Zonya responded, as the Challenger dropped below the horizon and contact was lost.

Chapter Two

TIME: Day 29

On Pioneer Island, Alpha Centauri A had just risen to begin a new day. Dianne was standing at the south end of Stellar Plateau looking down on the cargo shuttle, which was preparing to leave South Bay.

Michelle and her husband, Mike Johnson, chief engineer, had joined Moose and two crew members for the return flight to the Challenger. Mike was an expert at dropping landing capsules from the Challenger and guiding them to precise locations on Alcent. He had guided the first robot lab to a perfect landing on top of a 35-foot-high rock formation measuring only 35 feet wide by 60 feet long. There, it was protected from possible destruction caused by stampeding dinosaurs attempting to escape hungry T-Rexes.

The needs of Zonya and her family were not yet known. But if they urgently needed weapons or medical supplies, Mike was the perfect individual to deliver them.

Dianne enjoyed watching the shuttles take off, especially, the large, powerful cargo shuttle. She noted how low it rested in the bay. Its propellant tanks were filled with water, and it looked heavy and deceptively sluggish. It was lifting anchor and preparing to taxi out of South Bay.

Using binoculars, Dianne focused on the flight deck windows. She saw her husband busy at the controls. Before joining the mission to Alcent, Moose had spent several years ferrying cargo between Earth and Moon. He was comfortable sitting in the captain's seat. He and Mike were the pilots for this flight.

Dianne beeped Moose with her communicator and said, "Have a safe flight my love."

With the early morning sunlight warming his face, Moose looked out the window, smiled broadly, and said, "See you tonight, honey."

With the anchors lifted and stowed, Moose fed power from the shuttle's nuclear reactor to its propeller. Water started churning under the shuttle's tail. Slowly, the shuttle began to move. Moose turned it around and headed south. He needed the wide open space of Clear Lake.

Once out of South Bay, Moose applied full power to the propeller. In just a few seconds, the shuttle accelerated to 45 mph, rose out of the water, and glided on its hydrofoils. Then, the NTR (nuclear thermal rocket) boomed into action. The water stored in the propellant tanks was pumped through the reactor's heat exchanger, where it was instantly transformed into hot, high-pressure vapor, which expanded out the shuttle's rocket nozzle with a thundering roar. The shuttle quickly reached flight speed and pitched into a steep climb. In less than a minute, it reached the cold upper atmosphere, and the water vapor blasting out of the rocket nozzle condensed into a brilliant white trail, clearly showing the shuttle's rapid ascent.

Dianne silently watched in spellbound fascination. Will I ever grow tired of seeing our shuttles take off, she wondered. It's such a spectacular sight. It looked so sluggish in South Bay, but in just a few minutes, it will carry my husband into orbit.

Dianne turned and stepped into the ATV (all terrain vehicle). She took one last look at the vapor trail rising high in the sky. Then, she drove the short distance back to camp.

She went directly to the habitation capsule. Its second floor contained a kitchen, bathroom, and the bedroom where she and Moose slept. The medical lab and other research equipment occupied most of the first floor. Also, Jerry and Connie's bedroom was located on the first floor. Soon, everyone would have a small temporary home, and the entire habitation capsule would become a research lab.

Dianne entered the capsule and found Connie, Denise, and Matthew attending the baby pterodactyl. "How is our patient doing?" she asked.

"He's awake and alert," replied Connie.

"I think he's hungry," added Denise.

"What do you think he wants to eat?" asked Connie.

Denise wasn't quite sure how to answer the question, so she turned to Matthew for help. "In a movie, I saw Queen feed him pieces of fish," he said.

"We have some raw fish in our refrigerator," Connie said.

"I'll go upstairs and get some," offered Dianne.

When she returned with several small pieces of fish, the infant pterodactyl looked in her direction and started squawking loudly. "Apparently, he can smell the fish," Dianne said.

"It sure looks that way," agreed Connie. "And it looks like he's trying to tell us that he's hungry. He reminds me of a nestling begging his parents for food."

"Can I feed him?" Denise asked.

Facing her daughter, Connie asked, "How are you going to get the food into his mouth?"

Denise looked at the impatiently squawking chick and considered the problem. Before she could answer, Matthew said, "I know how. I saw Queen feed him in the movie."

With Denise watching, Matthew boldly picked up a piece of fish and held it above the infant. It squawked loudly while holding its mouth open. Matthew dropped the small piece of fish into the wide open mouth. The infant quickly swallowed it and started begging for more. Following Matthew's example, Denise dropped a piece of fish into the chick's mouth. The children took turns feeding the baby until the fish was gone, but it still begged for more.

"How much can this thing eat?" Dianne asked.

"I don't know," replied Connie, "but I think we should feed it until it shuts up."

"I'll get some more fish."

Meanwhile, on the Challenger, Jerry and Zeb were awaiting the arrival of the shuttle. With their communicators and Michelle's help, they were discussing their next meeting with Zonya.

"There are some questions that we need answered on our next pass over that island," Jerry said.

"I have some questions too," replied Zeb, "but what information do you want?"

"We need to find out what their situation is. Specifically, do they urgently need some critical items, such as weapons or medical supplies? Also, do they want to continue living on their island, or do they want to join us on Pioneer Island?"

Pleased with the implication of Jerry's final question, Zeb said, "You would be willing to undertake a hazardous mission to rescue people who aren't even a part of your species?"

"It is the right thing to do. But we don't know if they want to be rescued. They might be happy on their island. They might be expecting you to join them."

"What they're hoping for is the biggest question in my mind," responded Zeb.

At that moment, Jerry received a call from Moose. "We're entering the hangar deck," he said.

"Let me know when you have the shuttle tied down," requested Jerry.

"Will do."

Jerry entered the parameters for a new orbit into the Challenger's flight control computer and waited for Moose's call. The current orbit had been optimized for docking with the cargo shuttle. The new orbit would take the Challenger over Zonya's Island.

Three minutes later, Moose called, "We're ready."

Jerry fired the antimatter engines. In just a few minutes, the flight control computer maneuvered the Challenger into the requested orbit and shut the engines down.

"We'll be over Zonya's Island in a half-hour," Jerry said.

"I can hardly wait," Zeb responded, barely able to contain his excitement.

"We need to send down some communication equipment. I respect your telepathic ability, but it is limited by line-of-sight. If they had communicators, you could talk to them anytime, and we wouldn't have to keep adjusting our orbit to pass over them."

"Great idea."

"Why don't you find out what else they need. I'll have Mike put the stuff in a capsule and send it down later today."

"Is there room in the capsule for me?"

"I don't think that's a good idea. The g-forces in a landing capsule are much higher than in our shuttles. Your broken ankle is still healing. My wife said it was a nasty multiple fracture, and it did take her several hours to put the pieces back together. Going down in the capsule could jeopardize the repair work she did."

"Unfortunately, you are right, but I had to consider the possibility."

Holding up her communicator, Michelle entered the flight deck and said, "You don't need to talk through these things anymore. Now that I'm here, I can translate for you directly."

"Soon, you won't have to translate for me. I am working hard at understanding English," Zeb said.

"You are making great progress," agreed Michelle.

"I am lucky to have such a good teacher."

"Thank you," responded Michelle.

Turning to Jerry, she said, "Mike will join us shortly."

"Good! I have a special job for him."

"I've already told him about the capsule you want to send down. He agrees with you. Zeb should not be on it. The g-forces are just too high."

"But Zeb and Zonya do have my sympathy," Jerry said. "After being apart for 30 years, I can understand their eagerness to get back together. Zeb had no one during that time. At least, Zonya had the children."

"What an awesome responsibility that must have been. Imagine caring for two youngsters on this hostile planet with no help. Just keeping them alive must have been quite a challenge."

"She must have been very well trained in survival skills."

"Even so, she needed a strong will to survive," stated Michelle.

"After all that they've been through, I think we should get them back together as soon as we can."

"Zeb will like to hear that," commented Michelle, as she turned to tell him.

Michelle talked with Zeb for a few minutes. Then, he went to the observation deck to prepare for his next meeting with Zonya.

Shortly after Zeb left, Mike arrived on the flight deck. He saw that Jerry was studying a topographical map of the area around Zonya's Island. The map was displayed in 3-D on a wall-sized video screen. The natural colors were enhanced to bring out additional detail.

"Rescuing them or delivering Zeb will present us with some problems," commented Jerry.

"To start with, how do we get there?" questioned Mike.

"That's the most obvious difficulty. I've never seen a river with so many bends. There just aren't any straight stretches long enough to safely land on and take off from with a shuttle."

"The nearest large lake is 80 miles away."

"The ocean is closer than that," stated Jerry. "Traveling the river, it's 89 miles, but by air, it's only 40 miles."

"Are you suggesting we land on the ocean and fly in with our helicopter?"

"Gaining access to inaccessible areas is the reason it was designed to fit inside the cargo shuttle."

"But to use it, we need to install the elevator deck on the shuttle's floor."

"That's not a big job," responded Jerry.

The elevator deck that Mike and Jerry were talking about allowed the shuttle to operate like a flying aircraft carrier. After landing, the shuttle's upper cargo bay doors could be opened wide. Then, the elevator deck would rise to the top of the shuttle and lock in place. In this position, it could serve as a platform for the helicopter to take off from and land on. It took only a couple minutes to deploy the rotor blades and make the chopper ready to fly.

"Maybe we should be installing the elevator deck instead of loading the shuttle with cargo," suggested Mike.

"Not yet. For one thing, we don't know if Zonya and her people want to leave their island. Also, our people need the building materials we're putting on the shuttle."

"But we know that Zonya and Zeb want to be together, and the chopper would be an easy way to deliver Zeb and whatever supplies they might need."

"That's true, but I think they can wait until tomorrow. That will give us today to decide how we're going to get there."

While looking at the video display of the area, Mike said, "Even though it's twice as far away, I think we should land on the lake. It's four miles across, which is more than big enough, and it will never have the large waves that the ocean can have."

"That's all true, but we don't know how deep that lake is or if it has any underwater obstacles that lie close to the surface, like rocks for example. They could wreck the hydrofoils or even cut a gash in the hull."

"I'd better load a marine explorer in a capsule and send it down, so I can explore the lake."

"Good idea. If the lake proves to be unsuitable for shuttle operations, we'll try to find a nearby, sheltered ocean bay."

"I don't think that will be necessary," commented Mike.

"Why?"

"Take a look at the lake. Its most obvious feature is that it is round. That suggests that it might be an ancient crater filled with water. An impact crater could be very deep. A volcanic crater might be deep or shallow, depending on whether or not there was a slow dome-building eruption after the explosion that formed the crater."

"How do you think this crater was formed?"

"Judging from the lay of the land, I believe that it's a deep impact crater."

"Why don't we call it Crater Lake, and if your guess is correct, it should be ideal for shuttle operations."

"I will send the marine explorer down on our next orbit, so I'll know for sure by tonight."

The marine explorer Mike planned to send down was a simple research tool. When deployed, it consisted of an inflated pontoon with cameras, sonar equipment, and batteries mounted on its underside. On its topside, it had a radio antenna, solar cells, and more cameras. For propulsion, it had an electric motor and a propeller.

Meanwhile, on the observation deck, Zeb was thinking about his next visit with Zonya, now only minutes away. His thoughts were interrupted by the beeping of his communicator. It was Michelle. She told him what Jerry and her husband were planning.

Zeb became very excited by the prospect of being with Zonya in as little as 24 to 30 hours. He couldn't wait to tell her. "Thank you for the good news," he said to Michelle.

With Zonya's Island now in sight on the distant horizon, Zeb focused his mental energy and slipped into a deep trance. His mind was searching for Zonya's mind. In less than a minute, he found her and established contact. "Good morning! How are you?" he asked.

"I've been waiting for you. Now that I know you're alive, I really miss you. When will I see you?"

"Tomorrow, I think."

"Really! That's wonderful! I can't wait. It's been so long."

Zeb told Zonya what Mike and Jerry were planning. Then, he said, "We have a big decision to make. Will I live with you on your island? Or will you and your family join me and live with the Earth people?"

"Do they want us to live with them? Will they welcome us?"

"Yes, they will. They are friendly and treat me like I am one of them."

"That means it would be possible for us to fit into their society."

"We could do that, but what is it like to live on your island?"

31

"We've found ways to be comfortable, but living here is a difficult struggle."

"Jerry has offered to give us weapons, medical supplies, and whatever else we need, if we decide to stay on your island."

"If that's the case, we do have a big decision to make. I never dreamed I'd be faced with this choice. Right now, all I want to do is see you."

"Maybe some of us could live with you for a few days while you decide. We want to explore the area and try to discover what is there that caused our Captain to undertake a long, dangerous journey. What was he looking for?"

"There is a crashed starship somewhere in this area."

"What!"

"There is a crashed starship somewhere in this area."

"I heard you the first time, but I am shocked by the news. Tell me more."

"When we arrived here, we set up camp. Our Captain's wife and I maintained the camp while everyone else went out in search of the starship. They wanted to find advanced technology that their country could use in the war against our country, but they never returned."

"Looking for advanced technology must have been the reason their country was so aggressive about sending a mission to this planet. Using in-the-name-of-peace politics, they even got our nation to help pay for it, so they could use the money saved for weapons. They probably decided, even before leaving B-2, that they would get rid of me at the earliest opportunity. Since I was the pilot, I became expendable when we landed. But how could they've known about the starship before we left B-2?"

"They didn't. They came here hoping to find an advanced civilization that they could steal technology from. The starship was discovered by our leader after we arrived here, and he kept it a secret from everyone until after you were deserted."

"I am glad he suffered an early death. How did he die?"

"I don't know how any of them died. None of them came back from the expedition to the starship."

"I need to change the subject. I am going to lose contact with you very soon. What items are you urgently in need of?"

"Guns! There is a small carnivorous dinosaur here that hunts in packs. Early on, we killed many of them with our rifles and pistols, and they learned to fear us, but we used up our ammo years ago. Now, we kill them with arrows and spears. This works as long as we are never ambushed by them. But they are clever, aggressive hunters. Sooner or later, they will kill one or more of us. We urgently need guns, especially, large-caliber handguns. They are effective and easy to carry."

"I will relay your request to Jerry," responded Zeb, just before losing contact.

Zeb went directly to the flight deck. Speaking through Michelle, he told Jerry about the crashed starship and Zonya's request for weapons.

Jerry listened attentively. Several questions entered his mind. Where did the starship come from? Why did it crash? Were there any survivors? If there were, are any of them still alive? Where are they? What are their capabilities? Are they a threat? "We have to find that ship and investigate," he said.

He called Moose and Mike and asked them to report to the flight deck. When they arrived, he briefed them.

"It seems like our lives are now a bit more complicated," commented Moose.

"That might be the understatement of the day," responded Mike. "It's possible that there might be creatures on this planet that are far more advanced than we are. And they might even be hostile."

"None of Zonya's abductors returned from their expedition to the starship," commented Jerry. "Something killed them. Before we go down, I would like to determine how they died."

"That's going to be difficult," Moose said. "Thirty years have gone by. The whole area is covered by dense jungle. It seems like their bodies and any clues would have disappeared long ago."

"That may be," replied Jerry. "But, we must locate that starship. Our investigation will start there. Also, we need to look at the jungle between it and Zonya's Island. Perhaps we can determine what route Zonya's abductors followed and what hazards they encountered. I don't know how long this is going to take, so I want to send some essential items down to Zonya, even before we drop the marine explorer."

"I have the explorer ready to go," stated Mike.

"That was quick. Since you have it ready, we might as well drop it on our next orbit. How long will it take you to load a capsule for Zonya?"

"What all do you want on it?"

"Guns, communication equipment, three RPVs (remotely piloted vehicles), and if there's any space left, let's give them some modern conveniences."

"What conveniences do you have in mind?"

"Why don't you take Zeb with you. I'm sure he'll have some definite ideas about what to send down."

"Good idea," responded Mike. Then, he turned to Michelle, "I'll need you to be our interpreter."

As the trio left the flight deck, Jerry turned to Moose, "I need your radar skills. On our next pass over that area, I want you to find that starship. After all these years, it must be totally concealed by vegetation, so our radar is our best chance to find it."

"Using the appropriate frequency, we can certainly penetrate the jungle, but we don't know what materials that starship was made out of. It might not give us a good radar return."

"That's true, but it should reflect radar differently than the surrounding terrain. We should be able to see that difference."

Moose considered some possibilities. "If it's made out of metal, it should give us an easy-to-identify return. If it's made out of stealth materials, it won't give us any return, but it will then appear as a blank area and still be easily detectable. The worst case is if it is made out of a combination of materials that reflect radar pretty much like the surrounding terrain."

"That's possible, but it's unlikely."

"I'll use the computer to work this problem. When it comes to radar recon, we do have some very sophisticated software. If there's a starship down there, I'll find it."

"That's what I was hoping to hear from you, but the ship might not be intact. It might not be anything other than widely scattered wreckage."

"I will have the computer consider that possibility too. But Zonya said that their mission leader discovered a crashed starship. That implies that the ship did not disintegrate, but came down in some sort of controlled crash, which would mean that it should be mostly intact."

"That sounds reasonable, but we have to consider all possibilities. The ship could have come down in one piece, or it could have disintegrated. In either case, the crew might have landed in an emergency escape vehicle. You should search for such a craft. It could be a capsule, a lifting body, a blended wing-body, or it might even be shaped like our shuttles."

"I'll look for an escape vehicle, along with everything else. It's going to take me a while to set this up, so I need to get started."

A little over an hour later, Zeb was on the observation deck preparing for contact with Zonya. Jerry, Moose, Mike, and Michelle were on the flight deck. Moose was ready to conduct the radar search.

Mike had already launched both landing capsules. Speaking to Jerry, he said, "The capsule carrying the marine explorer is heading for Crater Lake. Its flight control computer should be able to handle the entire landing sequence, but maybe you could keep an eye on it, in case something goes wrong."

"I have time to do that," replied Jerry.

"Good, because I need to closely monitor the flight of the capsule heading for Zonya's Island. I want to set it down on the beach fairly close to their landing capsule. That gives me a small target, but if the wind doesn't play any tricks, I should be able to do it."

"I've already seen you do several precision landings," commented Michelle, "and you always make it sound like a simple routine matter."

"The flight control computer does all the work. All I have to do is program it."

"I don't believe it's as easy as you're trying to make it sound. Our orbital speed is about five miles per second, and you're planning to take a capsule from that speed to a precise landing on Zonya's Island. That seems like a tough challenge."

"It is, but I have lots of technology to work with. The weather satellite over this area constantly updates the capsule's flight control computer with wind speed and direction, and control vanes give it enough cross-range ability to adjust for changes in the wind. During the final phase of landing, the capsule is suspended from a large para-wing, which can be flown much like a low speed glider. This allows for a circling descent until the capsule is low enough for final approach, which brings the capsule right over the target. Then, the para-wing is pitched up to kill its speed, and the capsule slowly drops to a landing."

"That sounds good, but I am not convinced that it's just technology. I think you have a special talent."

"That's possible, but maybe I've also had a little luck." Mike appreciated the confidence that his wife always had in him. He smiled at her. "We'll soon know if I can pull it off one more time."

On the observation deck, Zeb looked down on the vast ocean they were traveling over from west to east. He noted its beautiful blue color and a few widely scattered clouds that looked like tufts of cotton. Far to the east, the coastline was starting to become visible. Soon, he would again be in contact with his beloved Zonya. He had exciting news to tell her.

As the distance to the coastline steadily decreased, Zeb started to recognize familiar landmarks. The mouth of the river that led to Zonya's Island became visible. Zeb decided it was time to make contact. He dropped into a deep trance. Telepathically, his mind searched for Zonya's mind. In a few seconds, he found her.

"A capsule full of supplies has already begun its descent," he told her. "If all goes as planned, it will land on your island shortly after I lose contact with you. It contains three pistols, two rifles, and one shotgun, along with an ample supply of ammo. There are five communicators, so you can talk with each other when you are separated. The landing capsule has a receiver and a transmitter able to contact the communication satellite in geosynchronous orbit over this location."

"That means you and I can be in continuous contact," exclaimed Zonya. "We will no longer be dependent on telepathic communication and limited by line-of-sight. I love it."

"Also, we'll be able to see each other, because the capsule is equipped with video cameras. Mike uses the cameras, along with radar, to guide the capsule to a precise landing."

"You haven't seen me for 30 years. I've aged some, and I don't even have any makeup to fix myself up."

"You will when the capsule lands. Michelle insisted on including a makeup kit and a nice selection of personal hygiene items. You will also find kitchen utensils."

"Extend my sincere thanks to Michelle."

"I am not done yet. When I told Connie that you were our mission doctor, she insisted on putting some basic medical supplies in the capsule."

"I am very happy about all of this, but I get the feeling that you're not coming down anytime soon."

"The Earth people want to find the starship and investigate it before coming down. Also, they want to explore the area."

"How are they going to do that without being here?"

"The capsule contains three RPVs that are equipped with cameras, microphones, and radar."

"If they'll teach me how to fly one, I'll show them some interesting sights."

"They're easy to pilot. I can show you how."

"I promise you that I will be an eager student."

A few minutes later, Zonya lost contact with Zeb. Filled with anticipation, she began searching the sky for a para-wing, but she wasn't alone. Her entire family was as thrilled as she was. All were scanning the sky.

For several minutes, they searched in vain; then, Zonya's daughter, Ricki, cried out, "I see it!" With an outstretched arm and forefinger, she pointed at the red, white, and blue para-wing that had just dropped below a large cumulus cloud. Everyone quickly spotted it and watched its graceful gliding descent.

It was a perfect morning to land a capsule. There was very little wind. As time slowly ticked by, the para-wing circled the island, dropping ever lower. Finally, it was low enough to make its landing approach. It banked into a gentle turn and established a glide path over the island's southern shore. When the para-wing's cargo was only a few feet above the beach, it pitched up just enough to kill its forward velocity. Then, it dropped straight down. The small capsule full of supplies landed only ten yards away from the large capsule already on the beach. It immediately released its para-wing, which collapsed onto the beach only a few yards away.

A small hatch opened in the capsule's top. A video camera, supported on a mast, rose out of the capsule. It slowly panned the area; then, it returned to Zonya and her family. A hatch in the side of the capsule popped open. The door that had just swung open had a video screen and speakers mounted on it. On the screen was an image of Zeb. He smiled and said, "Here are the guns you ordered, along with the additional items I promised you."

With the video camera now focused directly on Zonya, Zeb said, "I am very happy to finally see you again. You look so good. I wish I were there with you."

Zonya moved closer to the small video screen and feasted her eyes on the father of her daughter. "You look great, and I wish you were here too," she said.

"Jerry thinks we'll be coming down in no more than just a few days. First, he wants to locate the starship and determine what we need to bring down to investigate it."

"I know where it might be. Our Captain told his wife where they were going before they set out on their ill-fated journey. When they didn't return, she tried to talk me into going with her to look for them. But I convinced her that it was too dangerous."

"Where did they go?"

"About two miles upriver from here, there is a stream flowing in from the south. They were going to follow it for about 15 miles. Then, they had to hike east for about five miles through the jungle."

"Jerry and Moose are using radar to search the area. I will tell them to concentrate their search at that location."

"No need to," interjected Michelle. "I've been listening to you. I will let them know."

"Thank you," replied Zeb. Then, speaking to Zonya, he said, "Why don't you start unpacking this capsule. I will tell you about everything as you unload it."

"Sounds good," she responded.

Meanwhile, the flight deck was bustling with activity. Moose was excited by the possibility of finding an intact starship to explore. He directed the computer to analyze the radar data for the area indicated by Zonya. If a starship was hidden in the jungle, the computer would generate an image of it from the data.

Mike was happy that he had delivered supplies to Zonya and her family. With this mission done, he turned his attention to the capsule he had sent to Crater Lake.

"The flight control computer did its job," stated Jerry. "The capsule landed near the middle of the lake, and the flotation collar has already inflated. It's now your baby."

"Thanks," replied Mike, as he popped open the capsule's hatch. A spring-loaded mechanism ejected the folded marine explorer, and it immediately inflated. Mike tested its instruments and electric motor. Everything worked properly, so he started exploring the lake to determine its suitability for shuttle operations.

Mike had barely begun the exploration, when Moose announced, "I've found the starship. At least, I think that's what it is."

"You seem to have some doubts," commented Jerry.

"I am trying to figure out why a starship would have this kind of shape. It looks more like an aircraft, a huge flying wing with a body blended into the middle of it. You simply don't need that kind of streamlined shape to fly through the vacuum of space."

"Perhaps it's not a starship. It might be a landing craft that fulfilled the same function as our shuttles."

"It seems too big for that. It looks like it could haul a lot more payload than our cargo shuttle. If this was their shuttle, then their starship must have been much larger than ours."

Jerry studied the image and said, "Maybe they followed a different design philosophy than we did."

"What do you mean?"

"Let's assume that they came here on a one-way mission like we did, but they had no intention of keeping their starship functional and traveling between it and this planet with shuttles. Maybe the living quarters of their ship contained all of their supplies and equipment, and they shaped it like an aircraft. When they arrived here, they detached it from the propulsion section and landed."

"If that's what they did, they gave up the kind of operational flexibility that we have."

"But the design would be greatly simplified. Their starship would not have had a large hangar deck filled with shuttles, which means they skipped the challenge of designing a shuttle that could return to orbit."

"I can see the logic of doing it that way," agreed Moose, "but I am glad we have shuttles that allow us to return to our starship or visit any part of the planet where there's enough water to land on."

"We don't know if they gave up operational flexibility for a simplified design, but it is a possible explanation for what we're looking at. In any case, I would like to know where that ship came from and why they came here. I would like to know what its inhabitants looked like and how advanced they were technologically. To get these answers, we need to look inside that ship."

"How do you plan to do that?"

"Very cautiously," replied Jerry.

"Surely, you don't think that ship is still inhabited."

"Why not? It came down intact."

"It looks deserted."

"But we're only looking at a computer image generated from radar data."

"That's my point," stated Moose. "It's overgrown with vegetation. It's completely concealed. If it were inhabited, it seems like they would've cleared away some of the jungle, so they could have some open space."

"That's what we would've done, but we can't assume that they would think like us," argued Jerry. "Somehow, we need to get inside that ship and snoop around."

Even though Mike was busy exploring the lake with the newly deployed marine explorer, he had overheard much of the discussion between Moose and Jerry. He put the marine explorer on autopilot and said, "The largest RPV I sent down to Zonya has enough range to reach that ship, especially, if we make the flight during the middle of the day when Alpha Centauri A is high in the sky. Its solar cells will generate maximum energy, which will minimize the drain on its batteries."

"It's pretty close to mid-day right now," stated Jerry.

"Are you trying to tell me that you'd like to launch the RPV?"

"Nice guess."

"If I can drag my wife away from the conversation between Zeb and Zonya for a few moments, I'll have her explain to Zeb which RPV we need Zonya to take out of the capsule, if she hasn't already done that."

Michelle overheard Mike's remark and explained, "I can't help listening to their conversation. They have 30 years of harrowing survival stories to tell each other. They're happy to be alive and overjoyed that they'll soon be back together."

"You're just a hopeless romantic," Mike teased.

"Look into my eyes and tell me you're not touched by their reunion," Michelle demanded.

Mike smiled at his wife. She read the expression in his eyes and said, "I know you very well, and you are also a hopeless romantic." Then, Michelle explained to Zeb what Mike wanted Zonya to do.

After Zonya unpacked the RPV, Mike gave it the coordinates of the starship and launched it. The RPV followed a flight path that was only a hundred feet above the thick forest.

Excellent video from the small aircraft was displayed on a wall-sized screen. Digital signals from two cameras separated by the width of the RPV were combined and enhanced by computer software to create the video. When viewed on a large screen, it had a very real three-dimensional appearance. Watching the video gave one the sensation of being inside the RPV.

"We're looking at a sea of green," commented Jerry.

"I am glad we don't have to hike to that spaceship," Moose said. "A jungle that dense could be a very dangerous place."

"When we reach the spaceship, we'll drop down into the jungle and find out how hazardous it is," stated Jerry.

After a 15-minute flight, the RPV reached its destination, and Jerry took control of it. Slowly circling the derelict starship, he noted that trees had grown up next to it on all sides. Their long branches nearly closed the airspace above it. Concealment of the spacecraft was completed by a layer of fallen leaves that littered its upper surface and by vines sporting dense foliage that had climbed all over it.

"Even knowing where to look, we would never have found it without radar," commented Jerry.

"It would've been difficult," agreed Moose.

"There's something about this that is puzzling."

"What?" Moose asked.

"The image generated from our radar data shows this starship to be intact. How did it come down among all these trees without getting demolished? We should be looking at widely scattered wreckage."

"Maybe it was capable of landing and taking off vertically," suggested Mike.

"As large as that thing is, it would take immense power to pull that off," responded Jerry.

"Maybe the trees weren't there when the starship came down," suggested Moose. "They look young. They are quite tall, but their trunks are small, indicating youth. In this wet tropical area, they could easily have reached their present size in less than thirty years."

"That sounds reasonable," agreed Jerry. "Perhaps, there was an open meadow here when the ship came down."

"Either that or a shallow lake."

"Do you have any evidence indicating a lake?"

"No, I just threw out the idea for the sake of discussion, but we can easily determine if it was possible. All we have to do is look at the topography of the area."

Moose asked the computer to display the topographical data for the area around the starship. "This is interesting," he said. "That ship is resting near the east end of a flat depressed area that is about two miles long, and there's a small river running through it. Near the west end of the depressed area, there's a raised ridge cutting across it that has been breached on the river bed. It's definitely possible that there was once a lake there, and it could have been created by a dam built by animals. In early America, numerous lakes and swamps were created by beaver dams."

"If there was a lake there when that starship came down, it could have landed on hydrofoils," commented Jerry.

"Or it could have landed with lift fans, if the lake was too shallow to land with hydrofoils," added Mike.

"The lake could easily have drained after the starship landed," suggested Moose. "A flood could have opened a breech in the dam. If the animals that built the dam were no longer living there to repair it, the lake would've drained, leaving the starship high and dry. Then, trees quickly seeded into the area and grew up. Now, we have a spaceship surrounded by a forest."

"A large ship floating on a lake could easily have been seen from orbit using only low power optical instruments," commented Mike. "Zeb's Captain probably spotted it, then, used his telepathic powers to search it for occupants."

"If Zeb and Zonya were sleeping at the time, he could have kept it a secret from them," suggested Moose.

"It all adds up," stated Jerry. "Now, I would like to get inside it and look around."

"There are two small mechanical bugs on the RPV you're flying," Mike said. "If we can find a small opening somewhere, we could get them inside."

Jerry slowly flew the RPV around the spaceship, looking for an opening in its hull. But there were no holes resulting from damage, and all hatches were tightly sealed. "It looks like we aren't going to see the inside today," he said.

"But we have proven my lake theory," stated Moose. "The ship is resting on hydrofoils. The bottom of the hull is about eight feet above the ground, indicating they could even have handled rough water."

"Your lake theory does look pretty good," admitted Jerry. "I will take one more look into the wells the hydrofoils retract into, just to make sure that there isn't a small opening that I missed."

"I don't think you're going to find one," commented Mike. "Those wells have to be watertight."

"You're right, but I'm going to look anyway." One by one, Jerry carefully inspected the hydrofoil wells. Finally, he said, "They're tight. There's no way in."

"Maybe the creatures who own the ship are still there," suggested Mike. "They might be living inside it. The hull might be rugged enough to protect them from whatever predators live in this area."

"That's possible," Jerry agreed, "but it sure looks deserted. Also, the area under the ship looks trampled down. It looks like it might be a sleeping area for a bunch of animals."

Jerry inspected the area for clues as to what kind of animals might be using it for their home. A few minutes into the search, the RPV's tiny, but powerful, computer notified Jerry, "Park me in a sunny area. My batteries are getting low."

Jerry immediately piloted the RPV to the top of the spaceship. He found an area where the radiant energy from Alpha Centauri A was pouring down between tree branches and landed the RPV for a recharge. "While the batteries are charging, I am going to try something," he said.

"What?" Mike asked.

"We're going to listen for internal activity," Jerry replied, as he deployed the RPV's sensitive microphone. He pushed it down through the litter of leaves, and nested it against the starship's hull. "Other than listen, there's not much we can do for the time being. I need to let these batteries charge for at least an hour. Occasionally, I will move it to keep it in the sun, and that will allow us to listen to a different part of the ship."

"I am going back to exploring the lake," stated Mike.

"I'll analyze radar data to see what else I can learn about this ship and this area," Moose said.

"What are you hoping to discover?" asked Jerry.

"If the owners of this starship are alive, but not living in it, maybe, I can find them."

"Good luck," responded Jerry. "I need to call my wife. It seems like this is about the time of the day when King and Queen should return to pick up their infant. If they actually do that, I think that will demonstrate that they are quite intelligent."

Jerry picked up his communicator and beeped Connie.

"Hello," she answered.

"How's your patient?"

"He's ready to be released to his parents."

"I am still amazed that his parents even delivered their infant to you. That's tremendous trust on the part of fierce wild creatures."

"Don't forget that we solved a big problem for them once before. To them, we might look like benevolent gods."

"If they understood your hand signals and return to pick up their chick, I wonder how they're going to react when they see that he's healthy."

"We'll soon find out. Take a look at the video from the camera on Western Island."

Jerry did as instructed. "It looks like they're trying to decide if the time is right to visit you. They keep switching their gaze back and forth between Stellar Plateau and Alpha Centauri A."

King stepped to the edge of his cliff-top home, jumped off, spread his wings, and headed toward Pioneer Island. Queen immediately followed.

"They're on the way," Jerry said. "How are you going to present their chick to them so that they can carry him home?"

"I've made a sling with a couple wide belts, and wrapped it around the chick a couple times to immobilize him. The loose ends are tied into a loop for King to grasp with his beak. If these pterodactyls are as smart as we think they are, they will quickly figure out how to unwrap the infant when they return home."

"So, you're going to step outside, walk up to a 400-pound predator, hold his chick in one hand, and the open loop with the other, so he can grab it with his beak?"

"Do you have a better idea?"

"I haven't given it any thought, but your plan sounds very dangerous. This creature could kill you in an instant."

"Why should he? I just saved the life of his infant."

"I know, but I cringe at the thought of you being so close to such an awesome killing machine."

"Dianne will be with me, and she will have her pistol ready."

"She is quick and accurate," Jerry acknowledged, "but I don't believe she'll have to use her gun."

"If that's what you think, what are you worried about?"

"I just don't want anything to happen to you. I almost lost you a couple weeks ago, and once is enough."

"Don't worry," Dianne assured Jerry. "I will be alert."

"Thanks," Jerry replied.

"I'll wear my communicator," Connie said. "That way, we can stay in contact."

"They've just landed," announced Dianne. "It's time to step outside."

Connie picked up the chick. Its wings and legs were secured by the wide straps wrapped around it. Only its neck and head were free to move. The chick alertly watched its surroundings as Connie headed for the front door.

Dianne stepped out first with her gun ready for use, but the big pterodactyls were standing about five yards from the front door and came no closer. They patiently waited. They did not yet know if the Earth people had cured their infant.

When Connie stepped onto the front porch with the infant, they looked at it very closely and made some soft squawking sounds. The infant recognized his parents and enthusiastically squawked back.

Instantly aware that their infant was no longer deathly ill, King and Queen squawked joyously, but they kept their distance. Noticing this, Dianne said, "Apparently, they don't want us to feel threatened. Is it possible that they know we can kill them?"

"They've seen us descend out of the heavens and go back up into the heavens. If they think we are gods, it would be easy for them to believe we could kill them."

"Just the same, let's not test their patience. Let's just get their infant back to them."

"I don't think they're going to attack me, but please be alert." Connie took a deep breath, as if to summon her courage. Then, holding the infant in front of her, she looked into King's eyes and calmly approached him. He waited for her.

When Connie was less than a yard away from the huge raptor, she reached out with her right arm, which supported the chick. With her left arm, she held the open loop and reached toward King's beak.

King made no menacing moves; instead, he looked at the chick, first, at one side, then, at the other side.

"He seems to be studying the sling," observed Dianne.

As Dianne finished speaking, the big pterodactyl looked into Connie's eyes. The gaze was fixed for a few moments. Then, he squawked softly and nodded his head.

Speaking softly, Connie said, "I don't know what you just said, but it looks like you approve of the sling and thanked me for curing your chick."

Connie shifted her gaze to the loop on the end of the sling. King followed her example, so she moved the loop closer to King's beak. He opened his beak a small amount and slipped his lower beak through the loop. Connie slowly dropped her right arm away from supporting the chick. It now hung from King's beak. Connie backed away from him until she was standing beside Dianne on the front porch.

Queen stepped forward and closely inspected her infant. Then, she looked into Connie's eyes, clapped her wings against her sides, and nodded her head. She squawked softly and lingered for a few moments. Then, she turned to the south, started running, spread her wings, and took off. King followed her.

Connie sat down and said, "I'm glad that's over."

"Not as glad as I am," Jerry said.

"You were never in any danger," teased Connie.

"But you were, and I was helpless to assist you."

"I was here," stated Dianne.

"I appreciate that. Both of you handled the situation very well. You showed tremendous courage. And, as a result, we've gained new knowledge about pterodactyls. They sure seem to be intelligent."

"How smart do you think they are?" asked Connie.

"I think we should treat them the same way that we would treat Stone Age humans, if there were any around. Pterodactyls have no technical ability, but it is obvious that they can think and communicate. If they had hands to work with, I believe they would develop tools and technology over a long period of time."

"You're giving them credit for considerable intelligence," commented Dianne.

"Based on what we've seen so far, I think my conclusions are justified. They might very well be the smartest animals on this planet.

One thing that is certain is that pterodactyls are the only animals that can quickly and easily visit Pioneer Island. They have the physical ability to make our lives miserable. Combine that ability with intelligence and communication skills and it is easy to see that they could be a force to be reckoned with. It is important that we learn as much about them as we can."

"So, you definitely approve of what Dianne and I did yesterday and today?"

"Yes! Both of you showed great courage, and I commend you for a job well done."

"Thank you."

Jerry returned his attention to the alien starship. He asked the computer for an analysis of the sound waves detected by the RPV's microphone. It concluded that all sounds recorded were generated by external sources. I am not surprised, thought Jerry. This ship looks like it was deserted years ago, but was it? Maybe its inhabitants became ill when they arrived here. Perhaps their immune systems were unable to cope with this planet's germs. But it seems like their medical technology should have been able to successfully treat any illness. What if they did get sick? They could have reacted by sealing themselves inside their ship for protection while fighting the disease. If they failed, they would've died in the ship; in which case, we would find their skeletons, if we could look inside.

What if they left the ship to build a home somewhere else in the vicinity? But that doesn't make any sense, Jerry thought. Why would they leave the security of living inside the ship along with leaving behind all the technology that it must contain? What could cause them to leave? And where would they have gone? Have they survived and prospered?

Turning to Moose, Jerry asked, "Have you learned anything that might give us a clue about what happened to the owners of this ship?"

"Nothing conclusive, but I have a theory."

"I'd like to hear it."

"I took another look at the radar data for the top of that ship to see if I could find an opening that is concealed by the leaves and plant life; specifically, I looked for a door outline. I looked at the sub-millimeter wavelength data to get the resolution I needed. Take a look at the computer-generated image when this information is incorporated into it."

Jerry did as directed, and said, "I see what you mean. There is the unmistakable outline of large clamshell-type doors in the top of the fuselage. That means they could've had some type of vertical takeoff aircraft."

"If that's the case, they could be living hundreds of miles from here. A VTO aircraft could easily have an operating radius of 500 miles."

"That's true," agreed Jerry. "If they're alive and not living in their ship, they might be difficult to find. But, whatever it takes, I do want to know where they came from, why they came here, what happened to them after they arrived here, and what their current status is. Getting answers to these questions starts with getting inside that ship."

"How do you plan to do that?"

"That's something we need to discuss."

"I have something to add to the discussion," interjected Mike.

"What?" Jerry asked.

"Crater Lake is suitable for shuttle operations. It is deep and relatively free of heavy driftwood. We could land on it as early as tomorrow. With our helicopter, we could fly to that starship and explore it in person."

"That could be dangerous," stated Jerry. "I know it looks deserted, but if it is inhabited, we might not be welcomed as guests. They might shoot us. We don't know how Zonya's abductors died. It's possible that they were killed by the inhabitants of that starship."

"We could fly the chopper by remote control and use it to deliver the equipment needed to explore that ship," suggested Mike.

"What equipment do you have in mind? And how long will it take you to assemble and package it?"

"If I keep it simple, it won't take long, perhaps, no more than a day or two."

"What can you put together that fast?" asked Jerry.

"The cleanest way to get into that ship would be to drill a small hole through the hull and insert a probe with a lamp and camera mounted on its end. Depending on what we see, we might drill a larger hole and drop in a couple mechanical bugs that we can fly from room to room and look around. This could be done with a simple design consisting of nothing more than a metal frame large enough to support a drill press, a camera probe, a manipulator arm, a battery pack, a couple bugs, and a remote control unit. This is all off-the-shelf equipment. It's just a matter of sticking it together."

"Can you have it ready by tomorrow morning?"

"If I start now, and if you help me, we might be done by midnight."

"Why don't you get started, and I'll join you after I fly this RPV back to Zonya's Island. But I want to add one more capability to your design."

"Is it something time consuming?"

"I don't think so. All I want is the ability to plug the hole when we're done. That starship must contain something of great value, or its owners wouldn't have locked it up so carefully before leaving, if they left. I don't want to leave an open hole when we're done exploring it."

"Good idea and that won't take long," Mike said, as he headed for the machine shop.

Speaking to Jerry, Moose said, "I guess you'll be spending another night up here."

"You guessed right."

"I just talked to my assistants. The shuttle is loaded and ready to go. I need to take it down soon, so we can get unloaded yet today. I am assuming you want us back up here early tomorrow, so we can install the elevator deck and load the chopper."

"Another good guess," said Jerry with a smile.

Moose returned the smile, gave Jerry a jovial salute, and said, "Aye, Aye, Captain." Then, he turned and headed for the hangar deck.

Chapter Three

TIME: Day 30, Early Dawn

Moose stepped out of the habitation capsule, stretched straight and tall, and took a deep breath of the early morning air. He noted its pristine freshness and exhaled. He shook his arms and shoulders to rid himself of the last bit of sleepiness.

His eyes quickly adjusted to the dim light, and he looked out over the plateau. The tents the recent arrivals were sleeping in caught his attention. This looks like a remote campsite back on Earth, Moose thought. However, on my last two shuttle flights, I brought down everything needed to build small temporary homes. But they're still having too much fun exploring this place to get serious about home building.

Moose surveyed the sky. To the east, there was just a hint of brightening near the horizon, indicating that night would soon come to an end with the rise of Alpha Centauri A, closely followed by Alpha Centauri B. High in the southeast, he observed Aphrodite, currently in a quarter moon phase. Almost overhead, a little to the southwest, he viewed Nocturne, with its face a little over half lit.

Even with both moons shining, Moose noted that many stars were visible. It sure is great to have a sky that is free of pollution and city light, he thought, as he searched the heavens for known points of interest.

Eventually, his attention settled on a bright star, the Sun. Earth is so far away, he thought. I wonder what I would be doing right now if I were still living there. Life is so very different here.

Deeply engrossed in thought, Moose failed to notice that his wife had joined him. He was startled when she said, "Good morning. Care to share those distant thoughts with me?"

"What do you mean?"

"I've been watching you stare at the Sun. I assume there are some nostalgic thoughts in your mind."

"I was just thinking about how far we've come, and I was wondering what my life would be like if Jerry hadn't found a way to sneak me onto this mission."

"You would be very lonely if you were still on Earth."

"Why do you think that?"

"You would never have met me, and we would be light-years apart."

"I wouldn't like that," Moose said, as he put his arms around his wife and gave her an affectionate hug. For a few moments, they silently enjoyed the warmth of their loving relationship.

"Other than Earth, there's something else I've been thinking about this morning," Moose said.

"What?"

With an upward sweeping motion of his right arm, he said, "Somewhere out there is a star with a life-bearing planet that sent a starship here."

"Where do you think it came from?"

"I don't know. It could have come from anywhere. Maybe we'll find some clues to its origin, when we look inside of it later today."

"This could be a very exciting day for you."

"In more ways than one," Moose responded.

"What do you mean?"

"If the owners of that starship are still around, they might be living somewhere in its vicinity. We don't know if they're friendly or belligerent. Even if friendly, they might mistake our intentions and react with lethal force. Also, we're going to land on Crater Lake. It looks safe, but we've only briefly explored it. Who knows, the owners of the starship might even be living near it."

"You seem apprehensive."

"Not really. We just need to consider all possibilities and be prepared."

"I'm sure Jerry has thought about that too."

"He does seem to have a special talent for anticipating the unexpected," agreed Moose, as he looked at his watch. "I need to get to the shuttle."

"I'll drive," volunteered Dianne, as they walked to the ATV. "Where's your crew?" she asked.

"They might be swimming in South Bay. They told me last night they would go for a moonlight swim before we take off."

"That's understandable. They've only been here three days. After being in space for nearly seven years, something as simple as swimming is quite a thrill."

"Not to mention that it's a refreshing way to wake up."

"I like the way you woke me up better."

"I'm sure glad to hear that," responded Moose.

A short time later, Moose was rapidly climbing away from Clear Lake, heading for rendezvous and docking with the Challenger. In just a few minutes, he reached orbital speed and altitude. The shuttle's flight control computer had done a perfect job of navigation. Moose arrived in orbit only a few hundred yards from the Challenger. Its hangar doors were wide open, and Moose guided the shuttle into the spacious cavern. The doors closed and the hangar began pressurizing.

When pressurization was complete, Jerry and Mike joined Moose and his crew. The shuttle's upper cargo bay doors were opened wide. The elevator deck was lowered into it and latched in place. Electrical connectors were joined.

With this installation complete, the helicopter was loaded into the shuttle and secured. The instrumentation package that Mike and Jerry had built the previous evening to explore the alien starship was already attached to the chopper. Finally, three cartons of supplies were put into the shuttle.

Mike looked at his watch and said, "In a few minutes, we'll be in position to exit this hangar and drop down to Crater Lake."

"I haven't had breakfast yet," protested Jerry.

Mike grinned and playfully said, "So, we're going to delay an important mission just because the Captain's hungry."

"Can you think of a better reason?" asked Jerry.

"I am hungry too," exclaimed Moose.

Mike stared at Moose and Jerry and said, "Well, I suppose I could take another look at Crater Lake while you late sleepers eat breakfast. I didn't find any hazards yesterday, but I may have missed something."

"Good idea," agreed Jerry. "In about an hour and a half we'll again be in position to go down. Let's use that opportunity."

When he finished breakfast, Jerry called his wife. After exchanging pleasantries, they discussed their plans for the day.

Then, Denise appeared on the video screen, "Daddy, when are you coming home? I miss you."

Jerry looked at his daughter's beautiful blue eyes and golden blonde hair. He thought about how well she'd handled interstellar flight and landing on an alien planet. Born in space, the Challenger was the only home she had known until arriving on Alcent. I haven't spent much time with her since arriving here, he thought.

Denise grew impatient for an answer, "Daddy, what are you thinking about? When are you coming home?"

"I was thinking about you and how lucky I am to have such a wonderful daughter. If everything goes well, I should be home tomorrow."

"Will you take me sailing? I want to go to Zeb's Island and see the cave he lived in."

Connie appeared on the screen. "Both children have been curious about Zeb. I've told them where he came from and where he's lived all these years. They're intrigued by the idea of living in a cave, and they want to see it."

"After I get back, we might take them there and camp out for the night."

"That would be fun," declared Denise.

Jerry checked the time. "Right now, I need to get to the shuttle. We'll begin our descent shortly."

"You face lots of unknowns today," commented Connie. "Please be extra careful."

"You can count on that."

A short time later, the shuttle exited the Challenger. With its aft end facing into the direction of flight, Jerry fired its main engine for several seconds. This reduced its speed to less than what was required to maintain orbit, and it began its descent. Jerry turned the shuttle's nose into the direction of flight to prepare for atmospheric entry.

When the shuttle entered the upper atmosphere, friction with the thin air slowed it down and heated its leading edges to a hot glowing cherry red. The shuttle gradually lost speed and altitude. At about 30,000 feet, its speed became subsonic, and it began circling Crater Lake while continuing its descent.

While looking at the landscape far below, Michelle said, "It looks mysterious. I wonder if the starship aliens are still around."

"If they are, we don't have a clue as to where they might be," replied Mike. "Maybe Moose will discover something today. He's doing additional radar recon."

"If they're in this area, they know where we are," stated Jerry. "Until a few moments ago, we were traveling supersonically and generating a strong shock wave. That sonic boom would have alerted them to our presence. Then, they could've spotted us visually and might now be tracking our descent."

"Do you think they'll attack us?" asked Michelle.

"I don't think so," replied Jerry, "but we don't know anything about them, so we can't say for sure."

"Even if they're hostile, I don't think they would attack immediately," commented Mike.

"Why?" asked Michelle.

"It just seems like a species smart enough to achieve interstellar travel would want to spy on us and learn our capabilities before attacking."

"That sounds reasonable," agreed Jerry, "but they are aliens, and we don't know how their minds work."

A few minutes later, the shuttle was in its final approach glide at 225 mph, with Crater Lake directly ahead. Looking out the window to the right, Michelle said, "What an endless sea of green this jungle is."

Abruptly, the green was replaced by blue water. Jerry pitched the shuttle to a slightly higher angle of attack and reduced its speed to 195 mph. Its small stab-con (stability and control) hydrofoils entered the water, followed immediately by its large main hydrofoils. Within seconds, the hydro-drogues were deployed, rapidly slowing the shuttle. When it dropped under 40 mph, it settled into the water and glided on its hull.

"We're here," Michelle announced. "What's next?"

"We're going to the center of the lake," replied Jerry. "Staying there will keep us about two miles away from any of the shores. If the aliens are living nearby, keeping our distance should make us look less threatening. I don't want them attacking us because they think they're defending themselves."

"It would be nice to know if they live on this lake," stated Michelle.

"I agree," replied Jerry, "so I want you and Zeb to launch two

RPVs and explore the shoreline. If they live here, you should be able to find a boat, a canoe, ashes from a campfire, … something."

"I love investigative work," replied Michelle. "Maybe I can remove part of the mystery shrouding this mysterious area."

"I am counting on your talent and Zeb's experience with living on this planet," stated Jerry.

"We won't let you down."

"Good! Also, record everything on video, so we can study it later."

"You got it," replied Michelle, as they arrived at the center of the lake, where the depth was 2,300 feet.

Because of the depth, Jerry could not drop anchor, so he instructed the navigation computer to maintain position with the propeller. Then, he opened the large doors at the top of the fuselage, and activated the elevator deck, which slowly rose to its top position and locked in place. The shuttle now served as a floating air base for the helicopter. Mike and Jerry left the flight deck and went to the chopper to prepare it for takeoff.

Zeb and Michelle launched their RPVs. They flew them to the northern shore and started their exploration at the same place, but Zeb headed toward the east while Michelle went west. They would cross paths on the southern shore; then, each would take a look at the territory explored by the other.

Before working on the chopper, Mike and Jerry scanned the lake in their vicinity for signs of danger. Not finding any, Jerry used binoculars to view more distant parts of the lake. Finally, he said, "I don't see anything that looks threatening."

"That doesn't surprise me; I didn't find anything dangerous with the marine explorer either, just lots of fish."

"Just the same, let's stay alert. Things aren't always what they seem. In fact, why don't you get the chopper ready for flight, while I stand guard."

"What do you expect to bother us out here?"

"I don't know," replied Jerry, "but I have an eerie feeling that we're being watched."

"By what or whom?"

"The obvious answer is the aliens we're looking for, and it would be easy for them to spy on us. All they would need is a small telescope."

"That's certainly possible," Mike agreed. "Maybe our RPV pilots will discover something to shed some light on your suspicions."

"If not, maybe we'll find some clues in that starship."

Mike went to work on the helicopter. In just a few minutes, he had the rotor blades deployed. He checked the instrument package and the winch that would lower it down to the starship. Satisfied that everything was in working order, he said, "It's ready to go, and it's such a beautiful day, I wouldn't mind piloting this thing in person."

"That would be fun, but I think we'd better stick with the plan and fly it by remote control."

Mike and Jerry returned to the shuttle's flight deck. Jerry seated himself at the helicopter's remote control council and immediately started the chopper's powerful, but fuel-efficient, turbine engine. The whine from the inlet compressor joined the muffled roar from the exhaust nozzle to shatter the stillness over Crater Lake. As the engine approached full power, Jerry added a positive angle of attack to the chopper's rapidly spinning rotor blades. The sudden generation of lift caused the helicopter to leap off the shuttle.

Jerry was wearing a video headset, which accessed signals from the many cameras carried by the helicopter. Being sensitive to his head motion, the headset tuned in to the video from whatever direction Jerry faced. Images from the various cameras were smoothly joined by computer software. Thus, Jerry had the very real illusion of actually being in the helicopter's cockpit and felt like he had just taken off.

He flew the aircraft nearly straight up to about 500 feet. Slowly circling, he visually inspected the lake and countryside in every direction. Unable to detect any evidence of the beings he felt were watching them, he headed the helicopter toward the alien starship.

Twenty minutes later, the helicopter arrived over it. Slowly circling the area, Jerry looked for anything suspicious, but all he saw was dense jungle. "It's time to take a look inside that spaceship," he announced, as he brought the chopper to a hover directly above it.

Mike turned on the winch and lowered the exploration package through the jungle canopy. In less than a minute, it was resting on the starship's fuselage. He released it and retrieved the winch cable.

With no place to land, Jerry began the return flight, while Mike started the procedure for entering the derelict starship. Using the robot arm, he cleared debris from a small area and placed a microphone against the hull. He tapped the surface with the robot arm and listened. Then, he transmitted ultrasound at various frequencies and observed the data. Wanting to get a feeling for the kind of structure he was about to drill through, Mike repeated this procedure for three additional locations. He wanted to avoid drilling through a support member or an electrical cable.

Finally, he found a spot he liked and said, "I think this would be a good place to drill an entry hole."

By this time, Jerry had returned the helicopter and joined Mike. "What kind of material do you think we're drilling through?" he asked.

"It looks like some type of composite. It might be carbon fibers imbedded in a special high-temperature epoxy."

Mike drilled a one-half-inch hole. With a small vacuum, he picked up the chips from around the hole and said, "We can examine these later and learn something about their materials technology."

"Good idea, but right now, I'm anxious to see what's inside."

"Let's take a look," stated Mike, as he inserted the camera probe with its small, but intense, spotlight.

After several minutes of looking around, Jerry said, "No surprises here. It appears to be exactly what we expected, a hangar deck."

"That theory is supported by the fact that the floor looks like a retracted elevator."

"But there's no flying machine here, which means they survived their landing and flew away."

"Either that, or they didn't bring an aircraft down," commented Mike.

"I believe they brought one down. This ship doesn't appear to be equipped with any kind of propulsion, which means they could not return to orbit, which means they brought everything down."

"I'm not yet ready to conclude that this is nothing more than an unpowered landing craft. It might have some novel form of propulsion that is far more advanced than anything we're familiar with."

"That's possible," conceded Jerry. "Let's see what we can find."

"It sounds like you're telling me to drill a three-inch hole for the bug."

"You guessed it."

Mike cut the hole and lowered the mechanical bug through it. Jerry deployed its wings and turned on its lights and instruments. He flew the bug forward, hoping to find the starship's flight deck. It was there that he thought he could gain the greatest amount of information. Jerry wore a video headset, so he could see what the bug's cameras were aimed at.

After leaving the hangar deck, Jerry flew into a room that looked like it might have been someone's apartment. He was astonished by what he saw. "You have to see this," he exclaimed.

Mike turned on a video screen and tuned in to the signal from the bug. What he saw, securely attached to a wall, were framed portraits of people. "I can't believe those pictures," he exclaimed. "They look like humans. How can that be? There should be some differences."

"Maybe these pictures were taken on Earth."

"Are you suggesting that these aliens visited Earth en route to here?"

"It's possible," stated Jerry.

"If they had visited Earth, I think they would've been seen. A landing and takeoff would've been hard to hide."

"I'm not saying that they landed on Earth. I'm only suggesting that they could have visited Earth en route to here. They could have obtained pictures of people, along with a wealth of other information, by simply intercepting TV signals from the many communications satellites orbiting Earth."

"With all of the radar systems and optical equipment monitoring the near-Earth environment, I think they would've been discovered," argued Mike.

"What if they detected radio signals from Earth when they were still outside the Solar System and decided to investigate without revealing their presence?"

"I guess that's possible," admitted Mike. "They could have hidden their starship inside a balloon designed to look like a small asteroid."

"What a simple but clever idea. With a little work, they could even have made that balloon reflect radar like an asteroid."

"What's troubling about this is that there might be an advanced race out there somewhere with detailed knowledge about Earth."

"Why does that bother you?" Jerry asked.

"It disturbs me because the people on Earth know nothing about this. Who knows what these creatures have planned for Earth."

"Let's keep in mind that the only evidence we have are pictures that look like they could have been taken on Earth. It's possible that the owners of this starship look exactly like us and that they haven't been anywhere near Earth."

"What's the probability that an intelligent species that closely resembles humans could have evolved on another planet far removed from Earth?"

"I don't know, but it is possible. Zeb's race doesn't look that different from us. Their heads and ears are slightly larger, and their hands have a thumb on either side. Otherwise, they look like us."

"But this is weird. The first things we find in a derelict starship are photos that look like they were taken on Earth. What a shocking surprise. What's next?"

"Let's find out," stated Jerry, as he flew the little bug around the apartment. After examining the furniture, he said, "It appears that two people lived in this room."

"What makes you think that?"

"The bed appears to be designed for two people. In fact, it's about the same size as the bed Connie and I sleep in, which indicates that these people are about the same height as us."

Jerry flew the little bug from room to room and discovered six additional apartments. All appeared to have been inhabited by two people. He found two bathrooms, one for men and one for women. He also found a cafeteria and a small recreation room containing some exercise equipment. "It looks like this ship had a crew of fourteen," he said.

Finally, he reached the flight deck. After investigating it for a few minutes, he said, "This must have been the nerve center for the entire starship. There's far more here than would be needed to land a shuttle."

"Apparently, they simplified their design by incorporating their living quarters, life support systems, supplies, and all essential equipment into this vehicle, which was also designed to be their landing craft. When they arrived here, they separated from their starship's propulsion section and landed with no provision to take off and go somewhere else."

"If that's what they did, they gave up a lot of operational flexibility for a simplified design," commented Jerry.

"To me, it seems like they gave up too much, especially, when you consider all the unknowns that you might have to deal with at an alien destination."

"Maybe they had no choice. Their starship may have been designed and built with severe budget restraints."

"That's possible, but it's also possible that their mission was different from ours. Perhaps they never intended to land here or anywhere else. Maybe their intent was to journey from star to star and report their findings back to their home planet. Landing here might have been the result of an emergency."

"If their mission was to explore the local part of the galaxy, then I wonder, what was the purpose of that exploration? Was it purely scientific, or were they looking for planets to colonize?"

"That second objective could have ominous implications for humans if they reported Earth as a suitable place to inhabit," commented Mike.

"Likewise for us if they made a similar report about Alcent," added Jerry. "What's especially worrisome is the timing. This ship landed here just over 30 years ago. If they visited Earth before coming here and if their speed was limited by the speed of light, then they would have visited Earth about 36 or 37 years ago. So whatever plans their home planet has for Earth or Alcent could be close to realization by now."

"The possibilities are disturbing, but we are just speculating."

"My gut instinct tells me that this is something we need to be seriously concerned about."

"You might be right, but we don't have any hard evidence to go on."

"I believe we're going to find some," stated Jerry.

"Technically advanced societies tend to store everything in their computers. Unless we can figure out how to get into them, I don't think we're going to get the information we need."

"Even if we are able to enter their computers, we won't be able to understand their language. So we need to find another way to understand their mission. We've only investigated one of their apartments. Let's look at the other six."

"What are you hoping to find?" Mike asked.

"I want to take a look at their artwork. People generally decorate their walls with paintings and photographs, sometimes, even maps and charts. Maybe these creatures also decorated that way."

Jerry flew the little bug out of the flight control room and into the nearest apartment, which was somewhat larger than the others. "This may have been the Captain's quarters," he speculated.

On the first wall that Jerry looked at, he found pictures that shocked him and Mike into silence. After staring at the images in disbelief for several moments, Jerry asked, "Do these pictures qualify as hard evidence that these creatures have been to Earth?"

"I'm not sure," replied Mike, as he looked at a picture of the starship Enterprise, then at pictures of Captain James T. Kirk, Spock, and Scotty.

"Where else could they have gotten them?"

"The original Star Trek episodes are classics that are still being broadcast by TV satellites in geosynchronous orbit. Those satellites have plenty of power. It's possible that these creatures could have picked up the signals without getting near Earth."

"If they recorded the hundreds of channels broadcast by one satellite, the end result is still the same: they have detailed information about Earth."

"That, I agree with," stated Mike.

"The big question is: what are their intentions toward Earth?"

"Answering that question might be impossible."

"We have to try," responded Jerry, as he flew the little bug to the next wall decoration, which turned out to be a local star chart.

"It looks like we now know where they're from and where they've been," commented Mike.

"The obvious interpretation of the arrows connecting some of these stars indicates that they are from a planet orbiting Delta Pavonis."

"That is a Sun-like star."

"It looks like their first destination was Tau Ceti," Jerry noted.

"That's another Sun-like star, and it's more than 20 light-years from Delta Pavonis."

"From there, it looks like they went to the Sun."

"That's about 12 light-years," stated Mike.

"Then, they came here. However, it looks like they did not intend to stay here. There is an arrow leading from here back to Delta Pavonis, and that arrow is formed by a dashed line, indicating that part of the trip was not yet made."

"From the Sun to here is a little over four light-years, and from here to Delta Pavonis is about 15 light-years. That means they were on a round trip journey of more than 50 light-years. In terms of our technology, that seems very ambitious."

"Are you implying that their technology might be more advanced than ours," Jerry asked.

"Their journey required them to go through four cycles of acceleration and deceleration. Assuming that they cruised between 80 and 90 percent of light speed, they would have to have left home with several times more fuel than we started with. With our technology, antimatter fuel is very expensive to manufacture. It is possible that they are 50 to 100 years ahead of us and have found an inexpensive way to make the fuel."

"What if their cruise speed were only 15 to 20 percent of light speed? Then, they could have left home with about the same amount of fuel we left with."

"But then, there is another problem," argued Mike, "and that is time. Their journey would have required several centuries to complete. How did they handle that?"

"Maybe they've learned how to control the aging process."

"Again, that would mean that they are scientifically more advanced than we are. People have been trying for centuries to slow and even stop aging, but so far, the knowledge needed to double or triple a human life span has eluded us."

"It's also possible that there's no science involved. Evolution may have simply treated them differently than humans. Their normal life span might just be much longer than ours."

"I can't argue with that," responded Mike. "As far as that goes, they might not even look like humans. Those portraits we saw in that first apartment may be from a TV program from Earth."

"While that's possible, I believe they do look like us."

"You sound convinced."

"When we explored the flight deck, it looked like it was designed for humans. I could be comfortable in there. The same is true for these apartments."

"I get that same feeling," Mike said. "I also get the feeling that no one has lived in this ship for a long time. I wonder where they went."

"I haven't seen anything to even give us a clue where they might be, and we can't snoop around much longer. We need to bring this bug out soon for a battery recharge."

"You have about ten minutes left."

"Good! I'll record the contents of each room on video for future study and take a quick look at the rest of the hangar."

Seven minutes later, Jerry finished the project and flew the bug to the hangar's aft end. There, he discovered a closed door that looked quite sturdy. The door was red, and above it, there was a light panel that was also red. "What do you suppose is on the other side of that door?" he asked.

"Something valuable, something hazardous, or both," Mike replied.

"An exotic type of propulsion system might fit that bill."

"That bulkhead is far enough away from the end of this ship to provide enough room for a propulsion system."

"My bug's batteries are almost dead," Jerry said.

"I think we need to find out what's on the other side of that door."

"Let's do that this afternoon."

"Are you that anxious to deliver Zeb to Zonya for their long awaited reunion?"

"Well, they have been apart for 30 years."

"I didn't know you were such a romantic."

"There's more to it than that."

"Like what?" asked Mike.

"I'd like to give our people a few hours to look at the pictures we already have. If they see something that we need to take a closer look at, we can do that this afternoon when we go back. I don't think that starship's going to go anywhere by then."

"That sounds good, but I think you're just a hopeless romantic," teased Mike.

"Until a couple days ago, Zeb and Zonya didn't even know that each other were still alive. Now, they're overjoyed to find out that they haven't lost each other. You tell me that you aren't happy for them and don't want to see them together soon."

Mike grinned and said, "Of course I do, but I still enjoy pulling your leg now and then."

Jerry flew the bug to the entry location, folded its wings, and retrieved it. Then, while Mike plugged the entry hole and prepared the exploration package for flight, Jerry launched the helicopter to pick it up.

After the chopper left, Michelle and Zeb landed their RPVs. "We've finished exploring the waterfront, and we've found nothing to indicate that the aliens have ever been here," Michelle reported.

"So, we know where they're from and where they've been, but we still don't have any idea where they are," commented Mike. "In fact, we don't even know if they're still alive."

"Have you seen any evidence that they might all be dead?" asked Michelle.

"Only a star chart that indicates they traveled more than 35 light-years to get here. This was the third star they visited, so they had three cycles of acceleration and deceleration. If we assume their cruise speed was 80 to 90 percent of light speed, it could easily have taken them 50 years to come here. They arrived here more than 30 years ago. If they were 30 years old when they left home, they could now be 110. Either they live much longer than we do, or they're dead."

"What if they were able to travel at a speed very close to the speed of light?" Michelle asked.

"That would have drastically slowed down their aging process," responded Mike, "but reaching that high a speed requires a level of technology much more advanced than we have."

"Do you have reason to believe that they didn't have the technology to accelerate to near light speed?"

"No hard evidence, just a gut feeling."

"What do you think that feeling is based on?"

"We just explored their ship, and I felt that I was looking at the kind of technology that would be present in a first generation starship."

"But you only saw their landing craft. You did not see the propulsion section of their ship."

"That's true, but I'm guessing that they were not able to approach the speed of light and slow down the aging process; therefore, they could be around 110 years old."

"If you're correct, I have to believe that they live much longer than we do and that they are alive and healthy."

"Why?"

"I don't believe they would have departed on a long interstellar journey without the expectation of being mentally sharp and physically healthy throughout the trip. Therefore, they live much longer than we do."

"Your logic is pretty good, and you sure asked a lot of pointed questions," commented Mike.

"Have you forgotten that before we left Earth, I was a nationally recognized science reporter, as well as, an investigative reporter?" Michelle asked.

Mike smiled at his wife and said, "I haven't forgotten, and I respect your ability."

"Thank you."

"Despite their possible age, our safest policy is to assume that they are alive and a potential threat to us," stated Jerry. "We simply have no choice but to find them or evidence that shows they perished."

"That could take a long time," commented Mike.

"Why?" asked Michelle. "The Challenger's reconnaissance equipment is very good."

"I know," replied Mike, "but their hangar deck implies that they brought along an aircraft. If it had an operational radius of 500 to 1000 miles, we have a large area to search."

"While that's true, I don't think they would've relocated to the limit of their aircraft's range," Jerry said. "For one thing, they would've had a limited fuel supply."

"You're suggesting that they would have gone only as far as need-ed to find a suitable place to live," Michelle said.

"Unless they had a way to manufacture fuel, it seems reasonable to assume that they would have conserved what they had," responded Jerry. "It seems like they would've wanted to retain the ability to return to their starship if the need arose."

"Their ship looks like they haven't been there in a long time," remarked Mike.

"I get that feeling too," agreed Jerry, "so either they have every-thing they need where they're living or they lost the ability to return."

"Or they're all dead," added Michelle.

"They are alive," stated Jerry.

"Why are you so certain about that?" Michelle asked.

"Earlier, I had the uncanny feeling that we were being watched. During the exploration of the starship, I forgot about that, but the feeling has returned."

"Zeb and I found nothing on the waterfront to indicate they've ever been here."

"There are mountains to the east, and we have clear air this morn-ing. From the high ground, all they would need is a telescope that is equipped with digital image processing and they would have a very good view of us."

"I wonder if they did move to the mountains," questioned Mike.

"That's a possibility we have to consider. If they didn't like the lowland jungle they landed in, mountainous terrain would certainly provide a different environment."

"For one thing, the jungle thins out with altitude," stated Mike.

"And the climate is cooler," added Michelle.

"We believe these people look like us; maybe, they also think like us," speculated Jerry. "Let's find locations within 500 miles where we would like to live and search those areas first."

"I'll relay that to Moose," responded Michelle.

"Good," replied Jerry, who was still busy piloting the helicopter on its return flight. As the chopper passed over the lake's northwestern shore, he said, "Before I land this bird, I will circle the lake and get some additional video, in case you and Zeb missed something."

Less than ten minutes later, Jerry had the chopper hovering above the shuttle. Slowly, he brought it down for a gentle landing. "It's time to deliver Zeb to Zonya's Island," he said.

Michelle translated the message to Zeb, who became very elated. He would soon be with his family.

Speaking to Mike, Jerry said, "I'm going to have you and Michelle fly Zeb to the island. I want to stay here to guard our shuttle."

"Are you expecting trouble?" Mike asked.

"No! But this bird is a critical piece of equipment, and I'm just not comfortable leaving it unguarded."

"I'm with you on that," responded Mike.

"Also, I want to make a good impression on the aliens who are watching us."

"How are you going to do that?" Michelle asked.

"Just being here armed and alert creates a different impression than leaving our shuttle unguarded. Being careless doesn't earn much respect, being ready for trouble does have to be respected."

"I'm good with weapons," stated Michelle. "Would you like me to stay here with you and help put on the show of strength?"

"Thanks for the offer, but I don't think that's necessary; besides, Mike needs you as a translator. You people should get going, and I need to talk to Moose."

While Jerry discussed his reconnaissance ideas with Moose, Mike loaded three cartons of supplies for Zeb and Zonya onto the helicopter. Zeb and Michelle climbed aboard. Mike waited for Jerry to finish his discussion with Moose; then, he said, "See you in a couple hours."

Mike boarded the chopper, started its engine, and took off. The flight would last only 20 minutes.

Meanwhile, on Zonya's Island, an air of excitement was brewing.

Zonya had not had a single visitor in thirty years. Now, her first visitor would be the man she loved.

Zonya received a call from Zeb, who gave her the estimated arrival time. "See you soon," he said.

"Your father's on the way," Zonya said to her daughter Ricki.

"I hope he's not disappointed with me. I'm just a primitive woman, and he's a space traveler from a modern society."

"Don't worry, he is a wonderful man. He will love you and be proud of you."

"I hope so."

"Don't forget that despite all of his training, he has also lived a primitive life for a long time. He knows how difficult it is just to survive, let alone, care for two children. He will respect you."

"But will dad accept my husband? I know what his father did to you and him."

"Your father will not punish Ron-Y for what his father did to us. You worry too much."

"I just want dad to like me and my family." Ricki paused, gazed at her mother, and said, "It looks like you're also concerned about having Zeb like you. You've bathed, fixed your hair, and you're wearing makeup and new clothes from Earth."

"I've aged some over the years, but I want to look as good as I can."

Ricki appraised her mother, who was wearing shorts, a halter top, and tennis shoes. She noted her mother's lean, but ample, figure and her excellent physical condition. "I think you look great," she said.

"Thank you, honey."

Ricki continued discussing her hopes and fears with her mother until the distinct sound of an approaching helicopter interrupted them. They looked toward the southeast and momentarily, it appeared, gracefully flying about a hundred yards above the treetops. It circled the island while Mike looked for a good spot to land. Ricki, Ron-Y, and their children watched it in total fascination. They had never seen a chopper. Zonya stared intently, looking for Zeb. She spotted him looking out a side window, wearing a broad smile.

Mike found an open area on the beach, a short distance from Zeb's large landing capsule. He swooped in, brought the chopper to a hover, and gently set it down. He shut down the engine, and the whining, spinning turbine wound down to a dead stop. Except for the sound of small waves washing the beach and a gentle breeze rustling leaves in nearby trees, silence surrounded the chopper.

Zeb opened the side door, swung his legs out of the cabin, and smiled in the direction of his family, who were more than 100 feet away. Zeb's smile was all that was needed to spark the welcoming committee. Zonya returned the smile and started walking toward him at a fast pace. Her grandchildren threw caution to the wind and raced toward Zeb. They had been told that he was a good man. They wanted to meet him and have a close look at the strange bird that brought him.

After meeting Zeb, the children quickly asked, "What's it like to fly?"

"It's fun," he replied.

Speaking to Mike, Michelle said, "There's a possibility that these kids are going to beg you for a short flight before we leave here."

"That's okay. We have plenty of fuel, and I want to take a look at this area anyway. Maybe I can spot something that will help us find the starship aliens."

Then, Zonya arrived. Ricki and Ron-Y were close behind her. Zonya stopped about two steps away from Zeb, who was still sitting on the seat inside the chopper. They made eye contact and telepathically read each other's thoughts. Their emotions took over. Zeb eagerly reached out for Zonya, and she quickly stepped forward into his welcoming arms. They embraced warmly for quite some time. Then, they separated by about a foot, while still grasping each other. They again made eye contact, and each noticed tears of joy streaming down the other's face. They quickly returned to a tight embrace. "It is so wonderful to be back together," Zeb whispered. "I've been so lonely for so many years."

"Feeling your arms around me has lit a fire inside me that I haven't felt for a long time," responded Zonya, softly. "But we need to save that for later. Our daughter wants to meet you."

Zonya moved to Zeb's right. "This is Ricki," she said, as the young woman stepped forward to meet her father.

Zeb and Ricki appraised each other for a few moments; then, Zeb said, "You are every bit as beautiful as your mother."

Ricki smiled and stepped into her father's embrace. "I am happy you're here," she said. "I have so much I want to tell you, but right now, I want you to meet my husband, Ron-Y."

Ricki moved to Zeb's left. Her husband stepped forward, reached out with his right hand, and firmly grasped Zeb's right hand. "Pleased to meet you," he said.

"Zonya tells me that you've been a good husband for our daughter."

Ron-Y glanced at Zonya and said, "Thank you." Then, he turned to Ricki, who smiled warmly. Turning back to Zeb, he said, "Your daughter inspires me. Motivating me to please her seems to be a natural talent of hers."

"She probably learned that from her mother," responded Zeb.

"And what's wrong with that?" demanded Zonya.

"Nothing! I think it's great," Zeb quickly replied.

"Would you like a tour of our campsite?" Zonya asked.

"Yes, but you'll have to be patient with me. I'm not too speedy on these crutches."

"That's okay. We have lots of time, since you're going to be living with us now."

"That's the best thing that's happened to me in a long time."

"Me too," agreed Zonya, warmly.

"Why don't we start the tour by looking at the capsule that brought us to this planet."

"Good idea! It's going to be our home for a while."

Zeb supported himself with his crutches and stepped away from the helicopter. Accompanied by Zonya, he headed for the capsule.

With Zeb no longer sitting in the entrance, the children stepped right up to the chopper and looked inside. Michelle smiled at them and asked, "Would you like to come in?"

The children turned to their parents and asked, "Can we?"

Ron-Y and Ricki both nodded their approval, and the children eagerly climbed in. Fascinated by the chopper's interior, they looked at everything. Finally, Ricki's son, Joeby, the older of the two children, asked, "Can we go up? I want to fly like the birds."

His sister, Tara, said, "I want to fly too."

Ricki quickly said, "These people have done so much for us. I don't think we should ask them for more."

"It's okay," Michelle interceded. "In fact, why don't you and Ron-Y hop in too?"

"I've had a simple life. I'm not sure I'm ready to leap into the modern world."

"Maybe you're afraid to fly," teased Ron-Y.

Looking a bit anxious, Ricki admitted, "That's possible."

"I have some concerns too, but I don't think we should let it be known that our children have more courage than we do."

"I assure both of you that it's perfectly safe," stated Michelle. "Come on, climb in, you'll enjoy it."

The assurance and the invitation was all that Ricki needed. She seemed worried, but she didn't want to miss out or appear frightened. She entered the chopper, closely followed by her husband. Michelle showed them how to fasten their seat belts; then, she locked the door.

Ricki beeped Zonya on her communicator. "We're going flying. I hate to leave you alone with Zeb, but I'm sure you'll figure out how to keep him busy while we're gone."

"Don't worry. It's been a very long time, but I haven't forgotten how."

"Have fun! See you when we get back."

"Don't come back too soon."

Having overheard the conversation, Michelle grinned at Ricki and said, "I don't think we should disturb them for a while."

Ricki smiled naughtily and nodded.

"Is everyone ready to go?" Mike asked.

Michelle checked everyone's seat belt and said, "They seem a bit nervous, but they're ready. Let's give them a thrill."

Mike started the turbine and brought it up to full power. The muffled roar flowed through the helicopter's structure and filled the alien passengers with anxiety. They looked out the windows and wondered if it was too late to jump out. Mike read their expressions and decided to take off immediately. With the rotor spinning at maximum rpm, he added positive angle of attack to the blades, and the chopper sprung into the air. Mike immediately climbed to 3000 feet and slowly circled Zonya's Island while surveying the countryside.

Michelle turned and looked back at the passengers. They seemed filled with mixed emotions. They appeared fearful about the altitude, but even so, they were enjoying the thrill of a lifetime. They had only dreamed of being able to fly like birds, and now, they were doing it. Excitedly, they looked around and pointed at things that caught their attention.

When Mike was satisfied that he had a feel for the lay of the land, he put the chopper into a dive that he felt was steep enough to scare his passengers. He abruptly leveled off at 600 feet, then, slowly descended to 300 feet. "We're going to follow the river to the ocean and then explore the coast on both sides of its mouth," he said to Michelle.

As Mike followed the meandering river, he and his passengers saw much lush jungle but nothing indicating the presence of the starship aliens. At the ocean, Ron-Y and Ricki stared at the vast body of water in disbelief. Zonya had told them about it, but they were unprepared for its vastness. The children were even more amazed. Their adrenaline was still flowing freely from the delightful excitement and imagined dangers of flying, and now, a vast water world confronted them.

"Is it real?" Joeby asked.

"It sure is," replied Ron-Y.

"Where did all the water come from?" Joeby asked.

"Our river filled it up," answered Tara.

"No way!" objected Joeby. "Our river doesn't have enough water."

"This ocean is where the rain comes from," Michelle told the children. "Many, many rivers carry the rain back to the ocean."

The children thought about Michelle's comment, struggling to understand this new concept. Being primitive, they had never considered this possibility, but how could they disbelieve Michelle. She was from Earth and knew how to travel between stars.

By this time, Mike had turned south. He wanted to explore the coast for about 40 miles. The children continued staring at the ocean, attempting to comprehend its size. Finally, Joeby said, "I want to touch the ocean."

Michelle relayed the request to Mike and added, "I wouldn't mind stretching my legs a bit. It might be fun to wade in the surf."

"It might also be dangerous," responded Mike.

"Where is your sense of adventure?" teased Michelle.

"I have more than enough guts to keep up with you, but this is a new area for us. We don't know what dangers are down there."

"That's true, but there's a large, open beach directly ahead. If we circle it and check it out, we should be able to land on the wet sand near the water. All of us adults are armed. If we stay alert, we should be safe."

"Okay, but I am going to leave our turbine idle, and we're not going to go very far away from this bird."

"I can live with that. I just want to walk barefoot on the sand and let the surf wash over my feet."

"I think the real reason you want to land is so the children can get their feet wet."

"Well, they've never seen an ocean. Why not let them run in the surf for a few minutes."

"Okay, but I don't want anyone getting into water more than a few inches deep. We don't know what kind of predators live in this ocean. There could be salt water piranhas here."

"I think you're being overly cautious."

"Just trying to keep everyone alive."

Mike dropped down to 50 feet above the sand and flew along the edge of the jungle, which was about a hundred yards back from the water's edge. With the trees stretching to a height of 200 feet or more and with the foliage being quite dense, it was difficult to see into the jungle for any significant distance. "It's impossible to see if any predators are hiding in there," Mike said.

"Except for various kinds of seabirds, the beach is deserted," noted Michelle.

"We'll land near the water, and I will stand guard while the rest of you play in the surf."

While Mike looked for a landing site, Michelle explained the plan to their passengers. "It'll be fun!" exclaimed Joeby.

A few moments later, Mike found a suitable landing spot and set the helicopter down. He brought the rotor to a stop but left the turbine idling. After staring at the jungle, he stepped out of the chopper. He checked his rifle and pistol. The other adults were armed only with 10.5 mm pistols. All checked their weapons.

Michelle took off her shoes and socks, picked up a small bottle, and headed for the ocean to collect a sample for analysis. When she judged that she was close enough, she stood still and waited for the incoming surf. In just a few seconds, the water came racing in. It covered her feet up to her ankles. She reached down and filled her sample bottle. Then, she walked back to the chopper and put the bottle inside.

Zonya's family had never seen ocean waves crash onto a beach, the water race in, only to race back out moments later. The roar of the surf added to their new experience. Awestruck, they stood still, staring at and listening to the huge ocean in front of them. The children seemed almost frightened by it, but when they saw Michelle nonchalantly walk back toward the roaring monster, they decided to join her.

Tara grasped Michelle's right hand while Joeby grabbed her left hand, and together, the trio approached the incoming surf. The children seemed fearful of the rapidly approaching water, but they were thrilled when it washed over their bare feet. When it went racing back out, they released Michelle's hands and chased after it. When the retreating water stopped and came charging back in, the children screamed in delight and ran to stay ahead of it.

Seeing their children wildly excited was too much for Ron-Y and Ricki to just watch. They decided to join the chase-and-escape game that their children had invented. The fun continued for several minutes until it was suddenly brought to a halt by the sharp report of a gunshot. Michelle quickly ordered the children and Ricki into the chopper; then, she went to her husband's side. Ron-Y had already joined Mike.

They were looking at a pack of small dinosaurs that were strolling out of the jungle. "They are dangerous animals," Ron-Y said to Michelle. "They are intelligent hunters. Even though they never get bigger than about 150 pounds, they are able to kill animals that weigh several thousand pounds with well-coordinated group attacks."

"Are they going to attack us?" Michelle asked.

"This pack has probably never seen people or a helicopter. I think they will study us first."

"Why is the pack splitting? Some are going to the left, while others are going to the right."

"They will form a semicircle to trap us against the ocean while they investigate us with probing attacks and plan their final assault."

"Are they smart enough to do all that?"

"Like I said, they are very intelligent hunters."

Michelle translated Ron-Y's comments to Mike.

"There are 23 of them," stated Mike. "If they're hungry, their first probing attack should come soon."

Mike had hardly finished speaking when an animal directly in front of him broke from the ranks of the semicircle and aggressively approached, snarling hideously. Quickly raising his rifle, Mike aimed and fired, killing the animal instantly.

The sharp report of the rifle caused the rest of the pack to stop growling. They looked at their fallen comrade, but they did not break position. "It looks like they're thinking," Michelle said.

"Since they're not making any more probing attacks, they've apparently figured out that we can easily kill them," commented Mike.

"Maybe they'll leave."

"I hope so. There are too many for us to kill if they all attack at once."

"Can we leave without provoking an attack?" Michelle asked.

"I don't know. We have to back away from them to get into the chopper. That might look like weakness and invite an attack. I don't think we can get into the chopper before some of them would be on top of us."

"Maybe we should kill a few more. That might cause a few of them to panic, break ranks, and charge into the jungle. The rest might follow."

"It might also cause an attack. I think we have to boldly face them and hope they leave."

"I was afraid you'd say that. I've never faced the prospect of violent death before. I want out of here."

"Don't panic! Staying in control is our best chance."

"How can you be so cool in the face of death?"

"I don't see that we have any choice. We have to wait for an opportunity to leave."

"They aren't in any hurry to attack. Some are even settling down into a resting position."

"Ron-Y has lifelong experience with these brutes. Ask him if he knows what they're doing."

Michelle discussed the situation with Ron-Y. Then, she reported to Mike. "Ron-Y said these animals aren't just clever hunters; they're also patient. Once they select their prey, they don't usually give up. He thinks they're planning to keep us trapped until nightfall. They have excellent night vision and will try to sneak up on us during the darkness."

"That's just great! We need to get out of here long before then."

"What are we going to do?"

"If Ron-Y is right, we aren't in danger of immediate attack unless we provoke it, so let's stay cool and think this through."

"Those brutes are sure ugly. Just looking at them sends a chill up and down my spine. They look like something out of a nightmare."

Mike carefully appraised the creatures. "They almost look like a cross between a dinosaur and a wolf. They have canine bodies, except they don't have fur; they have dinosaur hide. Their heads look like a small version of a T-Rex head. Their tails are much smaller than dinosaur tails, but larger than a wolf's tail. I think lupusaurus would be a fitting name for them."

"They sure are hideous."

"That they are, but they look like quick, efficient killers. We could try to shoot our way out of this, but if just one of them gets through, one of us will surely die. I feel like a deer surrounded by a wolf pack."

"I hate this waiting game," stated Michelle.

"Maybe we can lull them into a state of reduced vigilance by staying relaxed. If they believe they have us trapped, we might be able to slowly move closer to our chopper without alarming them."

"What if they attack?"

"Then, we open fire and hope for the best, but the closer we get to the chopper, the greater the distance some of them have to cover to get to us. Buying an extra second or two might give us the margin we need. If we make it all the way to the chopper, we should be able to hop in and close the doors before they get to us."

"Your plan seems to be our best chance."

"Talk to Ron-Y and let me know what he thinks."

"OK!"

While Michelle talked with Ron-Y, Mike's communicator beeped. It was Connie. "I'm worried about Jerry," she said. "He won't answer his communicator."

"Maybe he's busy doing something."

"I've called three times in the last ten minutes. He should've answered one of those calls."

"I think it's too soon to worry. He might simply be tied up."

"I don't think so."

"Why?"

"He would've answered the call if at all possible. He wouldn't worry me unnecessarily."

Mike thought about possible reasons why Jerry didn't answer. Then, he admitted, "I think your concerns are justified."

"Can you get to the shuttle right away and investigate?"

"We have a little problem of our own at the moment, but I believe we have a way out."

"What's your problem?"

"We're surrounded by a lupusaurus pack."

"You're surrounded by what?"

"A lupusaurus pack, I'll explain later. I'm worried about Jerry too, so we've got to get out of here and check on him."

"Ron-Y has misgivings about your plan," Michelle reported. "He thinks the pack will attack before we can climb into the chopper."

"We've got to try it anyway. Jerry might be in trouble, and we need to get to the shuttle. Ask Ron-Y if he's any good with that pistol. He only had yesterday to practice."

A few moments later, Michelle said, "He and Ricki fired several dozen rounds in practice. He said they will have no problem hitting charging lupusaurs."

"Okay, here's what I want to do. The turbine is still idling. I want you to slowly slip into the chopper and put the rotor in gear. When it starts turning, the eyes of the pack will be fixed on it. Since they don't know what it is, they might be confused into inactivity for a few moments. That's all the time Ron-Y and I will need to hop in and slam the doors. I want you and Ricki to have your windows open and your guns ready. Shoot any animal that makes a threatening move. Hopefully, that will put doubt in the minds of the other animals and further confuse them into inactivity."

Michelle explained the plan to Ron-Y, then to Ricki. All readied their weapons for instant action.

Trying to act inconspicuous, Michelle slowly scanned the pack that encircled them. They seemed all too confident that they would eventually kill and eat their prey. While alertly watching them, Michelle inched her way toward the helicopter. She reached it without incident but did not immediately enter it. Mike and Ron-Y needed to get closer, and they were slowly closing the distance.

One of the animals, apparently the pack leader, was watching closely and seemed to sense that the quarry might be attempting escape. Menacingly, it growled out an alarm. Instantly, every animal in the pack came to full alert.

"I think they're going to attack!" Mike yelled. "Hop in! Kick the rotor in gear! And jam the throttle to full power!"

As he finished speaking, Mike quickly raised his rifle and aimed at the pack leader. The animal yelped out a command. Mike fired, instantly killing the lupusaur, but it was too late. The rest of the pack had already heard the command and broke into an attack. Realizing that they could not kill all of the animals, Mike and Ron-Y bolted for the chopper. Ricki opened fire, killing the two closest animals. Having completed her tasks, Michelle risked hitting Mike when she shot a lupusaur that was only a few feet away from grabbing him as he jumped into the pilot's seat.

Ron-Y had lived his entire life on this savage planet. His survival instincts were sharp, and he sensed that a lupusaur was closing in. So when he leaped for the open passenger door, he did a mid-air spin. He entered the chopper backwards, but he was able to face and shoot his attacker in the chest as the animal landed on him. With his left forearm, Ron-Y struck the lupusaur's neck, thereby keeping the animal's open, teeth-filled jaws away from his neck.

Alarmed by the way their father was pinned by a lupusaur, Joeby and Tara screamed while Ricki fired her pistol into the animal's open mouth. The bullet passed through the animal's brain and out the top of its head. Assured that it was dead, she helped her husband shove it out the door. Mike had already lifted off, so the dead animal crashed into the midst of the yelping pack that had been cheated out of its prey.

Ron-Y's upper body and face were covered with blood. His children were terrified. "Daddy! Are you all right?" they cried out.

"I might look like a bloody mess, but it's all lupusaurus blood, and I'm okay," he smiled reassuringly.

Tears streamed down Ricki's face. "I am so happy that we're all okay," she said, weakly.

Worried about Jerry, Mike quickly cleared the lupusaurus attack from his mind and climbed to only 400 feet. He brought the helicopter up to full power. He wanted maximum speed, which was well over 200 mph. In less than 15 minutes, he landed on Zonya's Island. Ron-Y and his family jumped out, and Mike immediately took off for Crater Lake at top speed.

Chapter Four

Shortly after taking off from Zonya's Island, Mike received a call from Moose, who was onboard the Challenger. "I've just passed over Crater Lake. I called Jerry and got no response, so I trained our optical instruments on the shuttle. He's not on deck, so unless he's inside with his communicator turned off, he's disappeared."

"He wouldn't turn off his communicator," insisted Mike.

"What happened to him?"

"I aim to find out as soon as I get there."

"I hope you don't find out the wrong way."

"What do you mean?"

"Suppose Jerry was captured by the starship aliens, they could be waiting for you."

"I am armed."

"So was Jerry."

"That's what makes this so puzzling," commented Mike. "He was not only armed, he was also on full alert. All morning, he kept saying that we were being watched. Apparently, he was right."

"We don't know that for sure, and we don't know that Jerry's been abducted. I was only throwing that out as a possibility. He could be unconscious inside the shuttle."

"That doesn't seem likely," responded Mike.

"I know that Jerry's been in excellent health, but things do happen. He could've had a heart attack, a stroke, a burst aneurysm, food poisoning, a lethal sting from an insect . . ."

"OK! You've made your point," Mike interrupted. "But, in case he was abducted by aliens, I am going to land a short distance away and investigate the shuttle with an RPV."

"After what we've just been through, I don't think we should land on a beach," stated Michelle.

"We're not going to," responded Mike. "This chopper's landing gear is equipped with inflatable pontoons."

"That's convenient."

A few minutes later, Mike and Michelle arrived over Crater Lake. Mike piloted the helicopter toward the shuttle, which was still near the lake's center. Michelle studied the shuttle with binoculars. "It looks deserted," she reported.

Five hundred yards from the shuttle, Mike stopped approaching it and began circling it. "The hatch to the flight deck is open," Michelle said.

"Good! Let's look inside," stated Mike, as he inflated the helicopter's pontoons and set it down.

Michelle put on a video headset, launched an RPV, and flew it into the shuttle's interior. Quickly looking around, she said, "He's gone! What happened to him?"

"I don't know, but we're going to investigate and find out."

"Are we going to land on the shuttle?"

"No! If there are any clues to be found, the downwash from our rotor could blow them away."

Mike deployed the helicopter's marine propeller. With the turbine still idling, he shifted the propeller into gear.

A couple minutes later, he tied up to the shuttle's left wingtip. He and Michelle stepped onto the wing and walked to the wide open cargo hold. They stepped onto the elevator deck. "Jerry had planned to be on this deck with his rifle," Mike said. "He wanted to look alert and ready for action."

"He wouldn't have just looked alert. He would've been alert, because he was convinced that we were being spied on."

"That rules out a couple possibilities."

"Which ones?" Michelle asked.

"He could not have been carried away by a pterodactyl. He would've seen its approach and shot it or taken cover. And if the starship aliens had tried to capture him, he would've seen them. We have good visibility in all directions. It would be impossible to not see an approaching boat."

"So where does that leave us?"

"Maybe he's still onboard. There are some compartments that you couldn't get into with the RPV, like the reactor room, for example. Let's look everywhere."

"I don't like this," Michelle said, as she checked her pistol to make sure it was ready to fire. "Why don't you investigate, while I cover your backside."

"I'm ready. Let's go."

Pistol in hand, Mike cautiously entered the flight deck. As expected, it was deserted. He approached the restroom, its door was closed. "A perfect place to ambush us from," he said.

"That's true, but we have to look inside."

After directing Michelle to the left, Mike stepped to the restroom door's right. He made eye contact with Michelle. She was ready, so he reached out, grasped the door latch, turned it, and quickly flung the door open. Instantly, Mike pointed his pistol into the restroom; then, he looked in. It was empty.

Compartment by compartment, Mike and Michelle searched the rest of the shuttle, but to no avail, Jerry was gone, and nothing had been disturbed. "How could he have just vanished?" questioned Michelle.

"I don't believe he did. There has to be some evidence to indicate what happened to him. Let's inspect the elevator deck."

Several minutes later, Michelle said, "It looks clean."

"That just means that there aren't any obvious clues," responded Mike, "but Jerry could not have just disappeared into thin air. Whatever captured him had to leave something behind."

"What should we be looking for?"

"I don't know, but we have to consider all possibilities and think about what clues each capture scenario might have left."

"We don't think he was captured by a pterodactyl or by the starship aliens, so what does that leave?" Michelle asked.

"I think the starship aliens have him."

"But earlier you said that wasn't likely, because Jerry would've spotted their approach."

"What I said was that Jerry would've seen an approaching boat."

Michelle's eyes lit up as the implication of Mike's remark dawned on her. "Are you saying that they have a small submarine?" she asked.

"We do, and their landing craft is certainly big enough to have carried one down."

"That means they could've been watching us from right under our noses."

"That's possible, and it would've been easy. All they needed was a tiny camera pack floating on the surface connected to the sub by a fiber-optic cable. Had it been disguised to look like a small piece of driftwood, we would've ignored it."

"And they could've watched our every move without us even being suspicious." As Michelle finished speaking, she began staring intently at the water around the shuttle.

"What are you looking for?"

"Suspicious looking driftwood."

"I don't think you're going to find any. They're long gone by now."

"What if they want to capture us too?"

"That's possible," admitted Mike.

"Maybe we should leave and come back with a lot more people."

"I'd sure like to give this deck a more thorough inspection first. We need some clues. Right now, all we have to go on is speculation."

"I'd like to get out of here, but you're right. I'll stand guard, but I want more firepower. Let me grab a rifle from the gun locker."

Mike's communicator beeped. It was Connie. "Have you found my husband?" she asked, sounding very worried.

"Unfortunately, we haven't, but we're not giving up. I believe he's still alive, and we are going to find him."

"Thanks for being so positive, but I need something concrete. Why do you think he's still alive?"

"I think the starship aliens have him, and to them, he's a lot more valuable alive than dead."

"Why?"

"By keeping him alive, they can get information about us. If they kill him, they gain nothing."

"But how can they learn anything from Jerry? There has to be a huge language barrier to overcome."

"There may not be a language problem. These aliens have been to Earth. They've undoubtedly recorded jillions of TV programs and other communications. They probably understand the most common languages used on Earth."

"I hope you're right, because other explanations for my husband's disappearance don't leave me with any hope for getting him back."

"I need to search for clues, and that will take my full attention. Michelle will stand guard, but I want more eyes watching the area around this shuttle. We have a couple RPVs. I want you and another person to fly them. Circle this shuttle about 50 to 100 yards out. If something happens to us, you'll have it on video."

"Dianne is with me. She can fly one of the RPVs. We'll scream if we see anything."

"Good!"

Mike went into the shuttle and brought out the two RPVs. By remote control, Connie and Dianne launched them and began circling the shuttle.

Dropping to his hands and knees, Mike began a meticulous search of the elevator deck. Believing that Jerry was taken by something that came out of the water, he decided to start his search on those parts of the deck with easiest access from the water.

Five minutes into the search, Mike found what he was looking for. At the front end of the deck, on its right side, he found several splotches of faint discoloration. He examined the spots very closely. "If I'm not mistaken, this is algae," he said. "It looks like something came out of the lake and left puddles of water while capturing Jerry. Then, the water evaporated, leaving behind traces of algae."

"But how could Jerry have been caught unaware?" asked Michelle. "It seems like he would've put up a fight."

"That depends."

"On what?"

"If he were faced by one or more large marine predators, he would've shot them or fought them any way that he could. If the aliens got the drop on him, and he suddenly found himself looking into the barrel of a rifle, he would've surrendered peacefully. Then, he would play along with them and look for an opportunity to escape."

"Do you see any sign of a struggle?" Michelle asked.

Search as he might, Mike could not find any evidence of a fight: no blood stains, no bits of skin, no hair, no scales, no scuff marks, no shell casings. "Except for the traces of algae, this deck is absolutely clean," he said.

"Does that mean Jerry's still alive?"

"The chances are a lot better than if we were looking at abundant evidence of a life and death struggle."

"I hope you're right, but we know so little about this planet that I don't think we can rule out capture by a large marine predator."

"What kind of carnivore could've taken him without leaving any sign of a struggle?"

"Back on Earth, there are frogs that nab insects by flinging their long sticky tongues at them," replied Michelle.

"Are you suggesting that a giant frog captured Jerry? You can't be serious."

"No! I'm only citing that as a capture technique that might be quick enough and clean enough to not leave any clues. This lake is four miles across and very deep. It could certainly harbor a species of large predator equipped with a long octopus-like arm. If the arm had suction cups and stingers and were, let's say, 50 feet long, such a creature could stay submerged and make a good living by grabbing animals that come to this lake to drink. The creature could have eyes at the ends of small tentacles. If these tentacles had a camouflage color scheme, that made them look like driftwood or seaweed, they would be easy for a thirsty animal to overlook."

"Such a creature could exist," agreed Mike.

"Jerry was convinced that we were being watched. Maybe he sensed the presence of a hungry predator."

"I sure hope you're wrong, because such an animal could've taken Jerry without a struggle. If Jerry were pacing the deck, all it would have to have done was wait until Jerry was near the water. Then when Jerry turned his back to walk in the other direction, the creature could've flung the long arm out at lightening speed, wrapped it around Jerry, and yanked him into the lake. It would've been over so quickly that Jerry would not have had a chance to put up a fight. And the only clue as to what happened might be some lake water carried onto the deck by the long arm."

"I was feeling hopeful, but now, I feel empty," commented Connie. Mike and Michelle had left their communicators turned on so that everyone could tune in to their investigation.

"I wasn't trying to smash your hopes," responded Mike, "but we have to consider all possibilities. I still feel in my heart that we are going to find Jerry alive."

"Thanks Mike! I needed that."

"I think we're going to find him too," added Michelle, "but we sure don't have much to go on."

"Just these algae stains," stated Mike, "and I'd better make sure that this is algae from this lake."

Mike went into the shuttle and returned with a small jar of pure water. He poured some of it onto the algae stains. Then, he picked it up with a suction device and put it back into the jar. He lowered a second bottle into the lake and filled it. "It shouldn't take Dianne very long to determine if water from the lake made the splotches here on deck," he said.

"Does that mean we're ready to leave?"

"Almost."

"What's next?"

"We need to go to Pioneer Island to pick up our sub and bring it here, so we can explore the depths of this lake. But before we can leave, I need to get our chopper onboard."

"Maybe we should leave it here, so we can use it to search for Jerry. We could fly it to Zonya's Island and leave it there until we need it."

"That's a good idea, except that I need it when we get back to Pioneer Island."

"What for?"

"I need to lift this elevator deck out of the shuttle to make room for our sub. Since we don't have a crane, I have to use the chopper."

"It sure would be convenient to have it here. These aliens have to live somewhere. Maybe we could find them with the chopper."

"After we get the sub here, I'll have someone go back and get it. Unfortunately, it's getting late. It's going to be dark before we get back here."

"Let's wait until morning, so we can get some sleep," suggested Michelle.

"Our night surveillance equipment is very good," argued Mike. "We could search for the aliens tonight."

"That's true, but the aliens are aware of our technology. They're not going to reveal themselves just because it's dark."

"You're probably right about that," acknowledged Mike. "We might as well get some sleep and start out fresh tomorrow."

"I won't be getting much sleep tonight," Connie said, sounding brokenhearted. "If there's any way to find Jerry tonight, please do it. I can't wait until tomorrow."

"I know how you feel," responded Mike. "But if the aliens have Jerry, they're not likely to kill him until after they get all the information they want. Jerry will figure that out. To buy time, he will stall and negotiate over every bit of info he gives them. He will also try to find a way to tell us where he is."

"How can he do that?" asked Connie.

"I don't know right now, but Jerry is aware of the Challenger's recon capabilities. He will try to do something that will get our attention."

Moose had been listening to the discussion. "I will be up all night," he said. "Every time we pass over this area, I will be searching for any little thing that might tell us where Jerry is."

"Thank you!" replied Connie.

"Before we leave for the night, I want to take another look at the beaches," Mike said. "If the aliens have a small sub in this lake, they have to be living nearby. There should be tracks on the beach, a hidden canoe … something."

"While you do that, Dianne and I will keep an eye on the shuttle," stated Connie.

"I'm going with you," exclaimed Michelle.

"I would not even consider leaving you behind," Mike said.

Two minutes later, Mike and Michelle took off and flew to the south shore of the lake. "I want to get back to Pioneer Island early enough to load the sub yet today," stated Mike. "That gives us about a half-hour to search these beaches."

"What do you expect to find that Zeb and I didn't find with the RPVs this morning?"

"I don't know, but evening shadows are different than early morning shadows. We have video from this morning, and we'll get more video now. We'll have people meticulously compare this morning's video to this evening's video."

"That will give Connie something to do and help her deal with her anxiety."

"It will give all of us something to do tonight. None of us are going to be able to sleep much anyway."

"Why are we flying so close to the ground? Aren't you worried about crashing?"

"If the aliens are here, they might have boats or something hidden in the bushes. I am hoping that our rotor downwash will blow away the cover or move branches around enough, so we can see anything that might be hidden."

"Clever idea, but dangerous. One of our rotor blades could hit a tree, and we could crash."

"I know, but we have to find Jerry, and right now, we have no clues except algae stains and speculation. We have to take the risk. If anything's hidden along this waterfront, we need to find it."

"OK! But you are scaring the daylights out of me."

"It can't be helped. You can take your mind off the danger by focusing on the search. Look straight down and try to see through the bushes when our downwash whips them around."

"I'll try, but I don't like flying only a couple feet above the shrubs."

"Concentrate on the search, and I'll make sure we don't crash."

"OK!"

Mike and Michelle steadily worked their way around the lake. A little over a half-hour passed by and Mike said, "We're back where we started."

"And I haven't seen a thing to indicate that the aliens have ever been here," stated Michelle.

"Maybe a careful look at our video will reveal something."

Two minutes later, Mike brought the helicopter down for a soft landing on the shuttle's elevator deck. He secured it and nested its rotors. Then, he lowered the elevator deck, dropping the helicopter into the shuttle's interior. "As soon as I close the doors and put some water in our fuel tanks, we'll be ready to take off," he said.

"I wish you didn't have to leave and could just keep looking for my husband," Connie said.

"I wish we could too, but we need our sub for the next phase of the search," responded Mike.

"I know, but when you leave, I will feel like Jerry's being abandoned."

"If Jerry's able to hear or see us depart, he'll figure out what we're up to. In the meantime, there's something you can do for me."

"I'll do anything that will help find Jerry. What do you have in mind?"

"As soon as we take off, I want you to bring our marine explorer to the center of the lake and search the depths with its sonar and cameras. Set up a search pattern of expanding circles from the lake's center."

"Anything specific you want me to look for?"

"A midget submarine, large animals, and anything that might lead us to Jerry."

"I will help her," insisted Dianne.

"Good! Now, it's time to land the RPVs. We need to take off."

Dianne and Connie returned the RPVs, and Mike closed the upper cargo bay doors. Drawing power from the shuttle's nuclear reactor, Mike pumped lake water into the shuttle's fuel tanks. Since this was a brief sub-orbital flight, covering a distance of only 1600 miles, Mike filled the tanks to only one-third of their capacity.

In less than ten minutes, the fueling was complete, and Mike fed power to the shuttle's marine propeller. Quickly, the shuttle reached 40 mph, rose up out of the water, and rode on its hydrofoils. The nuclear thermal rocket thundered into action. Water pumped through the reactor's heat exchanger instantly became high-pressure vapor and expanded out the rocket nozzle. The shuttle rapidly accelerated to 200 mph, pitched into a steep climb, and headed for Pioneer Island.

Twenty minutes later, Mike landed on Clear Lake and taxied into South Bay. He opened the upper cargo bay doors and moved the elevator deck to its top position. He prepared the helicopter for flight while his crew from Pioneer Island entered the shuttle. As soon as Mike took off, they disconnected the elevator deck and its associated equipment. When it was ready for removal, Mike lifted off from Stellar Plateau, dropped down to the shuttle, and hovered over it. He lowered the winch cable from the chopper and waited for it to be hooked to the elevator deck. The helicopter strained as Mike steadily increased power and slowly lifted the deck out of the shuttle. Mike hauled it to Stellar Plateau and landed the chopper nearby.

It had been a long tiring day, and Mike was hungry. But before he could eat dinner, he wanted the submarine loaded on the shuttle, so he joined the crew on South Bay. By the time he arrived, they had already closed the upper cargo bay doors and opened the lower cargo bay doors. Even with these doors open, the shuttle remained afloat because all of its wing fuel tanks contained only air.

The little submarine was slowly guided to a position directly under the wide open doors. Then, it was carefully brought to the surface. This put the top of the sub inside the shuttle.

Mike, who was inside the shuttle waiting for the sub, stepped onto its deck. He connected a winch cable to an anchor point on the sub's forward deck. Then, he connected a winch cable to the aft deck. The winches were mounted in the ceiling of the shuttle's cargo bay. Mike turned on the winches and slowly lifted the sub into the cargo bay. When this was done, he closed the shuttle's lower doors.

A significant quantity of water was now in the cargo bay. This was pumped into the wing fuel tanks; then, the sub was securely anchored in place. It would not break loose, even if the shuttle encountered severe turbulence in its flight back to Crater Lake.

With an overall length of 36 feet and a maximum internal diameter of seven feet six inches, the little submarine could accommodate four people on an extended voyage of exploration. Additional people could be carried on shorter voyages.

Most of the submarine's batteries and ballast were contained in its keel, which had a maximum width of 54 inches and a depth of 46 inches. The electric motor, essential equipment, facilities, and instrumentation occupied about half the space inside the main hull, leaving the other half for human occupants.

The most appealing feature for users of the submarine was its transparent plastic hull. Advanced plastics technology made it possible to have a strong, tough hull that was as transparent as high quality window glass.

With the sub loaded, Mike headed home. Michelle had dinner waiting for him. However, they weren't alone. Denise and Connie had joined them.

Speaking to his father, Matthew asked, "Where is Jerry?"

Before Mike could answer, Denise quickly repeated the question, "Where is daddy? I want him to come home."

Seeing how worried the children were, Mike wondered how best to answer the question. He turned to Connie and saw despair written on her face. Mike wanted to reassure everyone, but did not want to mislead them. He looked into his wife's eyes. She was good at this sort of thing. After a few moments, Mike realized that although Michelle understood what he wanted, she was unable to help.

Turning to Denise, he said, "Your father is lost, but we are going to find him."

"How did he get lost?" Denise asked.

"I don't know, but we're going to figure that out."

"Maybe a bad animal got him."

"I don't think so," Mike said.

"But then, what happened to him?"

"There are people from another star living on this planet. I think they captured him."

"Will they hurt him?"

"I don't think so."

"Do you know where those people are? Can we go there and get my dad back?"

"We don't know where they are, but we are going to find them, and then, we'll find a way to get your father back."

"Can I help?"

"I want to help too," Matthew offered.

Mike didn't think the children's efforts would lead to anything, but he wanted to keep them busy doing something positive. "After dinner, you can help us look at video of Crater Lake's beaches," he said.

"Will we find Jerry on a beach?" Matthew asked.

"Probably not, but we might find something that will help us find him."

"Like what?" Denise asked.

"You and Matthew can look for a boat hidden in the bushes, footprints in the sand, or anything that Jerry might have dropped for us to find."

"I'm not very hungry," Denise said. "Can I start looking now?"

"I am just as anxious to find Daddy as you are," Connie said, "but we have to finish our dinner first."

Reluctantly, Denise complied with her mother's wish. There was little conversation, and everyone ate in a hurry. When they were finished, they went to the habitation capsule, where Dianne and several others were studying video looking for clues. "Find anything?" Mike asked.

"So far, not a thing," Dianne replied.

"How much of the waterfront have you looked at?"

"About half."

"We're here to help."

"Good! My eyes need a break. I'm starting to see things that aren't there."

"How do you know that?"

"On a second look, I didn't see what I thought I saw."

"I'd like to do a computer analysis of the video where you thought you were seeing things."

"I flagged those parts of the video, and I wrote down the file locations." Dianne handed Mike a notepad and said, "Check these."

"Will do," replied Mike. Turning to Michelle and Connie, he said, "Why don't you and the children continue with what Dianne is doing, so she can take a break. I'll look for the mirages Dianne saw."

90

Turning to Dianne, he asked, "What exactly do you think you saw?"

"I'd rather not say right now," she replied.

"Why?"

Dianne quickly rolled her eyes toward the children, then back to Mike. He concluded that what Dianne thought she saw was not good and that she didn't want to alarm the children. "I'll study the video," Mike said. "When you're finished with dinner, we'll go for a walk and discuss it."

"Okay."

Mike had video from three cameras; the helicopter's forward-looking camera, the downward-facing camera, and the rear camera. Mike looked at the video Dianne had marked from the forward camera's imagery. Nothing here but sandy beach and thick brush, he noted. Then, he looked at video from the downward camera. The downwash from the rotor violently pushed the foliage around, but concentrate as he might, Mike was unable to see anything under the shrubbery. He switched to the rearward camera and saw nothing but sandy beach and thick green shrubbery. Mike switched to the second area that Dianne had marked, went through the same analysis and saw nothing unusual.

Wondering what the two areas looked like earlier in the day, Mike called up RPV video and closely scrutinized it. The scenes now had early morning shadows instead of late afternoon shadows, but Mike still did not see anything unusual. What did Dianne see? He silently asked himself. What do these two areas have in common? They look the same, and they're both on the south side of the lake, barely 50 yards apart.

By this time, Dianne had returned from dinner. "Anything grab your attention?" she asked.

"Absolutely nothing."

"Let's go for a walk."

"Okay."

When they were far enough away from the habitation capsule so that the children could not hear them, Mike said, "Tell me what you think you saw."

"I was watching the video and seeing nothing but water, sandy beach, and thick brush along the edge of the jungle. I wanted so much to see something that would help us find Jerry. I was concentrating so hard that I was almost in a trance. Then, I saw him."

"Saw who?"

"Jerry."

"You saw Jerry," Mike responded in disbelief.

"I saw him wading ashore, but before he stepped out of the water, he was grabbed by a creature with a long snake-like arm that wrapped around him. It dragged him into the water, and he disappeared beneath the surface."

"I studied the video intently and did not see that."

"What I saw were fleeting ghostlike images, almost like a signal that came from somewhere else."

"Maybe it did," suggested Mike. "I looked at our video and saw nothing unusual."

"Are you saying that what I saw isn't on our video, but was a signal transmitted here from somewhere?"

"I don't know. I'm only saying that I didn't see Jerry or the monster."

"But who would send that signal to us and why?"

"The aliens we're looking for might want us to think that Jerry's dead so that we'll stop looking for him. They might not want to be found, and searching for Jerry could lead us to them."

"If they're behind this, they picked a bad way to convince us that Jerry's dead. Do they really expect us to believe that Jerry jumped off the shuttle and swam two miles to the south side of the lake? There's no way he would've done that."

"That's true, but if they think that we believe they captured Jerry, then, they might want us to believe that Jerry found a way to escape and was subsequently killed by a monster of the deep."

"But if they used a small sub to get to our shuttle to capture Jerry, how could he escape from the inside of a sub?"

"Their sub might not be as luxurious as ours," responded Mike. "It might be nothing more than a torpedo-like device that people wearing diving gear ride on externally."

"So it is plausible that Jerry could've died the way the images I saw depicted?"

"It's possible."

"I get the feeling that you're not convinced," commented Dianne.

"You're the only one who has seen the images. And they were ghostlike, possibly a figment of your imagination."

"But they seemed real."

"I don't want to disregard them, but I'm not convinced either. What else do you think you saw?"

"A pair of ostri-dinos wandered to the water to drink. One of them was grabbed by a monster with a long snake-like arm. It wrapped the arm around the ostri-dino's legs and dragged it into the lake. The doomed creature put up quite a struggle, but it was pulled under just the same."

"You sure remember a lot of details in spite of this being ghost-like imagery."

"It grabbed my full attention."

Mike and Dianne walked in silence while Mike thought about everything that she had told him. After a few moments, he said, "I'd sure like to know who sent us those images and what they're hoping to accomplish with them. Also, why can't I see them?"

"I think we should show the video to Zeb," suggested Dianne.

"Why?"

"Let's assume that the ghostlike images came from the aliens. It's possible they might be skilled with telepathic communication. They may have altered our video in a way that stimulates my mind to create images but not yours. Don't forget, I have received telepathic communication from Rex and Zeb."

"But why would they communicate to us that way?" questioned Mike. "Why wouldn't they just get on the radio and talk to us?"

"Maybe they don't want to be found. Talking to us on the radio would give us an opportunity to pinpoint their location."

"There are easy ways to get around that. Also, it seems to me that if they were serious about getting a message to us, they would not use telepathic means. How do they know that we're even capable of telepathic communication?"

"It's possible they tuned into the telepathic communication between Zeb and Zonya and think that all of us have that ability."

"Computer analysis of the raw data that goes into producing our video should reveal if an outside signal is superimposed on it."

"Wouldn't it be quicker to just show the video to Zeb and Zonya?"

"Maybe, but I don't think they're going to see anything."

"Why?"

"Because you've only seen it once. If there's something there, you should see it every time you look at it."

"Not necessarily."

"Why?"

"My telepathic ability isn't very good. All I've ever been able to do is receive messages sent by others. I'm not able to send anything. Zeb and Zonya communicate very well telepathically."

"We'll show them the video as soon as we get back, and I hope they see what you saw. If they don't, there's another possibility we need to look into."

"You sound very concerned. What's on your mind?"

"The telepathic images you saw could have been transmitted by a bug planted on our shuttle and have nothing to do with the video you were looking at."

"That means I might've seen them no matter what I was doing. The fact that I was looking at video was just coincidental."

"That's true, and the possibility that our shuttle might be bugged concerns me. They could even have planted a bomb on it. Think about it. They don't know if we're hostile or friendly. A bomb that they could detonate by remote control would give them some extra insurance."

"That's a frightening possibility," exclaimed Dianne.

"You show the video to Zeb and Zonya. I'm going to grab whoever I can, and we're going to inspect the shuttle."

"I'll call you as soon as I find out anything."

A half-hour later, Dianne contacted Mike. "Both Zeb and Zonya saw what I saw," she reported. "For them, the images weren't ghostlike; they were quite clear. Also, Zeb is convinced that they were seeing telepathic images from a signal that was superimposed on our video. His people believed that it was possible to do this, but they never succeeded in accomplishing it."

"I think that confirms that the aliens sent us those two sequences of images. The question is, why? Are they trying to convince us that Jerry's dead? Or are they trying to tell us that there are monsters in Crater Lake that we need to be wary of?"

"I don't think we can answer those questions tonight."

"That might be, but I am going to consider the possibilities and make plans for tomorrow."

"Zeb and Zonya are looking at the rest of our video to see if there are any more messages."

"Good! Keep me informed."

An hour and a half later, Dianne reported, "They've finished the video and haven't found anything unusual."

"That means the aliens are relying on two messages to make us think whatever it is they want us to believe."

"Have you found any bombs or bugs on the shuttle?"

"No, but we haven't yet completed the search."

"Are you going to stay up all night?"

"I don't think so. I don't know what challenges I'll have to face tomorrow, but I'd better get at least a few hours of sleep, so I'll be sharp enough to meet them. I have to rely on my crew to complete the search."

"That shouldn't be a problem. They are intelligent and capable. If there's a bomb onboard, they'll find it."

Chapter Five

TIME: Day 31, Early Dawn

Mike, Dianne, and Connie were on their way to the cargo shuttle, which was still anchored in South Bay. "I spoke to my crew chief a few minutes ago, and they haven't found a bug or a bomb," Mike said.

"You sound surprised," responded Dianne.

"I'm convinced that a bomb was planted."

"Why?"

"I fell asleep last night thinking about the aliens. I believe they have Jerry and that message showing him killed by a monster was nothing more than an attempt to mislead us. I don't know what they hope to gain by holding Jerry. It could be that they just want to question him. Or they might want something critical to our success, like our starship."

"My husband would never give them our ship," stated Connie.

"What if they told him that you were on the shuttle and that they could blast it to pieces, thereby killing you?" Mike asked.

"He would never part with our starship. He is very resourceful, and he would find a way to keep me alive while retaining our ship."

"That's possible, but we have other things less valuable than our starship that Jerry might relinquish in return for your life or to prevent shuttle destruction. Having a bomb on our shuttle would be a powerful bargaining chip for them; therefore, I believe they planted one, and we can't take off until we find it."

"But that could take forever," protested Connie. "We need to get going, so we can find Jerry and rescue him."

"I want that as much as you do, but we have to stay alive to do that. Also, we must avoid putting Jerry in a situation where he has to issue orders that he doesn't want to give."

"If there's a bomb, and we find it, Jerry will still be in that situation, because he won't know that we found it, and there's no way we can tell him, since he's not responding to his communicator."

"That's true," responded Mike, "but the aliens also won't know that we disarmed their bomb. We can pretend to go along with their demands; then, at a crucial moment, we attack. In any case, the shuttle must be grounded until we find the bomb."

Shortly, the trio arrived at the shuttle. Mike, again, discussed the bomb search with his crew. "There must be some obvious place where you haven't looked," he said.

Detail by detail, they went over their search with Mike. Finally, he admitted, "You've been thorough, but I know that there's a bomb, there just has to be."

Then, the bomb's location hit Mike with the force of a lightening bolt, and he exclaimed, "Of course! There's only one place it can be! It's mounted on the underside of the elevator deck!"

Without saying another word, Mike left the shuttle, closely followed by his crew chief. They stepped into the small inflated boat, rowed to shore, and took the elevator up to Stellar Plateau. Quickly, they jogged the short distance to the stowed elevator deck. With a flashlight in hand, Mike crawled under the right forward part of the deck, the location where Jerry had been captured. Sweeping his flashlight back and forth, he searched the underside. In less than a minute, he exclaimed, "I found it!"

The crew chief crawled to Mike's side and looked up at the bomb. "We'll remove this and dispose of it," he said.

"I want you to use Charlie for that job. He's a very valuable robot, but if there's an accident, he is replaceable. In fact, using Charlie, you might be able to disassemble this thing and learn something about the explosives technology of our potential adversaries."

"We'll give it our best shot."

"Good! I have to get going, but I need to take some people along to guard the shuttle. Do you have anybody that's fresh, or have they all been up all night?"

"The guys who had been helping me during the night were relieved about an hour ago. My replacement crew had a pretty good night of sleep."

"How many can you spare?"

"You can take all three of them. I only need Charlie for removing and dismantling the bomb."

"I'll give them twenty minutes to get their weapons and some food; then, we'll take off."

A short time later, Mike and his crew taxied out of South Bay. Mike quickly accelerated the shuttle to 200 mph and pitched it into a steep climb. In less than two minutes, the shuttle reached a speed just over 5,000 mph and exited the atmosphere. Mike shut down the powerful nuclear thermal rocket, and called Moose who was still on the Challenger. "Good morning old buddy. Do you have any news for me?"

"I've been up all night searching the area around Crater Lake," Moose replied.

"Did you find anything?"

"I found something for you to investigate."

"What?" Mike asked.

"There's a small lake about a half-mile south of Crater Lake, which I'll call Sandstone Lake. On the east side of it, there's a sandstone cliff set about a hundred yards back from the water's edge. There are some holes in the cliff's face that don't look natural."

"Do you think they were cut by the aliens we're looking for?"

"That's a possibility. With their technology, they could easily have excavated caverns in a sandstone cliff. Homes of that type would offer protection against large carnivores."

"Have you seen any evidence that the aliens might be living there, like a campfire, a fishing boat ... anything?"

"No, but I believe those holes in the cliff were dug out. They just don't look like a creation of nature."

"Okay, let's assume that they're living there. How did they get from those cliffs to the middle of Crater Lake to capture Jerry?"

"During the time that you and Jerry were investigating their starship, they could've hiked through the jungle and swam out to the shuttle using nothing more than diving gear. Underwater propulsion equipment would've been helpful, but they could've made the trip without it."

"I think we should launch a couple RPVs after we land, one to investigate the openings in the cliff and the other to search the jungle for a trail."

"I'll investigate the cliff," volunteered Connie.

"I'll look for the trail," offered Dianne.

"I've made a radar map of the topography between the lakes," stated Moose, "and I've plotted a couple routes of least resistance that a trail might be expected to follow. You might begin your search by checking them out."

"Sounds good," replied Dianne.

"We're approaching atmospheric entry," Mike said. "I need to get back to being a pilot."

"Talk to you later," responded Moose. Addressing Connie, Moose said, "I have some ideas on how to investigate the cliff openings."

"I'd like to hear them," she responded.

"If the aliens are in there, and if they have Jerry, you must avoid tipping them off that we're watching them, so you need to be sneaky."

"How do I do that?"

"The area between the cliff and the lake is fairly open. It is mostly slabs of rock and doesn't have much growing on it. About 30 yards away from the cliff, there's a huge rock, more than 20 feet tall. Two scrubby bushes have taken root in cracks on its top. If you could fly the RPV undetected to the top of that boulder, you could use the bushes for cover."

"The trick will be to hide the RPV while giving its cameras a clear view of the openings in the cliff."

"That would be ideal. If the aliens are living there, we'll be able to spy on them without them knowing that they're being watched. But first, you have to fly the RPV to the top of the boulder without being seen."

"I can do that. I'll use a small RPV, approach the cliff from the lake, and use the large boulder for cover. That will make it difficult for cliff dwellers to spot my RPV, unless someone happens to be outside."

"That plan should work, and I can help."

"How?"

"In about ten minutes, I will have that area in sight. I can train our optical instruments on it, and if any of them are out and about, I will spot them and let you know."

"Sounds good."

A few minutes later, Mike guided the huge cargo shuttle to a soft landing on Crater Lake and brought it to a stop at the middle of the lake. He immediately opened a door in the side of the fuselage, so Dianne and Connie could launch their RPVs.

The next task was to unload the submarine, so Mike opened the lower cargo bay doors. This did not put the shuttle at risk of sinking, because its wing fuel tanks were empty. These tanks and the water-tight compartments making up much of the fuselage gave the shuttle excellent buoyancy.

Mike released the locking devices that held the sub securely in place. Then, he turned on the winch and lowered the sub about four feet. "I'm going to enter the sub and take it to the bottom," he announced.

"What do you expect to find?" Connie asked.

"I don't know, but as near as I can tell, this is where the shuttle was when Jerry disappeared. I believe the aliens have him. If they dropped anything, and I'm able to find it, that would confirm my suspicion. Also, it's possible that Jerry may have dropped some selected item in an effort to tell us something. He knew at the time of his capture that we would probably bring in our sub and begin our search on the bottom."

"I'd like to go with you," stated Connie.

"How long before you have your RPV on top the boulder?"

"I'm approaching the clearing now. Put on a headset, and you can see what I'm looking at."

Mike put one on, and because of three-dimensional viewing, felt like he was sitting inside Connie's RPV. He saw the jungle racing by beneath him and the clearing directly ahead. He saw and almost felt the tight banking turn that Connie made as she headed the RPV toward Sandstone Lake. Then, he saw the water rushing toward him as she dropped the RPV down to a few inches above the lake. Mike felt the RPV's speed as Connie piloted it straight ahead. She wanted to minimize the time that the RPV could be seen if there were aliens dwelling in the cliff. When the large boulder was between the RPV and the cliff, Connie turned inland and slowed down. When she reached the boulder, she slowed the RPV to a hover and slowly climbed to its top.

The shrubs were just as Moose had described. They were less than three feet tall and were about five feet apart. Their branches joined at the top, forming a small arch. A few weeds were growing out of the crack between the shrubs.

Connie inched the RPV forward, nosing it up against the weeds. "This is perfect," she said. "This RPV is so well concealed that it would take a very keen eye to spot it from that cliff, yet we have an excellent view of those openings. And there's no doubt in my mind that those holes were cut by intelligent beings."

"It sure looks that way," agreed Mike.

"However, this place does look deserted," noted Connie. "Maybe they're not living here anymore."

"It's early. First sunrise is still a few minutes away, and they might be sleeping."

"That could be, but when I flew in, I didn't see any boats anywhere. It seems like there should be some. And take a look at their front yard; there are no outdoor tables or cooking facilities. I just don't see any evidence that anyone is living here."

"Keep in mind that these creatures are aliens, and we don't know what kind of campsite they would maintain. They might eat their food raw."

"But you and Jerry explored their starship and decided that they look like humans. It seems like their campsite would look like what we would have."

"We don't know that for sure. Consider the various lifestyles lived by the different cultures on Earth."

"But most of Earth's people, whether primitive or modern, enjoy outdoor cooking or engage in it out of necessity."

"That's true," agreed Mike. "But these are aliens, and we don't know what lifestyle they live. I admit, this place does look deserted, but I'm not yet ready to go get our chopper, land in front of that cliff, and explore it in person."

"Now that you put it that way, I'm not either. Let's have someone watch this place while we go search the lake bottom."

"I'm ready."

"By the time you two return, I should be done searching for a trail," Dianne said. "Why don't you pick me up. I'd like to go with you to explore the sites where the telepathic images occurred."

"Okay," replied Mike.

A few minutes later, Mike and Connie were in the sub. Operating the winch by remote control, Mike lowered the sub out of the shuttle and released it. Turning on the sub's electric motor, he put it into a steep dive. He explored the bottom with sonar and found the rock formation that he intended to use as a reference point. Mike believed that the shuttle was 170 yards northwest of this formation at the time of Jerry's disappearance.

"It seems like we're diving too fast," commented Connie.

"I'm not trying to scare you; I'm just anxious to start searching for clues. I'll slow our descent when we near the bottom."

"How deep is it here?"

"Twenty three hundred feet. You're not worried about the depth, are you?"

"No! Jerry has assured me that this sub can safely dive to at least 5,000 feet. I just don't want to crash into the bottom. It's awfully dark down here."

Mike checked the sonar data. "We're 800 feet from the bottom," he said.

"Isn't it time to slow our descent?"

"Almost."

Several seconds later, Mike began lifting the little sub's nose to decrease the dive angle. Also, he throttled back the electric motor and turned on the searchlights.

"I wish this lake were as clean as Clear Lake," Connie said.

"Few lakes are that clean, but we should be able to see the bottom pretty soon."

"How extensive a search do you plan to do?"

"I want to spend about an hour slowly cruising back and forth over this area."

"That should be enough time to alleviate my worst fear."

"I believe the chance of your worst fear being true is very small," Mike said, softly.

"I hope and pray that you're right. My life with Jerry has been wonderful. If we find him here on the bottom, I will be heartbroken for a very long time."

"I think the bomb we found this morning proves the aliens have him."

"But they could've killed him and dumped him overboard."

"I know that you're worried. I am too, but killing Jerry would be incredibly stupid on their part. They would have to realize that we would retaliate. Once we find them, we could use our antimatter particle beam gun to annihilate them. With Jerry held hostage, we can't do that."

"But why did they take him in the first place? What do they want?"

"Hopefully, nothing more than information about us."

"They could have gotten that by contacting us on the radio. Since they've been to Earth, they probably understand our language. They didn't have to take my husband and plant a bomb on our shuttle. I believe they want a lot more than information."

"We won't know what they're after until they tell us. In the meantime, we're going to do everything we can to find them and rescue Jerry. We're going to begin right now by searching this lake bottom for clues."

"What a barren, rocky place," commented Connie.

"There's so little light down here that I really didn't expect to see much plant life. For the sake of our search, that's good. If Jerry or his captors dropped anything, it would be hard to find in an underwater jungle."

"What do you want me to do?"

"We're going to slowly cruise back and forth over this area, just a few feet above the bottom. I've aimed our spotlights forward and downward. I will look ahead and to the left. I want you to search ahead and to the right."

After a half-hour of tedious observation, Connie said, "I'm starting to get the feeling that we're not going to find anything."

"That might be, but we have to finish the job anyway. I want to be thorough, so that when we go back to the surface, we can be confident that we didn't miss anything."

Connie pointed to her right and asked, "What's that thing?"

"Let's take a closer look," replied Mike, as he turned the sub toward the object and slowed to a barely perceptible crawl.

"It's a skeleton," stated Connie.

Mike slowly circled the bony structure. "It looks like a skeleton of a creature like the aliens showed us in the telepathic images," he said.

"Maybe such a predator really does live in this lake."

"That skeleton certainly indicates that."

"And it has an arm that's nearly fifty feet long," Connie noted.

"That skeleton sure lends credibility to the images the aliens sent us."

"I wish I knew why they sent us those images."

"Maybe they were trying to warn us that there are dangerous creatures in this lake."

"Why would they do that? After capturing my husband and planting a bomb on our shuttle, it makes no sense to warn us about dangerous predators."

"Maybe it does," responded Mike.

"How?"

"First, they capture Jerry to use as a hostage. Then, they demonstrate goodwill by warning us about the fierce marine predators. But to protect themselves, they plant a bomb on our shuttle to use as a last resort in case we respond belligerently to their demands. Since we use our shuttle to ferry our sub and helicopter into action, blowing it up would certainly hurt our ability to find and attack them."

"When you put it that way, it does make sense, but I'm still confused. If they need help, why didn't they just get on the radio and ask us?"

"It's possible they want something that they don't think we would be willing to give," Mike replied.

"If that's the case, we will be fighting them, because we certainly aren't going to give up anything that's crucial to our success."

"I hope it doesn't come to that. Our numbers are too small to risk losing anybody."

"I want my husband back, and if they have him and refuse to release him; then, like it or not, we are going to have a fight on our hands, because we will find a way to rescue him. I am damn good with weapons, and I will volunteer for the most dangerous part of the mission."

"No way!"

"Why not?"

"You are our doctor, and you're too valuable to risk. All of our people are experts with weapons, and if the need arises, there will be no shortage of volunteers for a rescue mission. But we're getting ahead of ourselves. Let's finish searching this area."

Fifteen minutes later, Mike and Connie headed for the surface. "Except for the skeleton, we didn't find anything," stated Connie.

"Yes, but that was a frightening discovery. The long arm we saw indicates that these predators can strike from a distance of 40 to 50 feet, and that makes them very dangerous."

"All of a sudden, I feel a sick emptiness. My husband could've been savagely eaten by one of them."

"I don't believe he was."

"Why?"

"Yesterday, I found no evidence of a struggle when I inspected the elevator deck. Today, we found nothing on the bottom. If one of those creatures had eaten Jerry, we should've at least found his rifle.

The animal would've found that gun to be pretty tough chewing and would've spit it out. Also, I believe other things would've been dropped. Eating prey in the wild is pretty messy business. If Jerry had been eaten, we should've found something on the bottom, his pistol, a boot, his communicator … something. I am more convinced than ever that the aliens have him."

"I sure hope you're right, but how did the aliens elude these creatures while capturing Jerry? It seems like a two-mile underwater swim with nothing more than diving gear would've been extremely dangerous."

"They've lived here for a long time and should know how to deal with these animals. A spear gun should be effective, especially if the spear carries a small explosive charge."

"But they might not see them in time to use such a weapon," argued Connie. "The water in this lake isn't very clear."

"Maybe their diving gear is equipped with sonar to warn them of the approach of one these predators."

"Wouldn't our marine explorer have heard the beeps?"

"Not necessarily. They could've used covert surveillance sonar. The pings could've been sent out erratically, rather than at a regular rhythm. Each ping could've been sent at a different frequency with an irregular wave shape. In short, their sonar computer could've disguised its signals to sound like background noise. When I deployed a marine explorer to this lake, I didn't program it to discover sophisticated sonar; I was looking only for hazards to shuttle operation."

"If they had nothing more than diving gear, how did they get Jerry to go with them?"

"They could've put a neck collar on him and put him on a leash between two of them. But I think they had more than scuba gear. I think they had underwater propulsion units, maybe even a small sub."

"How would they've put that in this lake?" Connie asked.

"We think they have a helicopter. They could've seen our marine explorer two days ago and brought in a small sub to investigate it."

"Would they have been able to figure out why it was here?"

"From the kind of data the marine explorer was gathering, they certainly had to consider the possibility that we would be landing on this lake."

"If they came to that conclusion, then their best strategy would have been to stay out of sight and patiently wait for our shuttle."

"And while spying on us, they probably saw me leave with Michelle and Zeb. Then, they assumed Jerry was alone, and by capturing him, they could roam the shuttle undisturbed."

"That sounds so plausible that I think that just might be what happened," commented Connie.

"There's one thing that bothers me about this scenario," stated Mike.

"What?"

"Why did they plant their bomb in such an easy-to-find location if they had time to roam the shuttle?"

"There's an easy answer to that question," replied Connie.

"Tell me."

"They didn't know when you would return, so they quickly planted a bomb in an out-of-sight, easy-to-get-to location just to make sure they had one onboard."

"And then, while exploring our shuttle, they looked for a difficult-to-find place to hide a second bomb," added Mike.

"We're in a terrible bind, if your suspicion is correct. Even if we're fortunate enough to find Jerry, we cannot confront the aliens for his release, because they could blow up our shuttle."

"Having the means to put us in that kind of predicament would be such a big advantage for them that it seems there must be a second bomb," stated Mike.

"It seems that way, but they might not have had time to install one. After capturing Jerry and hiding the bomb that we found, they might've heard the approach of your chopper and made a hasty retreat."

"I don't think so, because when you called him and he didn't answer, you called me. I was tied up with a lupusaurus pack at the time, and it was about 45 minutes before I got back to the shuttle. So they had at least that much time to do their dirty work, and they may even have had a couple hours."

"How likely is that?"

"I don't know, but all morning, Jerry felt that we were being watched. The aliens could've seen me take off with Michelle and Zeb. If they captured Jerry shortly after that, they had a couple hours."

"With that much time, it seems certain that there is another explosive device," Connie reluctantly admitted.

"But where is it? The shuttle has already been carefully searched."

"If you were an alien stepping onto our shuttle, where would you put a bomb?" Connie asked.

"That would depend on how powerful my bomb was and what my objective was."

"What if you wanted to destroy the shuttle, but for easy conceal-ment, your bomb was too small to do that on its own?"

"Then I would have to wreck the shuttle by blowing up a critical system. For example, a very small bomb hidden on the flight deck could kill the crew, disable the flight control computer, and cause a crash. But we've already been over all of this. We've looked in all the conceivable hiding places, and we haven't found anything."

"Maybe that's it!" exclaimed Connie.

"What do you mean?"

"The bomb's not hidden."

"Are you trying to tell me the thing is setting right out in the open, in plain view of everyone?"

"I think it is."

"But that doesn't make any sense," argued Mike.

"Maybe it does. The aliens might've anticipated exactly the kind of search you've made. Therefore, they didn't hide their bomb that way, because they knew you would find it."

"So what do you think they did?"

"I think they disguised their bomb to look like some common ordinary object. Consequently, we're ignoring it."

"Do you really think that they would leave a bomb where we would see it and overlook it every time we walk past it?"

"I think so, and your expression of disbelief tells me that such a strategy would work."

Mike thought about Connie's idea for a few moments. Then, his eyes lit up. "Those sneaky devils," he exclaimed. "We've been look-ing in all the wrong places while their bomb has been right in front of our eyes."

"Sounds like you know where it is."

"I believe I do, and I am going to check it out."

A few seconds later, Mike and Connie surfaced a short distance from the shuttle. "Before I go looking for the bomb, I want to search this lake for a small sub, so we aren't left open to a surprise attack," Mike said.

"Do you think their sub is still here?" Connie asked.

"We don't know if they have one, but if they do, it's probably still in this lake."

"That would mean that Jerry might still be here."

"Maybe, but I think they came in last night with their chopper and picked him up for questioning while leaving the sub here to spy on us. I have to find out."

Mike accessed computer software for covert sonar surveillance. He instructed the computer to listen to Crater Lake's background sounds and create sonar signals to mimic them. After two minutes went by, the computer said it had a sonar search program that would be nearly impossible for others to identify. Mike immediately activated the search.

As the seconds ticked by, the results came in. "I've located several monsters that might fit the skeleton we found, but I haven't found a sub," he announced.

"Does that mean they're not here anymore?"

"Not necessarily. They could be parked on the bottom somewhere. That would make them difficult to differentiate from a rock formation."

"If they're still here, do you think they'll attack us?"

"I don't know, but we aren't going to let them do what they did yesterday. I am going to have this computer do a continuous covert sonar search of this lake. To make things more difficult for our adversaries, I am also going to use the sonar equipment on our marine explorer. This computer will communicate with the marine explorer and use its sonar to transmit some of the signals. Having more than one transmitter will make it easier to mimic background noise. Also, if we find them, we can pinpoint their location and even get some idea about their size and shape." Mike set up the sonar program and instructed the computer to sound an alarm if anything large enough to be a threat approached the sub or the shuttle.

Satisfied with the security arrangements, Mike opened the hatch and climbed out of the sub. He went to the on-deck controls and piloted the sub toward the shuttle. Gently, he nudged it against the left wingtip.

Dianne stepped out of the shuttle and walked on the wing to the waiting sub. After boarding the sub, she reported, "I've explored the jungle on the south side of this lake, and I found some trails. They look like game trails. In fact, I found a rather large lupusaurus pack on one of them. I counted 31 animals."

"That's a big pack," commented Mike. "I would hate to encounter that many animals on my own. It's very likely that I would not survive a determined attack. I could empty my rifle and pistol, and there would still be several of them left. If the aliens are living in the sandstone cliffs, it doesn't seem likely that they would make a risky hike through the jungle just to capture one of us."

"You might be right," responded Dianne. "I flew up and down the only trail that runs from Crater Lake to Sandstone Lake, and I found no evidence of humanoid travel. There were some places where the trail was wet, and there were no boot prints in the mud."

"What about the RPV I landed in front of the cliff? Has it detected any activity?" Connie asked.

"No! The place looks deserted."

"Maybe they don't live there anymore," suggested Connie.

"It's possible they never did," Mike said.

"I am convinced they did and maybe still do," stated Dianne.

"Why?" Mike asked.

"Because every entrance is closed by a stout door set about four feet back from the cliff's face."

"That indicates that they built homes there, but I think they've locked up and moved on," Mike said.

"Why do you think they're not here anymore?" Dianne asked.

"There's no indication of any recent activity, and there's the sheer size of that lupusaurus pack. A band of vicious predators that large would be a threat to even well armed humanoids. Their survival would depend on killing these animals whenever they see them. For that reason, I don't think a pack could grow to 31 animals if the aliens are still living here."

"What if the aliens found a way to coexist with them?" Connie asked.

"That's not very likely. Yesterday, I had a terrifying encounter with these killers, and I can tell you with certainty that they are very aggressive, cunning, and capable."

"Michelle told me about that. You're lucky you didn't lose anyone."

"I know, and I definitely would not want to live in an area frequented by a large pack of these animals."

"But we can't say with certainty that the aliens have left," stated Dianne.

"That would be a dangerous assumption," agreed Mike. "We simply don't know where they are. Right now, I have to go look for a bomb, and I think I know exactly where it is. You two keep an eye on the sub."

"We will," replied Dianne.

"Be careful with the bomb," cautioned Connie.

"You can count on that," stated Mike, as he left.

A minute later, Mike entered the shuttle and went to the flight deck. He faced a commemorative plaque on the back wall and studied it intently. It depicted the space shuttle Challenger and the seven-person crew for its final mission. The shuttle had been destroyed by an in-flight explosion on January 28, 1986. All seven astronauts were killed.

This does not look like our original, thought Mike. It looks like a good copy, but the copper color isn't quite right. It appears slightly faded, but it's so close that it hasn't attracted any attention. Is this fading natural, or have I found plastic explosives molded in the shape of our plaque? They could've used our plaque to make a mold. Then they could've used the mold to make a plastic shell to contain their explosives. This would've been easy to do.

Mike reached toward the plaque, then, changed his mind. I'd better not take it off the wall; it might be booby trapped. But I have to inspect it. Maybe there's another way.

As he continued to stare at the plaque, he thought, something other than the color is wrong. Our original had four attachment points and was mounted about a sixteenth-inch away from the wall. Mike put his head against the wall and tried to peer behind the plaque. There was no air space; it fit tight to the wall. "This is a bomb," he calmly stated to the guard who had entered the flight deck with him. "I want everyone off this shuttle while I remove it."

"You might need help," responded the guard.

"I don't want to risk more lives than my own."

"I understand, but you might need help. How do you plan to get rid of that thing?"

"It would be dangerous to just take it off the wall," replied Mike. "We need to remove the panel that it's mounted on."

"That's a two-person job," stated the guard.

"I can do it alone," argued Mike.

"That may be, but it would be safer with two people. I can hold the panel while you remove the screws. We certainly don't want this thing to drop when you take out the last screw."

"You've convinced me, but I want the other two guards on the sub and at a safe distance."

Mike gave the order and waited for it to be complied with. Then, he turned to his assistant and asked, "Are you ready?"

"We might as well get this over with," he replied.

Mike picked up a power screwdriver from the tool closet and quickly removed the screws holding the small wall panel in place. "Okay, it's loose," he said. "Now, I want you to move the left side of the panel out from the wall just enough, so I can look behind it."

When this was done, Mike beamed a light into the interior wall space and intently peered into it. After a few moments, he said, "It's clear."

"Were you expecting it to be booby trapped?" his assistant asked.

"It would've been easy for them to attach a trip wire to the opposite wall panel. Then, when we pulled the bomb away from the wall that wire could've triggered it to explode."

"Is it safe for me to remove this panel?"

"It looks safe, but I don't know, so I want you to leave." Mike called Connie. "I have a passenger for you to pick up," he said.

"I'll pick him up off the left wingtip," she replied.

"Let me know when you are again at a safe distance."

"Will do."

Mike put his right hand on the panel and held it firmly in place while his assistant left. "I'll be glad when this is over," he said.

"It won't be over until I get my husband back, and then, we need to punish the aliens for what they've done."

"First things first. Before we can do anything, I have to get rid of this bomb without blowing my head off."

"What are you planning to do with it?"

"I am going to send the aliens, and maybe even Jerry, a message."

"How?"

"I'll explain later. Which way is the wind blowing?"

"We have a gentle breeze out of the east."

"When you've picked up my assistant, I want you to head into the wind. Let me know when you're a couple hundred yards away."

"Okay."

A couple minutes later, Mike received a call from Connie. "We're clear," she said.

"Say your best prayer for me," replied Mike.

"You have that from all of us. Please be careful."

Very cautiously, Mike pulled the panel away from its mounting structure. "So far, so good," he said. Slowly, he turned and headed for an open hatch in the left side of the fuselage. When he reached the hatch, he stepped through it and onto the shuttle's left wing. Very carefully, he set the panel down; then, he went back into the shuttle. He grabbed a life jacket from emergency supplies, took it outside, and inflated it. He placed the panel on top the life jacket and tied it in place. After picking it up, he walked to the wingtip. It was close enough to the water, so Mike could place his package into the water without having to drop it.

Almost immediately, the gentle breeze caught the life jacket with its lethal cargo, and it began to slowly drift away from the shuttle. Mike watched it for a few moments; then, he returned to the shuttle's interior. He went to the weapons locker and picked up his rifle. He selected a clip of explosive bullets and inserted it into the rifle.

Mike stepped out of the shuttle and stood on its left wing. He noted that the bomb had drifted about a hundred feet away. Since I don't know how powerful that thing is, I'd better wait for more distance, he thought. While I'm waiting, I can get ready for takeoff.

After shouldering his rifle, Mike reached for his communicator. With it, he contacted the shuttle's flight control computer and began checking the status of various systems. Also, he instructed it to pump water into the wing fuel tanks. The lower fuselage cargo bay doors had already been closed. Satisfied that everything was in order, Mike returned his attention to the slowly receding bomb. It's still not far enough away, he thought.

Returning to his communicator, Mike shifted the shuttle's propeller into reverse. He backed the shuttle away from the floating bomb. When he judged the distance to be about 150 yards, he stopped the propeller.

After removing his rifle from his shoulder, he turned on the laser spotter and dropped to a prone position. He chambered a cartridge, supported the gun in his left hand, and aimed at the bomb. It was a small target bobbing up and down with the gentle waves on the lake. This is a difficult shot, Mike thought. He refocused his telescopic sight for greater magnification and turned on his rifle's computer driven fire control system. It was designed to make this kind of tough shot easy. When turned on, it had final control over firing the gun. Mike could squeeze the trigger, but the rifle would not fire unless its computer determined that the target would be hit. Using the laser spotter, the computer calculated the distance to the target and sensed its relative motion.

Mike aimed at the bomb and pulled the trigger, but the rifle did not fire. He held the gun steady and waited. Several seconds ticked by. Suddenly, the rifle boomed. The bullet struck the bomb and exploded. The bomb detonated with a deafening blast, sending out a shock wave that jarred Mike from head to foot.

"WOW! That was powerful," he exclaimed.

He contacted Connie. "Meet me at the left wingtip and I'll explain what I am about to do."

"You got it," she replied.

A minute later, the sub nudged against the left wingtip. Mike stepped aboard and said, "As loud as that blast was, the aliens should've heard it, if they're anywhere in this area, and I believe they are nearby. Since there's no good reason for us to explode a bomb in the middle of this lake, they have to assume that we found one of theirs and set it off."

"Maybe Jerry heard it too," speculated Connie.

"Let's hope so," Mike replied. "I don't know what these aliens want from Jerry, but with the sound of that explosion, they might decide to terrorize him by telling him that they blew up our shuttle and killed some of us. To prevent that, I need to takeoff and circle this area at supersonic speeds at about 5,000 feet. Jerry will hear the powerful sonic boom and the roar of the NTR, and he will know that our shuttle has not been blown up."

"That will put his mind at ease," responded Connie.

"I am hoping that he will also figure out something that the aliens won't be able to deduce," stated Mike.

"What are you trying to tell him?"

"The aliens might think that we found only one of their bombs, but Jerry should be able to determine that we found both of them."

"How?"

"Let's assume that the aliens forced Jerry to watch them install their bombs for the sake of intimidating him."

"I can picture them doing that," replied Connie.

"The aliens don't know how big our submarine is. They don't know that we had to take the elevator deck out of the shuttle to load the sub. One of their bombs was mounted on the underside of the elevator deck. Since Jerry would assume that we brought our sub here this morning, he would know that the elevator deck and its bomb are back on Pioneer Island. Jerry will assume that the bomb we just exploded was the one from the flight deck. Unless there are more than two bombs, Jerry will know that our shuttle is now free of bombs, greatly reducing the leverage the aliens have over him."

"How long before the shuttle's ready for takeoff?"

"It's ready now."

"Let's go! I'm coming with you," stated Connie.

Mike and Connie boarded the shuttle and went directly to the flight deck. Mike revved the propeller to full speed, quickly bringing the shuttle to 40 mph. It rose out of the water and rode on its hydrofoils. Mike fired the powerful NTR. In a matter of seconds, the shuttle accelerated to 200 mph, and Mike pitched it into a steep climb. He leveled off at 5,000 feet but left the NTR at full power. Shortly, the shuttle passed through the speed of sound and continued to accelerate. At mach 1.5, Mike throttled back the NTR a bit. He rolled the shuttle into a banking turn and said, "I am going to circle Crater Lake several times in ever expanding circles out to a distance of about 15 miles."

"Do you think the aliens are somewhere within that area?"

"I think so, and I don't believe the bomb blast was heard any farther away than that anyway."

"I want to compliment you on the ingenious way you found to communicate with Jerry," Connie said.

"It's just an attempt, but I hope it will work."

"Why do you think it might not?"

"They could be holding him in a deep cave, or they might've picked him up with a helicopter and flown a couple hundred miles from here."

"Let's hope for the best."

"Whether or not we reach Jerry, there's something else I'm hoping to accomplish."

"What?" Connie asked.

"In a sense, we're thumbing our noses at any aliens in this area."

"How?"

"This shuttle is a large vehicle. Flying it at mach 1.5 at only 5,000 feet will subject anything under us to a very loud sonic boom. To maintain this speed, our NTR must operate at close to full power. That produces a thundering roar. Hitting them with all this noise right after setting off one of their bombs is kind of like telling them to go to hell. I'm letting them know that we're still here and that we're coming after them. If they get the feeling that we might be willing to plaster them, even at the risk of losing Jerry, they might decide that their best course of action is to release Jerry and quietly disappear."

"That would be wonderful. Do you think your strategy will work?"

"I don't know, but psychological warfare can be quite effective. In the game of poker, some professionals become champions because they excel at the art of bluffing."

"But this isn't a poker game; my husband's life is on the line."

"That makes this a high-stakes poker game."

"Why do I get the feeling that you have a dangerous trick up your sleeve?"

"Probably, because I do," replied Mike, while entering some instructions into the shuttle's computer.

"What are you doing now?"

"I am activating the Challenger's antimatter particle beam gun."

"Why?"

"If the aliens don't release Jerry by 5:00 PM, I am going to incinerate them."

Mike's communicator beeped. It was Moose. "What's going on?" he demanded.

"What do you mean?" asked Mike.

"Our particle beam gun has just been turned on. Why?"

"I intend to vaporize the aliens if they don't release Jerry by 5:00 PM."

"But we don't even know where they are," protested Moose.

"I think I do."

"But what about Jerry? He'll be killed too."

"That can't be helped."

"You sure have a callous disregard for the life of my best friend."

"He's my best friend too, but we don't know if he's still alive. The aliens may have killed him by now, or worse yet, they might be torturing him. I just can't let that continue. At 5:00 PM, I am going to blast them into smithereens."

"You can't do that! You have to change your mind!"

"I just might change my mind. I might blast them sooner."

"I don't like it," stated Moose. "I can't let you do this."

116

"You cannot stop me. I've programmed the instructions into the fire control computer, and I've locked it up. Only I can stop it."

"I will disconnect the computer."

"You can't. I've put it in a self-defense mode. The hatches to the gun operation area have been closed and locked. If they are tampered with, the fire control computer will know and immediately attack the aliens. Also, I must contact the computer periodically, or it will begin the attack."

"I don't like your plan. It's premature. We shouldn't risk Jerry's life until all possibilities have been exhausted. I want you to reconsider."

"My mind is made up. I will not reprogram the fire control computer."

"Then, you leave me no choice. I have to find a way to deactivate it."

"I was one of the engineers who helped design and test the system. Believe me; you are wasting your time. You cannot shut it down."

"I am going to try anyway." Moose abruptly ended his call.

Connie was silent for a couple minutes while she thought about the conversation between Mike and Moose. She thought about Jerry. Was he still alive? Was he being tortured? Finally she said, "I don't know what they're doing to Jerry, but I agree with Moose, I don't think we should attack until all possibilities have been pursued."

"My mind is made up."

"I can't talk you into waiting a day or two longer?"

"No!"

"I hope you know what you're doing."

"I am getting Jerry back."

"I hope you're right."

"The aliens have no choice. If they want to live, they have to release him in good health."

Lost in their own thoughts, Mike and Connie finished the flight in silence. After landing, Mike taxied to the center of Crater Lake and waited for the sub. When it approached the left wingtip, he and Connie left the flight deck, walked out on the wing, and greeted the people arriving on the sub.

Dianne approached Mike. "I just talked with my husband. He said you're planning to blast the aliens. He's worried about Jerry and wants me to try to change your mind."

"Good old Moose. He's done exactly what I wanted him to do."

"What do you mean?"

"He talked to you about my bluff."

"I don't understand."

"I can't blast the aliens, because I don't know where they are."

"But you convinced my husband that attack instructions are already programmed in."

"Moose knows that I haven't done that, and his worried call to you was made to help convince the aliens that I have."

"But he sounded so concerned. He made me believe that you're ready to attack."

"Good! Maybe the aliens will believe that too."

"If they heard you guys talking."

"Don't forget, they have Jerry's communicator. They have to be listening to try to keep tabs on us. And they've been to Earth, so I have to believe that they understand our language."

"How did Moose know that your attack plans are just a ruse?" asked Connie. "I listened to you guys talking, and you convinced me you were serious."

"Moose is on the Challenger, and he knows that he can prevent my attack. He quickly figured out that I'm bluffing and played along with me."

"Will the aliens fall for it?"

"You and Dianne did."

Chapter Six

With the bluff discussion finished, Dianne, Connie, and Mike went to the south side of the lake. They planned to investigate the site where Dianne had seen the telepathic images of Jerry wading ashore and being dragged back into the lake by a monster.

While looking at the shore with binoculars, Connie said, "I hope we find something that will lead us to my husband."

"I hope so too," stated Dianne, "but I don't relish the idea of going ashore. That lupusaurus pack I saw earlier scared the hell out of me. Yesterday, Mike was almost killed by lupusaurs."

"I did have a close call," admitted Mike, "but we need to find Jerry. I don't know why the aliens showed you those images. I've been assuming that it was an attempt to mislead us, but there are other possibilities."

"Like what?" questioned Dianne.

"Maybe they wanted us to come here."

"What for?"

"There might be something here they want us to see."

"Or they might be trying to lead us into a trap," added Connie.

"Unfortunately, that's a possibility," agreed Mike. "Before we go ashore, we're going to investigate the area with an RPV. I want you to stand guard while Dianne does that. I am going to explore the underwater world with sonar. I don't want any surprises from that arena."

"Don't you already have the computer doing sonar surveillance to warn us of anything suspicious?" Connie asked.

"It's looking for an alien sub. I want to see what else might be down there."

"I think your plan is risky," commented Dianne.

"In what way?" Mike asked.

"Jerry was armed and alert when he disappeared. If I'm preoccupied with RPV recon and you're searching the depths, Connie will be our lone guard."

"Good point. Let's have both of you stand guard while I play with the sonar. When I'm done, I'll help Connie protect us while you do the RPV search."

"I like that plan better," responded Dianne.

Mike dropped into the sub's interior. He did not alter the ongoing covert sonar surveillance; rather, he used a different set of signals to explore the bottom. He made no attempt to disguise these signals, because he wanted the aliens to know that he was exploring their domain. Also, by boldly using loud pings, he was hoping to mislead them into thinking that he did not have the capability to do covert sonar surveillance. If the aliens had a small sub in the lake, they might think they could move around undetected whenever they didn't hear the pings.

A few moments into the bottom search, Mike made a surprising discovery. He checked and rechecked his data. Then, he went to the deck and exclaimed, "You can't believe what I just found."

"What?" both women asked.

"There's a large hole in the bottom of this lake."

"A hole in the lake?" Dianne exclaimed in disbelief.

"Actually, the hole isn't in the bottom, it's in the side. This lake is nothing more than a crater filled with water, and the south wall of this crater has a hole in it. It's about 175 feet below the surface."

"How big is it?" Connie asked.

"Fifty to sixty feet across."

"How deep is the hole?" Dianne asked.

"Impossible to tell from here."

"Let's go down and take a look," Dianne suggested.

"I know what you're thinking," commented Connie. "You're wondering if this hole is the entrance to an underground river that extends to Sandstone Lake."

"Well, it might be," responded Dianne. "If it is, the aliens might've used it to get from that lake to this lake. A small sub could certainly navigate a large tunnel filled with water."

"That's true, but I can't believe they led us here to show us how they got from that lake to this lake. They must have some kind of trap set up."

"We don't know if they needed to travel from that lake to this lake," stated Mike. "You're assuming they live in the sandstone cliff."

"I know the RPV I parked over there hasn't spotted any activity, but those holes in the cliff have closed doors. With us looking for them, they may've decided to stay out of sight. They certainly don't want us to find them while they have my husband."

"That's true," agreed Dianne, "but if they live there, it makes no sense for them to lead us to an underground river connecting these lakes."

"You're both jumping to conclusions too fast," stated Mike. "We don't know if this is an underground river. We have to go down and check it out."

"It could be a trap," warned Connie.

"I know," replied Mike. "We'll have to be careful."

"We have company," exclaimed Dianne, while pointing ashore to the left.

"Looks like the lupusaurus pack you spotted earlier is thirsty," noted Mike.

"Those animals sure are hideous," commented Connie, as a cold shiver ran up and down her spine.

"They're also vicious," added Mike. "They might even be the dominant predator in this area."

"Why do you think that?" asked Dianne.

"It's their attitude. Look at the fearless way they're lining up on the water's edge to drink."

"Maybe they're being a little too careless," Connie said.

"I don't think so. I've encountered them, and I think they're cunning enough to deal with whatever risks they face."

Mike had hardly finished speaking, when a long arm shot out from just beneath the surface and wrapped its end around the neck of a lupusaurus. It began pulling the animal into the water, but the lupusaurus struggled valiantly trying to escape. The few seconds that its resistance bought was enough. The lupusaurs on either side of it leaped at the arm with wide-open mouths. Their attack was right on target, and they clamped their teeth on the arm with bone-crushing strength and violently shook it, attempting to rip out chunks of flesh. The monster of the deep released its struggling victim and contemplated its own escape as additional lupusaurs entered the water and latched onto its attack arm. Desperately, it struggled to gain deep water. Being a strong swimmer, it slowly began dragging the lupusaurs into the lake. One by one, they released it and returned to shore.

"See what I mean," commented Mike.

"That long-arm is lucky to escape with its life," Connie said.

"It'll be a long time before it attacks another lupusaurus," added Dianne.

"Unless it has amazing healing powers, it may even die," Connie said. "Look at all the blood it lost. The water is red over there. If it doesn't bleed to death, it might starve. I don't think it's going to use that arm to catch food for a long time."

"So why did the aliens show me images of one of those monsters attacking Jerry?" Dianne asked.

"Maybe they were hoping we'd come here and see a battle like the one we just watched and conclude that they're not living here because this place is too hostile," suggested Connie.

"In other words, they're trying to mislead us into thinking that they don't live here and don't have Jerry," stated Dianne.

"Let's go down and investigate that hole and see if we can find some answers," Mike said.

"That could be very dangerous," warned Dianne. "That hole might be a tunnel to an underground base."

"That's possible," agreed Mike, "and since they led us here, they must not be worried about our capabilities. That means they've set up a way to deal with whatever we do, but I may've short-circuited their plans."

"How?" asked Connie.

"If they monitored my conversation with Moose and believe my bluff, they can't attack us."

"Why?"

"Because I told Moose that I had to contact the fire control computer periodically, or it would begin the attack."

"So if they believed you, they can't kill you."

"That's right."

"Does that mean you're planning to take us into that hole to see where it leads?" Connie asked.

"No, at least not right now. We're going to learn what we can without going into it; then, we'll decide what to do next."

Mike reached for his communicator and entered the number for the fire control computer. When it responded, he sent it a sequence of 20 random numbers and letters. "Let them try to make sense out of that," he said while grinning.

"I think you enjoy toying with them," noted Connie.

"What makes you say that?"

"I watched you enter those characters. It looks to me like you sent the computer a bunch of gobbledygook."

"I did. There's no sense to it at all. No matter how hard the aliens look for a hidden code, they're not going to figure out when I'm suppose to contact the computer again and what signal I'm suppose to send. So I'm hoping they'll leave us alone while we explore the underwater hole. Let's dive."

A few minutes later, the submarine was at a depth of 200 feet with its nose facing the hole. Mike sent sonar signals into it. "It extends horizontally for just over 200 yards," he said, "but it doesn't end there. It makes a gentle turn."

"How do you know that?" Connie asked.

"I'm getting a weak sonar return, indicating that a large part of the signal is being deflected around a bend. A dead end would give me a strong return."

"Are we going in to find out where it leads?" questioned Dianne.

"It might lead us to the aliens," replied Mike.

"If that's the case, it might take us to my husband," stated Connie.

"But if we close in on their homes, they might defend themselves with deadly force. I don't want to fight them on their turf."

"I want my husband back."

"I believe we should give them until 5:00 to return him. It isn't even lunchtime yet, so we have several hours of waiting ahead of us."

"You mean we're just going to sit here and wait."

"I didn't say that. There are ways we can put pressure on them without confronting them."

"What do you have in mind?" Connie asked.

"I am going to send a small reconnaissance torpedo into that tunnel to explore it."

"I'd forgotten that we have those."

"You've been busy with your medical research. Enhancing the capabilities of the recon torpedoes is one of the things I did during our long voyage from Earth."

Mike selected the sub's largest torpedo. It would trail a fiber-optic cable, providing a secure line of communication. He tuned a monitor to the torpedo's sonar and a video screen to its low-light-level camera, which was aided by headlights. Mike went through a checklist. When he was satisfied that all equipment was operational, he launched the torpedo and guided it into the cavern at low speed. He controlled its direction and speed with a small joy stick.

As expected, 200 yards into the tunnel, it gently turned to the left. One hundred fifty yards later, it curved back to the right and was again headed south toward Sandstone Lake. Shortly thereafter, Mike announced, "We've reached a fork in the tunnel. There's a branch heading to the left."

"Which way are you going to send the torpedo?" Connie asked.

"I think we should go straight ahead. That appears to be the way to Sandstone Lake. I'd like to find out if this tunnel goes there."

"How much range do these torpedoes have? Can we explore the side tunnel on the way back?"

"We can easily do that."

"We need to investigate that fork," stated Connie.

"You sound very determined," commented Dianne. "What do you expect to find?"

"We haven't seen any activity in front of the sandstone cliffs. Maybe the activity is underground. Maybe that side tunnel leads to an underground base."

"You might be onto something," commented Mike. "The cliffs are big enough to contain a fairly large cavern."

"That's what I'm thinking," responded Connie. "And their cliff homes might even have backdoors that open into the cavern."

"That would be a safe, secure setup," commented Dianne.

"The side tunnel does have a gentle upward slope," added Mike. "And in about 300 yards, it curves to the right."

"It sure looks like it heads toward those cliffs," stated Connie.

"If it really does go there, the aliens now realize that we know where they are," commented Dianne.

"You're assuming that they're listening to the sonar signals I'm beeping into the side tunnel," Mike said.

"If they live here, they have to be listening."

"We might be getting too close for their comfort," commented Mike, "but that might be what convinces them to release Jerry."

"What are you going to do to up the pressure?" Connie asked.

"To make sure they hear us, I'm going to turn up the volume and stay put for a minute; then, we'll leave. If they're in there, they should be relieved. But on the way back, we'll turn up the heat by sending the torpedo in there again."

After sending out several loud pings, Mike headed the recon torpedo down what seemed to be the main tunnel. Several minutes of uneventful exploration passed by; then, the torpedo's camera detected light. As the seconds ticked by, the light grew brighter.

"It looks like the tunnel does lead to Sandstone Lake," commented Dianne.

"My sonar data indicates that the tunnel opens into a lake a couple hundred yards straight ahead," responded Mike.

A minute later, Mike announced, "Our torpedo has just entered Sandstone Lake."

"Let's find some evidence that the aliens are living in those cliffs," suggested Connie.

"We might start by searching the lake bottom offshore from the cliffs," Dianne said.

"First, I want to see if there are any of the long-arm monsters in this lake," Mike said, as he turned up the power and panned the lake with sonar pulses.

After a few moments of searching, he said, "I see five of them swimming around. I have no way to know how many are resting on the bottom or lurking in their lairs, but the long-arms definitely live in this lake."

"I wonder if they swim back and forth between the two lakes," questioned Connie.

"That's possible," responded Dianne. "All they would need is simple sonar to navigate the dark tunnel. Back on Earth, bats do very well flying around in total darkness by emitting high frequency sounds and listening to the echoes."

"We didn't see any long-arms in the tunnel," noted Mike.

"That's true," responded Dianne, "but I would be surprised if they don't have the ability to migrate back and forth between these lakes."

"If that's true, they have the ability to prey upon the aliens in their underground cavern, if one exists, and if that side tunnel leads to it," commented Mike.

"I would hate to have to live with that possibility," Dianne said.

"I wouldn't like it either," stated Mike, as he headed the recon torpedo toward the cliffs. When he thought he might be halfway there, he put the torpedo into a 45-degree climb. It soon broke the surface and leapt out of the water like a fish. At the apex of its leap, it was momentarily horizontal. In that instant, its camera returned a sharp image of the sandstone cliffs directly ahead. Then, the little torpedo dove back into the water and resumed its journey.

A short time later, it arrived offshore from the cliffs. Mike piloted it back and forth along the bottom, but search as they might, Mike and his colleagues found nothing unnatural on the lake bottom.

"We're going to have to bring this thing back soon," stated Mike. "I have to save enough power for the return trip."

"I am disappointed we haven't found anything," Connie said.

"I have an idea," Dianne said.

"I'm open to suggestions," responded Mike.

"My husband is a fishing nut, and he recently lost a lure when it snagged an underwater obstacle. I wonder if these aliens do any fishing."

"I think you want me to search for sunken tree trunks and inspect them for lost tackle."

"It's worth a try."

"That's something we can do on the way back," stated Mike, as he started a sonar search for underwater obstacles. He located several and headed for the first one. It was an old waterlogged tree that had sunk to the bottom in about 20 feet of water.

"The sonar indicates there are plenty of fish milling around in that area," commented Mike. "If the aliens do any fishing, we just might find something hooked into that old dead tree."

"I will be surprised if we do," stated Connie.

"Why?" asked Dianne.

"Would you be comfortable fishing in a lake where the long-arms live?"

"They would certainly add some excitement to a fishing trip."

"Yeah, some deadly excitement."

"I can't deny that, but the aliens might have a way to deal with them."

A few minutes later, the torpedo arrived at the deadhead and the search began. All were eagerly watching the video. Almost immediately, Dianne exclaimed, "Look at that!"

Displayed on the screen was a red and white lure sporting a pair of triple hooks. One of the hooks was firmly imbedded in the sunken log.

"That lure looks fairly new," commented Mike.

"I would guess that it's been there no longer than just a few weeks," noted Dianne. "It's not covered by the kind of algae that has coated the tree trunk."

"If they were fishing here that recently, they must be living here," concluded Connie. "And that means my husband is probably a captive inside those cliffs."

"It sure looks that way," agreed Mike.

"I wish we could go in there and get him," stated Connie.

"I do too," responded Mike, "but we have to give them until 5:00 to release him."

"I don't want to wait until then."

"I don't either, but I believe that's our best chance to get him back alive. Essentially, I've given them a 5:00 PM ultimatum. I've put our cards on the table. We have to play the hand out. It is now their move, but we need to find ways to keep the pressure on."

"Let's explore that side tunnel," suggested Connie. "I am convinced it will lead to an underground base."

"If it does, we can expect them to grab our torpedo before it gets there," commented Mike. "And that will give us additional hard evidence that we've found them."

"Also, they will know that we've found them," stated Connie, "and that should strengthen our position."

A short time later, the little torpedo was back in the underground river. When it reached the fork, Mike piloted it into the side tunnel. In less than 100 yards, the torpedo's progress was blocked. On the video screen was a clear image of one of the long-armed monsters. Except for its long attack arm, it looked like a huge octopus.

"Is it just coincidence, or is that thing intentionally blocking our progress?" questioned Mike.

"Why don't you try to go around it," Dianne suggested.

Mike turned the torpedo to the right, but the long-arm also moved to the right. Mike tried to dive under the creature, but it immediately dropped to the tunnel's floor. "I don't think it's going to let us pass by," he said. "I wonder why."

"It's acting like a wild animal guarding its nest," commented Dianne.

"It reminds me of a guard dog protecting its owner's property," stated Connie.

"Are you suggesting that the aliens are able to train and control these things and that they're using them as guard dogs?" Mike asked.

"Back on Earth, various kinds of marine animals are captured and trained, why not these monsters?"

"If they're able to do that, it would turn the existence of these creatures into an advantage," Mike said.

"Why don't you turn off the torpedo's light and sonar and just listen for a few moments," recommended Dianne.

"Good idea," replied Mike, as he turned them off.

In just a few seconds, the little torpedo started detecting pulses of sound. "That animal does have its own sonar and doesn't want to lose track of us," stated Mike.

Wanting to see the long-arm, Mike turned the headlight back on. "We have a decision to make," he said. "Do we try to find a way past it, or do we back out and leave?"

"If it's a capable guard dog, you're not going to get past it," stated Connie.

"If it's an animal protecting its nest, you're not going to get past it either," added Dianne.

"Let's find out if it will allow us to leave," Mike said, while slowly backing away from the monster. As time ticked by, the long-arm maintained its position. Eventually, the torpedo was back in the main tunnel, and Mike turned it toward Crater Lake.

"Any thoughts?" Mike asked his colleagues.

"I think this was an animal guarding its den, and it was content to leave us alone when it saw us leaving," commented Dianne.

"I tend to agree," stated Connie. "If it were a guard dog for the aliens, it seems like they would've used it to grab our torpedo and take a look at our technology."

"That's an interesting point," commented Mike. "But for that reason, the aliens might've avoided grabbing our torpedo. By not taking it, they might be hoping to mislead us into thinking that they aren't in there and that this animal was just protecting its lair."

"Do you really think these aliens have enough control over these long-arms so that they could have one of them take or not take our torpedo?" Dianne asked.

"We don't know what kind of mental powers they have," replied Mike. "What if they're able to telepathically get into the brains of the long-arms?"

"Then they might be able to get them to do whatever they want," Dianne replied. "In fact, they could then safely fish or even swim in these lakes."

"If they have that much mental power, I shudder to think what they may've already done to my husband," commented Connie. "Who knows what evil things they might be programming into his brain?"

"It's too soon to worry about that possibility," advised Mike. "We don't know what mental powers they have. Anyway, we have to hope for the best."

"They damn well better release him unharmed by 5:00," stated Connie. "If they don't, we're going to go in there and get him, and they are going to pay a big price."

"We don't know for sure that they're in there," responded Mike. "So if they don't release him by 5:00, the first thing we need to do is send a recon torpedo into that side tunnel all the way to wherever it goes."

"How do you plan to get past the long-arm?" Dianne asked.

"I'll send in a pair of torpedoes. The first one will be rigged with an explosive charge."

"How many torpedoes do we have?" Connie asked.

"Only two, this sub wasn't designed for warfare; it's a research tool."

"Two torpedoes might not be enough," commented Connie.

"If we have to mount a rescue mission, we'll need a day or two to bring in people and weapons. I will definitely want our helicopter here and armed. And we'll have the Challenger overhead, in case we need the antimatter particle beam gun."

"If it comes to that, I'm not likely to get Jerry back alive," stated Connie.

"That's not necessarily true. We could use that gun's capability to intimidate them."

"How?" Connie asked.

"If I were to fire a small charge into the middle of Sandstone Lake, it would demonstrate the gun's awesome power and our resolve."

"If you do that, you will kill everything in the lake, and much of the water in the lake will evaporate into a mushroom-shaped cloud," warned Dianne. "Do you really want to annihilate the creatures that live in the lake?"

"No, I don't, but that kind of brutality would demonstrate our willingness to brutally punish them."

"If that's what it takes to get my husband back, we should do it. Water will flow back into the lake, and life will return."

"Hopefully, it won't come to that," Mike said. "In a couple minutes, I'll have our torpedo back; then, we'll surface and eat lunch. I'm starving."

"How can you be hungry at a time like this?" Connie asked.

"I had a very early breakfast, and it's well past lunch time, I should be hungry. I need to eat, or I won't have the energy for clear-headed thinking."

"I just think we need to keep the pressure on our adversaries," responded Connie.

"Our very presence here tends to do that, but if you're not hungry, there's something you can do."

"What do you have in mind?"

"You can fly an RPV over to the sandstone cliff, fly right into the entrances, and inspect their front doors. Try to find evidence indicating how recently they've been opened."

"I'm not hungry, and I'll do that."

Several minutes later, the submarine was back on the surface. Connie eagerly launched an RPV and flew it toward the cliff. Dianne stood guard, and Mike started wolfing down a sandwich while helping with the guard duty.

"Aren't you going to send some gibberish up to the fire control computer?" Dianne asked Mike.

"I'll wait awhile on that. Sending such a message now might increase our danger of being attacked."

"Why?"

"I've let the aliens know that the fire control computer is programmed to attack them if I miss a check in deadline. Immediately after I make a check in, they might think they have a window of opportunity to take action against us."

"Why?"

"Suppose they think I need to check in every hour or two. Right after I check in, they might think they have an hour or two to kill us and clear out of this area."

"Do you think they would take that chance?"

"I don't know, but I am going to wait until Connie's done inspecting their front doors. In case they feel threatened by her activity, I don't want them doing something foolish, like attacking us."

"Maybe we would be safer if we were farther away from shore or even submerged."

"To keep them believing my bluff, I think we need to boldly stay right here and act like we have no fear of them attacking us."

"That's a risky strategy," warned Dianne.

"I know, but I want Jerry returned, so I need to keep them convinced that I really do have the particle beam gun programmed to attack them."

"I'm approaching the cliff now," Connie announced.

Speaking to Dianne, Mike said, "You're going to be our only guard for a while. I need to watch the video coming from the RPV we parked over there earlier today. If the aliens take any action against the RPV Connie's flying to their front doors, I want to see that."

"I think this is a critical time," stated Dianne. "I will be extra alert with an itchy finger on the trigger."

"Try not to look overly anxious; in case, they're watching us."

"You're asking quite a lot. I don't exactly have nerves of steel."

"Do your best to act like we hold the winning hand. Try to display an air of confidence."

"All of these openings are cut into the cliff about 20 feet above ground level," commented Connie. "I am heading for the cave farthest to the north."

A few moments later, she said, "My RPV is inside the opening. I am looking at a solid wood door, and I don't think it's been opened recently. There are lots of spider webs here that haven't been disturbed for a long time. They're loaded with the carcasses of long dead insects. Now, I see a large spider that seems to be upset by the presence of my RPV. This thing has a body that is three inches across and legs that are four inches long."

Connie backed the RPV out of the opening and flew south to the next cavern. "This door has been opened recently," she said. "I see only one spider web attached to both the door and its frame. This is a fresh web. It has only two dead insects, and they look like they may've died earlier today."

After inspecting the sandstone floor in front of the door, Connie said, "This rock is worn smooth. There's been traffic in and out of this door for a good many years. Also, there are several metal hooks bolted into the rock floor. They might be used as anchor points for a hanging ladder, among other things."

One by one, Connie inspected the remaining doors. All indicated recent use, but not as much traffic as the second door she had inspected. She returned to it. "I believe this door is their main entrance," she said. "It shows the heaviest wear, and it has more anchor points than the others. In fact, it even has anchor hooks bolted into the ceiling. Maybe they're attachment points for systems of pulleys to hoist things up from below."

Connie continued her inspection. When she was satisfied that she had been thorough, she asked Mike, "How rugged are these RPVs?"

"Even though they're lightweight vehicles, they are very sturdy," he responded. "But what motivated that question?"

"I'm wondering how hard I can repeatedly crash into the door. In case they're unaware that we're inspecting their castle, I want to let them know that we are here."

"I like it. The psychological value of knocking on their main door is worth risking an RPV."

Connie crashed into the door three times at ten mph; then, she backed the RPV away from the door and waited. After half a minute, she said, "That didn't get any response. Maybe no one is home."

"I think they're in there. Try it again; only this time, do it at 12 mph."

"I don't want to wreck the RPV."

"Twelve mph should still be in the safety margin."

Connie did as instructed, and after three crashes, she said, "Based on what I heard, that was definitely a harder knock, and the RPV is still operational."

"Wait a minute, and if there's still no response, do it again."

"You don't expect them to open the door, do you?"

"No, but I want to bug them a little bit."

Connie repeated the crashes, and as expected, there was no response. After a brief pause, she banged the RPV into the door six more times before backing away.

After waiting a minute and not getting a reaction, Mike said, "I believe we've made our point, and we've learned all we can. Let's bring back the RPV. It's time to back off and wait until 5:00 before we do anything more."

Cruising on the surface, Mike headed the submarine toward the shuttle, which was still in the middle of the lake. He cruised at a leisurely pace.

Upon arriving at the shuttle, he said to Dianne, "I want you to pilot the sub to the north side of this lake. I'll bring the shuttle."

"Why are we moving so far away from them?" Connie asked. "If they release Jerry, I want to pick him up right away."

"I want to put as much distance as possible between us and them."

"Why?"

"I want it to look like we're getting out of the danger zone. If they aren't yet convinced that they will be blasted at 5:00, leaving the area might help persuade them."

"But 5:00 PM is still a couple hours away," protested Connie. "It seems like we should be doing something other than just waiting."

"Getting as far away as we can is doing something. It lends credibility to our bluff."

"I wish I had your nerves of steel. You're so calm about this."

"What choice do I have? We've played our hand; now, we have to wait. But while we're waiting, we have to look confident; just in case, they have some way to watch us."

"With a telescope, they could easily observe us from the top of one of those foothills to the east," acknowledged Connie.

"I believe we're being watched from much closer than that; in fact, I think we're being watched from right here in this lake."

"What makes you think that?"

"Ever since we left the south shore, there's been a long-arm within a hundred yards of us. Quite a number of those animals have taken turns shadowing us. It looks like an intelligently directed relay of responsibility from one animal to the next along our path. I think the aliens are watching us through the eyes of those monsters."

"It's scary to think that they have the mental ability to get into the brains of these animals and not only control them, but also, see and hear what they see and hear," responded Connie.

"That's an ominous possibility," commented Dianne. "If they've been listening to us, they know that the bluff we've been trying to play so strongly is nothing more than a bluff, and consequently, they might keep Jerry."

"Now, I'm really worried," stated Connie.

"We don't know if they've had access to our conversation, and even if they have, they have no way to know with certainty whether or not I will incinerate them at 5:00. In any case, we've done what we can, and now, we need to go to the north shore and wait."

"I'll bring the sub," Dianne said.

"I'll ride with you, and watch the sonar," Connie said to Dianne. "I want to see if the long-arms shadow us the rest of the way."

"I'll be watching that too," Mike said as he headed for the shuttle's flight deck.

Wanting to find out if the long-arms would continue to shadow them, Mike and Dianne piloted their vehicles at only five mph to make it easy for the monsters. The distant shore was two miles away, and the journey took about 25 minutes.

When they arrived, Mike joined Connie and Dianne on the submarine. "They stuck with us all the way," he said.

"It sure looks like these animals are being intelligently directed," responded Connie.

"Either that, or they're intelligent and did this on their own," suggested Mike.

"But that doesn't make any sense," argued Connie.

"Why?" Mike asked.

"Suppose they are intelligent, what reason would they have to track us?"

"I don't know," replied Mike. "But this is their home, and they might not like our presence."

"They didn't track us this morning, why this afternoon?"

"Maybe that side tunnel we weren't allowed to explore is important to them. The fact that we tried to go in there might be the reason they now see us as a threat."

"I guess that's possible," conceded Connie. "But I just can't believe those ugly monsters are smart enough to use team relay tactics to keep tabs on us."

"Why?" asked Mike.

"This morning, one of those brutes was almost killed when it tried to prey on a lupusaurus. If these animals are smart enough to use team effort to track us, it seems like they would know better than to attack a lupusaurus when the rest of the pack is there to rescue it."

"That animal could've been a teenager that made a dumb mistake, but for the sake of discussion, let's assume that these creatures are being controlled by the aliens. Maybe we can use that to our advantage."

"How?"

"Let's assume the aliens are seeing everything we do, and then, let's figure out what we want them to see and show it to them."

"They've already seen us put maximum distance between us and them. What else do we want to do?"

"I think *maximum distance* is the key," responded Mike.

"We've already moved as far away as we can without leaving the area." As she finished speaking, Connie read the expression in Mike's eyes. What she saw alarmed her. "I can see that you are planning to leave, and I just cannot leave here without Jerry. I want him back."

"I do too," stated Mike. "That's why we are going to load the submarine. Then, we'll begin filling the shuttle's fuel tanks. At 4:15, we'll take off."

"I don't want to leave here without my husband."

"Getting out of this area is the best way to convince the aliens that a truly devastating attack is about to hit them."

"I wish I had your nerves of steel."

As time slowly dragged on, Connie thought about all the things she and Jerry had done since leaving Earth. She recalled their first encounter in the medical lab so many years ago. How exciting that was. She thought about their happy relationship and their wonderful daughter. Now, they were thinking about having a second child. The future seemed so bright, despite Alcent's many dangers.

Then, she thought about the shock of Jerry's sudden disappearance. Her heart skipped a beat, and she felt sick at the possibility that she might not get him back. Involuntarily, she gripped her rifle so hard that her knuckles turned white. She stared to the south and shouted, "You had better release him, or all of you will die!"

She searched the water around the shuttle for a long-arm. When she spotted one about 50 yards away, she faced it and shouted, "I know you can hear me, so let me repeat: If I don't get my husband back in good health, all of you will die! This, I promise you!"

She raised her rifle and aimed at the long-arm. She held the gun steady for several seconds. The long-arm disappeared beneath the surface. She beeped Mike and said, "I have more evidence that they're using the long-arms to keep tabs on us."

"What did you find?"

"I believe they just moved one out of harm's way in response to my threat."

"That's possible," agreed Mike, "but it's also possible that the animal submerged on its own because it felt threatened by you."

"Maybe so, but I am now completely convinced that the aliens are controlling them."

"I am too, but just in case they aren't, I am going to make sure they know we're leaving. I am going to do a full power takeoff to the south, and we are going to buzz their sandstone cliff on the way out."

"The sound will be deafening, but will they hear us underground?"

"They have to have cameras and microphones to monitor the vicinity of their home. They will hear us."

"When are we leaving?"

"As soon as you come in, we'll close the hatch and take off."

"I'm on the way."

A few minutes later, Mike headed south at full power. The shuttle quickly reached 45 mph and rose up on its hydrofoils. The NTR thundered into action, accelerating the shuttle to 200 mph. It became airborne, but Mike kept it at low altitude while it continued to gain speed. He instructed the flight control computer to use the shuttle's radar to clear ground obstacles by only 50 feet. He headed toward the sandstone cliff. When he arrived, he pitched into a vertical climb with the thundering NTR pointed at the cliff top. He blasted the aliens with the ear shattering roar of the NTR at full power.

In less than five minutes, Mike had the shuttle at an altitude above 100 miles and in a ballistic trajectory that would take it to Clear Lake. He hoped that shortly after arriving on Clear Lake, he would receive a message to return to Crater Lake to pick up Jerry.

Less than 25 minutes after takeoff, the shuttle was in its final approach glide for a landing on Clear Lake. Connie's communicator beeped. "Hello," she answered.

"Hi, sweetheart. Can you pick me up?"

"Jerry! Where are you?"

"I am on Zeb's Island."

"How did you get there?"

"I don't know. I was standing guard on the shuttle. I blanked out and woke up here. What day is it?"

"You disappeared yesterday."

"I've lost a whole day. What happened?"

Mike broke into the conversation and said, "We're trying to fig-

136

ure that out, and we'll pick you up shortly." Mike fired the NTR only seconds before the shuttle's hydrofoils would've hit the water, instantly aborting the landing. He turned the shuttle toward Zeb's Island, which was located just a few miles south of Pioneer Island. "Where on the island are you?" Mike asked.

"I'm in the cave that Zeb lived in for so many years. I'd sure like to know how I got here."

"I would too," responded Connie. "But right now, I just want you back in my arms. Are you okay?"

"I feel fine, but I have no memory of the last day-and-a-half."

"I am going to give you a complete physical as soon as I get you home."

"I don't think you're going to find any problems," Jerry replied. "Why?"

"Apparently, whoever put me here was concerned about my safety. They could've put me anywhere, but they put me in a secure cave."

"They could've done that out of concern for their own safety," argued Connie. "I am going to give you a thorough medical exam. I don't trust them."

"Why would they be worried about their safety?" Jerry asked.

"Mike threatened to annihilate them at 5:00 PM."

"That's only minutes away," responded Jerry.

"I'd better call off the attack," commented Mike, as he contacted the Challenger's fire control computer and sent it random series of letters and numbers.

The shuttle's hydrofoils entered the water. "We've landed," Mike said.

"I'll meet you at the shoreline," Jerry responded.

"I would prefer that you stay in the cave until we get there," stated Mike.

"I agree," Connie said. "You might feel fine, but you might be disoriented in a way that you're not aware of. Please wait for us."

"I'm okay," responded Jerry, "but I'll trust your judgment and wait."

"Thanks," replied Connie.

A couple minutes later, Mike, Connie, and two guards beached a small inflated boat and headed for Zeb's cave. When they reached the huge tree in front of the cave, Mike posted the guards and began climbing the tree. Thirty feet up the tree, he came to the large branch that led to the cave entrance. He walked on the branch to the entrance.

He shined a light into it looking for traps. Not seeing any, he turned to motion Connie up the tree, but she had not waited for his signal; she was already on the branch and was right behind him. "Let's go in," she said.

"That won't be necessary," Jerry said, as he crawled out of the cave and stood up.

Connie squeezed past Mike and grabbed Jerry in a tight embrace. Tears of joy streamed down her face when she felt Jerry's strong arms holding her tight.

Chapter Seven

TIME: Day 32, 8:30 AM

It was a pleasant morning on Pioneer Island, and everyone was happy to have Jerry back. Connie, Dianne, Mike, and Michelle were sitting at an outdoor table discussing his capture and release.

"How is Jerry doing this morning?" Mike asked.

"He's still sleeping," Connie replied.

"Sleeping late is rare for him."

"Yeah, it is, but the nightmare he's just been through would wear out anybody."

"What do you think the aliens did to him?"

"I don't know yet, but I did give him a thorough medical exam last night, and I didn't find anything."

"Maybe they used drugs to make him talk," suggested Mike. "His fatigue might be a side effect of that."

"I didn't find any drugs in his system, but they may've used chemicals that don't leave telltale traces."

"Is there any way to determine if they did that?" Mike asked.

"Since there aren't any traces I can measure directly, I will try an indirect approach."

"How are you going to do that?" Mike asked.

"I'll examine the function of key body organs. If I find even the slightest deviation from what has been normal for him, I'll run tests to determine the cause of the deviation."

"But haven't you already run quite a bunch of tests without finding anything to worry about?" Mike asked.

"That's true, but I don't know what the aliens did to him, so I have to look at all possibilities."

"Well, I think it's encouraging that Jerry seems to be in good health," Michelle said.

"Physically, it looks like he's okay, but I want to make sure. Then,

I'm going to tackle the next problem, his lack of memory. I am worried about what they may've done to his brain. He isn't able to remember anything from just before he was captured to when he woke up in Zeb's cave. We need to find a way to recover his memory, so we can find out what they did to him."

"That might be impossible," commented Dianne.

"I know, but we have to try," stated Connie.

"We also need to figure out how they were able to put him in Zeb's cave," added Michelle.

"My guess is that they have an aircraft with much greater capability than our helicopter," Mike said.

"Why wasn't it spotted by the radar we use to track pterodactyls?" questioned Dianne.

"Apparently, it is a long-range stealth aircraft," responded Mike.

With obvious anxiety in her voice, Michelle said, "It really worries me that the aliens know where we live and have the means to get here."

"Maybe that's what they were trying to tell us when they delivered Jerry to Zeb's Island," commented Mike.

"I don't like this one bit," stated Michelle. "This is a scary situation. Which one of us will they capture next?"

"Maybe no one," responded Mike.

"Why do you say that?" asked Michelle.

"It's possible that they captured Jerry and planted bombs on our shuttle because we provoked them. Think about it. If they really are living in that sandstone cliff, then we landed practically in their front yard. They may've felt threatened by us. If we stay out of that area, they might be content to leave us alone."

"But we're peaceful people. We meant them no harm."

"They had no way to know that," argued Mike. "Don't forget, they've been to Earth and had access to TV programs. They have good reason to think we are a violent people."

"That might be, but I don't trust them," stated Connie. "They took away my husband's memory for the time they held him captive. What are they trying to hide?"

"I don't know," replied Mike, "but maybe they don't trust us and don't want us to know anything about them."

"That's not exactly true," argued Connie. "They've made it clear that they know where we live and that they can come here."

"The fact that they did that supports my belief that they're worried about us. I think they're trying to tell us to leave them alone."

"If they don't want trouble from us, they better not have harmed my husband."

"I don't believe they have," responded Mike. "When they returned Jerry, they apparently could've put him most anywhere, but they chose to put him in Zeb's cave, one of the safest places you're going to find around here."

"They had to put him in a safe place," commented Dianne. "Have you forgotten your threat to incinerate them?"

"No, I haven't, and that's why I believe that they haven't harmed Jerry. They had to consider the possibility that we would punish them if Jerry's been hurt in any substantial way."

"That makes sense," agreed Dianne. "But if they truly believe we are a violent people, your threat to blast them yesterday at 5:00 PM presented them with a real dilemma."

"How is that?"

"If they didn't release Jerry, they were to be blasted at 5:00 PM. If they did release him, they would no longer have a hostage, thereby leaving you free to attack them as punishment for kidnapping Jerry."

"By putting Jerry on Zeb's Island, they handled that dilemma quite well," stated Mike. "In effect, they've told us to leave them alone, because they know where we live and have the ability to get here."

"Are they threatening to attack us if we harass them?" asked Connie.

"I believe that's what their message is," replied Mike.

"That means that they could've injured my husband and then went out of their way to tell us that we'd better not retaliate."

"Unfortunately, that is possible," agreed Mike, "but I just don't believe that Jerry's been hurt."

After a few moments of silence, Dianne said, "There is a sinister possibility that we need to consider."

"What?" Connie asked.

"I don't want to alarm you, but maybe they returned Jerry in perfectly good physical condition to hide their real plan."

"What are you getting at?" asked Connie.

"We have reason to believe that these aliens have telepathic ability. Remember the images they showed us of Jerry being attacked by a long-arm?"

"Of course I do," replied Connie.

"I know from experience with Rex and Zeb how effective telepathic communication is. If the aliens who took Jerry are that good, we need to consider the possibility that things may have been telepathically planted in his subconscious."

"I am worried about that," admitted Connie.

"I wish you didn't have to be worried," responded Dianne. "But we are dealing with unknown aliens, and all sorts of bad possibilities exist. For example, Jerry could be programmed to deliver one of our shuttles to them. With it, they could capture our starship. Our very existence could be put in jeopardy."

A stunned silence fell over the small group while each thought about the full implications of Dianne's comment. The silence continued until Mike said, "We have to keep Jerry under observation until we figure out what the aliens have done to him and what their objectives are. Also, we have to keep him off the shuttles. I hate having to treat my most trusted friend this way, but we have no choice."

"I don't like it either," stated Dianne, "but I agree. We have no choice."

"How do you propose to keep Jerry off the shuttles?" asked Michelle. "He loves to fly, and he is our Captain. He can go wherever he wants."

"I know," replied Mike, "but we have to find a way." Turning to Connie, Mike said, "Maybe you can help us."

"How?" she asked.

"You are his wife and doctor. How much influence do you have over him?"

"He always listens to reason."

"If you tell him that you don't want him doing any flying, will he honor that request?"

"You're asking me to ground him?"

"That's right," Mike replied.

"I might be able to keep him home for a week or two, but if he's feeling great, he won't tolerate being grounded any longer than that."

"Buy us as much time as you can."

"I'll do it, but there's one thing that's confusing me about this."

"What's that?" Mike asked.

"If they want one of our shuttles, why didn't they take the big one when they had the chance? Why did they take Jerry and leave the shuttle behind with bombs planted on it? It doesn't make sense to sabotage a shuttle that they would like to take away from us."

"To start with, they would not have known how to fly the shuttle, and knowing what the stakes are, there's no way that Jerry would've cooperated with them. He would've sacrificed his life rather than fly the shuttle to the Challenger, thereby, letting them capture it."

"You know my husband very well."

"I've worked with him for a long time. But I want to continue with what I think could've happened. When faced with Jerry's stubborn refusal to cooperate, the aliens may've said, OK, if you're not going to help us now, we're going to take you home and program your brain, so that you will help us in the future. And just in case your people decide to mount a rescue mission, we're going to plant some bombs on this shuttle. Also, they probably made Jerry watch them do that, so they could make him behave by threatening to explode the bombs."

"You make the aliens sound so ruthless, it's frightening," stated Connie. "I think we're lucky to have Jerry back."

"Ruthless people understand ruthless tactics. I did threaten to annihilate them."

"Apparently, that was the right strategy. It did work. I got my husband back. I just wish I knew what they did to him."

"If we knew what their objectives are, we could make some intelligent guesses about that," commented Mike.

"If you were them, what would your objectives be?" Michelle asked Mike.

"If I were in their shoes, the first thing I would want to know is: are the people from Earth a threat to my survival?"

"That would suggest that they captured Jerry only to get firsthand information about us by picking his brain with whatever mind probing techniques they have," commented Michelle.

"They sure used brutal tactics if they wanted nothing more than information," stated Connie. "Why didn't they just call us and ask us some questions?"

"I don't know," replied Michelle, "but if they think we are a barbaric people and don't trust us to tell the truth, they may've thought it necessary to capture one of us and use mind probing techniques. Thirty years ago, they were attacked by Zeb's people, and based on Earth's movies and TV programs, they would have to wonder how violent we are."

"I sure hope they didn't damage my husband's brain while pumping information out of him."

"That's definitely something we need to be concerned about," commented Dianne, "but he did seem perfectly normal last night."

"I'll give him some mental and psychological tests, just to make sure he's okay," stated Connie, sounding worried.

"I can help by presenting him with engineering problems that I know he can solve," offered Mike. "If he can still handle them, we'll know that part of his mind hasn't been messed up."

"Thank you," replied Connie, "and I'll get Moose to test his long-term memory by asking him questions that go back to their college football games."

"They were best friends back then," added Dianne. "Moose should be able to think of plenty of things to ask him, starting with the key plays in some of their games."

"The only problem is, Moose is on the Challenger," stated Connie, "and I don't think he should probe Jerry's mind from there. We have to assume the aliens are listening."

"That's not a problem," responded Mike. "We can use line-of-sight communication methods that will be impossible for them to listen in on. And we can use regular channels for the stuff we want them to hear."

"What kind of information are you planning to feed them?" asked Dianne.

"If we let them hear all of the chatter in our normal everyday life, they should come to the conclusion that we're only trying to build a home here and are not a threat to them."

"Hopefully, they would then leave us alone," commented Michelle.

"That would be nice, but I am worried about them," stated Connie. "I think we have something they want."

"That's possible," agreed Mike, "and that's why we have to find a way to recover Jerry's memory for the time he was their captive. Then, he might be able to tell us what they're up to."

"Speaking of Jerry, he's about to join us," announced Michelle.

Everyone turned toward the habitation capsule. Jerry had just stepped out the front door. Connie stood up and greeted him with a hug. "How do you feel this morning?" she asked.

"I don't know what you did to me last night, but I could swear I feel ten years younger."

"I didn't do anything to you last night. In fact, you were so exhausted that I could hardly keep you awake. I'm glad you feel so rejuvenated this morning."

"That just shows what a little sleep can do for you," commented Jerry.

"What do you mean, *a little sleep*? You just slept almost eleven hours."

Jerry looked at his watch. "I did sleep a long time, didn't I?"

"You definitely needed the rest. I hope you slept soundly."

"I did most of the time, but I sure had some weird dreams."

"Tell me about them."

"You're not going to believe this, but I dreamt I was captured by aliens."

"You were captured by aliens."

"I was?"

"Yes, you were."

"Then, I wasn't just dreaming."

"No, you weren't. It actually happened. I told you all about it last night. Don't you remember?"

Jerry looked puzzled while searching his brain. Finally, he said, "I'm sorry, but I really don't remember much from last night. I guess I really must have been tired."

"You were, but don't worry about last night, just tell me about your dreams."

"This is really wild. You and I sailed into Mystery Lagoon to explore the place and enjoy an overnight campout. We took the sub down to look at the underwater world, and we found a sunken spacecraft that was shaped like a landing capsule. While we were studying it, hideous monsters with long arms attacked us from every direction. They wrecked our sub's propeller. Then, they towed it to an underground base, where we were taken captive by aliens. They put me to sleep and some really weird hallucinations happened to me while I was out."

"What do you remember about them?"

"Right before my eyes, they transformed you into one of them."

"What do you mean?"

"Your blonde hair became black, your blue eyes became brown, and your facial features became Asian."

"How did they do all of that?"

145

"I don't know how they did it, but I watched them change you. In just a few minutes, you turned into one of them."

"You said I looked Asian?"

"You looked like a Chinese woman I dated when I was in college."

"Are you saying that the aliens in your dream looked like Chinese?"

"Yes."

"What did I do after they transformed me?"

"You hugged me and kissed me. Then, you told me not to worry, that you were still the same person."

"How did you feel about that?"

"I was skeptical. I wanted to believe that you were still the same wonderful woman I married, but I couldn't understand why they changed your appearance. Why did they make you look like a woman I dated a long time ago?"

"Did you ask the aliens that question?"

"I couldn't, they were out of the room."

"Were we alone?"

"Yes."

"What did we do?"

"You were very affectionate with me while you were asking me questions. It was almost like you were seductively trying to coax answers out of me."

"How did you react to that?"

"I was confused."

"Why?"

"Because you had assured me that you were still the same person, but you were asking me questions that you know the answers to. That made me think that you weren't you, but had actually become the woman I was in love with many years ago."

"Did you answer my questions?"

"You were able to get the answers out of me."

"There is something that bothers me about your dream."

"What's that?"

"How do you know you were dreaming?"

"What do you mean?"

"It seems to me that all of the things that happened to you while you were a captive are recorded somewhere in your subconscious mind. Whatever the aliens did to block your memory of that might be effective only when you're awake. When you're asleep, it's possible that your subconscious mind might feed memories of your captivity into your conscious mind in the form of dreams."

"Are you saying that my dream was actually a memory of part of what happened to me while I was a captive?"

"It's possible."

"If it was real, then, who was the woman in my dream?"

"It had to be one of the aliens. Didn't you say they looked Asian?"

"Yes."

"So she could've been one of them."

"That's what's confusing, because I saw them transform you into one of them, but they made you look like a girlfriend from long ago."

"I wasn't there, so that had to be a delusion, a trick to disarm you. Obviously, you would be more willing to answer questions if you thought you were talking to me or a past girlfriend."

"That does make sense."

Connie's serious demeanor changed as a mischievous grin lit up her face. "Just how cooperative were you with your interrogator?" she asked.

"What do you mean?"

"Well, if you thought you were with me or a past girlfriend, you might have been your usual masculine self."

Jerry smiled broadly and said, "I only remember answering questions."

"Some of your earlier comments make me believe she used her female charm to get those answers."

"She had to do that to be in character."

"What do you mean?"

"That's what you what have done, and the aliens were trying to convince me that she was you transformed into one of them."

"I am suspicious."

"Don't worry," responded Jerry. "This was only a dream."

"I don't think so," stated Connie. "I think we've just had a glimpse of how the aliens interrogated you. The questioning was done by a cunning young woman willing to use her female charm to full advantage."

Mike, Michelle, and Dianne hadn't said anything, because they didn't want to interrupt Connie's effort to retrieve information from Jerry's mind. But Mike had an idea that he thought was pertinent.

147

"The theory that this was more than a dream doesn't make sense in one important respect," he said.

"What?" Connie asked.

"Jerry was captured in Crater Lake, which is 1,600 miles south of here. Mystery Lagoon is in the northeast corner of this lake. It's about 35 miles from here, and none of us have ever been there."

"Dreams are frequently filled with symbolism," responded Connie. "We know that Jerry was captured on a spacecraft in a lake. Also, the long-arms may have played a role in the capture."

"Are you saying that Mystery Lagoon is irrelevant in the dream, that it only represents a body of water?"

"Jerry was captured in Crater Lake, which is a body of water."

"But why would his dream place him in Mystery Lagoon at the time of his capture?" questioned Mike.

"I don't know," replied Connie.

"I guess what's bothering me about this is your suggestion that this wasn't just a dream. You said that this dream might actually be revealing memories of what the aliens did to Jerry."

"That's something we have to consider."

"I agree, and that means that Mystery Lagoon might be more than a symbol representing a body of water."

"In what way?"

"Maybe the aliens want us to go there and investigate the site of Jerry's dream," replied Mike.

"Why?"

"I don't know, but it's possible that the downed spacecraft isn't just a symbol representing our cargo shuttle."

"Are you suggesting that there might actually be a landing capsule resting on the bottom of Mystery Lagoon?" asked Connie.

"It's possible."

"There's only one way to find out," stated Jerry. "Let's go take a look."

"Not so fast," objected Connie. "I have a full day of medical tests planned for you."

"I feel great. I think those tests can wait until tomorrow."

"He might be right," commented Mike. "Besides, there might be some medical reasons to take Jerry to Mystery Lagoon."

"This, I have to hear."

"Look at it this way," argued Mike. "Suppose Jerry is able to find a place in the lagoon that looks like the site where he was captured in his dream. Suppose we actually find a spacecraft there. Isn't it possible that these events could stimulate his memory? He might be able to tell us more about the aliens and what they did to him. Wouldn't that help your diagnosis?"

"That's all possible, but I would like to run the tests first."

"I feel great," stated Jerry. "I don't think the aliens did anything bad to me. I think they want to be our friends."

"They picked one hell of a way to express friendship," exclaimed Connie. "After what they did, I don't trust them."

"I don't either," agreed Mike. "But we have to go to Mystery Lagoon to see if there's anything there. Also, just being there might help Jerry remember more of his dream. We might be able to determine if it was just a dream."

"OK! I agree; we have to go. But before we leave, I want a half-hour to run some basic medical tests."

"You worry too much. I feel fine."

"I know, but I am convinced the aliens did something to you, and I am going to find out what, however long it takes me."

Jerry grinned at Mike and said, "I guess I'm stuck with another exam before we can go sailing."

"It's for your own good," Connie quickly declared.

Jerry smiled at his wife, reached out, and affectionately held her hands. "I know you're worried about me, but your mind will be at ease when you see the good results you're going to get."

"I don't know how you can be so confident. You've been a captive for a day-and-a-half, and you can't remember anything."

"I know, but I feel like a bundle of energy. Let's get the tests done, so we can go sailing."

"I'll get the sub ready," stated Mike.

"I'd like to come along," Michelle said.

"Good, it should be a fun day, and we all need a break. Why don't you get our supplies together. Better pack enough food for two days, in case we stay overnight."

"Good idea."

"Also, I am going to take some fishing gear along, so bring what we need for a fish fry."

"Okay."

"I want to come along," exclaimed Matthew, who had just

joined the group, closely followed by Denise. Not wanting to be left out, she said, "I want to see the dinosaurs. Can we sail over to where they are?"

Jerry dropped down to one knee and gave his daughter a big hug. "We have a big mystery to solve," he said, "but when we get back, I'll take you to see the dinosaurs."

"But you're always gone," protested Denise.

"I know I've been gone a lot, but I have to go to Mystery Lagoon. I promise I'll come back no later than tomorrow afternoon."

"Then can we go see the dinosaurs?"

"I will take you there the day after we get back."

"It'll be fun to go sailing with you all day," responded Denise. "I miss you when you're gone so much."

"I want to see the dinosaurs too," stated Matthew.

"You can come along," Jerry said.

"Will we go ashore to see them?" Matthew asked.

Remembering Connie's brush with death the one time they had gone ashore at Sauropod Meadow, Jerry said, "We'll watch the dinosaurs from the safety of our boat."

"How close will we get to them?" asked Matthew.

"Close enough to scare you," replied Jerry.

"I wish we could go today," Matthew said.

"I know you do, but we have to wait, and I promise we'll go the day after tomorrow," Jerry assured both Denise and Matthew.

"You kids must be hungry," Dianne said. "Why don't you let me fix you some pancakes with fresh maple syrup?"

Responding enthusiastically, both children eagerly followed Dianne to the second floor of the habitation capsule. Jerry and Connie went to its first floor for the medical tests, while Mike and Michelle prepared for the voyage to Mystery Lagoon.

Chapter Eight

TIME: Day 32, 10:30 AM

Jerry, Connie, and Michelle arrived at the submarine just as Mike finished converting it to its sailboat configuration. The conversion was quite simple. All Mike had to do was deploy the boat's sails and inflatable outriggers. These pontoons were mounted at the ends of 21-foot telescoping beams on both sides of the hull.

A telescoping mast supported the boat's sails. But since there wasn't any wind, Mike did not deploy them. Instead, he deployed the solar sails. These large arrays of solar cells were rolled out on top the outrigger beams and faced skyward. They could produce up to 45 kilowatts of electrical power at midday when Alpha Centauri A was high in the sky.

One feature that helped make sailing the boat enjoyable was its spacious deck. Mounted just above the hull, it was eight feet wide by 28 feet long.

"It's about time you people got here," commented Mike.

"We've been busy," responded Michelle.

"Me too," Mike said.

"You had the quick, easy job," stated Michelle.

"What do you mean? I had to convert our sub into a sailboat."

"Tough job pushing the right buttons to get that done."

Mike smiled at Michelle. "Well, I guess I'll have to admit that the people who designed this boat did make it easy to operate."

"That's true," agreed Jerry. "We have a terrific boat and a great day for sailing."

"If it weren't for the dark cloud hanging over our heads, we could enjoy it," responded Connie.

"What dark cloud?" Jerry asked.

"The aliens are every bit as threatening and unpredictable as a big dark storm cloud."

"I think you should forget about them and enjoy our day on the lake. It's not good for you to worry all the time."

"After what they did to you, I don't know how you can be so calm and unconcerned."

"Other than loss of memory for the time I was their captive, I don't believe they've done anything to me. I feel great, and you said the tests you just did came up with the best numbers in several years. What are you so upset about?"

"The fear of losing you was a gut-wrenching nightmare for me, and I am mad as hell at them for putting me through that."

Jerry gave Connie a reassuring hug. "Your anger is certainly justified," he said.

"You darn right it is, and I'm not going to forget this anytime soon. In fact, I think we should find a way to punish them."

"I understand how you feel, but we are back together, and I am unharmed."

"We don't know that for sure."

"That's true, but I do feel pretty good."

"I'm happy about that, but I'm still mad at them for taking you in the first place. Why would they put us through that ordeal?"

"I don't know, but in time we'll learn more about them, and everything will become clear. I just don't think they mean us any harm."

"I don't know how you can be so sure of that. I think they want something from us, and they're not going to leave us alone until they get it."

"That might be, but I don't think they're going to bother us today."

"Why?"

"We know where they live, we have the means to annihilate them, and they no longer have me as a hostage. Why would they risk provoking us?"

"That sounds reasonable, but I am worried."

"Okay, here's something else for you to think about. If your suspicion is correct, and there is something they want from us. Don't you think it makes sense for them to leave us alone for a while, and maybe even do some fence mending, rather than harass us?"

"You might be right, but I think we should be vigilant anyway. Just in case, they use force to try to take from us whatever it is they want."

"I agree, and Mike and I will be alert for trouble of any kind. This lake might even have dangerous predators living in it, so we have to be on guard anyway. But I want you to forget about everything, kick back, and relax."

"Under the circumstances, I don't know if I can just forget about everything and relax. I might need your help."

"In what way?"

"I have a bottle of sunscreen, and you have a way of giving massages that always takes my mind off everything else. Maybe you could put your magical hands to work."

"Are those the doctor's orders?"

"It's definitely the medicine I need at the moment."

"I agree with her prescription," chimed in Michelle.

"This is beginning to sound like a conspiracy," commented Jerry.

"I don't know how you could call it a conspiracy when it was your idea," responded Michelle.

"How was it my idea?" Jerry asked.

"You said you wanted your wife to relax. All she did was tell you how to make that happen, and I agreed with her. That's hardly a conspiracy."

Jerry smiled at Michelle, then at Connie. Even though she returned the smile, Jerry noted that she didn't seem to be her usual vibrant self. My captivity must have been pure hell for her, he thought. "I think you do need some special attention," he said.

"I'll get the sunscreen, and you can roll out an air mattress for me."

Jerry went below deck to get an air mattress. While there, he viewed the underwater world through the boat's transparent plastic hull. He marveled at how clean the water was and how easy it was to see for great distances. He noted the multitudes of colorful fish slowly swimming around. He wondered if the water in Mystery Lagoon would be as clean as the water in Clear Lake. If so, exploring the bottom would be easy, and if there was a space capsule there, it would be easy to find.

Air mattress in hand, Jerry went back on deck. He noted that Mike was piloting the boat northward along the east side of Pioneer Island. Going to the forward part of the deck, he laid out the air mattress and pressed the inflation button. It quickly inflated to a comfortable firmness.

Connie stretched out on her back and looked up at the deep blue sky. "We couldn't ask for a more pleasant day," she said. "It's so warm and peaceful."

"I like the pristine quality of the air," commented Jerry. "It's refreshing."

Connie pointed up and to her left. "Look at that. There are a couple pterodactyls riding the thermal under that cloud. For such huge creatures, they sure make flying look effortless."

"It looks like they're just lazily enjoying themselves."

"That's what I need to do," commented Connie, while handing Jerry the bottle of sunscreen.

A couple minutes later, she said, "Your hands feel really good, and this warm sunshine is making me feel drowsy."

Connie turned over, and Jerry began applying sunscreen to her back. By the time he finished, she was sound asleep. That didn't take long, he thought. I hope she sleeps for a couple hours. The splashing sound of the waves breaking against the bow should have a relaxing hypnotic effect on her and help keep her asleep.

I wonder if the aliens used hypnosis on me. Are there any posthypnotic suggestions planted in my mind that will be triggered by certain events? What can I do to guard against that possibility?

While looking at Connie, Jerry thought, I have such a beautiful wife. I love her so very much. I have to discover what the aliens have done to me. I cannot allow them to make me do anything that will put her through any more hell. Maybe she can help me. She is a skilled psychoanalyst. After we get back from Mystery Lagoon, she'll be well rested, and together, we can delve into my mind. Hopefully, she can get past whatever mental blocks the aliens put there and discover what they're up to.

Quietly, Jerry stood up. Once again, he gazed at his peacefully sleeping wife. Then, he turned and walked to the aft deck, where Mike and Michelle were enjoying the voyage, while alertly watching their surroundings. Mike had programmed the desired course into the boat's navigation computer, and it required no further attention unless a new course or arrival time needed to be set.

"My wife is sleeping," announced Jerry. "In fact, she has really conked out."

"I'm glad," responded Michelle. "She needs it."

"It's going to take three to four hours to get to Mystery

Lagoon," stated Mike, "so she has plenty of time to get caught up on her rest."

"She won't sleep that long," commented Jerry. "I've never seen her sleep more than an hour or two during the day."

"When she wakes up, why don't we stop the boat for a while and go swimming," suggested Michelle.

"Good idea," responded Jerry. "I could use a little goofing around in the water."

"And I could use a nap, so I'm going to join your wife and leave the sailing up to you guys. But I do need a sunscreen application, so I don't get toasted."

"I believe I could do that for you," responded Mike.

"I'll stand guard," stated Jerry.

"I don't know if that's a good idea," commented Mike with a bit of laughter.

"Why?"

"The last time you volunteered for guard duty, you were kidnapped, and that caused all kinds of headaches for us."

"That's not going to happen today," stated Jerry.

"How do you know that?" asked Mike.

"Just a feeling I have."

For a few moments, Mike stared into Jerry's eyes trying to figure out what was going on in his mind. Then, he said, "I hope you're right, but we're going to stay alert anyway."

Mike turned to Michelle and applied sunscreen to her scantily clad body. "Your touch is putting me in the mood," she said.

"I'm not trying to arouse you; I'm just trying to keep you from getting sunburned."

"That might be, but you do have my attention."

"Good! Maybe you can forget our current problem, and soak up some rays for a while."

"All I need is an air mattress to lie on."

"I'll get you one. I want to go below anyway. I am going to set up a covert sonar surveillance program."

"Why covert?" asked Jerry.

"Just a precaution," replied Mike.

"I realize there might be dangerous predators in this lake, but why covert surveillance?"

"The aliens put you in Zeb's cave yesterday. We don't know how capable their aircraft is, but it's possible that they delivered a miniature submarine to this lake. If they're following us, I don't want them to know that we know where they are."

"You're being awfully cautious."

"I know, but we have two very good reasons to be cautious. One of them is already sleeping and the other soon will be. I don't want either of them to be worried about safety."

"I don't want them to be worried either, but I just don't believe the aliens are going to bother us."

"If you're right, we'll have a fun day," responded Mike, while going below deck.

A few minutes later, he climbed back on deck and said, "Sonar surveillance is now in progress. It will warn us of any underwater threats."

"And you and Jerry will keep an eye on things up here," commented Michelle, "so that means I can forget about danger and just let my mind wander into fantasyland."

"That sounds promising," responded Mike.

Michelle placed her air mattress next to Connie. She stretched out on it, closed her eyes, and listened to the soft washing sound of waves splashing against the boat. She heard the squawking sounds of distant pterodactyls. Opening her eyes and searching the sky, she spotted four of them high above her flying due north. Amazing creatures, she thought. They're so big, but yet so graceful. I wonder where they're going. After watching them for a few moments, Michelle again, closed her eyes.

She felt the warm radiant energy flowing into her body from Alpha Centauri A. This is just like sunbathing back on Earth, she thought. But when I was a teenager back on Earth, I never dreamed that I would one day enjoy sunbathing on a dinosaur planet. What an awesome experience.

Michelle noted the gentle breeze that was caressing her body. It provided a soothing, cooling effect that nicely balanced the heat from the rays she was soaking up. This sure feels good, she thought, as she drifted off into slumber land.

Mike and Jerry were silently lost in their own thoughts as they alertly gazed out over the lake in various directions. Mike's wandering gaze found Michelle and fixed on her for a few moments while he admired her beauty. I am so fortunate to have such a wonderful wife, he thought. He turned to Jerry and said, "We now have two sleeping beauties to protect."

"I don't think they're in much danger," commented Jerry, "but we're going to make sure nothing happens to them."

Jerry's communicator beeped; it was Moose. "How are you guys this morning?" he asked.

"Morning? It's almost lunch time," responded Jerry. "Do you always sleep 'til noon?"

"I needed to sleep in. I was up late last night."

"Doing what?"

"I was looking at recon data from the Sandstone Lake area."

"Find anything interesting?"

"I think so, but I'm not sure."

"Tell me about it."

"About three-fourths of a mile east of Sandstone Cliff, there's a flat open area in front of a big cave in a tall cliff."

"What's unusual about that?" asked Jerry.

"It looks like a perfect place to operate an aircraft with vertical takeoff capability. Assuming that the aircraft would be used sparingly, it would need to be safely stored for long periods of time. A large cave with a stout door would serve that purpose quite nicely."

"Do your pictures show a closed door?"

"No. But a door could be set back from the entrance a few yards, and I wouldn't be able to see it from orbit."

"We need to take a close-up look," stated Mike.

"How are you going to do that?" asked Jerry.

"While you were captive, your wife parked an RPV on a rock in front of Sandstone Cliff, hoping to spy on the aliens. But they never showed their faces. That RPV is still there."

"What are you waiting for?" asked Jerry. "Check it out."

Mike dropped into the boat's interior, and within seconds was back on deck with a headset and a remote control unit. The signals from the unit would go to a communications satellite, and then down to the RPV, which was 1,600 miles away.

Mike put the headset on and tuned in to the signals from the RPV's video cameras. "I'm looking at the face of Sandstone Cliff," he said, "and the doors are still closed."

"I could've told you that," Moose said. "I've been keeping an eye on those cliffs, and I haven't seen any activity."

"I wonder why they don't want to be seen," questioned Mike.

"I don't know," replied Moose. "Maybe they're ugly and would be embarrassed to show themselves."

"I doubt that," commented Jerry.

"I was just kidding," responded Moose.

"I have the RPV airborne," announced Mike. "I'm glad it's still operational."

"Was there any doubt?" asked Moose.

"We're dealing with aliens whose technical ability might be far beyond ours in some key areas. It's conceivable they could've fried its flight controls while leaving its cameras functional."

"Why would they do that?" asked Jerry.

"To mislead us," replied Mike. "By immobilizing the RPV, they could move around in areas out of view from its cameras. We would see no activity in front of the RPV, while they're busy elsewhere. We might think they're playing it safe by staying in their cave; while in reality, they're out and about causing all kinds of mischief for us."

"You're sure suspicious of these people," responded Jerry. "I just don't believe they mean us any harm."

"I'm willing to be convinced," stated Mike. "But until then, I am going to be suspicious."

A few seconds later, Mike said, "I'm approaching the area, and you're right, it would be ideal for a VTOL (vertical takeoff and landing) aircraft."

"I want to look in that cave," stated Moose.

"We'll be there in a few seconds," responded Mike.

When the RPV reached the cave, Mike flew it slowly into the entrance; then, he brought it to a hover. With its low-light-level cameras, he panned the interior. "There's no aircraft here," he announced, "but it looks like it's been here. I see cabinets and work benches."

After turning the RPV from side to side, Mike said, "There are doors here, and they're made out of some pretty heavy-duty timber. I wonder why they're open."

"Probably to deceive us," replied Moose. "If they were closed, my recon photos would've revealed them. By leaving them open, this looks like nothing more than a large cave, a natural occurrence."

"So where is the aircraft?" Mike asked.

"They must've used it to put Jerry in Zeb's cave yesterday. Where did they go after that?"

"I don't think we're going to find them," commented Jerry. "They could be anywhere, and it's obvious they don't want to be found."

"But why?" questioned Mike.

"Yesterday, you threatened to incinerate them. Maybe they took your threat seriously and moved on to another part of this planet. They may've feared retaliation after releasing me."

"Are you suggesting that their aircraft is so big that all of them were on it when they brought you to Zeb's cave?"

"That's possible. We don't know how many of them there are. Their numbers might be small. In that case, their aircraft wouldn't have to be big for all of them to leave their home."

Mike piloted the RPV to the back of the cave and looked around. He took a closer look at the cabinets, work benches, and tools, while flying the RPV back to the cave entrance. "It certainly looks like they left in a hurry," he said. "Too many valuable items have been left behind."

"That means that they're planning to return to pick up some of those items," commented Moose.

"When?" asked Mike.

"If they fear retaliation, the obvious time would be to return after the Challenger passes overhead and drops below the horizon," Jerry said. "They would then have more than an hour before the Challenger would again be in position to attack."

"Where on this planet could they move to that we wouldn't be able to find them?" asked Mike.

"Nowhere," replied Moose. "This starship's recon capabilities are so good that I could find them anywhere."

"We have to assume that they've figured that out, and that means they're not planning to move," stated Mike.

"So where are they?" asked Moose.

"One ominous possibility is that they're somewhere in this area," suggested Mike. "They might be on one of the islands right here in Clear Lake or on one of the islands in the big lake north of here. Who knows, they might even be hiding in the forests around Mystery Lagoon waiting for us."

"Sounds like I should do some intensive recon of Mystery Lagoon and the entire Clear Lake area."

"And I am going to find a hiding place for this RPV, so I can spy on this cave. If they return, we'll get a good look at them."

"You guys sure are suspicious," commented Jerry. "I just don't believe these people mean us any harm."

"You keep saying that," stated Mike, "but I don't know how you can know that when you're not able to remember anything about your captivity."

"You're right about my lack of memory, but somehow, I just know that they mean us no harm."

"Have you considered the possibility that you might be constantly reiterating a posthypnotic suggestion that they planted in your mind?"

"That is a possibility," admitted Jerry, "and obviously, there is no way that I can know whether it is or isn't, since I can't remember anything."

"That means that we have to consider all possibilities. We simply can't afford to take unnecessary risks."

Jerry thought about the situation for a few moments; then, he reluctantly said, "Because of the possibility there might be several posthypnotic suggestions planted in my mind, I want you to assume command until this situation gets resolved. That means ignoring anything I say that doesn't make sense."

"I will get us through this," stated Mike.

"You've done an excellent job so far."

"Studying military tactics has always fascinated me. I've looked at most of the major battles fought in the last few centuries, and I've analyzed the reasons why they were won and lost."

"I know. That's why you're the right person for this job."

"Thanks for the vote of confidence."

"I'll be over Mystery Lagoon in a few minutes," Moose said, "and I'll get started with the recon."

"Good," responded Mike. "Before we go in there, we're going to search the forests along the shoreline with RPVs. Let me know if you find anything for us to give special attention to."

"Will do. Talk to you later."

"I think the RPV search would be a good job for our wives," commented Jerry. "That will leave us free for guard duty."

"Good suggestion," responded Mike. "They should be well rested and sharp by the time we get close enough to launch the RPVs."

TIME: Day 32, 12:30 PM

Connie sat up and stretched. "I'm hungry," she said.

160

"How can you be hungry?" asked Michelle. "All you've been doing is sleeping."

"I know, but breakfast was a long time ago, and I didn't eat much. I wasn't hungry then, but I'm starving now."

"Well, I'm hot and sweaty, and that water looks refreshing. I need to go swimming before I eat."

"Our husbands are in a hurry to get to Mystery Lagoon. I don't know if they'll want to stop the boat, so you can go swimming."

Placing herself in a provocative pose, Michelle said, "I think I can get Mike to go swimming with me."

"That bikini you're wearing doesn't leave much to one's imagination," commented Connie.

"Your outfit's pretty skimpy too. Let's go convince our husbands to stop the boat."

"I don't know if I feel like going swimming."

"The way you've been laying around all morning, a good swim would do you good," commented Michelle, as she stood up and sauntered up to Mike. She snuggled up to him and said, "I need you to stop this boat, so we can go play around in the water."

"We're on an important mission," replied Mike. "I don't think we should delay it."

"Letting the boat drift for 20 minutes, so we can have some fun, isn't going to jeopardize our mission," argued Michelle, while pressing her nearly nude body against Mike.

"You're being awfully persuasive," responded Mike.

"I really haven't said all that much."

"It isn't your words that are convincing me."

"Does that mean we're going swimming?"

Mike cut power and the boat slowed to almost a dead stop. "Before we dive in, I want to take a quick look at our sonar data," he said, as he went below deck.

Turning to Connie, Michelle smiled smugly and said, "I knew I could convince him."

"I'm not sure that going swimming is what you convinced him of."

"What do you mean?" asked Michelle, while displaying an air of innocence.

"You know what I mean."

"The underwater world looks safe," commented Mike, as he appeared from below deck.

"Catch me if you can," stated Michelle, before diving in. A few seconds later, she surfaced and began swimming vigorously.

Mike dove in and followed her, but he was unable to catch her. About 50 yards away from the boat, she stopped and waited for him. When he came to her, she gave him a big hug and said, "Thanks for swimming with me."

"I'm glad you talked me into it. I'm having a ball."

"You needed a break. You've been pushing yourself pretty hard since Jerry's capture. I don't know what we're going to find in Mystery Lagoon, but we need to be fresh and alert when we get there."

"That's true, but we're still ten miles away, so let's forget about that for a while. I'm going underwater to look at the fish."

"How deep is the lake here?"

"About 280 feet, but don't worry, I'm not going down more than 15 to 20 feet."

"I'll go with."

About a minute later, they surfaced. "I didn't see any. Did you?" Michelle asked.

"No, but there's some seaweed floating over there. Let's look under it."

Mike and Michelle swam 20 yards to the floating vegetation. They dove under it. When they surfaced, Michelle asked, "What do you think of those fish?"

"They remind me of freshwater sunfish back on Earth."

"I wonder what they eat. I hope they're not voracious feeders like piranha."

"They don't seem to have the right mouth structure for that. Also, I saw one of them grab a snail off a plant."

"I wonder if we should try to catch some of them for tonight's fish fry."

"I think we should stick with fish that we've already tested for toxins," commented Mike. "We don't know if these guys are safe to eat."

"Maybe we should be getting back," suggested Michelle.

"You want to go back already. It seems like we just got in the water."

"We need to save some energy for after lunch."

Mike smiled at Michelle. "Sounds like you have one of those special desserts planned."

"I think that would add a nice touch to our day, don't you?"

"Maybe we've been in the water long enough."

"Sounds like you're agreeing with me."

"Definitely."

A few minutes later, Mike and Michelle climbed onto the boat. They sat down at a portable table on the aft-deck to enjoy their lunch. Their rifles were in easy reach.

Jerry and Connie were in the water playing self-invented games that seemed appropriate for the occasion. As time went on, their frolicking around gradually carried them farther away from the boat.

"This is fun," commented Connie, "but I think we should be getting back. I'm anxious to get to Mystery Lagoon. I can't get your dream out of my mind. I'm hoping to find out if it was just a dream or if the aliens were behind it."

"I wish you weren't so worried. In spite of what's happened, I believe everything is going to work out."

"I hope you're right, but I think we should get back and head for the lagoon."

"It looks like we might be about a hundred yards from the boat. Do you feel like racing me back?"

"Why would you want to race with me? I've always been faster than you in the water."

"Not by much. Besides, it's okay if you beat me. I just want to take your mind off of worrying. I am fast enough so that you will have to concentrate on your swimming if you want to beat me."

OK! You're on for the race. Are we going to use any particular stroke?"

"Let's make it freestyle."

"Are you ready?"

"Anytime."

OK! HIT IT!"

Jerry and Connie swam with power and gracefulness. By the time they were halfway to the boat, Jerry was slightly in the lead. During the second half of the swim, Jerry gradually lengthened his lead, arriving at the boat two full body lengths ahead of Connie.

After climbing onto the boat, she said, "That was quite a performance. This is the first time you've ever beat me in a swimming race. How did you do it?"

"I don't know, but I feel full of energy today."

"I do too. I just had a two-hour nap."

"But you haven't slept much in the last two days. I think I beat you only because your energy levels are lower than you think."

"That might be, but I have to consider some other possibilities."

"Like what?"

"I don't know right now, but I don't trust the aliens. Who knows what chemicals or drugs they put in you."

"But you haven't found anything."

"I know. That's what's puzzling."

"Are you two ready for guard duty?" asked Michelle.

"I'm starving," replied Connie.

"That's not a problem," responded Michelle. "You can watch for trouble while you're eating. We're going below deck to keep an eye on the underwater world."

"Want me to check on you in a few minutes to make sure everything is okay?"

"Actually, I think it would be better if you don't disturb us for a while."

Chapter Nine

TIME: Day 32, 2:15 PM

"We're only a mile away from Mystery Lagoon," announced Mike. "It's time to fly in the RPVs and look around."

"Moose hasn't found anything for us to be concerned about," commented Michelle. "He's passed over it twice now."

"The Challenger has immense recon capability," acknowledged Mike, "but Moose was 120 miles above the lagoon on both passes. You and Connie can fly in under the treetops for a really close look."

"If the aliens are in there hoping to ambush us, we'll find them," stated Connie.

"That's going to be difficult to do, if they're well hidden," commented Mike.

"If they're in there, it seems like there should be some clues to indicate that," argued Connie.

"We'll investigate anything that looks out of place," added Michelle.

Connie and Michelle put on video headsets and launched their RPVs. "I'll take the north shore," Connie said.

"I'll do the south shore," stated Michelle.

TIME: Day 32, 3:15 PM

"I just spent an hour looking at three miles of shoreline, and I didn't find anything suspicious," Connie said.

"I looked at about that much waterfront on the south side," stated Michelle, "and I didn't find anything either."

"One hour's not really enough time to do a complete search of that much territory," commented Mike.

"I know, but we had to bring the RPVs back," responded Michelle. "The batteries were almost dead."

"A recharge only takes a few minutes," Mike said. "Is there anything you want to take another look at?"

"I don't think so," replied Michelle. "I know that an hour isn't enough time to look for every possible hiding place, but much of the shoreline doesn't have any hiding places. The first mile or so on the way into the lagoon is mostly steep rock cliffs."

"Except for concealed caves, it would be tough to hide there," agreed Mike.

"Consequently, I concentrated my search on the next two miles, which is sandy beach backed by meadows, shrubs, trees, and rock cliffs. On the way in, I looked for footprints on the beach and didn't find any. On the way out, I snooped around in the forest, and I didn't see anything that grabbed my attention."

"It seems like you didn't have anywhere near enough time to search all that forest," commented Mike.

"There isn't that much to look into. The rock cliffs are never more than about a hundred yards from the beach. So what you have is a narrow band of trees, a couple miles long, that abruptly ends at the cliffs."

"So you're confident that none of the aliens are in there waiting for us?" questioned Mike.

"I didn't find any evidence to indicate their presence," responded Michelle.

"That's a safe answer that almost evades the question."

"It's the best answer I have at the moment."

Mike turned to Connie. "Tell me what you found."

"Pretty much the same thing that Michelle found."

"Give me some details," requested Mike.

"On the north side of the lagoon entrance, the cliffs are right at the waterline for about a half-mile. The next half-mile of waterfront is rocky beach with some really big boulders. I looked behind all of them. After that, I looked at two miles of sandy beach backed by thick forest that butts against steep cliffs. I found no humanoid footprints in the sand. I spent some time in the forest, but it's too thick and there's too much of it to search thoroughly in just an hour. At the far end of the lagoon, there's a rather majestic waterfall that I enjoyed looking at."

"Tell me more about the forest."

"The rock cliffs are 200 to 300 yards back from the beach, so there's a lot more forest than on the south side. There's too much to search in an hour, or even in a day."

"Why wouldn't a day be enough time?"

"Because it's too thick. It reminds me of a tropical rain forest. There are long strands of various kinds of moss hanging from branches everywhere. The undergrowth is lush. Giant ferns and other kinds of low-light-level plants crowd the forest floor. It's a real jungle."

"It sounds like it would be very easy for someone to stay hidden in there."

"Definitely."

For a few moments, Mike thought about everything that Moose, Michelle, and Connie had told him. "We have no evidence to show that any of the aliens are in the lagoon," he said, "but no matter how much we search, we aren't going to be able to rule out their presence. It's just too easy for them to stay out of sight."

"Some of them are in there," stated Jerry, "but they're not going to bother us. They're only going to observe us."

"How do you know that?" Mike asked.

"I don't know how I know; I just know."

Mike, Michelle, and Connie silently stared at Jerry wondering what was going on in his mind and what the aliens had done to him. Connie stepped up to her husband and put her hands on his shoulders. "I am worried," she said.

"Don't be," responded Jerry.

"How can I not be worried? You just made a statement with such total conviction that I have to believe that you think it's true. That means the aliens planted that information in your mind. How else could it be there?"

"I don't know, but it could be part of the dream I had last night, a detail that I just didn't remember until now."

"That means that you don't know with certainty that some of the aliens are waiting for us," commented Mike. "You only think they are, because they were there in your dream."

"That's possible," responded Jerry.

"But it's also possible that you heard the aliens discuss their plans when you were their captive," suggested Connie.

"They suppressed my memory of that time period," stated Jerry.

"I know," acknowledged Connie, "but their memory blocking techniques might not be 100 percent effective. Some isolated memories might slip through. I think we have to take seriously anything that you say with conviction, even if we can't explain it."

"He keeps saying that the aliens don't mean us any harm," commented Mike. "Should we believe that?"

"I think that would be dangerous," replied Connie. "The aliens might be trying to get us to believe that."

"That means we should sail into the lagoon expecting the worst."

"Why don't we convert this boat to a submarine," suggested Jerry. "Then, we can dive and slip into the lagoon unseen by anyone hiding in the forest."

"That's one plan," agreed Mike. "Another way is to boldly go in on the surface with our helicopter overhead carrying six well armed individuals."

"I like the stealth approach better," commented Michelle. "I think it's safer."

"I agree," stated Connie. "We're only here to search the bottom for a sunken spacecraft to find out if Jerry's dream really was a dream or something planted by the aliens. We have to dive to search the bottom, so we might as well go in that way."

"That makes good sense," agreed Mike. "I'll change this boat back to a submarine, and the rest of you can clear the deck."

"In my dream, we sailed in on the surface," commented Jerry.

"But you just suggested that we go in underwater," stated Mike.

"I know I did, but I just now remembered that in my dream, we went in on the surface."

"Are you sure about that?" Connie asked.

"Yes!"

"Why?"

"I just saw an image in my mind of us sailing between the rock cliffs that border the entrance."

"How do you know that image is from your dream?" Connie asked.

"What do you mean?"

"It might've come from somewhere else."

"Like where?"

"A few minutes ago, you stated that some of the aliens are in there."

"I believe some of them are."

"Isn't it possible that the image you just saw was from them and that it was telepathically transmitted into your mind?"

"I've never been involved in telepathic communication. That's all come through Dianne."

"That doesn't mean that your mind isn't able to receive it. Besides, you've just been a captive. Who knows what they did to you. They might've programmed your mind to receive telepathic messages and maybe even to transmit them."

"That's possible, but I don't know."

"It seems like our plan to do an underwater entry into the lagoon has just been changed," commented Mike.

"Sailing in on the surface could be very risky," Connie warned.

"That's true," agreed Mike, "but I don't see that we have any choice."

"What do you mean?" Connie asked.

"We're here to investigate Jerry's dream to find out if it was just a dream. That means we have to re-enact the parts we can re-enact and see where they take us."

"I am worried," stated Michelle. "I think we're being led into a trap."

"I can't deny that possibility," responded Mike, "but we have to sail in on the surface."

Mike called his friends on Pioneer Island and requested the presence of the helicopter with six heavily armed individuals onboard. "They'll be here shortly," he said.

"Thanks," responded Michelle. "I think the aliens will be less likely to bother us with the chopper circling overhead."

Mike headed the boat toward the lagoon. He rolled up and stowed the solar sails. Then, he deflated the outriggers, retracted them, and stowed them. "We're now a submarine," he said. "We can dive if we need to."

"I'm going below deck for a few minutes," Jerry said. "I need to check on something."

Two minutes later, Jerry poked his head up through the open hatch. "We've had a drop off in the lake bottom," he said. "It's about 1900 feet deep here."

"Evidently, that underwater canyon you found west of Sauropod Meadow extends to here," responded Mike.

"I think we're going to find that it runs into the lagoon," commented Jerry.

"Why?" asked Mike.

"In my dream, the sunken spacecraft I discovered was resting on the bottom in water 1800 feet deep."

"It sounds like you expect to find that your dream wasn't a dream, but was information planted in your mind by the aliens," commented Mike.

"I am starting to feel that way, but we'll soon know. We're only a couple hundred yards from the entrance."

"One thing we can do is cruise the lagoon from end to end and see if there is any water that's 1800 feet deep."

"If there isn't, you're going to conclude that my dream was just a dream and not something planted by the aliens."

"It will be one piece of evidence indicating that."

"I'm ahead of you on this one," responded Jerry.

"How?" Mike asked.

"When I went below, I put on a wrist monitor, so I can keep an eye on depth from up here."

"Let me know if you see anything interesting." Turning to Michelle and Connie, Mike said, "I want both of you to search the waterfront and the cliffs with binoculars."

"Will do," they responded.

To Jerry, Mike said, "I want you to observe our surroundings and keep your mind relaxed and open to suggestions. Maybe something that you see will trigger your memory to bring out more details from your dream, if that's what it was."

"Good idea," replied Jerry. Rifle in hand, he went to the front of the deck. As the boat moved into the lagoon entrance, Jerry shifted his gaze from left to right. He searched the cliffs for anything that seemed familiar, but he found nothing. He looked directly ahead at the long point of land that reached out from the south side. It totally blocked the view into the lagoon. That's what makes this lagoon so mysterious, Jerry thought. You cannot see into it from the lake. It's like a hidden world with its own unique ecosystem. It's completely different than the surrounding countryside. The 500-foot cliffs that surround it make it impossible for any of the dinosaurs to get into it. So, what kind of animal life inhabits the forests around the water? Is this a place where people could safely live? What interests do the aliens have in this lagoon? Why do they want us to come here?

Mike turned the boat to the left to sail to the north end of the long point. Even though lost in thought, Jerry continued his inspection of it, as well as the rest of the waterfront. He glanced at his wrist monitor. "The water's not as deep anymore," he announced.

A few minutes later, the boat passed the end of the point, and Mike turned to the right. "It's only 50 feet deep here," stated Jerry. "That long point extends into the underwater world."

Jerry now had a view of the entire lagoon. Looking across a couple miles of open water, he observed the waterfall at the far end of the lagoon. Even though it was quite distant, it captured his attention because of its height. The river tumbled over a cliff 500 feet high, and it was a large enough river to form an awesome waterfall.

Jerry glanced at his wrist monitor. "The depth is starting to increase again," he said.

"Let me borrow that monitor," requested Mike. "I want to stay on a course that constantly takes us to deeper water to see if we can find 1800 feet."

"You got it," replied Jerry.

Less than three minutes later, Mike said, "We're here. It's 1800 feet deep."

"Let's follow the deepest part of the lagoon and see where it takes us," suggested Jerry.

"Good idea," responded Mike.

Twelve minutes later, Mike said, "Our underwater canyon has come to an end. It's only 200 feet deep here."

"We're only a couple hundred yards from the waterfalls," commented Jerry, "so the canyon runs the entire length of the lagoon."

"That falls is really impressive," exclaimed Connie.

"It should be impressive," noted Jerry. "That's a pretty big river pouring over the cliff. It's at least 150 feet wide, and it drops 500 feet."

"It's a beautiful sight," stated Michelle, as she pointed at the top of the falls. "That rock formation up there divides the river in half creating a double falls. The left half strikes a ledge halfway down causing huge outward spray and a brilliantly colorful rainbow. I believe we should name this Rainbow Falls."

"I'm glad we came here," stated Connie. "Seeing this falls makes this whole trip worthwhile."

"It's an inspiring sight," agreed Mike. "But we only have a few hours of daylight left, I think we should dive and take a look at the bottom along the 1800-foot level."

"There's not much light at that depth," commented Jerry. "Since we're going to have to use our searchlights to explore the bottom, it doesn't matter if we go down now or after dark, so I think we should use our remaining daylight to enjoy the waterfalls. We can go ashore right over there and barbecue some fish over a bed of hot coals."

"I think that would be dangerous," Connie said. "I almost got killed the last time we went ashore. Who knows what we might run into here."

"You and Michelle spent an hour exploring the beaches and forests and didn't find any dangerous animals or even any footprints," responded Jerry. "What are you worried about?"

"The aliens."

"They're not going to bother us."

"You can't possibly know that for sure."

"I know you're concerned, but take a look at that beach. It's the biggest, most open stretch of sand in this area, and it's surrounded by rock slides that are backed by a cliff. The trees are very sparse in the rocky terrain. There are no places to ambush us from."

"I still don't like it."

"Why don't you and Michelle launch the RPVs and search the area while I catch a rainbow pike. If you find anything that looks dangerous, we'll cook our fish right here on the boat."

"There might be a good reason to boldly go ashore for a fish cookout," commented Mike.

"What would that be?" demanded Connie.

"It sends a message to the aliens that we aren't going to let their possible presence deter us from enjoying ourselves."

"Why do we need to do that?" Connie asked.

"Because it's not good strategy to give the impression of weakness in our own backyard."

"I still think it's risky," argued Connie.

"There is some risk involved, but we can put on a show of strength. Our helicopter can land and drop off some people to guard us and our sub while we eat, assuming that Jerry can catch our dinner."

"Rainbow pike are plentiful," responded Jerry. "I've seen several leap out of the water, and I brought along Moose's most effective lure."

"That's all well and good," commented Mike, "but you haven't caught one yet."

"By the time our wives finish exploring the waterfront, I'll have one."

"Enough talk," commented Mike. "Let's see you catch dinner. I'm hungry."

"I guess that means we really are going ashore for a fish fry," Connie said.

"I don't know," replied Mike. "Your husband hasn't caught anything yet."

Jerry ignored Mike's comment and calmly hooked Moose's specially designed, double-jointed lure to the end of the leader. For extra action, the lure had a small spinner in front of its nose and a second spinner mounted on its tail-end triple hook. "I would suggest you ladies get those RPVs airborne and explore our picnic area," Jerry said.

Jerry dropped the lure into the water and watched its action. Satisfied with its performance, he pulled it in and cast it out about 30 yards. "We're moving at about the right speed," he said to Mike, "but I want you to take us closer to the falls. Fish and other critters that are unlucky enough to drop over the falls will be easy prey for the big pike, so there should be plenty of them hanging around there looking for a meal, and I intend to catch one of them."

Mike turned the boat toward the falls. After several minutes went by, he said, "I hope this is close enough. I'm getting soaked with spray, and look at the way the water is churning."

"I can't hear you," Jerry yelled, in an attempt to be heard above the thundering roar of the massive falls.

"Never mind," Mike yelled. "I'm not going any closer."

Not wanting to miss the awesome, inspiring sight, Michelle and Connie landed their RPVs on rocks and took off their headsets. Two people onboard the helicopter circling overhead immediately took control of the RPVs and resumed the search for danger.

Connie and Michelle feasted their eyes on the magnificent falls. The roar was overpowering, so they didn't try to say anything. They just soaked up the spray and let their senses become totally saturated.

Suddenly, Jerry's fishing rod bent in half as he received a powerful strike. Line rapidly played out from the reel. Jerry began tightening the drag, hoping to turn the fish around before it pulled out all the line and snapped it.

The strategy worked. The fish leapt completely out of the water, briefly standing on its madly thrashing tail. Jerry's heart skipped a beat when he saw how big it was. "That ought to take care of dinner," he yelled at Mike.

"First, we have to land him," Mike yelled back.

Jerry worked the fish until his arms ached so much they practically screamed for relief. The fish struggled mightily to break free, but it was securely hooked. Then, with the same suddenness of its strike, it ran out of energy.

Jerry reeled in the exhausted fish. Mike reached into the water with a landing net and captured it. He lifted it onto the deck and said, "This guy must weigh at least 50 pounds."

Jerry pulled his hunting knife and plunged it into the fish's brain. The fish gave one last desperate thrash and the knife slipped in Jerry's fish-slime-coated hand, cutting through the skin over the main muscle to his thumb. The cut was about an inch long and an eighth-inch deep. It started bleeding profusely.

Connie had been looking at the large fish, but at the sight of Jerry's blood, she immediately became the concerned wife and doctor. She grabbed his hand. "Let me look at that," she said.

Connie examined the wound for a few moments. "The bleeding will clean it," she said, "but as soon as it stops, I need to close it. This cut is too long and deep to leave it heal on its own."

It took Connie a couple minutes to stop the bleeding completely and wash the area around the cut. Then, she held the cut skin together and secured it with gas permeable tape. "That should take care of you," she said.

"Good! Let's go build a campfire."

"There's a pretty good collection of driftwood right over there," Mike said, while pointing at it. "Also, it's out of the spray zone, so it should be dry."

A few minutes later, the sub was anchored 50 feet offshore. Jerry pressed the inflation button on a tightly packaged boat and shoved it into the water, where it rapidly inflated. Everyone piled in and rowed ashore. "I'll go back and get our fish and cooking supplies," Michelle said.

Jerry started collecting small pieces of driftwood, while Mike went to work arranging rocks into a fire pit. Connie, however, was suspicious. She stared intently in every direction, while holding her rifle in a quick reaction position.

"You worry too much," Jerry said.

"Can you blame me? You've said that some of the villains who captured you are in this area."

"We have four heavily armed guards onsite and two more on the chopper."

"I know, but I like to keep my eyes open too."

"Why don't you trust the guards to take care of us, so we can enjoy dinner?"

"I have a strong feeling that those aliens are closer than you think."

"After we eat, I'll help you find them."

"Why do I get the feeling you're not serious?"

"I am serious. I will help you look for them."

"But you're attitude tells me that you'll just be going through the motions to placate me."

"That's because we're not going to find them unless they want to be found."

"It worries me that you're so unconcerned about them. It makes me wonder what they did to you."

Jerry dropped the armful of wood that he had collected and turned to his wife. He took her rifle and set it down. Then, he gave her a reassuring hug. "I wish there were something I could say to ease your mind. I can only assure you that I feel perfectly normal; in fact, I feel really good. I can't be certain that they didn't plant things in my mind, but my mind seems to be as sharp as ever. Also, except for the period of my captivity, my memory is as detailed as ever. I just don't believe my mind has been damaged in any way."

"Thanks for the reassurance, but we have lots of life left to live, and I can't help worrying about our present situation."

"I understand your concern, but I think you should set it aside for a while, so we can live some of the life you just mentioned. Think about it, right here and right now, we have an opportunity to enjoy a cookout on the shore of a pristine body of water next to a truly awesome falls. Let's take advantage of this."

"Okay, but after dinner, I want to look around this area before we leave."

"What do you expect to find?" Jerry asked.

"I don't know. Let's just look around."

"Okay."

A short time later, Jerry had a roaring fire going. He had made a large pile of small pieces of driftwood. These were quickly consumed by the fire and reduced to a bed of red-hot coals.

Mike had already cut several choice fillets and placed them on a grate. He set the grate on the rock walls of his fire pit. In short order, the fillets were sizzling.

Mike's communicator beeped. It was Jim, the helicopter pilot. "Do you think it's safe for us to join you for dinner?" he asked.

"Have you seen anything to be concerned about?" Mike asked.

"Absolutely nothing."

"Come on down, but don't land too close, I don't want to be blown away by your downwash."

"We'll land on the water and taxi in."

Mike brazed the fillets for a few minutes on each side. Then, he announced, "Dinner is ready."

Everyone grabbed a fork and a plate. Mike served each a large fillet. After locating the most comfortable rocks and logs they could find, everyone sat down to enjoy the meal.

Twenty minutes later, Mike said, "That really hit the spot. I guess I was hungrier than I thought."

"It was just really good fish," Jerry said. "Apparently, I skillfully caught the best one in the whole lagoon."

"I don't know about that," responded Mike. "I think the wise choice of gourmet spices I used had something to do with how good it tasted."

"It was delicious," stated Jim. "While you guys quibble about how to divide up the credit, I think some of us should get back in the air."

"I agree," Mike replied, "and I'm glad you enjoyed my campfire cooking."

"Which was made possible by my fishing skills," commented Jerry.

Jim looked at Mike and Jerry. He chuckled in amusement; then, he turned away from them and headed toward the helicopter.

"I love this place," Michelle said. "We need to come back here now and then."

"I'd like to come back too," stated Connie, "but I think we need to resolve our current situation before we plan a return."

"I promised I'd go for a walk with you and help you find some aliens," Jerry said.

"Let's go," replied Connie.

"Where do you want to start the alien search?" Jerry asked.

"I wish you took this more seriously," Connie said. "How can you be so jovial?"

"I don't know why I'm not worried. I'm just in a good mood, and I feel like enjoying life. Where do you want to go?"

"Let's just walk the beach toward the falls."

"I'll help Mike wash dishes and put away the leftover fish," Michelle said. "I think we might need a midnight snack. Who knows how long we'll be exploring the bottom tonight."

"We won't be gone more than a half-hour," Connie said. "I just want to take a good look around."

"I already searched this area with the RPV, and didn't see anything suspicious," Michelle said. "Plus, the chopper crew has been up there looking around."

"I know, but you might've missed something. I just want to quietly walk the beach, look around, and let my intuition be my guide."

"Be careful and enjoy your walk," Michelle said.

Before Jerry and Connie left the picnic site, Connie spoke to two of the guards. "I would appreciate it if you would follow about 15 to 20 yards behind us and give us some backup if we need it."

"Will do," they responded.

Jerry and Connie strolled on the sandy beach toward the falls, which was only a couple hundred yards away. Halfway to the falls, the sandy beach gave way to a rocky slope. The rocks were covered with algae-like plants that thrived on the constant heavy spray from the falls. The wetness and the plant life made the rocks slippery and treacherous to walk on. Connie and Jerry were constantly losing their footing and catching themselves.

"Walking on this stuff is dangerous," Jerry shouted above the roar of the falls. "We're risking serious ankle and knee injuries."

"I know, but I think we should go on. Just be careful."

"I think we should go back and begin our bottom search."

"We need to get closer to the falls."

"Why?" Jerry asked.

"Something I read in a wild west novel a few years ago."

"What's that got to do with this?"

"The good guys were being pursued by a gang of killers. They escaped death by hiding in a cave behind a waterfall."

"And you think there might be a cave behind this falls?" questioned Jerry.

"There might be. Take a look at the top of the falls. The center of the river is curved outward."

"I see what you mean."

"Now, look at the bottom of the falls. The rock cliff appears to be curved inward. That suggests there might be an open area behind the falls. The rocky beach we're walking on seems to continue behind the falls. There doesn't even have to be a cave back there to make it an excellent hiding place. The area behind the falls is the one place in this whole lagoon that has escaped all of our surveillance."

"Ever since we arrived, I've strongly sensed that some of the aliens are here," Jerry said.

"They could be camped out behind the falls."

"If the aliens did motivate us to come here, it makes sense that some of them might be here to spy on us."

"I'm starting to think there really is a derelict spacecraft resting on the bottom," Connie said.

"If that's the case, there must be something in it that's really important to them," commented Jerry. "If we find it and bring it to the surface, they might attack us with the hope of taking it away from us. Some of us could be killed."

"I'm glad to hear you say that."

"You're glad that we might be killed."

"No! I'm glad to hear you admit that the aliens pose a danger. All you've been saying all day is they mean us no harm, and they're not going to bother us."

"Now, it's starting to make sense. They're not going to bother us until after we do what they want."

"All of this talk assumes that there is a sunken spacecraft," commented Connie.

"We need to get back to the submarine and find that capsule or prove there isn't one. I certainly don't want to step behind that falls. We might not be welcome."

"Before we leave here, look over there," directed Connie, while pointing at some rocks.

"I see what you mean. The algae have been scuffed off some of those rocks." Jerry turned around and looked behind him. "The rocks we slipped on are scuffed in the same way."

"Someone or something stepped on those rocks and slipped just like we did," stated Connie.

"I think we should take a closer look and see if we can find some evidence to indicate what kind of creature did that."

Jerry turned around and motioned the guards to join him and Connie. When they arrived, Jerry explained the situation and asked them to be especially alert. He called Jim and asked for the chopper crew to be extra watchful. Then, he and Connie cautiously approached the scuffed rocks.

When they reached the first scuffed rock, they were shocked by what they found. Next to the rock was an unconscious woman hidden under a couple bushes with thick overhanging foliage. Jerry instantly recognized her. "That's the woman who was in my dream last night," he said. "What is she doing here?"

"I don't know," replied Connie, "but it looks like she has a serious head injury."

Connie dropped to her knees and checked the woman's pulse. "She's alive, but that injury might be life threatening. I need to get her back to the medical lab right away."

"Earlier today, you said you wanted to punish the aliens for capturing me. Now, you want to take one to our home."

"She's in urgent need of medical attention. First, I'm going to save her life; then, I'm going to find out what she did to you."

"If the aliens value the lives of their own, they can't attack us while we have her."

"That's a pretty big if. We don't know what their values are."

"They released me when threatened with annihilation. Holding her hostage might have some value for us."

"First, I have to save her life. To do that, we have to get her out of here."

"As slippery as these rocks are, I don't think we should try to carry her out. We need to use the chopper."

"I think she also has a broken ankle," Connie said.

Jerry called Jim. "We have a rescue mission," he said.

"I'm on the way."

A minute later, the chopper arrived. Jim hovered overhead and lowered the center section of the helicopter's floor, which was configured for rescue missions. Connie and Jerry carefully lifted the injured woman onto the litter and belted her in place. Then, Connie lay down beside her and fastened the restraining belts. The winch operator began hauling them up. "Good luck with your spacecraft search," Connie yelled to Jerry.

"Good luck with your patient," Jerry yelled back.

Jerry and his guards returned to the picnic area. "Let's get our gear back on the sub and dive," he said.

"Why the urgency?" Mike asked.

"The presence of the alien woman tells me that I wasn't just dreaming last night. There really is a spacecraft here, and I want to find it."

"Do you think there are more aliens here?" Michelle asked.

"I don't believe they would've left the woman here by herself, so there must be others."

"That means we're being watched," commented Michelle with a sense of alarm.

"I think so," replied Jerry.

"What about our guards, are they going to be stranded here for the night?" Michelle asked.

"Jim will be right back to pick them up," Jerry replied.

"Good, they're my friends. I wouldn't want them stuck here overnight with who knows how many aliens."

"I don't want them here either," stated Jerry. "They could be in great danger."

"You sound like you know something we don't," commented Mike.

"The injured woman we just picked up is the oldest daughter of their commander. Her name is Akeyco (A-key-co). She holds a position of considerable power in their society. They might want to capture some of our people to hold hostage while we have her."

"That makes sense," agreed Mike. "But how do you know so much about her?"

"She was in charge of questioning me. She told me a great deal about herself, hoping to win my friendship and get me to talk about myself."

"Your memory seems to be coming back," commented Mike.

"Only a few bits and pieces of what happened."

"I have more questions, but let's dive first. I'll ask them on the way down."

It took the trio just a few minutes to stow their gear, climb into the sub, and close the hatch. They slipped below the surface and began their dive to the bottom.

"Any idea where to start our search?" Mike asked.

"A hundred yards north of the falls and 700 yards west."

"That's a very specific answer. How do you know that?"

"The obvious answer is the aliens told me."

"How would you remember that and not remember how you were captured and where they took you?"

"I don't know."

"Maybe that's why Akeyco was here," commented Michelle.

"What do you mean?" asked Mike.

"Maybe she has the ability to telepathically place information in Jerry's mind and was here to make sure that we do search for the spacecraft and search in the right place."

"That's an interesting thought," responded Mike, "but we haven't yet found a spacecraft. We don't know if there's even one down there."

"It's there," stated Jerry.

"How do you know that?" asked Mike. "Never mind, I know how. The aliens told you, but how do they know?"

"I don't know."

"What I'd really like to know," stated Mike, "is where did the spacecraft come from, and why did they land it here, instead of where they live?"

"There must've been a severe navigation malfunction."

"I'll buy that, but where did it come from? And what's on it that is so all-fired important that they would go through so much trouble to recover it? Why didn't they just ask us for help?"

"Maybe they think we are a violent barbaric people who would take advantage of them if we knew about a weakness they now have," commented Jerry.

"What weakness?" Mike asked.

"I don't know if they have a weakness. I'm only speculating."

"But that might be it. There might be something really crucial on that spacecraft; without which, they are vulnerable. If that's the case, they couldn't tell us about it without revealing their vulnerability. That could lead them to find a way to use us without telling us much of anything."

"That's a scary possibility," commented Michelle. "Our people on Pioneer Island might be in danger."

"How?" asked Mike.

"Think about this scenario. Let's say that Akeyco has fantastic telepathic ability. She could've subjected herself to a self-inflicted injury to gain a ride to Pioneer Island. We nurse her back to health;

then, at the appropriate moment, she strikes. Not with weapons, but with her mental ability to control those around her."

"I don't think Akeyco's head injury was self-inflicted," commented Jerry. "It's too severe. Connie thinks that she has a fractured skull, and that could be life threatening. Then, there's the treacherous footing on those slippery rocks and the broken ankle."

"Are you convinced she had an accident?" Mike asked.

"That's what it looks like. It appears that she was spying on our dinner party from behind those bushes. When she saw Connie and me heading toward her, she tried to make a hasty retreat and slipped on the slime growing on the rocks."

"How do you know the accident didn't occur earlier today?" Michelle asked.

"There wasn't any caked blood around her head injury. It was still fresh and flowing."

"If the accident just happened, that would explain why her colleagues hadn't picked her up, if they're here," commented Mike.

"Some of them are here," stated Jerry. "They wouldn't allow Akeyco to be here alone."

"If they are that protective of her, how are they going to react to us taking her to Pioneer Island?" Mike asked.

"If they need us to retrieve their space capsule, they aren't going to do anything to us," replied Jerry.

"We haven't found it yet," commented Michelle.

"That's true," responded Jerry, "but we're getting close to the bottom, and we can start looking shortly."

A few minutes later, Mike said, "We're here."

Speaking to Jerry, Michelle said, "You were right. It is dark down here."

"Fortunately, the water is fairly clean," commented Jerry. "Our spotlights allow us to see far enough to make our search quite easy."

"How far are we from the location where Jerry said we should start our search?" Michelle asked Mike.

"About 100 yards."

"The bottom sure is barren," commented Michelle. "It's almost like a rocky desert. But I guess that's to be expected because of the lack of light."

"We're fortunate it is barren," responded Mike. "Imagine how difficult our search would be if the water were only a couple hundred feet deep and we had a jungle of vegetation to look into."

Mike piloted the sub slowly forward, creeping along just a few yards above the bottom. One by one, the minutes passed by as time slowly dragged on. Then, Mike said, "We've passed over the targeted location."

"Let's go a couple hundred yards farther before we circle back," suggested Jerry.

"Okay," Mike replied.

Two minutes later, Jerry said, "Turn 45 degrees left, I think I see something."

"I see it too," responded Mike. "It's conical in shape, but it's so covered with crud, it's hard to tell what it is from this distance. It could be a rock."

A minute later, Jerry said, "I think we found their spacecraft."

"It sure looks that way," agreed Mike.

"What do we do now?" Michelle asked.

"I don't think there's any doubt about what the aliens want us to do," replied Mike

"They probably want us to haul it to the surface and turn it over to them," commented Michelle. "But why? What could that capsule possibly contain that would still be good after all these years underwater? Look at it. It's covered with so much gunk that it's obvious it's been down here for a long time."

"I have no idea what's in it," responded Mike, "but some materials handle long-term water exposure very well, so it could easily contain something that is still functional."

"Whatever is in there must be of crucial importance to the aliens," stated Jerry. "And that brings up a serious question, what will the aliens do if we raise this capsule to the surface? Will they try to take it away from us? Will they ask us for it? Will they allow us to take it home, open it, and see what's in it?"

"Until we get answers to those questions, we can't bring this thing to the surface," stated Mike.

"That could be a risky approach," commented Michelle. "If the aliens really want what's in the capsule, they could try to take our sub and raise it themselves."

"Not while we're holding Akeyco," responded Mike.

"She might be a part of their plan," argued Michelle. "Her injuries look accidental, but we can't be certain that they're not self-inflicted just to get into our midst."

"That's possible," agreed Mike. "Let's hope Connie can bring her back to consciousness. We need to demand answers."

"When it comes to that, let me ask her the questions," stated Jerry. "I believe she will talk to me."

"It might help if you make her understand that we're not going to risk our lives trying to salvage this capsule, unless she does give us some straight answers," stated Mike.

"If she regains consciousness and recovers to the point where she can talk, I'll explain the situation to her."

"Assuming you can get satisfactory answers, we'll then have the problem of hauling this capsule to the surface. Let's figure out the most practical way to do that."

"Before you guys start discussing that, we need to talk some more about Akeyco's presence," stated Michelle.

"What's on your mind?" Jerry asked.

"I am 100% convinced that she's been planted in our society."

"How can you be so certain of that?" Jerry asked.

"Something you said earlier keeps nagging at my mind."

"What?"

"You said she is the daughter of their commander, has a lot of power in their society, and that they would not have left her here alone. In other words, there are people here who were supposed to protect her."

"I believe so."

"If that's the case, why did they let us take her away? Why didn't they defend her?"

Michelle paused for a few moments, but she didn't get a response from either Mike or Jerry, so she continued, "I believe they wanted us to pick her up and take her to Pioneer Island."

"Akeyco's head injury is far too serious to be anything other than an accident," argued Jerry.

"You might be right," acknowledged Michelle. "But I think her injuries were planned, and she accidentally hurt herself more than what was intended."

"If they really do think we are barbaric, why would they put Akeyco in a situation where she would be at our mercy?" Mike asked. "How could they know that we would give her medical aid, rather than, torture her for information about them?"

"Maybe Akeyco was able to get into Jerry's mind and convince herself that we aren't barbaric, but she was unable to convince her father that we can be trusted. Maybe she volunteered to put herself at our mercy to convince her father. Maybe her father agreed because they desperately need our help."

"What problem could the aliens have that would be so serious that their commander would let his daughter put herself in our hands right after kidnapping Jerry?"

"That's a good question," replied Michelle. "Maybe Jerry should confront Akeyco on that matter."

"If my wife is able to nurse her back to health, I will try to get some answers," Jerry said. "Until then, what are we going to do about this spacecraft?"

"Before we leave here, we should get video of it from every possible angle," replied Mike. "We can figure out later how we're going to raise it. Then, let's go home, so we can keep an eye on Akeyco."

"Sounds like you don't trust her either," commented Michelle.

"It isn't that I don't trust her; it's just that I don't know what she's up to. What we do next is dependent on what kind of answers we get from her."

"Before we leave here, we have a decision to make," Jerry said. "Do we tell the aliens we found their spacecraft, or do we keep quiet until we get some answers from Akeyco?"

"I think we should quietly slip out of here underwater," replied Mike. "When we get home, we can let the aliens know we found their space capsule."

"How do you plan to tell them?" asked Michelle.

"We'll call Moose and discuss it with him. The aliens still have Jerry's communicator, so I'm sure they'll be listening."

"We have to decide what we want them to know," Jerry said.

"Let's talk about that on the way home," suggested Mike.

Chapter Ten

Jerry went to the medical lab. "How is Akeyco doing?" he asked Connie.

"She's stable now, but during the night, she dropped steadily deeper into unconsciousness."

"Is she going to live?"

"I don't know; her head injury is critical. She suffered a small fracture in her skull."

"How bad is it?"

"I'm not worried about the fracture, it will heal. What concerns me is possible swelling of brain tissue beneath the fracture. Too much swelling could cause permanent brain damage, even death."

"We cannot allow that to happen."

"I know. I've been up with her all night, and I've done what I can to prevent swelling."

"Has your treatment been effective?"

"The brain scans I've done look good."

"If she lives, do you think she'll have lasting brain damage?"

"I don't think so, but it's too soon to tell."

"How long will she be out?"

"I don't know. Her unconsciousness could be a normal part of the healing process for her species. Her pulse and blood pressure are both well below what we would consider normal. Also, her body temperature has fallen dramatically since last night. She reminds me of a bear going into hibernation."

"Maybe she's dying."

"That's possible, but I think she's passed into a state that aids the healing process."

"Why?"

"Reduced blood pressure, pulse, and temperature are all things

187

that would tend to reduce the swelling of injured brain tissue. It looks like her body is equipped with a survival mechanism to bring about these conditions."

"Are you saying that Akeyco could be out cold until her brain heals?"

"That's possible, but let me clarify something. In humans, brain cells don't regenerate. Once they're dead, they're not replaced. We don't know if that's the case in these aliens."

"Are you suggesting that they might be able to grow new brain cells and that she might be hibernating until that process has been completed?"

"I don't know, but that's possible."

"That means she could be out for several days."

"Again, I don't know. Their regenerative powers might be much faster and more capable than ours. I wish I could talk to her doctor and get some advice."

"Why don't you call her?"

"I tried calling them by dialing your old communicator, but I couldn't get through."

"That's because they changed the number," stated Jerry, as he picked up his new communicator, punched in 253926, and handed it to Connie. After two beeps, a voice speaking perfect English came through, "Hello! This is Geniya speaking. How is my daughter doing this morning?"

Connie stared at Jerry in stunned disbelief. "How did you know what number to call?" she asked him.

"I don't know; it just popped into my mind."

"We gave it to him," Geniya said.

"How come he didn't remember it until now?" Connie asked.

"His memory was triggered by what you said right before he called me."

"All I did was express a desire to get medical advice from Akeyco's doctor."

"We were hoping you would react that way to Akeyco's injuries, and we placed a posthypnotic suggestion in your husband's mind to call us if you did."

"That means her injuries were planned, and you planted her here to test us. How did you know we wouldn't kill her after what you did to Jerry?"

"What do you mean by what we did to Jerry?"

"You captured him and held him prisoner."

"We had to. You landed in our backyard. We had no way of knowing what your intentions were. But I assure you; we did nothing bad to your husband. We only got from him the information we needed."

"But he has no memory of his captivity."

"Again, we had to protect ourselves, but we haven't harmed him in any way. In fact, we did the opposite. We improved his health. Have you noticed?"

"Physically, he seems better than ever. He even beat me in a swimming race yesterday. Was that the result of something you did?"

"Yes! We gave him a special gift to demonstrate what we can do for all of you, if you will help us with a big problem that we have."

"Before we talk about helping you, I have to know what you did to Jerry."

"About 25 years before we left home on our interstellar voyage, our scientists learned the secret of controlling the aging process. We can slow it way down, and in some cases, even roll back the clock a bit."

"Are you saying that's what you did to my husband?"

"Yes!"

"How did you do that?"

"I'll explain later. First, tell me about my daughter."

"I am worried about my husband. When you gave him the age reduction treatment, weren't you worried about harmful side effects?"

"The biggest side effect is beneficial."

"How would you know that? We are a different species."

"Genetically, we are almost identical."

"How could you possibly know that?"

"I'll explain later. Tell me about my daughter."

"First, one more question, what big beneficial side effect are you talking about?"

"Yesterday, your husband cut himself."

"How did you know that?"

"My daughter saw it happen. Have you looked at the cut today?"

"Not yet."

"Why don't you take a peek at it?"

Connie removed the tape from Jerry's hand and examined the wound. "It's almost completely healed," she exclaimed.

"The chemicals we use to control aging have a very useful side benefit; they accelerate the healing process. In fact, they were originally developed to speed up healing. While being used for that purpose, it was discovered that people treated with them seemed to stop aging for a while."

"But I found no trace of drugs in Jerry."

"You wouldn't because they are quickly absorbed and converted into natural substances that are already present in the body. But enough questions, I need to know about my daughter. She is every bit as special to me as your husband is to you."

Connie briefed Geniya on Akeyco's medical condition. She concluded her remarks by saying, "It looks to me like her head injury is far more serious than you intended."

"You are right," acknowledged Geniya. "Akeyco wasn't supposed to fracture her skull or her ankle. Those injuries were accidental. She was only supposed to get a nasty bump on her head. Then, she was supposed to fake unconsciousness with her mental powers."

"Why have her vital signs gone down so much? Is that normal in your species for this kind of head injury?"

"Yes, but it's also a state that can precede death. She needs to be watched closely. If she falls too deeply into hibernation, I need to bring her out of it. I realize that you don't trust us, but if I come alone, could I get permission to treat my daughter?"

"I think so, but I have to find out."

"Our aircraft could deliver me, but if you're not comfortable with that, you could pick me up with your helicopter at a place determined by you."

"I will discuss this with Mike and Jerry and call you back in a few minutes."

Connie didn't have to go anywhere to find Mike, because he had walked into the medical lab only a couple minutes after Jerry. Mike had heard the entire conversation between Connie and Geniya. "I wonder how much they trust us," questioned Mike.

"What do you have in mind?" Jerry asked.

"I would like to see their aircraft, so I can judge its capability. I wonder if they trust us enough to land right here on Pioneer Island."

"If they do that, we could capture their aircraft, or even destroy it, if we wanted to," commented Jerry.

"I know," replied Mike. "Do they trust us enough to land here?"

"They allowed Akeyco to place herself at our mercy," commented Connie.

"That's true," responded Mike, "but militarily speaking, she's expendable. If they only have one aircraft, it's not expendable."

"If they only have one, they would have to trust us totally to land it here," stated Jerry.

"I don't know if we should invite them to land here," Connie said. "Let's not forget that they put bombs on our cargo shuttle just a few days ago."

"They had to as a matter of self-defense," stated Jerry. "They had no way of knowing what our plans were when we landed in their backyard. A lot has happened since then."

"That's true," agreed Connie, "but I really don't like the idea of bringing their airplane here."

"Why?" Jerry asked.

"We don't know how big it is, and we don't know how many of them there are. They could land here with a hundred well-armed troops onboard. Then, what do we do?"

"If they're that powerful, they wouldn't have to worry about trusting us," argued Mike. "They could attack us at a time of their choosing and try to achieve the element of surprise. They certainly wouldn't try to pull off an attack when we're armed, out of sight, and waiting for them. I say, let's invite them here and find out if they really do trust us."

"That's a bold plan," commented Jerry, "but I like it."

"I think it's risky," argued Connie.

"There's more risk for them than there is for us," stated Mike. "Our most valuable piece of equipment is our cargo shuttle, and we can get it out of here."

"Let's get our chopper out of here too," suggested Jerry.

"Sounds like you guys have decided to invite them here," Connie said.

"We have to meet them sometime," responded Mike.

"If we're going to invite them here, let's ask Geniya to bring her husband along," suggested Connie. "Then, you guys can find out what their big problem is and discuss what to do about it."

"Good idea," Jerry said.

Connie picked up the communicator and looked at both Mike and Jerry. They nodded, so she pressed the button for re-dial of the last number.

The immediate response from Geniya was, "Hello! What took you so long?"

"We had to decide how far we could trust you before giving you an invitation."

"You have my daughter, so it shouldn't be too hard to trust us. What kind of invitation did you come up with?"

"We've decided to invite you and your husband to land right here on Stellar Plateau."

After a few moments of silence, Geniya said, "My husband wants to bring along four people to give guided tours of our aircraft and answer questions about it."

That sounds like four guards, Mike thought, but he said, "That's a good idea. I would like to see the aircraft, and I will have plenty of questions." Jerry nodded in agreement.

"Your request is granted," Connie said. "When will you be here?"

"In about a half-hour," Geniya replied. "Where would you like us to land?"

"There's a clear area in the south half of the plateau that we use for our helicopter. We'll move it, and you can land there."

"Okay, we'll see you in a half-hour. Please call me if my daughter's condition changes."

"You can count on that."

"I guess they trust us enough to bring their airplane here," commented Jerry.

"The trust isn't complete," stated Mike. "They are bringing along four guards."

"To avoid any possibility of miscalculation, we'd better make sure those guards never feel threatened," Jerry said.

"I think the best way to do that is to keep everyone away from them except you and me. We can ask their commander to show us the airplane. I am especially interested in its propulsion system."

"I am too. They've been here for at least 30 years, and it's still operational without the benefit of a major maintenance facility."

"Discussing their aircraft will be a good icebreaker. After that, maybe they'll tell us about their big problem. Right now, we need to get our shuttles out of here."

"I don't think that's necessary," stated Jerry. "They already had an opportunity to blow up our cargo shuttle with the bombs they planted on it, but they chose not to. Whatever their big problem is, I think our shuttles are going to be needed to solve it, so in their own best interest, they can't destroy them."

"That might all be true," commented Mike, "but we need to send the cargo shuttle up anyway to pick up more materials, so we can finish building and equipping our homes. We can't live in tents forever."

"That, I agree with."

"Also, I think Moose might like to come back down here. He's been up there for a while."

"Okay, let's send it up."

"I've already made the arrangements, but I wanted your approval first."

"You don't need it. You're in charge until this whole thing with the aliens gets resolved."

"I know, but I wanted your approval anyway. We are a team."

Mike contacted the shuttle pilot and gave the order to depart. "We're ready to go," the pilot replied, as he began taxiing out of South Bay to the open water he needed to take off and begin the steep climb into space.

Meanwhile, Jim took off with the helicopter and made the short flight to the north end of Pioneer Island, where he landed on the water in Rocky Point Bay. He had two armed individuals onboard. They would watch the arrival of the aliens on video screens using the many surveillance cameras on Stellar Plateau. If needed, they could quickly return.

Mike and Jerry sent everyone else into hiding except Connie and Dianne. Connie would stay with Akeyco. Mike, Jerry, and Dianne would greet the aliens upon their arrival.

"I believe we are as ready as we can be," commented Mike.

Jerry looked at his watch and said, "They should be here shortly."

While pointing skyward to the southeast, Mike said, "That looks like an approaching aircraft."

"It could be a pterodactyl," Dianne speculated.

Mike looked at it with binoculars. "It's an airplane," he said.

The aircraft passed over Pioneer Island at about 5,000 feet. Then, it made a tight banking turn and went into a fairly steep descent from the north. As it approached Stellar Plateau, it pulled out of its dive and made the transition from fast forward flight to a hover. It seemed to float toward its designated landing area. Then, it descended nearly straight down to a gentle landing. The whine of the engine faded.

"Let's go meet our guests," Jerry said, as he pressed the accelerator of the all terrain vehicle (ATV) that he, Mike, and Dianne were sitting in. Wanting to give the aliens a couple minutes to scope out their surroundings, Jerry drove slowly to the aircraft, which was about 400 yards away.

"What's your first impression of their aircraft?" Jerry asked Mike.

"Judging from the whine and the roar that I heard, it's powered by some kind of turbojet. It might have two of them. Its shape indicates it could easily fly supersonically, perhaps as fast as mach three. For VTOL flight, it has lift fans in the wings."

"I would sure like to know what they use for fuel. It seems like any fuel they brought with them would've been used up long ago, which indicates that they have the ability to manufacture fuel."

"Maybe they used genetic engineering to design special organisms that can make sugar and then alcohol from virtually any kind of plant material. Our chopper does quite well with the modified alcohol that we make for it."

"Yes it does, but I think this alien aircraft has much greater range than what would be available from alcohol fuel."

"They promised to answer our questions," commented Mike. "Let's ask them about propulsion right up front and find out how freely the information will be given."

"I will let you handle that," responded Jerry. "There are some other things I need to talk to them about."

"Like what?" Mike asked.

"I want to know how they captured me, what they did to me, and why I can't remember anything. If they need our help with some big problem, they need to come clean about my captivity before that can happen."

"I'm glad to hear you talk that way," Mike said. "You're getting back to sounding like the Jerry that I've worked with for the last 20 years."

"They're opening a door," Dianne said. "I wonder how many will get out and how many will still be inside."

"It's a pretty small airplane," commented Jerry. "I don't believe there's room in it for more than a dozen people."

"Someone's getting out," Dianne said.

"That's Trang," stated Jerry. "He's their commander. The woman who just stepped out is his wife, Geniya."

"Seems like more of your memory is coming back," commented Dianne.

"Hopefully, it will all come back," stated Jerry.

A few moments later, Jerry brought the ATV to a stop near the aircraft. He stepped out and approached Trang.

"We meet again," stated Trang. "I apologize for taking you captive at our last meeting, but we had few choices. We did not know what you were doing so close to our home. In the interest of self-preservation, we simply couldn't take any chances."

"I guess one of your choices would've been to assume the worst and attack us," commented Jerry.

"That is not our way. We are not killers. We like to resolve a crisis with non-lethal means, if we can."

"That is also our way," replied Jerry.

"We've reached that conclusion," stated Trang. "You are trying to save my daughter's life. Could you take us to her, please?"

"Sure! This is Dianne, one of our doctors. We will take you and Geniya to your daughter. But first, I want you to meet Mike, our chief engineer. He is fascinated by your aircraft and has many questions."

"I brought some people along who can answer them."

Trang introduced Mike to his people and told them to show Mike whatever he wanted to see and answer his questions. "Let's go to my daughter," he said to Jerry.

"Hop in," Jerry said.

Two minutes later, they arrived at the habitation capsule, which contained the medical lab. Geniya quickly stepped out of the ATV and headed for the front door. Dianne opened it for her and showed her to Akeyco.

Geniya immediately checked her daughter's pulse, temperature, and blood pressure. "She's still in the normal range," she said. "Please show me pictures of her head injury."

After studying the images, Geniya said, "I believe she will recover completely. Can you show me her ankle?"

Connie put the images on the screen, and Geniya evaluated the broken bones. "We need to set these soon," she said. "Akeyco took the age-control drug before injuring herself because of its speeded-up-healing side effect. She sought to protect herself in the event that she hurt herself more than planned. She wanted to heal quickly."

"So, if we wait too long, there will be additional damage to correct, because the bones will soon begin to heal in the wrong position."

"That's correct."

"Can we set the ankle with her in the condition she's in?"

"Now is the best time. She won't feel a thing or even remember what we do."

"It sounds like you think our daughter's going to be okay," Trang said to his wife.

"I believe so," Geniya replied.

"I am very glad to hear that. We should never have allowed her to do what she did."

"We had to. Have you forgotten about our problem? We had to find out for sure if we could trust these Earth people to help us and not take advantage of us."

"I know, and while you are attending to our daughter, I will talk to Jerry about that."

"We need to include Mike in this conversation," stated Jerry.

"You're assuming that he's run out of questions about our airplane," commented Trang.

"For not knowing Mike, you sure have a good handle on his curiosity."

"This one was easy. It's not everyday that an engineer gets to examine a major piece of equipment built by people from another star. You must be curious too."

"I am curious," admitted Jerry, while he and Trang stepped into the ATV for the short drive to the airplane. "I would like to know how it's powered and what you use for fuel."

"It is powered by a pair of combined cycle turbojet/ramjet engines, and the fuel is antimatter."

"That means your airplane has global range."

"We can circle the planet dozens of times without refueling."

"What's your top speed?"

"In the ramjet mode, we can sustain mach ten at 135,000 feet."

"That's about 6500 mph."

"Aerodynamically, our airplane is optimized for high speed flight. As you've seen, we have lift fans in the wings for landing, takeoff, and low speed flight."

"Your airplane has fantastic capabilities. You must be proud of it."

"We are, but its technology was current on our home planet

at the time we left. Airplanes with this capability are numerous back home."

"Why do you feel vulnerable to us when you have such awesome mobility that could be used to either hide from us or attack us?"

"We've been here nearly 31 years, and we are almost out of fuel. But that's not our biggest problem."

At that moment, Jerry and Trang arrived at the airplane. Mike was actively engaged in conversation with its guards, but Jerry motioned him to the ATV. Mike stepped in and the trio drove to the south end of the plateau. They sat down at a picnic table overlooking South Bay, and everyone enjoyed the picturesque view for a few moments. Breaking the silence, Jerry said, "Tell us about your big problem and what you think we might be able to do for you."

"Do you want all the background information, or do you want the crisis in a nutshell?"

"Hit me with it," Jerry replied.

"Twelve of our people are marooned on the moon you call Aphrodite, and we have no way to rescue them."

Mike and Jerry were shocked by the pronouncement from Trang. Before either man said anything, Trang added, "Our starship is also stranded there, and we have no way to repair it, even if we had a way to get there."

"We were wondering what happened to your starship after you landed here," commented Jerry.

"It was flown to Aphrodite to refuel."

"How could you refuel on that barren moon?" Mike asked.

"We have equipment to manufacture antimatter fuel, and we discovered a rich source of the needed raw materials there."

"How long was the refueling operation supposed to take?" Mike asked.

"Two years."

"Why are they still there?" Jerry asked.

"A tragic accident befell our starship a few days before they planned to come here. It was hit by a meteor. Even though the impact was catastrophic, I guess you could still say we were lucky. If it had hit our antimatter fuel, the resulting blast would have incinerated everything and everyone. As it was, the meteor wrecked most of the equipment in our ship's machine shop, and it destroyed some of the ship's key structure. So now, we still have a fully fueled starship that can't go anywhere, because we have no means to repair the structure. Even worse, our people's life-support equipment is in serious need of repair. It's only a matter of time, and it will suffer a breakdown that is beyond the limited repair capability that our people on Aphrodite still have."

"Are you saying this meteor impact happened 29 years ago?" Jerry asked.

"Yes!"

"I am amazed that your people have stayed alive so long without a fully functional machine shop," commented Jerry.

"Our life-support equipment is rugged, but some key elements will soon fail."

"How much time do they have?" Mike asked.

"Impossible to tell. Failure could come at anytime, or it might not happen for several months."

"It sounds like we need to get some emergency supplies to them as soon as possible," commented Mike. "That will keep them alive while we figure out solutions to the rest of your problems."

"Then, you will help us?"

"We can't let them die," stated Mike.

"A couple days ago, you threatened us with annihilation."

"You were holding Jerry, and I found your bombs on our cargo shuttle. What did you expect me to do?"

Trang looked into Mike's eyes for a few moments, trying to see the depth of his character. "You are a strong man. You handled the situation with utmost self-control. Your strategy was effective, and you earned my respect. I most definitely would rather have you for an ally than an enemy."

"Thank you," replied Mike.

Turning to Jerry, Trang said, "You are fortunate to have such an effective, dedicated individual on your crew."

"I wholeheartedly agree with you," responded Jerry, "and I believe we can help you, but first, I need more information. I would like to understand your situation better."

"That's fair. What would you like to know?"

"I'm puzzled by why you felt the need to fully refuel your starship unless you never intended to stay here."

"You're right. We weren't planning to stay here. This was the last stop on a voyage of discovery. When we left here, we were going home."

"I assume your starship was going to pick you up here," commented Jerry.

"It would have entered orbit around this planet, and we would've flown our shuttle up to meet them."

"That means your landing craft isn't just a landing craft, like we thought it might be," stated Mike. "It actually is a powered shuttle."

"That's true."

"Since your airplane is fueled with antimatter, I assume your shuttle is too."

"That's also true."

"That being the case, it seems like it should be capable of going to Aphrodite," commented Mike. "Why didn't you go pick up your colleagues after the meteor impact?"

"That's the other half of our tragedy."

"You mean there's more," questioned Jerry.

"Yes! A group of people from the planet you call B-2 tried to steal our shuttle. They wanted to fly it back to B-2, so they could have the technology to use in a big war they were planning. We fought a battle with them. Fortunately, none of our people were killed. Some suffered critical bullet wounds, but my wife was able to save their lives. Unfortunately, the combustion chamber in our shuttle's antimatter rocket was damaged beyond repair."

"So you weren't able to rescue your people on Aphrodite," commented Jerry.

"At the time the battle was fought, the meteor hadn't yet hit our starship. The battle was about 30 years ago, about a year before the meteor impact. We weren't in any danger here, so we decided to finish the two-year project of refueling our starship before bringing it here to pick us up. That turned out to be a bad decision."

"You've certainly had more than your share of bad luck," stated Mike.

"Our long voyage of discovery was very successful before arriving here, but as you know, the life of an interstellar pioneer is filled with risk. Tragedy is always a possibility."

"We've had some close calls," acknowledged Mike, "but we've been lucky."

"I have one more question for you," stated Jerry.

"Only one," responded Trang.

"Actually, several, but at the moment, I'd like to know why

you motivated us to search for that capsule at the bottom of Mystery Lagoon."

"So you did find it?"

"Yes we did, but what is its significance?"

"It contains a new combustion chamber for our shuttle. We had planned to install it, so we could take off, climb into orbit, and link up with our starship."

"I don't understand why you landed it in Mystery Lagoon," stated Jerry.

"Why not? Our airplane has global range and hover ability. We were able to pick up the capsule anywhere on this planet."

"But why did you bring it down in Mystery Lagoon?" Jerry asked.

"It was just a matter of convenience. Some of us were on a two-week campout in the lagoon, and we had our airplane with us."

"What led you to go camping in Mystery Lagoon?" Mike asked.

"You were there yesterday. You had to notice how scenic that place is. We wanted to enjoy it for a couple weeks. Also, it has its own unique ecosystem that we wanted to study. For whatever reasons, it is free of dinosaurs and is populated primarily by small mammals and birds."

"So why didn't you pick up your capsule when it came down?" Mike asked.

"It made a hard landing and sank. We watched a pair of pterodactyls attack its para-wing and rip it to shreds. Even so, the capsule should have survived a hard landing on water, and its flotation collar should have deployed and kept it afloat. We don't know why it didn't."

"How did you know its exact location?" Mike asked.

"It released a tethered, radio-equipped buoy when it sank. Also, it emitted sonar signals for several weeks. Despair set in when we found out the water was 1800 feet deep. We had no easy way to retrieve the capsule from that depth. We tried a number of schemes to bring it up, but none of them worked."

"Why didn't your people on Aphrodite send you another one?" Jerry asked.

"We only had one spare. The combustion chamber is a very robust piece of equipment. There wasn't any reason to bring more than one spare along. But we weren't planning on the tragic events that beset us."

"So now your only spare is at the bottom of the lagoon," commented Jerry.

"We are hoping that you will bring it to the surface for us."

"Do you think it's still functional after being submerged all these years?" asked Mike.

"The materials it's made out of tolerate water very well. It will need some cleaning and polishing, but unless it was damaged in the crash landing, it should be operational. I might add that we aren't looking for charity. We are prepared to compensate you for your help."

"In what way?" Jerry asked.

"We have much to offer. To start with, we can share our medical knowledge with you. We can show you how to control aging. If that's not enough, we can refuel your starship. I would guess that you've probably used most of your fuel, since you came here on a one-way mission."

"We can use both of those," replied Jerry. "You've already treated me with the first dose of age-control medicine. How effective is it?"

"It needs to be taken once a month, and it's very effective. Take a good look at me. Would you believe that I am 147 years old?"

"You look like you might be 45 to 50," replied Jerry. "How long do you expect to live if you keep taking the medicine?"

"I don't know. We don't have any data to tell us how long we can live."

"What you are offering us is difficult to refuse," stated Jerry. "I believe we can do business, but first, I have to know what you did to me during my captivity. How did you capture me without injuring me?"

"We traveled to your shuttle with powered diving gear and surfaced under one of the big open doors. You were pacing the deck doing guard duty. When your back was turned to us, we moved into position and pointed our rifles at you. You saw us when you turned around, and you instantly realized that your best choice was to surrender. We fitted you with scuba gear and took you home."

"Why can't I remember any of that?"

"My wife is a doctor, a psychiatrist, and a skilled hypnotist. She gave you a drug to reduce your will to resist. Then, she hypnotized you and used her telepathic skills to get into your mind. She was able to evaluate your mental reactions and answers to the questions that Akeyco asked you. Before bringing you out of the hypnotic state, Geniya planted several posthypnotic suggestions. One of which was to convince you that you would not remember anything about your captivity. Also, Akeyco telepathically entered your mind to gain information and reinforce the memory block."

"I am impressed with your method of interrogation," Mike commented. "It seems like it would be very effective."

"It is, but it's not foolproof. We felt the need to plant someone in your midst with serious injuries to see if you would provide medical assistance. Akeyco was convinced that you would, so she volunteered for the job."

"She's a brave woman," stated Jerry. "It took courage to surrender herself to our mercy after you captured me and planted bombs on our cargo shuttle."

"She is a very gutsy individual. Besides that, after what we learned about you, she was convinced that you would figure out that we planted the bombs only for our own protection. We had no intention of detonating them unless we had to. We are still suffering the effects of what Zeb's people did to us so long ago. We had no choice but to do everything we could to protect ourselves."

"I can accept that," responded Jerry, "but you did put my wife through living hell for a couple days."

"I am sorry for the distress we put you and your wife through, but because of that battle 30 years ago, we simply could not take any chances. We had to know your intentions, and we had to take steps to protect ourselves."

"I can understand that," replied Jerry. "When will I get my memory back?"

"My wife can remove the mental block anytime you're ready."

"Great! Let's have her do that when she's done treating your daughter. Now, I am ready to talk about helping you. What's the first thing that you would like us to do?"

"With the equipment you have, it should be fairly easy for you to salvage our space capsule. Then, we can find out if we have a usable combustion chamber. If we do, we can install it and make our shuttle operational."

"How would you take off?" Mike asked.

"What do you mean?"

"Your shuttle is resting on hydrofoils, which implies that you landed on water, but the lake you landed on isn't there anymore."

"You're right," responded Trang.

"So how would you take off?"

"Our shuttle has the ability to take off and land vertically. There is an antimatter turbine engine in the root of each wing. These are used to power lift fans in the wings."

"Why would you land on hydrofoils if you have a VTOL capability?" Mike asked.

"We can land with a much greater payload when a suitable body of water is available. But sometimes, there might be compelling reasons to land in a desert, so a capability to do that was built into our shuttle."

"So where does the combustion chamber go?" Jerry asked.

"The shuttle has a rocket that uses water as a propellant, much as your shuttles do. But we use antimatter to heat the water to a high-pressure vapor. This process begins in the combustion chamber, but the one in our shuttle has bullet holes in it."

"So you can take off, but you cannot fly into space," commented Mike.

"That's true. We need a functional combustion chamber, and I believe we have one. However, it's at the bottom of the lagoon."

"Does the capsule it's in have any attachment points?" Mike asked.

"There is a large eyebolt inside the compartment where the parachute was stored. We had planned to hook into that with a cable under our airplane and haul the capsule to dry land, but it sank before we got to it."

"We could go down there with our sub and attach flotation bags to that eyebolt," stated Mike. "Then we could inflate them, and they would bring the capsule to the surface."

"There is another way we could do it," Jerry said. "Our cargo shuttle has winches that lift our sub into its fuselage. If we equip one of those winches with a couple thousand feet of cable, we could go down with the sub and hook the cable to the eyebolt. Then, we winch the capsule directly into the shuttle and deliver it to Crater Lake or wherever you want."

"If the combustion chamber needs refurbishment, we could take it up to the Challenger and do that in our machine shop," stated Mike.

Speaking to Trang, Jerry said, "Assuming we can deliver to

you a fully functional combustion chamber, what's next on your agenda?"

"We will need your help to repair our starship."

"That will be more difficult," responded Jerry. "Aphrodite has no atmosphere, and we don't have any way to land and take off from airless bodies."

"But Aphrodite's gravity is only about one-tenth g," commented Mike. "So we should be able to put something together to deliver whatever is needed to repair the broken structure. Then, the starship could take off. Once in space, it could rendezvous with the Challenger, and we could use our machine shop to repair everything."

"That sounds like a workable plan," commented Jerry. "The lander design should be easy. All we need is a sturdy frame to support landing pads, fuel tanks, a rocket engine, and a payload."

"That sounds like an easy project for an engineer of Mike's caliber," commented Trang.

Mike smiled. "I believe I can get the job done," he said.

Facing Trang, Jerry asked, "How long can your people on Aphrodite survive if they're hit with a major life-support failure?"

"They've been stockpiling supplies and should be able to hold out for a couple months. Oxygen will run out first."

"Two months should be more than enough time to get help to them," Jerry said.

"I'll design a rocket powered lander today," Mike said. "It won't be fancy, but it will perform the mission."

"How long will it take to build it?" Jerry asked.

"Like I said, it won't be fancy, so it shouldn't take too long to build."

"How long?"

"No more than a couple weeks."

"Good!" stated Jerry.

Speaking to Trang, Mike said, "Before I start, I will need to talk to your onsite chief engineer to find out exactly what I need to deliver, so he can make your starship able to take off."

Trang pulled his communicator from his belt and contacted Kon, his chief engineer on Aphrodite. "I have in my presence an engineer from Earth who is going to help us repair our ship," Trang said.

Kon had a difficult time controlling his emotions, but he managed to say, "This is too good to be true. We've been stranded here a long time. None of us thought we would ever leave here, but it appears our prayers have been answered."

"I believe these Earth people will help us," stated Trang. "I want you to work with Mike."

Trang handed his communicator to Mike. "You may keep this for as long as you need it," he said.

Before Mike spoke to his fellow project leader, Jerry said, "While you two are working that problem, I'll have Moose modify one of the cargo shuttle's winches. Tomorrow, we'll haul the capsule to the surface. Moose can operate the winch. You and I will go down and hook up the cable."

"Okay," responded Mike. Then, he began speaking to his new work partner, an engineer from another part of the galaxy.

Jerry looked at Mike and thought, wow, is he ever excited. But I guess he should be. He is the first engineer from Earth to work with an engineer from a civilization from another star. They have a challenging problem to solve and a wealth of information from their own societies to share.

Jerry turned to Trang, who had also noticed Mike's excitement. "I believe they will find solutions," Trang said. "In regard to tomorrow, I'd like to go to the bottom of the lagoon with you guys. I know the capsule and can be of assistance."

"Besides that, you might enjoy the dive," responded Jerry. "It's a very different world down there."

"It does sound like fun. I haven't been in a deep-diving submarine in about a hundred years."

"When was the last time you went sailing?" asked Jerry.

"That was also about a hundred years ago."

"I promised Denise and Matthew that I would take them to see the dinosaurs today. Since we can't raise your capsule until tomorrow, I thought I'd keep my promise. You're welcome to ride along. I have lots of questions for you, and an all-day sailing trip would give us time to talk."

"Your invitation is gladly accepted. I also have more than enough questions to fill up the day."

Mike broke away from Trang's communicator for a moment and said, "Sounds to me like this meeting is over."

Jerry turned to Trang and asked, "Anything else you want to discuss at the moment?"

"My most crucial concerns have been addressed. Let's let our engineers work the problems while we go sailing."

"That sounds like a vote of confidence," commented Mike.

"It is," responded Trang. "The last couple days have shown me what you're capable of."

"Thanks for the compliment," Mike said.

Turning to Jerry, Trang said, "I wish my wife could go sailing with us, but she needs to stay with our daughter until she recovers."

"Let's go check on her," Jerry suggested.

"I'm going to the personnel shuttle," Mike said. "I need the computer access that I can get from there. Enjoy your voyage, and I'll have a design roughed out by tonight."

A few minutes later, Jerry and Trang arrived at the medical lab. "Our daughter's going to be okay," Geniya said to Trang.

"I am really happy to hear that. How long do you think it will be before she is ready to come out of the healing state?"

"Probably, sometime tomorrow. Right now, she is resting peacefully, and her condition is steadily improving. But I will remain at her side until late tonight; then, Connie will take over."

"Where is Connie now?" Jerry asked.

"She helped me set the ankle; then, she went upstairs to get some sleep. As you know, she was up all night, and she is exhausted."

"She was very concerned about your daughter," Jerry said.

"We greatly appreciate the care she gave Akeyco," stated Geniya. "Thank God the worst is over, and a full recovery should occur."

"With that good prognosis in mind, I am ready to go sailing," Trang said to Jerry.

"What sailing are you talking about?" Geniya asked.

Trang and Jerry explained the sailing expedition. When they finished, Geniya said, "I would love to go with you, but I have to stay here."

"I think you need to take me along," Michelle said. "I can keep an eye on the children while you guys do your shop talk. Also, I haven't yet seen the dinosaurs, and I would like to see them."

"You're welcome to come along," responded Jerry. "You can help me pick Trang's brain."

"I would love to. It isn't everyday that a science reporter gets to interview an alien starship commander."

"You're a science reporter?" questioned Trang.

"Back on Earth, I was recognized as one of the best in the business."

"This promises to be an interesting day," responded Trang. "I look forward to your questions."

"Let's eat lunch, grab some supplies, and go sailing," stated Jerry.

Chapter Eleven

TIME: Day 33, 1:00 PM

Jerry, Trang, Michelle, Matthew, and Denise were sailing out of South Bay. Trang's interest in the boat was obvious. He looked closely at every detail. Finally, he said, "This looks like a very practical piece of equipment for people who live in the middle of a big lake."

"We use it every day," responded Jerry.

"That doesn't surprise me. I can think of several things that I'd use it for."

"Start your list with pleasure. It's just plain fun to take it out."

"I'm amazed by how quiet it is and the complete lack of vibration. It's like we're being silently moved by an unseen force."

"That's because it was designed by naval experts in silent running technology, and they gave special attention to the electric motors and propeller."

"My compliments to them. They did a great job, but I am curious, where does your electrical power come from?"

"It's from batteries that we recharge with solar cells. Also, when there's enough wind, we can deploy one or more sails to take advantage of it."

"Once we get out of this bay, we'll have plenty of wind," commented Michelle. "Look at the waves out there."

"We might be in for a wild ride," Trang said. "I hope this boat is seaworthy."

"It is," stated Jerry, "but if the ride is too rough for your land legs to handle, we can always retract everything and dive."

"I can handle anything you can," responded Trang.

"Well, considering your age, I wasn't sure."

"Despite my age, I am willing to bet that I can keep up with you."

"Are you guys going to be swaggering all day?" asked Michelle. "Or do you think we can hoist the sail and do some sailing?"

Trang turned to Michelle. "Are you a reporter or a slave driver?" he asked.

"You sound like some men I knew back on Earth," Michelle said. "Is it possible that our cultures aren't that different, in spite of being light-years apart?"

"Many nations on my home planet have unique cultures, but the nation I am from has a multicultural society very much like America."

"It's amazing to me that great nations with similar cultural diversity could evolve on planets so far apart," commented Michelle.

"I have some theories about that," stated Trang, "but I would like to discuss them some other time. Right now, I agree with your request. Let's raise the sail and get going."

A couple minutes later, Jerry had the outriggers and main sail deployed. The wind was from the north and was strong enough to move the boat at a pretty good clip, but Jerry wanted to show off more of his boat's capability. So he deployed the solar sails to take advantage of the radiant energy from Alpha Centauri A, which was high in the sky. Forty-seven kilowatts of power flowed from the solar sails to the electric motors.

"I see why you like your boat so much," stated Trang. "Solar power and wind power together really make this thing move. This is more fun than I've had in a long time. It's definitely a needed break from the tension of the last few days."

"It sure is," agreed Michelle, as she turned away from Trang to watch Matthew and Denise. They were at the front of the deck tightly grasping the rail to maintain their balance as the small boat rolled and pitched on the rough water. They screamed with delight every time they were hit with spray from a crashing wave. Fortunately, it was a warm afternoon, because the children were already soaked, and the voyage had barely begun.

"Is this their first sailing trip?" asked Trang.

"It's the first time they've been out on rough water," replied Michelle.

"They're sure thrilled by it," observed Trang. "What a contrast to the sterile environment on a starship."

"Isn't that the truth. They've only been here a few days, and each day brings them one exciting adventure after another. Today, it's a wild ride on the lake, followed by seeing huge dinosaurs up close."

"This is more than just a children's adventure," stated Trang. "I'm also having a good time."

"Me too! But I am not yet soaked enough, so I am going to join the children up front."

"You were smart enough to dress for the occasion," noted Trang. "I wish I had brought a swimsuit along."

"How could you have known you would need one today?"

"You're right about that. I wasn't planning on this."

"I thought you might be unprepared, so I brought along a pair of Mike's swimming trunks. They should fit. You guys are about the same size and build." Michelle reached into her waterproof travel bag and pulled out the red, white, and blue trunks. "You can go below and change," she said.

Trang held up the swimwear and looked at it. "This is colorful, but there's no way that it's going to make me look as good as you look."

Michelle smiled. "Thanks for the compliment," she said. "It's the first one I've ever received from an alien starship commander."

"Do I still sound like some of the men you knew back on Earth?" Trang asked.

"Definitely."

"I guess men are men, no matter where you find them," commented Trang.

"That's the way it should be," stated Michelle. Then, she went to the front of the boat to join the children. Trang looked at her for a few moments, then went below deck to change.

"Mom, this is fun!" Matthew exclaimed.

"I like crashing the waves," Denise yelled.

"I know it's fun," stated Michelle, "but I want you kids to hang on tight, so you don't fall overboard and drown."

"We are," replied Matthew.

"We have our life jackets on," Denise proudly proclaimed.

"I know how to swim," added Matthew.

"I can swim too," Denise said.

"I know you have life jackets on and can swim," responded Michelle, "but the lake is really rough today."

"We'll hold on tight," the children said in unison.

"Will you stay here with us?" Denise asked.

"Yes," replied Michelle.

"Good! You can have fun with us. I wish my mom were here, but

211

she's home sleeping. She's tired because she stayed up all night to save Akeyco's life. Is she going to live?"

"I think so."

"I hope so," stated Denise. "She's pretty."

Meanwhile, Trang emerged from below deck and joined Jerry. "I like the clear hull," he said. "Cruising underwater must be a fascinating sightseeing experience."

"It's a very different world down there," replied Jerry.

"I would like to see it."

"We're going to be at Sauropod Meadow hours before the giant sauropods arrive, so while we're waiting, we may as well go underwater and look around. We haven't yet explored that part of the lake. In fact, we haven't yet explored most of the lake."

"Maybe we'll make some interesting discoveries."

"I would be surprised if we don't," commented Jerry. "This planet is filled with an abundance of diverse life forms."

"Yeah it is, and some of them are really bizarre."

"The long-arms in Crater Lake are more bizarre than anything we've ever encountered. How do you avoid being attacked and eaten?"

"We discovered that they are fairly intelligent animals and that we could telepathically get into their minds. Once we demonstrated the power of our rifles, we were able to convince them to leave us alone. And when we need to, we can even get them to do things for us in return for a reward."

"Sounds like you can use them for guard dogs."

"We sometimes do."

"What about the lupusaurs, have you been able to control them?"

"No, but we've taught them to stay away from us, and as long as they keep their distance, we leave them alone. But if they get too close or threaten us in any way, we shoot them. Consequently, they avoid us."

"In other words, they fear you."

"I don't know that it's fear. I sense that it's more a matter of them having a healthy respect for our killing ability."

"Sounds like an uneasy truce," commented Jerry.

"That's a very good description of the situation. They keep their distance, but we know they spy on us a lot. We've been here more than 30 years, and we recently ran out of ammunition. Soon, the lupusaurs will realize that we are no longer using our guns, and they will know we are vulnerable. We've already made very capable bows and arrows, and we've become skilled in their use."

"A well placed arrow is lethal, but it doesn't have the instant shock effect of a bullet."

"We are planning to relocate. Living with lupusaurs without the killing power of guns is just too hazardous. Sooner or later, one or more of us will be killed."

"Zonya and her people have survived a good many years without guns," commented Jerry.

"We believe she has stronger telepathic powers than we do and is able to instill strong fear directly into their minds. Also, she and her people live on an island and lupusaurs do not like to go into deep water. Their body density is high, and they sink easily. Swimming is very difficult for them."

"Even so, I am amazed that she not only survived on her own, but was also able to care for two babies and raise them to adulthood."

"Despite the fact that the rest of her party caused us so much grief, I have to admire her for her toughness and her accomplishment."

"Both Zeb and Zonya had no part in what was done to you. In fact, they were opposed to it."

"I know. You told us the complete story about them and what you were doing in our backyard."

"I need to get my memory back, so I can know what all I told you."

"When we get back tonight, let's ask my wife to restore your memory."

"Thank you."

"But I want to tell you that we are pleased that you rescued Zeb, saved his life, and brought him and Zonya back together. That required much effort on your part and convinced my daughter that you could be trusted to help us, rather than, take advantage of us."

"How about you?"

"I wanted additional proof and a spy inside your society. My daughter insisted on being the one to do the mission. She has complete trust in you and refused to believe she was in any danger. Then, the accident happened. Fortunately, it looks like she's going to make a complete recovery."

"I hope so."

Fifteen minutes later, Jerry and his passengers arrived in the one-mile-wide bay offshore from Sauropod Meadow. They sailed in along the north shore and were in calm water. Jerry lowered the sail and stowed it. He retracted the telescoping mast. Then, he slowed the boat to three mph and cruised 60 yards offshore. Finally, he retracted and stowed the solar sails and the outriggers. He wanted the boat to look small so as not to spook any animals into running away.

"When will we see some dinosaurs?" Matthew asked.

"Pretty soon," responded Michelle.

"How close to them will we get?" Denise asked.

"Close enough to scare you," replied Michelle.

"Will they try to eat us?" Matthew asked.

"Some dinosaurs are meat eaters, and some are plant eaters. We'll stay away from the meat eaters."

"Can they swim out to our boat?" Matthew asked.

"Some can. I'll get my rifle, just in case there's a problem."

Michelle retrieved her rifle from the on-deck gun rack and slipped its strap over her right shoulder. She also belted on her 10.5 mm pistol.

"It looks like you're prepared for trouble," commented Trang.

"We have to be. The countryside is a very dangerous place."

"You're right, but I left my weapons back on the airplane."

"No swimsuit, no weapons, what did you bring along?"

"My adventuresome personality."

"I suspect you do have that."

"It would be difficult to be in our profession without it," commented Trang.

"Isn't that the truth," stated Jerry. "You can even be captured by aliens when you're doing guard duty."

"You don't think that's going to happen to us this afternoon, do you?" asked Trang while grinning.

"Not with you standing guard," replied Jerry, while handing Trang a rifle.

"You're going to trust me with this after recent events?"

"Is there some reason why I shouldn't?"

"None that I can think of."

"Do you know how to use it?" Jerry asked.

"Do you want to have a marksmanship contest sometime?"

"What kind of prize would we be competing for?"

"Bragging rights would be enough," replied Trang, "but if you have something else in mind, I am open for suggestions."

"I'll give it some thought."

While searching the countryside with binoculars, Michelle said, "There are some T-Rexes on the beach about a half-mile ahead."

"What are they doing?" Jerry asked.

"It looks like they're eating something, and they're really tearing into it."

Wanting to observe the feeding frenzy, Jerry cranked up the speed. "We'll be there in a couple minutes," he said.

"There aren't any T-Rexes where we live," Trang said.

"I wonder why," questioned Michelle.

"It might be too hot, or it might be because there isn't any easy prey for them. Most of the plant eaters are small and fast. Some species don't get over fifty pounds, and the biggest top out at only 800 to 900 pounds. All are so fleet-footed that I doubt the T-Rexes could successfully hunt them. The pack-hunting techniques of the lupusaurs are effective though."

"Do you have an explanation for the lack of big dinosaurs in your area?" Michelle asked.

"Most of the terrain is quite rough. I don't think the really big dinos can handle it. Also, it is a warmer climate than here. It might be too hot for them."

"One of our objectives is to study this planet and discover all of its life forms, along with mapping out the territory each lives in."

"That's a very big job."

"I know, but we have to tackle it anyway. This is our home now, and we need to learn as much about it as possible."

"We can help. We've already done a great deal of exploration. We'll share our discoveries with you, and you can build on them."

"Thanks! That will be helpful."

"We've been looking at other parts of this planet with the idea of relocating."

"Have you found any places you like?"

"We like Mystery Lagoon. Also, one of the islands in the big lake north of this one looks attractive."

"If you move to one of those places, we'll be neighbors."

"Would that be a problem for you?" Trang asked.

"I don't think so; in fact, I think it would be fun to visit back and forth and learn about each other's home planet."

Just then, two of the T-Rexes decided to challenge each other for a choice piece of meat. Since they were now only a couple hundred yards away, their roaring bellows were extremely loud and had a spine-chilling effect on everyone. Matthew and Denise were terrified into a stunned silence. They gripped the deck rail so tightly that their knuckles turned white. They were virtually paralyzed in place, too scared to move.

Jerry slowed the boat and continued to approach the T-Rexes. He brought the boat to a halt about 30 yards offshore. "This is as close as I care to get," he said.

"What's the matter, is your courage waning?" Trang teased.

Jerry grinned. "Actually, it's the children I'm worried about. They're already frozen in place."

Returning Jerry's grin, Trang said, "I'm sure that's it."

Michelle joined the children. Her rifle no longer hung from her shoulder. She now held it in a quick-reaction, ready-to-fire position.

As the huge T-Rexes continued their challenge and counterchallenge, they made some feints and charges at each other. These had to be dodged or blocked. Their horrific struggle carried them some 50 yards away from the carcass, right to the water's edge. Occasionally, they were even thrashing about in the shallow water just offshore.

"How is your courage now?" Jerry asked Trang.

"I think we should back out a bit."

"Why? They're so preoccupied with each other that they could care less about us. I think it's the thrill of a lifetime to be only 20 to 30 yards away from this battle. Besides, I've been led to believe that you're a crack shot with a rifle. As I recall, there was something about a marksmanship contest."

"This isn't the contest I had in mind!"

"That might be, but this kind of situation does present the ultimate test of one's shooting ability under pressure."

"How much killing power does this gun have?"

"It's armed with high-velocity, explosive bullets, but you won't have to use it. They're after each other, not us."

"I'm glad you're so confident about that, but I think you should back away. I really don't want to kill these guys."

"He's right," yelled Michelle. "Let's back up! We're too close. Our kids are in danger."

"In a minute, I want some video of this," yelled Jerry, as he grabbed a camera and started recording.

A minute later, the T-Rexes stopped fighting. They held their positions and tried to stare each other down. After a few moments of this, one of them very slowly began backing away from the other. Seeing this, Jerry immediately kicked the boat into reverse while continuing to record video of the T-Rexes.

When the victor was confident that his opponent had conceded the fight, he turned his head toward the retreating boat. He stared at it for a few moments; then, he took two steps forward and stood as tall as he could. He filled his lungs with a deep breath and let it all out in a fierce, ear-shattering roar. He stared at the retreating boat a bit longer. Then, he returned to the carcass.

"Do you still think he was too involved in the fight to be aware of us?" Trang asked Jerry.

"Apparently, he was aware of us, but was too busy to do anything about it."

"That would be my guess," commented Trang.

"Now, I know how Moose felt when he faced one of these brutes," stated Michelle.

"Not quite," responded Jerry. "Moose faced a whole pack of them, and he was armed only with a knife."

"How did he stay alive with only a knife?" asked Trang.

"He was sitting on the back of a styracosaurus herd leader. The herd successfully defended itself, and Moose had a front row seat for the entire encounter."

"I would sure like to know how he got onto the back of a big dinosaur," Trang said.

"It's a long story, and I am going to let him tell you. He'll be home this evening, and we can all exchange stories around the campfire."

"I have some incredible stories, but I don't know if I can top that one."

Finally, recovering from the overwhelming terror that she felt, Denise released her grip on the deck rail and ran to her father. "I don't like dinosaurs," she cried. "They're mean. They could kill me and eat me. Can they come to our island?"

"No, and if they could, they couldn't climb to the plateau we live on."

"Are all dinosaurs so terrible?"

"No, some are very peaceful and eat only plants. But the T-Rexes are killers. They eat other dinosaurs."

"I want to stay away from them."

"What do you think?" Michelle asked Matthew.

"It was fun watching them fight."

"Were you afraid?"

"They couldn't hurt us, because you and Trang had guns to kill them. I wasn't even scared."

"You were scared," insisted Denise.

"No, I wasn't!"

"It's okay if you were," Michelle said. "We live on a dangerous planet. You need to be afraid of some things, because that will make you be careful."

"Were you afraid?" Matthew asked.

"Yes, I was," Michelle replied.

"But you had a gun."

"That's true, but I was afraid anyway."

"But I want to be brave like my dad and Jerry and Moose."

"You can be brave and have lots of courage while being afraid," Michelle assured her son. "Were you brave when you watched the fight?"

"Yes!"

"Were you afraid?"

"Well, maybe I was, but I have enough courage to watch another fight."

"Good! When we get home tonight, you can tell your father the whole story."

"I'll tell him how brave I was."

"He'll be proud of you."

"I was scared, but I had courage too," stated Denise.

"Yes, you did," responded Michelle, "and tonight, I want you to tell your mother about the dinosaur fight."

"I will."

"That fight looked like a full-fledged battle," commented Jerry, "but were they really trying to kill each other, or was it just a lot of huff and puff?"

"They had me convinced it was a fight to the finish," stated Trang.

"Me too," agreed Jerry.

"Maybe that's why one of them didn't have to kill the other," Michelle said.

"What do you mean?" Trang asked.

"Convincing each other that it was a fight to the death might have put some sanity into their brains. Each might have concluded that even the victor might end up with serious injuries. In the interest of the future strength of the pack, the fight was over when one of them elected to bow out."

"You're giving them credit for a lot of intelligence and the ability to think," commented Trang.

"I am only speculating on what we just saw. Also, we've seen a sauropod herd drive away a pack of T-Rexes, and we've seen a styracosaurus herd successfully defend itself against a determined attack by seven of these brutes. It's possible that the animals that live in this area are equipped to either defend themselves or to evade these killers. Despite their size and ominous killing ability, obtaining food might require the coordinated action of a strong healthy pack. That would mean that they must have a set of rules to settle disputes among themselves."

"It's difficult to argue with your logic," stated Trang. "I can see why you were a top-notch science reporter back on Earth."

"It sounds like I just received another compliment from an alien starship commander."

Trang smiled at Michelle and nodded. His growing respect and admiration for her was obvious.

"I wonder what started that fight," questioned Michelle.

"Maybe they were arguing over a choice piece of meat," commented Jerry.

"If that's what provoked the fight, then I would have to say that their emotions overshadowed their intelligence," responded Michelle.

"Why?" asked Jerry.

"Because the two smaller members were busy eating while the two big guys were busy fighting. It seems like they would've eaten the choice pieces of meat first, including what the big guys were arguing about."

"You're saying that the two big guys should've been smart enough to realize that's what would happen," commented Jerry. "Therefore, they were fighting about something else."

"I suspect they are rival bulls," stated Michelle. "So any little thing can provoke a fight, but the real issue is herd dominance."

"That makes as much sense as anything," responded Jerry. "Also, there's no reason why they should be fighting over the kill, if it was a kill. That dead styracosaurus is as big as any we've seen. It must have weighed up around ten tons. That should be enough meat to feed four T-Rexes for several days."

"Are you suggesting they didn't kill the animal they're eating?" asked Trang.

"The herd Moose got involved with defended itself very well against seven T-Rexes," replied Jerry.

"Are you suggesting that this animal died a natural death, and that in this case, the T-Rexes are scavengers?" Trang asked.

"That's a strong possibility. Every time these brutes find a meal of opportunity, they can avoid the work and risks involved in making a kill."

"They're mean brutes," stated Denise. "I think they killed the animal they're eating. When will we see some nice dinosaurs?"

"In a couple hours," replied Jerry.

"Where will we see them?" Denise asked.

"Over there," Jerry said while pointing to the shoreline where the local sauropod herd came to drink water in the late afternoon.

"Can we go there?" asked Denise. "I want to get away from these monsters."

"Of course we can," responded Jerry. "We'll cruise slowly, about 40 yards offshore, keep an eye on the land, and see what we might discover."

"May I use the binoculars," requested Matthew. "I want to make some discoveries."

After handing the binoculars to Matthew, Michelle asked Denise, "Do you want to explore the countryside too?"

"I'll watch it without binoculars."

Speaking to Matthew, Michelle said, "If you find something interesting, be sure to let us know."

"Sure mom."

Turning to Trang, Michelle said, "We might have some quiet time, so there are a few questions I would like to ask you."

"It sounds like I'm going to be interviewed by a reporter."

"Something like that."

"What's your first question?"

"Your wife said that Jerry was given the age control treatment after determining that our races are genetically compatible. How were you able to determine that so quickly?"

"We took advantage of an opportunity."

"What opportunity?"

"Akeyco was ovulating when we captured Jerry. My wife harvested her egg and placed it in a test tube with Jerry's sperm. Normal fertilization occurred. This could happen only if we are genetically compatible."

"What a quick, easy way to determine genetic compatibility," commented Michelle. "The normal lab process would have taken a long time."

"I know, and we didn't have a long time. Your husband was putting the heat on us, but we desperately need your help. We felt that we needed to give Jerry the age control therapy to demonstrate what we can do for you in return for helping us. To do that, we had to seize the opportunity to quickly determine whether genetic compatibility exists."

"I must say you came up with an innovative way to do that. Being scientists, Dianne and Connie will be interested in the results of that experiment."

"The experiment is still ongoing," Trang said.

"What do you mean?" Michelle asked.

"When my wife determined that fertilization was normal, Akeyco decided she wanted the baby, so my wife planted the embryo in her uterus."

"What motivated her to do that?" Jerry asked.

"My daughter was looking at the embryonic beginning of a human life in a test tube. She did not want to let it die."

"But it seems like she's taking a big risk," commented Michelle.

"In what way?" Trang asked.

"How does she know it will develop into a normal baby? She could end up giving birth to something grotesque."

"She understands the risks, and her pregnancy will be closely monitored. Anyway, Akeyco has a vision for the future and decided to take the risk."

"What is her vision?" Michelle asked.

"She sees a brighter future for our races if we join together. She believes the child will be normal, healthy, and intelligent. She thinks it will be a constant reminder that our races should unite."

"Besides all of that, it must be exciting for her to be carrying a child that is the result of an interstellar connection," commented Michelle.

"I think it's especially exciting because of a theory that she would like to prove."

"What theory is that?" asked Michelle.

"She thinks the human life we discovered at Tau Ceti, humans from Earth, and humans from our planet have a common origin. She believes that, a long time ago, humans with technology more advanced than ours traveled from star to star looking for fertile planets to start human colonies on."

"Does she have any proof?" Michelle asked.

"The human life at Tau Ceti is quite primitive, but genetically, it is identical to us."

"Genetically compatible human life on three different planets does seem highly unlikely, unless it does have a common origin," commented Michelle.

"That's what Akeyco thinks. My wife has other explanations, but Akeyco is steadfast in her common origin belief."

"If her theory is correct, why didn't this ancient race plant a colony here?" asked Michelle. "This is certainly a fertile planet."

"She believes they did."

"What happened to them?"

"Akeyco thinks they became extinct."

"Why?"

"Let's assume the ancient race put people here and gave them plenty of technology to get them off to a strong start."

"That sounds reasonable."

"However, in a relatively short time, no more than a century or two, a big problem could have developed."

"What?"

"They lost their technology."

"How?"

"Food is bountiful on this planet. It is easy to live off the land. The early people could have grown lazy, and consequently, neglected to maintain their technology, or they may have been unable to maintain it. It is difficult for a tiny population to have a large enough industrial base to maintain technology. On some planets, that would not be a problem, but this planet is fierce and unforgiving."

"I get the picture," commented Michelle. "Your daughter thinks the early humans became extinct because they did not maintain their technology, and they could not survive the dangers here without it."

"That's what she believes, and that's why she's so convinced that our future depends on us uniting and combining our strengths."

"But I thought you want to repair your starship, so you can return to your home planet."

"We haven't decided that yet. We've been stranded here for so long that we had pretty well resigned ourselves to staying here. Then, you people arrived and renewed our hope. But the main reason to repair our starship is to rescue our people on Aphrodite."

"That is our most urgent priority," agreed Jerry, "but I am interested in your daughter's common origin theory. Have you found any evidence to support the theory that humans once lived here?"

"I assume you're asking if we've found any artifacts."

"Have you?"

"No, but we haven't made a determined search either. Where would we start looking?"

"If we could figure out approximately when they came here, then we could turn to our expert geologist and ask him to figure out what this planet's climate might've been like in that era. With that information, we could determine what parts of this planet might've been the most hospitable places to live. Then, we could search those areas for evidence that people had once lived here."

"That sounds like a lot of guesswork to me," responded Trang.

"It is," admitted Jerry, "but we have to start with something."

"I will be absolutely blown away if we find evidence that people lived here long ago," stated Michelle.

"If we find very old technological artifacts, I too will be blown away," commented Jerry. "Once we get our more immediate problems taken care of, we'll have to devote some time to this."

"If we find evidence for an ancient human colony, it will not by itself prove my daughter's theory, but it will sure add some additional credibility to it."

"The possibility is exciting," stated Michelle, "but there is something that tends to cast doubt on Akeyco's theory. And that is, why haven't any artifacts been found on Earth to indicate that the human species came from a small colony that had advanced technology?"

"Advanced technology that existed in a small area for only a few generations could easily have vanished without a trace," commented Jerry.

Speaking to Trang, Michelle asked, "Have the people back on your home planet ever found any ancient artifacts to indicate the presence of advanced technology?"

"No, but Jerry's right; it could easily have vanished."

"The theory that humans on Earth evolved from primates will have to be seriously questioned, if we find such artifacts here," commented Michelle.

"I don't know that we even have to find high-tech artifacts to throw the evolution-on-Earth theory into question," stated Jerry. "It seems like all we have to do is find evidence that a small group of humans once lived somewhere on this planet for a few generations. If we can find no evidence for the existence of a lesser creature that the humans might have evolved from, then it would be reasonable to conclude that they came here from somewhere else."

"This is exciting," Michelle said. "What we are talking about is the origin of the human race. Where did our ancient ancestors come from? Where did we come from?"

"We need to search for evidence that humans once lived here," stated Jerry. "Also, for the sake of doing the research, let's assume that Akeyco's theory is correct and take a look at all nearby stars and try to determine which ones make good candidates for the origin of our ancestors."

"There's no way you could prove our ancestors actually came from one of them," commented Michelle.

"I'm not so sure about that," responded Jerry.

"How would you prove it?" asked Michelle.

"That depends on what kind of artifacts we find."

"What do you mean?"

"If human colonies actually were planted on various planets long ago by an advanced civilization, the people in those colonies would certainly have known where they came from. It's possible that someone in the colony would have wanted to leave a permanent record of that for all future generations. That could have been done by carving a map of local stars on a rock wall inside a cave and indicating on the map where the colonists came from."

"Wow! You're right," exclaimed Michelle. "Finding something like that would be even better than finding technological artifacts."

"That's the way I have it figured," stated Jerry.

"Let's hurry up and get Trang's starship repaired, so we can start the search," Michelle said.

"You need to talk to your husband about that," Jerry said.

"He's very capable," stated Trang. "I don't think you'll have to prod him."

"When I tell him what we've been talking about, he will be eager to start looking for artifacts. That's something he can be aware of while studying this planet's geological processes and climate history. He might be able to figure out where it would've made sense to plant a human colony in any given time period."

"Even so, it seems like we'll be searching for the proverbial needle-in-a-haystack," commented Jerry.

"That's true," agreed Michelle, "but we have to explore this planet and discover its secrets anyway, so while we're doing that, we might as well be alert for evidence of an ancient human colony."

"If we find clear evidence for that, the news will hit Earth's scientific community like a bomb," stated Jerry.

"That also will be the case on Proteus," Trang said.

"That must be the name of your home planet," commented Michelle.

"That's right, and we are called Proteans. The country we are from is Angea, so you can also refer to us as Angeans."

"I wonder how your planet came to be called Proteus," questioned Michelle.

"It's a very ancient name, but why are you interested in its origin?"

"On Earth, Proteus is the name of an ancient sea god that could easily transform itself into different forms. It's curious that this would be the name of your planet."

"Seventy percent of my home planet is covered with water. Mythology holds that in the beginning, it was ruled by a sea goddess named Proteus who changed her form to suit her moods. Mythology teaches that she named the planet Proteus before ascending into the heavens on a chariot of fire."

"This is truly astounding!" exclaimed Michelle. "How could an identical name arise on planets light-years apart and have essentially the same meaning?"

"This just might be a piece of evidence supporting my daughter's common origin theory."

"At first thought, it seems that way, but why would advanced beings traveling from star to star planting human colonies teach that kind of mythology? It makes no sense."

"I can't answer that question," responded Trang, "but I think you and Akeyco should study and compare the ancient teachings of our home planets. Find out if there are any other similarities."

"I'd love to do that."

"So would Akeyco."

Speaking to Michelle, Jerry said, "I think it's time to dive and show the underwater world to our Protean guest."

"Yes Sir!" Michelle saluted smartly with a broad grin. Then, she turned to the children and said, "Let's get everything put away. We are going to dive."

"I like going underwater," exclaimed Denise. "It's fun, and the fish are pretty."

"Are there any monsters down there?" Matthew asked.

"We haven't found any yet," responded Michelle, "but maybe you can help us find some."

"Let's dive," stated Matthew. "I want to look for monsters."

A couple minutes later, the submarine slipped below the surface. To avoid spooking the fish, Jerry planned to cruise silently at a very slow two mph. He set the navigation computer to maintain a distance of ten feet from the bottom.

"How deep is it here?" asked Trang.

"Only about 40 feet," replied Jerry.

"Is this whole bay that shallow?"

"No, it's about 250 feet deep out in the middle, and that's where we're headed."

"Good! We can see how life along the bottom changes as it gets deeper."

"It should be interesting. There is a large diversity of life in this lake."

"This is already fascinating," commented Trang. "You are definitely going to be getting some requests for underwater tours from my people."

"This is a popular piece of equipment, but we'll work the tours into the schedule on one condition."

"What's that?"

"I want a ride in your airplane; in fact, I want to fly it."

"You've already done that."

"I have!"

"When we delivered you to Zeb's Island, you asked if you could sit in the copilot's seat and pilot the airplane for a while."

"You allowed me to fly your airplane while I was your captive."

"Why not?"

"Weren't you worried about what I might do?"

"What was there to worry about? You are a top-notch pilot."

"But I was your prisoner."

"You flew the airplane for ten minutes while we were taking you home. We didn't think you would do anything stupid to interfere with that."

"I need to get my memory back, so I can find out what else happened while I was your captive."

"We were hoping for a good outcome, so you were not mistreated. In fact, your stay with us was quite pleasant for you. Your interrogation was handled by my wife and daughter. And Akeyco turned out to be quite talented at persuading you to answer questions."

"How did she do that?"

"Well, let's just wait until you get your memory back. Then, you can talk to her about what she did."

"That's one conversation I would like to listen in on," commented Michelle.

"Before I agree to that, I would like to get my memory back and have some idea about what happened."

"What are you trying to hide?" asked Michelle, while displaying a naughty grin.

"I honestly don't know," replied Jerry.

"I hope you won't be in trouble with your wife when your wayward adventures come to light," teased Michelle.

"I hope so too," replied Jerry, "but I don't believe I would have done anything out of character."

"I'm not the one you have to convince," responded Michelle, while maintaining her mischievous grin.

"You seem to be enjoying my misfortune."

"I am beginning to think that your captivity wasn't exactly a misfortune," Michelle said.

"I will have to get my memory back before I can respond to that comment."

Michelle tried to come up with a really good emotionally charged wisecrack to throw at Jerry, but her thoughts were interrupted by Matthew. "When are we going to see some monsters?" he asked.

"I don't know," replied Michelle. "There might not be any in this lake."

Jerry looked at the sonar data and said, "There aren't any large creatures swimming in this bay, only lots of fish. If there are any monsters, they would have to be lurking on the bottom."

"But I want to see some monsters," stated Matthew.

"You should be happy we've never found any in this lake," Michelle said. "You like to go swimming, and if there were monsters, you couldn't do that because they might eat you."

"There are monsters in the lake where I live," Trang said.

"I would like to see them," stated Matthew.

"Someday, you will," responded Jerry.

An hour later, Jerry took the submarine to the surface. He opened the hatch, and everyone climbed out onto the deck.

"What a marvelous research tool this boat is," commented Trang. "It's infinitely better than the scuba gear we use."

"We believe in doing things in comfort," stated Jerry.

"Our mission didn't allow for bringing along a submarine," Trang said. "A small, high-performance airplane with global range was deemed more useful for our needs."

"We knew before we left Earth that we would live on a small island, so a multipurpose boat was considered essential equipment."

"The big dinosaurs are coming!" exclaimed Matthew, while pointing at the huge sauropods.

Everyone watched the gigantic animals majestically march toward the lake. "They are giants," stated Matthew. "How close to them are we going to go?"

"They won't hurt us," Denise said.

"How do you know?" Matthew asked.

"My dad walked underneath the biggest dinosaur and reached up and touched him," Denise said, "and he didn't do anything to my dad. These dinosaurs aren't mean like the T-Rexes."

"When I get older, I will be brave enough to walk under one of them too," stated Matthew.

"You can be brave without doing that," Michelle said.

"I know, but Moose rode a dinosaur into battle, and Jerry walked under one and touched him. I want to do something wild and exciting too."

"There are exciting things for you to do that are far less dangerous. I want you to stay alive. That means you must avoid danger as much as possible."

"She's right," stated Trang. "This is a savage planet. You will encounter plenty of dangerous excitement without looking for it."

Matthew looked at Trang, then at his mother. "I will stay out of danger until I am old enough to have my own gun," he said.

"That's a good plan," stated Michelle.

Jerry brought the boat to a stop only 25 yards offshore. The huge sauropods continued their march toward the lake with the dominant male in the lead.

"It looks like they're coming straight to us," Matthew said.

"You wanted excitement," responded Jerry. "Pretty soon, you will be very close to them."

"Good!" exclaimed Matthew.

Two minutes later, the lead dinosaur was 20 yards from the water. Overwhelmed by the animal's immense size, Denise and Matthew were silently staring at it. When the huge sauropod was only ten yards from the water, Matthew found his voice. "Mom, are you sure they won't hurt us? Maybe we're too close."

"You said you wanted excitement."

"But he's huge. He's bigger than our cargo shuttle. He's monstrous."

"You said you wanted to see some monsters."

"But I don't want to be so close."

"Don't worry," Jerry said. "They won't hurt us. Just watch them and be brave. You might be looking at the largest animals that live on this planet."

"Okay, I'll try."

When the herd leader reached the water's edge, he looked from side to side for a few moments. Satisfied that there weren't any threats in the vicinity, he started drinking. Three females and their youngsters lined up on the herd leader's right, with the largest female on the far right. The herd's only other male faced the countryside and alertly watched the surrounding area.

"Despite their size, they are wary," commented Trang.

"They have three juveniles to protect, so they have to be on guard," commented Michelle. "T-Rexes are fierce predators, and they hunt in packs."

"I can't argue with that," Trang said, "but these sauropods look very capable of defending themselves, even against the T-Rex. The horns at the ends of their long muscular tails must be lethal when delivered with full force. Also, they have horns on their heads and long muscular necks to whip them around with."

"It isn't just the horns," commented Jerry, "there's also a tremendous size difference. A full-grown T-Rex weighs about ten tons compared to about 100 tons for the sauropod herd leader."

"That's an awesome amount of bone and muscle power with which to drive the horns into a T-Rex," noted Trang. "If the blow didn't kill the T-Rex outright, it would surely cripple him and knock him down."

"In which case, it could be stomped on by an angry 100-ton animal, and that would have to be fatal."

"That's all true," Michelle said, "but if the T-Rexes were ever able to isolate a juvenile, it would be easy prey."

"I don't believe they would be allowed to enjoy the meal," commented Jerry.

"Are you saying that these sauropods would attack a T-Rex pack in retaliation for killing one of their youngsters?" Trang asked.

"I think so."

"Do you have a basis for that opinion?"

"Yes, we've seen them attack T-Rexes."

"That must have been an awesome sight. Did you have a front row seat?"

"We had a very good view of the entire confrontation."

"How did you pull that off?" Trang asked.

"Before we set foot on this planet, we landed a robot research station on that rock formation over there. Using its cameras and microphones, we watched and heard this herd leader bellow out some very crisp orders. The other male and the largest female immediately lined up with him and went into an all out charge toward a T-Rex pack. The T-Rexes quickly turned and fled."

"From just looking at these giants, I'm not surprised that even the awesome T-Rex respects their fighting ability. And with that in mind, I think we might be a little too close to these guys."

"Why do you think that?" Jerry asked.

"Take a good look at that big guy. He is at least 100 feet long. Right now, we are only 60 to 70 feet away from him."

"That's true, but we don't look like T-Rexes. Do you really think that a 200,000-pound animal and his herd would feel threatened by creatures as small as we are?"

"Apparently, they aren't. I haven't seen them give us any attention at all."

"As far as I can tell, the only danger we face from them is to get between them and wherever it is that they want to go. Getting stepped on by a sauropod would be like a human stepping on a large beetle. It would be crunch, squish, lights out."

"I don't want to be stepped on," stated Denise.

"We aren't going to get stepped on," Jerry assured his daughter.

"But dad, weren't you afraid of being stepped on when you walked under him?"

"I thought about it, and I was ready to run if I as much as saw one of his leg muscles twitch."

"Why did you do something so dangerous?" Denise asked.

"I wanted to prove my theory that these animals would tolerate our presence, and I wanted to touch a dinosaur that might be the biggest on this planet."

"I don't want you to do things that are so dangerous. You could get killed. Then, I won't have a dad."

"I promise you that I won't get killed anytime soon."

Denise gave Jerry a big hug and said, "Thanks Daddy!"

"Why did you want to know if these animals would tolerate your presence?" Trang asked. "Are you planning to roam with the herd?"

"I'm not planning to, but someday we might have a need to be in the countryside. When that happens, it would be nice to know which animals we can hang out with."

"If you could avoid being stepped on, it appears that you would be safe from T-Rexes while traveling with the sauropods."

"Based on Moose's experience, that's also true for the local styracosaurus herd."

"How adventuresome is Moose?" Trang asked.

"What's that question leading up to?"

"Would he be willing to approach the animal he rode to see if it remembers him and will still tolerate his presence?"

"If there were a crucial reason to do so, I'm sure he would. What do you have in mind?"

"Nothing important enough to justify the risk. Mainly, I'm just curious about the animal. Will it remember Moose and accept his presence?"

"I believe it would. Those animals are big, up to ten tons. Relative to them, we are small, and they've never been taught to fear us."

"So if they are mild-mannered, rather than, mean-tempered, humans should be able to move around within the herd and be ignored."

"That's the theory Moose put to the test, but when the T-Rexes showed up, he ended up with a lot more excitement than he bargained for."

"That's one story I'd like to hear."

"Be prepared to listen for a while, because Moose doesn't like to leave out any details."

"Good! I love a wild story that's true."

"Speaking about true stories, there's one you can tell me."

"What's that?" Trang asked.

"Earlier, you said that you recently ran out of ammunition."

"That's correct."

"How did you capture me without guns?"

"I didn't say we ran out of guns; I said we ran out of ammunition."

Jerry's face turned red with a big grin of embarrassment. "Am I to believe that you captured me by pointing empty guns at me?"

"That's what we did."

"That's unbelievable. What if I'd hit the deck and started shooting?"

"Then, we would've died."

"You took a big chance, just to capture me. You had no way of knowing how I would react."

"We had to take the risk. When you landed on Crater Lake, you put us in a desperate situation. We didn't know what your intentions were, but we had to consider the possibility of attack. We would have had to use bows and arrows to defend ourselves against your guns. We could not possibly have won such a battle. We felt our only chance was to capture you and put some bombs on your shut-

232

tle, so we could have a stronger bargaining position. As it turned out, none of this worked, because we totally underestimated Mike's military mind."

"Mike is pretty sharp when it comes to military strategy; in fact, he's pretty sharp in lots of ways. If you'll take a close look at the main horn on that big sauropod's head, you'll notice that there's a camera pack attached to it. Mike put it there."

"How did he do that?"

"He attached an instrument pack to a specially designed clamp and delivered it with a couple modified RPVs when the animal was sleeping."

"When did he do all of that?"

"He did it before we landed here."

"Why did he take it upon himself to pull off a stunt like that?"

"We were trying to learn as much about this planet as we could, and seeing the sauropod's world from the head of the herd leader seemed like a good way to view the landscape, as well as, learn about herd behavior."

"I would like to see some of the video from those cameras."

"Sure, anytime. Also, you might want to pay attention to the sound effects. The natural sounds of the countryside are interesting. It's also interesting to listen to communication between herd members. They seem to have a fairly sophisticated language as far as animals go."

"It sounds like that instrument pack has gained a great deal of information for you."

"It has. We have well over a month of video and sound from the wanderings of this herd. We've gained a great deal of insight into what goes on in the countryside."

"All because Mike used his talent and ingenuity to pull off a stunt."

"And he made it look easy," added Jerry.

"How about the project Mike's working on now, will he be able to deliver to Aphrodite the things my people need to fix my starship?"

"He will improvise a workable lander. You can count on it."

"Good! In the meantime, I have a small favor to ask."

"What would that be?"

"My people desperately need some guns and ammunition."

"We could spare a couple rifles and pistols."

"That's great. I will send them home as soon as you give them to us."

"If you've seen enough here, we can head on back and take care of that."

"You'd better talk to Michelle and the kids before we take off. Their eyes are still glued to the big dinos."

Jerry followed the suggestion and gave them more time. When they were ready to leave, he set sail for home.

Forty-five minutes later, they arrived in South Bay to the sound of a sonic boom. "I guess our cargo shuttle is about to arrive," Jerry said.

"Is Moose on it?" Trang asked.

"I think so. He's been in space for a few days, and he was planning to come home on this flight."

"I need a firsthand account of his dinosaur ride, but first I want to see my daughter and talk to my wife."

Ten minutes later, in the medical lab, Trang looked at his daughter. "How much longer do you think she'll be out?" he asked Geniya.

"She's already started her recovery. I believe she'll be conscious in about a half-hour."

"That's very good news. I am so very happy that she's going to be okay."

"I am too," responded Geniya.

Turning to Jerry, Trang said, "If your offer to provide guns is still good, I would like to send my people home."

"Let's take care of that."

A few minutes later, Trang and Jerry delivered two rifles, two pistols, and ammunition to Trang's airplane. Trang ordered his people to return home. He and Jerry cleared the area and watched the airplane take off. "My people will be happy to receive the guns," Trang said.

"If I had the specifications for your guns, we could manufacture some ammunition for you," Jerry said.

"That would solve a serious problem that we have. Actually, we can make the job easy for you, because we've saved most of the empty shells."

"We can easily make the gun powder and the bullets."

"That will allow us to return your guns," Trang said.

"You can keep them for as long as you need to. You live in a more dangerous area than we do."

"Only because of the lupusaurs. They are vicious, intelligent hunters. But then, you have to contend with pterodactyls."

"We've developed a friendly relationship with the local pair."

"That is something I would like you to tell me about, but let's save it for another time. Right now, we should go back to my daughter. She should be regaining consciousness soon, and I would like to be at her side when she wakes up."

"I would too," responded Jerry.

A few minutes later, Trang and Jerry arrived in the medical lab, and their timing was perfect. Akeyco opened her eyes and looked around the room. "Where am I?" she asked.

"You are in the Earth people's medical lab on Pioneer Island," replied Geniya.

"How did I get here?"

"They brought you here with their helicopter."

"Why am I here?"

"You slipped, fell, and hit your head on a rock. You were unconscious when Jerry and Connie found you."

"How bad is my injury?"

"You have a small fracture in your skull."

"How long have I been unconscious?"

"About 24 hours."

"And the Earth people took care of me?"

"Yes, they have, and they called me for assistance."

Akeyco looked at Jerry, Connie, Dianne, and Michelle. Then, she looked at Trang and said, "I was right. They are good people, and they will help us."

"They already are helping us," responded Trang. "All of our most urgent problems are being addressed."

Akeyco briefly gazed at each of the Earth people. Then, she said, "Thank you."

Chapter Twelve

TIME: Day 34, 8:00 AM

Jerry and Connie were eating breakfast with their guests, Trang and Geniya. They were at the kitchen table on the second floor of the habitation capsule. Most of the capsule's first floor was occupied by the medical lab.

"This breakfast is fantastic," Trang said to Connie. "It's fit for a king."

"It isn't everyday that we have guests from another star. I just thought that a special breakfast would make you feel welcome."

"Be careful you don't make us feel too welcome," warned Trang. "We might never leave."

"That might not be such a bad idea," responded Connie. "Our numbers are small, and our future might be brighter if we can find a way to live together and combine our strengths."

"Akeyco feels very strongly about that," stated Geniya, "and she thinks her baby can help tie our societies together. She also believes our individual species have a common origin and that it is destiny for us to come back together."

"That might explain why she had the embryo implanted," commented Connie. "The baby symbolizes our races coming back together. In her mind, the baby is the fulfillment of destiny, and in a sense, proves her theory."

"I don't know that the baby is enough to prove the common origin theory," stated Geniya. "It's a strong piece of evidence, but I think we need to find some additional proof."

"That's a search we can take up after we get our more urgent problems taken care of," commented Trang.

"Speaking about urgent problems, when do I get my memory back?" Jerry asked.

"You'll have to talk to Akeyco about that," replied Geniya.

"Trang said that you could remove the block."

"I could try, but Akeyco's telepathic powers are greater than mine. She entered your mind rather deeply to plant the memory block and to get answers to our questions."

"How much personal information did she dig out of my husband's mind?" Connie asked.

"No more than necessary."

"That might be, but I think I have to assume that she knows my husband quite well."

"In some ways, that's true."

"What bothers me is that Akeyco might know my husband in ways that I don't."

"That's definitely possible. Since you don't have telepathic ability, you can't get into his mind in the intimate way that she did."

"I need to talk to her about that."

"I know my daughter, and I can guarantee that she will not try to deceive you. She will be open and honest."

"Good! I will talk to her after she recovers from her head injury."

"That won't take long. The age control drug does accelerate healing rather remarkably."

"I hear someone hopping up the stairs," Jerry said.

A few moments later, Akeyco arrived on the scene. "Good morning everyone," she said.

"How are you feeling?" Geniya asked.

"My headache is gone, and my ankle doesn't hurt anymore, but I am hungry."

"You haven't eaten in a couple days," responded Geniya.

"I know, and your breakfast smells so good I couldn't stand it. I had to get out of bed and come up here." Looking at Connie and Jerry, she asked, "May I join you?"

"Of course," replied Connie. "Our table is pretty small, but I am done eating, so you can sit here."

Connie stood up and pulled the chair back for Akeyco. "I hope you're staying off that ankle," she said.

"I made it up the stairs okay, but I could use some crutches for a week or two. By then, I should be healed, but at the moment, I am starving. What have you been eating that smells so good?"

"Blueberry pancakes, smoked meat, smoked fish, and fresh fruit. You can start with everything except the pancakes. I'll have them ready for you in a couple minutes."

"Thank you," replied Akeyco, who dove right into the food. A few moments later, she said, "This meat is really good. What's it from?"

"Moose and I went hunting," Jerry said. "I shot an ostri-dino. Moose marinated some of the meat in his special spice concoction. Then, he slowly smoked it for six hours."

"It is delicious. I'd like to find out exactly how he made this. When do I get to meet him?"

"He's going with us to Mystery Lagoon," replied Jerry, "so he should be here pretty soon."

"I wish I could go with you, but for medical reasons, I don't think I should."

"I agree," stated Geniya. "You should sit around and relax for a few days."

"If you stay here, I'll show you around," offered Denise, who had just arrived and immediately put her hands on Akeyco's right forearm.

"It looks like I have a new friend," responded Akeyco.

"I like you, and I'm glad you didn't die."

"I'm happy about that too. I guess I did hit my head pretty hard, and I could have died."

"My mom's a good doctor, and she made you get well. When Zeb was sick, she saved him too. She even made the sick baby 'dactyl get well."

"Your mom must be pretty special."

"She is. When I grow up, I'm going to be just like her."

"Your daughter really admires you," Akeyco said to Connie.

"She is my pride and joy, and I worry about her a lot. This is a savage planet loaded with dangers that we'll need a lifetime to discover."

"I understand your concern, but I was born here, and my parents successfully raised me. You should let us help. We've lived here a long time, and we have knowledge we can share with you."

"I appreciate your offer," replied Connie.

"Right now, you can help me in a big way," Jerry said to Akeyco.

"How is that?"

"Remove the memory block you put in my mind."

"Are you sure you want me to do that?"

"Why do you people keep asking that question? Did something happen that you don't want me to be aware of?"

"Sometimes tensions can be prevented between individuals by keeping some things secret."

"I can't deny that, but if my people and your people are going to work together and maybe even join together to form one society, I need to know what happened when I was your captive. I promise I won't do anything that will cause tension for anyone."

"Okay, I'll take your word for that. Now, I need you to totally relax and clear your mind. Look into my eyes and focus on me. You must completely relax and focus only on me. I need to enter your mind. Do not resist in any way. Just relax and open your mind to me, relax even more… You're resisting me. You must allow me in, drop your resistance, relax more completely… That's better. Close your eyes, but stay receptive to me."

Akeyco closed her eyes. Everyone was silent. Akeyco seemed to go into a trance for a few moments. Then, she opened her eyes and said to Jerry, "You can now remember your capture. Let your mind roll forward to the next event, and the next, and the next. Keep going forward."

A couple minutes passed by. "You can now open your eyes," Akeyco said. "Your memory block is gone."

Jerry smiled at Akeyco. "Thank you," he said.

Turning to Trang, he said, "That was a very good acting job you and your cohorts put on when you captured me with empty guns. You quickly convinced me that you were trigger-happy commandos."

"We expected you to react that way, but I did breathe a lot easier when you dropped your weapons."

"I admire your guts for pulling it off. Just think what you could do with loaded guns."

"Yeah, we might even be dangerous."

"I definitely want you on my side."

"That's the plan."

Facing Akeyco and Geniya, Jerry said, "If I ever need to interrogate anyone, I am going to turn the job over to you two. You really did a number on me."

"What do you mean?" Akeyco asked. "We didn't torture you in any way."

"I know, but the methods the two of you used were more effective than torture. You've turned persuasion into an art form. Was there anything at all that you wanted to know that you failed to get out of me?"

Akeyco looked into her mother's eyes. They exchanged smug smiles. "Not a thing," they said in unison.

"I don't know if I like the sound of that," commented Connie.

"Don't worry," Akeyco assured Connie. "We aren't trouble makers."

"Just the same, I would like to discuss this with you."

"I don't have a very demanding schedule for today. In fact, it's wide open."

"Good! I would like to find out exactly what you did to draw out the information you wanted."

"We'll answer your questions," stated Akeyco, with Geniya nodding in agreement.

"Now that I have my memory back, I can also discuss their interrogation techniques with you," Jerry said to Connie.

Connie affectionately put her hands on Jerry's shoulders from behind and said, "Thanks honey, I appreciate that."

"It seems like I am being ignored in this whole conversation," Trang protested.

"I'm getting to you," Jerry said. "I want to compliment you on your airplane. That's a pretty amazing machine."

"You should know. You really put it through its paces. I was impressed with your piloting skills."

"When you allowed me to fly it, I couldn't pass up the opportunity to have some fun. And you did assure me that it was a very forgiving airplane and that I couldn't get into trouble with it."

"I know I did, but when you started doing your daredevil stunts, I started having second thoughts about what I told you."

"Are you saying that I put the fear of God into you?"

"Let's just say that you got my attention and held onto it."

"After capturing me with empty guns, I'd say you had that coming."

"Are you guys going to be gabbing all day, or are you about ready to go?" Moose asked, as he entered the room.

"What's your hurry?" asked Jerry. "It's only going to take a few minutes to get there."

"It sounds like you had the sub loaded into the cargo shuttle," stated Moose.

"Flying it to the lagoon with the shuttle is the quickest way to get it there, but someone will have to sail it back. There'll be a space capsule in the shuttle, and there won't be room for the sub."

"If you twist my arm a little bit, I could volunteer to bring it home," offered Moose.

"I don't know about that. You've been really busy lately, and I hate to ask you to do one more thing. You might get stressed out from overwork."

"I appreciate your concern, but I think my wife would like to do some recreational sailing, so I'd better take the job."

"I'm sure that's it."

"Well, we haven't been sailing in quite some time."

"Yeah, it's been a whole week, hasn't it?"

"Something like that. Maybe I'll pick up a couple fish while we're out there and fire up the smokehouse when we get back."

"I would like you to show me how you made this smoked fish," Akeyco said. "It's a real delicacy."

"I'll be happy to," replied Moose.

"Be prepared to listen for a while," warned Jerry. "When it comes to food, he doesn't like to leave out any details."

"Good! After hearing him out, I'll be just as good at smoking fish as he is."

"That's not possible. No one's as good as the master," boasted Moose.

"He's also a bundle of humility," commented Jerry.

"Credit must be given where it's due," responded Moose.

"In his defense, the fish and the meat are excellent," Akeyco said with a big smile.

"You and I are going to get along quite well," stated Moose. Turning to Jerry, "I am going to go talk to my wife about a day on the lake and pack some supplies. We'll meet you on the shuttle shortly."

A half-hour later, with Jerry and Moose at the controls, the cargo shuttle taxied out of South Bay to open water, where Jerry accelerated to just over 200 mph and took off. At 300 mph, he stopped accelerating and cruised for a few minutes. Then, he began the landing approach to Mystery Lagoon.

After landing, Jerry guided the shuttle to the space capsule location and brought it to a stop. He opened the bottom cargo bay doors and lowered the sub a few feet. "Trang and I are going to the boat," he said. "Drop us when I give the okay."

A few minutes later, Jerry said, "We're ready. You can release us."

"You got it," replied Moose, as he lowered the sub a few more feet and cut it loose.

Jerry let the sub free fall until it was well clear of the shuttle; then, he put it into a steep dive. "If all goes well, we'll soon have your capsule in the shuttle," he said.

"We shouldn't have any problems," responded Trang. "It seems like a simple job."

"It is, but the capsule's been submerged for a long time, and it may've deteriorated. We might pull it apart when we try to lift it."

"I guess that's possible, but the composites it's made out of should be okay, even after all these years."

"But it might have been damaged on landing. For it to sink, it had to spring a leak and fill up with water."

"We'd better take a good look at it before we attempt to haul it to the surface," commented Trang.

A short time later, Jerry and Trang arrived at the bottom and quickly located the capsule. They gave it a thorough inspection while circling it and beaming a spotlight on it. "It looks structurally sound," stated Trang.

Jerry aimed the light at the top of the capsule. "There's the eyebolt your parachute was attached to," he said.

"It looks solid," stated Trang. "I think it's time to attempt what we came down here for."

Jerry contacted Moose. "Send down the cable," he said.

A few minutes later, Jerry spotted a flashing strobe light approaching the sub from directly above. "You're right on target," he said to Moose.

When the strobe light and the hook it was mounted on hit the bottom, Jerry said, "It's here." Then, he approached the hook with the sub and grabbed it with the sub's mechanical arm. Jerry moved the hook to the top of the capsule and slipped it into the eyebolt.

"Take the slack out of the cable," Jerry said to Moose.

A few moments later, Moose replied, "It's done."

"Add a few hundred pounds of tension to the cable," requested Jerry.

"Done."

"It hasn't moved yet, so let's slowly increase the pull."

Several seconds later, Jerry said, "It's starting to budge. Increase the tension a bit more."

"Done."

"Okay, I think this is going to work. One side of the capsule is a few inches above the bottom. Slowly reel in a bit more cable... That's good. The entire capsule is off the bottom. Continue to gradually haul it to the surface. We'll keep an eye on it."

"It looks like we've got it," observed Trang.

"I think so," agreed Jerry.

"I can't wait to look into the capsule to see what condition our combustion chamber is in."

"Is there anything else in the capsule?"

"Some specialized tools to install the combustion chamber and a few rocks from Aphrodite."

"Why the rocks?"

"Our geologist is here. My people on Aphrodite thought the rocks would be of interest to him."

"What's special about the rocks?"

"It's been so long that I don't know anymore. We've had so many other things to worry about, like staying alive."

"I can relate to that, but I'm curious about those moon rocks. I'd like to see them."

"Next time I talk to my people on Aphrodite, I will find out if they remember why they sent them."

"Good."

"So far the capsule retrieval is smooth," commented Trang. "It looks like we have it."

"You may have spoken too soon," stated Jerry. "A small crack has opened up on this side."

"It doesn't look big enough to be a problem."

"Does the structure have crisscrossed ribs, or is it uniform thickness?"

"It has crossed ribs on the inside, and they should prevent the crack from spreading."

"I hope so, otherwise, the capsule could break in two, and the piece we want will sink back to the bottom."

"I don't think that's going to happen on the way up," commented Trang. "The danger point will be when we try to lift it out of the water. Since the capsule's full of water, it's very heavy and could break apart."

Jerry contacted Moose and explained the problem. "As a precaution, let's slow the rate of ascent," Jerry said.

"I'm currently lifting it at 100 feet per minute. I'll cut that in half."

"Good."

"I have an idea how to safely get the capsule out of the water," Moose said, "but somebody will have to get wet."

"Let's hear it."

"This shuttle has an eight-person life raft that's tightly packaged. If we could roll it out, drag it under the capsule, and press the inflation button; it should act like a flotation collar."

"That raft will easily support a couple thousand pounds, but I'm not sure that's enough to keep the capsule from sinking if the top breaks off."

"Maybe not, but it might give it enough support, so that I can lift it partially out of the water. Then, we can drill a hole in it, stick in a hose, and pump the water out."

"That should work."

"Where are you going to get a pump?" asked Trang.

"The shuttle has several emergency pumps and plenty of hose," responded Jerry.

"They are high capacity pumps," added Moose. "It won't take long to get the water out of your capsule."

"Our shuttle doesn't have any backup pumps," commented Trang, "but it should. When we operate from water in wilderness areas, it would be easy to collide with a piece of debris and rip a hole in the fuselage. We rely on our primary pumps to never fail, but a couple reserve pumps would be nice to have."

"They are a good safety feature," commented Jerry.

Twenty minutes later, the capsule reached the surface, and Moose stopped the winch while the capsule was still submerged. This left the capsule hanging from the end of the cable between the cargo hold's lower doors.

Jerry brought the submarine to the surface near the shuttle; then, he and Trang went to the top deck. After slowly nudging the submarine against the shuttle's left wingtip, Jerry stepped onto the shuttle, closely followed by Trang. Dianne stepped aboard the submarine.

"Please move the sub a short distance away," Jerry said to Dianne.

"You got it," she replied.

"Are you ready to get wet?" Jerry asked Trang.

"The sooner we do this, the better. I will breathe a lot easier once we get the capsule in the shuttle with the doors closed."

A few minutes later, Jerry and Trang entered the cargo hold. They looked at the still submerged capsule, which was supported only by the winch cable.

"Why do I get the feeling this is a time capsule from the past?" Trang asked.

"Thirty years might have something to do with that."

"Even though I know what's in it, there's almost a sense of mystery to opening it."

"You don't expect any surprises, do you?"

"No, but just looking at it makes me feel like there's something mysterious here."

"Well, let's see, it was sent here by your people on Aphrodite. It contains a combustion chamber, specialized tools, and a few moon rocks. And it has rested undisturbed on the bottom of the lagoon for 30 years. What's mysterious about that?"

"How do you know it's never been disturbed?"

"It's been on the bottom, covered with 1600 feet of water. Who or what would've disturbed it?"

"I don't know if anything has. It just seems mysterious."

"I think you're letting your imagination get the best of you. Let's get this life raft under it," Jerry said as he unrolled it.

Trang and Jerry slipped into the water, and each grabbed a corner on one end of the raft. "Let's dive and pull this under it," Jerry said.

A few seconds later, they surfaced on the other side of the capsule. Jerry hit the inflation trigger, and the raft quickly inflated.

"I believe we have it," Trang said. "Let's get the water out of it and open it."

A half-hour later, the lower cargo doors were closed, and the capsule was secure inside the shuttle. "It's time to find out what kind of shape your combustion chamber is in," Jerry said.

"It's not in the capsule," stated Trang.

"How do you know that? We haven't opened it yet."

"I don't know how, I just have a sinking feeling that it's not in there."

"Before you panic, why don't you just open the capsule and look inside."

Trang grabbed the recessed latch handle and twisted it ninety degrees. He pulled on the door, and it popped open. Jerry immediately looked inside. "You're right!" he exclaimed in shocked surprise. "It's empty."

Trang glanced inside. "It's not entirely empty," he said. "The moon rocks are still there."

Jerry stared into the capsule. "I can't believe your equipment really is missing. What happened to it?"

"I don't know. The capsule hasn't even been broken into. It looks like the thief opened the door, took the equipment, and closed it. Why would he close it after the theft?"

"If we could figure that out, we would know something about the thief," responded Jerry.

"We do know something. The thief was smart enough to figure out how to open the capsule and close it. Also, the thief had an appendage able to grip the door latch."

"There might be a member of the animal community smart enough to do that."

"What would an animal want with our equipment?"

"I don't know, but some animals are curious. What did your equipment look like? Was there anything about it that would attract an animal's attention?"

"The combustion chamber has a polished metallic surface, highly reflective."

"As glossy as a mirror?"

"You could see your reflection in it."

"If an animal was smart enough to find a way into your capsule, they could easily want to run off with that. Are you familiar with the habits of pack rats?"

"No, what are they?"

"They are a species of rats that like to carry away odds and ends that attract their attention."

"Are you suggesting that there is an aquatic animal living at a depth of 1600 feet with the habits of a pack rat?"

"It's a possibility that we should investigate, but it's also possible that your equipment was stolen en route from Aphrodite."

"That seems very unlikely," stated Trang.

"I know, but we don't have any suspects, so we have to consider all possibilities."

"But who would've been in a position to take it, and why would they have taken it?" Trang asked.

"People from Zeb's planet were looking for technology. How do we know Zeb's mission was the only one?"

"Has Zeb ever mentioned other missions?"

"No, but maybe he didn't know. His enemies could've kept a backup mission a secret from him."

"I guess it's even possible that Zeb's country could have launched a secret mission to keep an eye on Zeb's mission. It was, after all, a politically inspired joint mission with their adversaries."

"Zeb's country certainly had reason to be suspicious," agreed Jerry, "but a separate mission just to spy on the joint mission doesn't seem likely."

"Maybe not, but let's run through the scenario anyway."

"Okay, let's consider the timing. How long after your battle with Zeb's enemies did your people on Aphrodite launch the capsule?"

"Three weeks."

"How much time passed between Zeb's landing on Alcent and the attack on your people?"

"I don't know, but they had to build a raft and sail 1600 miles to get to us."

"It seems like they could easily have built a raft in just a few weeks," speculated Jerry, "and with favorable winds, they could've made the voyage in about two months."

"So, if there was a second mission from B-2, and it followed the first by three to five months, it could have arrived here at the right time to rob our capsule," concluded Trang.

"That's right, but it seems like an awesome coincidence that they would've arrived here during that two-day window of opportunity when your capsule was en route from Aphrodite."

"Maybe they were here before that and were in a geosynchronous orbit over our location. They could have been listening to our communications and waiting for our ship."

"What's wrong with that theory is I don't believe they could've understood your language."

"They would not have needed to."

"What do you mean?" Jerry asked.

"From the direction of the communications, they could have learned that we had a base on Aphrodite. They could have observed both of our bases, looking for an opportunity to steal something of technological value."

"So they could've seen the capsule launch and intercepted it," commented Jerry.

"I'm suggesting that it was possible, but I'm not sure they had the ability to pull it off. Keep in mind; they didn't have antimatter propulsion systems, so their ability to maneuver was limited."

"Good point! They were barely able to get here, let alone, make the kind of orbit change required to intercept your capsule and rendezvous with it."

"Also, I don't believe they could have done an en route theft without us knowing about it. Unless they were extremely smooth, it seems like our spacecraft's inertial guidance system would have detected them messing around with it. The spacecraft might even have fired control thrusters to correct for the perturbations. That kind of erratic activity would have attracted our attention."

"Your arguments make it seem very unlikely that your capsule was robbed by people from B-2, but I don't think we can rule it out yet."

"Since we don't have any really good suspects, we can't rule out anything, no matter how farfetched it might seem," stated Trang.

"My pack rat theory is starting to look like the most likely explanation. I think we should go back to the bottom and look around. Let's see if we can find any kind of an animal that looks capable of opening and closing this capsule."

"What would live at 1600 feet?"

"I don't know, but on Earth, life has been found at depths far greater than 1600 feet."

"Well, we have to start our investigation somewhere. We may as well start where the capsule has rested for 30 years."

"We should ask Dianne to come along. She is our chief biologist and will be very interested in any life we might find down there."

Twenty minutes later, Jerry, Trang, and Dianne were at the site where the capsule had rested for such a long time. "Let's inspect this area thoroughly," Jerry said.

"What are we looking for?" Dianne asked.

"Anything that catches your attention. We have a big mystery to solve, and we need to explore these depths anyway. Clear Lake has a deep underwater canyon, and anything we find here might also exist there."

Jerry piloted the submarine over the area so slowly that it seemed to be just drifting. Using the sub's two searchlights, Trang and

Dianne meticulously searched the bottom. Jerry alternately viewed both search areas. He also transmitted sonar signals across the bottom. "I'm not getting any returns to indicate that anything is swimming around down here," he said.

"That doesn't mean your aquatic pack rats aren't here," commented Dianne. "They could be resting among the rocks or in their lairs."

"All of them?"

"Why not?" Dianne asked. "We don't even know what we're looking for, let alone, what its living habits might be."

"True enough," responded Jerry, "but we're looking for an animal big enough to run off with Trang's combustion chamber. If they exist, it seems like we should see some evidence to indicate that."

"I think we have," commented Dianne.

"What do you mean?" questioned Jerry. "All we're seeing is rocky, sandy lake bottom, no sign of life."

"That's the evidence."

"What are you getting at?"

"What happens to fish that die?"

"Something usually eats them," replied Jerry.

"That's right, but before that, depending on the cause of death, some might float to the surface, others might sink. Also, animals washed over the falls might sink, but this bottom is free of skeletons."

"Are you suggesting there are bottom feeders here that eat whatever sinks?"

"It looks that way," replied Dianne.

"Where are they?"

"Sleeping in their lairs or hiding."

"Hiding from what?" Jerry asked.

"Hiding from something that preys on them."

"How do you know those predators are here?"

"I don't, but if there are bottom feeders here, and I believe there are; then, it's likely there's something here that feeds on them. Since the bottom feeders are in hiding, I believe the predators are here."

"You are deducing all of this from the fact that we don't see any skeletons here," noted Trang.

"Yes! Do you see any flaws in my reasoning?"

"No, but if you weren't here, I don't believe I would've come up with all of that. I would've just assumed that we're not seeing any life because of the depth and darkness."

"I see a possible flaw," stated Jerry.

"What's that?" Dianne asked.

"How do you know that dead fish and animals falling to the bottom aren't being consumed by bacteria?"

"That's possible. Bacteria are very good at eating flesh. Eventually, it will completely decompose, but bones are difficult for bacteria to digest. We should see skeletons lying around if there are only bacteria here. I believe something is eating both the flesh and the bones."

"What kind of creatures could do that?" asked Jerry. "Could such creatures open Trang's space capsule and rob it?"

"A bottom feeder that eats dead meat is a scavenger. It's unlikely that it would have the intelligence or curiosity to go into a capsule. We need to find the creatures that prey on the bottom feeders. They are the hunters and might have the curiosity to go into a capsule."

"Why would they?" asked Trang.

"I don't know. We need to find them and see what they look like."

"The best place to look might be at the foot of the falls," commented Jerry. "There should almost always be doomed creatures there."

"It might be dangerous there," warned Trang. "When water falls 500 feet in huge quantities, it creates awesome turbulence. Can this sub handle that?"

"I really don't want to find out. The hull is tough, but I don't want to get banged into rocks. We'll approach the area cautiously and back off at the first sign of danger."

"Good plan!" stated Trang. "Large boulders have also been known to dislodge and tumble over falls. We sure don't need to get hit by one of nature's depth bombs."

Jerry, Trang, and Dianne slowly cruised along a zigzag course toward the falls, exploring the bottom as they went. Forty-five minutes passed by. "We're starting to feel the first bit of turbulence," Jerry said, as he halted forward progress and started to back off.

"Your suspected bottom feeders are nowhere in sight," Trang said to Dianne.

"I know, but I still believe they're here," she responded.

"I am prepared to watch and wait for up to an hour," stated Jerry.

"I don't think we'll have to," Trang said. "Right there, at the limit of my light beam, I see something falling. It looks like a small animal."

Dianne aimed her searchlight at it. With the illumination doubled, it was easier to see. "It is a small, dead animal," she said.

The carcass hit the bottom, and almost immediately, several crab-like creatures converged on it. "Where did they come from?" Jerry asked. "They just seemed to materialize out of nowhere."

"Apparently, they conceal themselves by digging into the sandy gravel between rocks," commented Dianne.

"How do they see when there's so little light down here?" Jerry asked.

"To us, it seems dark, but creatures living here might have eyes that are adapted to the low light level, or they might use echolocation to spot falling carrion."

"I've been listening to the sounds of the lake bottom, and I haven't heard any of the kinds of sounds that creatures might emit for echolocation."

"They have eyes," stated Dianne. "I can see them. Note the shiny spots on the tops of their heads."

"Where are the predators?" Trang asked.

"There must not be any around," commented Jerry. "All that activity on the part of the crabs would certainly attract them."

"I think we should be patient for a while," suggested Dianne.

As time slowly dragged on, the trio watched the large crabs devour the dead animal. First, they stripped away the flesh; then, they used their powerful jaw-like claws to begin the process of grinding and breaking the bones. "They are definitely more powerful than crabs back on Earth," commented Jerry.

"Now we know why we haven't seen any skeletons," Dianne said.

"Whatever preys on these things has to be good at avoiding those bone-crushing claws," stated Trang.

"I am beginning to think such a predator does not exist," Jerry said. "My pack rat theory doesn't look too good at the moment."

"Something stole our equipment, and I don't believe these crabs did."

"The people from B-2 might now be our best suspects," commented Jerry.

"I don't believe they had the maneuvering capability to do that," stated Trang, "so we need to consider the possibility that space travelers from somewhere else took the chamber."

"That's a real long shot. Why would beings smart enough to do interstellar travel want to rob your capsule? They would already have technology equal to or greater than yours."

"That's true, but they may've wanted to evaluate our technology. That combustion chamber is essential to our antimatter propulsion system and would have been a good high-tech find."

"If interstellar travelers took your combustion chamber, we'll never see it again."

"If people from Zeb's planet took it, we'll never see it again either," stated Trang.

"That brings us back to looking for a bottom dwelling creature with pack rat habits," Jerry said, "and so far, we don't have any evidence that such an animal exists."

"That's right," conceded Dianne, "but I still believe one does exist."

"Where do you propose we look for it?"

"I'm just guessing, but I have an idea that makes sense. We are currently at the bottom of a deep underwater canyon that has fairly steep rock walls. If the animals we're looking for happen to be reclusive, they might live in caves in the canyon walls."

"That makes sense," agreed Jerry. "We might as well go look for them now. This feeding frenzy is almost over, and we haven't seen any predators, so I see no point in staying here any longer."

"Let's look at the north wall first," Dianne advised.

"Okay," Jerry replied, as he turned the submarine toward it.

A few minutes later, they approached the rock wall. "I'll cruise a hundred feet off the bottom and a couple hundred feet away from the wall," Jerry said. "If there are any caves, our sonar will find them."

Trang and Dianne looked over Jerry's shoulder at the monitor displaying the sonar data. After just a few minutes, Jerry pointed at the screen and said, "We have a pair of caves. One's only 50 feet off the bottom. The other is nearly 200 feet above the bottom."

"Let's look at the lower one first," suggested Dianne.

Jerry took the submarine down to the level of the cave and slowly approached it. Trang and Dianne aimed searchlights into the cave, while Jerry beamed sonar pulses into it. "This cave is deep," Jerry said.

"The part that I can see looks empty," Trang said.

"A deep cave would make a good lair for animals with a reclusive nature," commented Jerry.

"It's also a safe place to rest," stated Dianne.

"I thought we were looking for a capable, intelligent predator," Jerry said. "Why would it need a safe refuge?"

"We don't know what the animal looks like or what its needs are. This might be a creature that needs to sleep. Maybe the crabs would attack it if it tried to sleep on the bottom."

"I guess that's possible," agreed Jerry, "and the crabs are certainly equipped to inflict serious injury."

"They might even be able to kill a sleeping predator. I was impressed with their bone crunching ability."

"I was too, but they have one shortfall, and that is they can't swim. They're bottom walkers. This means that our mystery creature should be able to safely sleep on any ledge."

"That seems like a reasonable assumption," agreed Dianne. "So before we take the time to explore these caves with recon torpedoes, why don't we scan the wall for ledges?"

"Good plan, but first, let's just take a quick look into the upper cave," stated Jerry, as he began piloting the submarine up to it.

When the trio reached the upper cave and looked into it, they discovered it was also deep and empty as far in as they could see. "There's something about deep caves that intrigues me," Jerry said. "We definitely have to come back and explore them."

Jerry took the submarine up to 400 feet above the bottom and piloted it westward along the rock wall. After five minutes passed by, he announced, "We've just found a ledge. It's 330 feet below us. That would make it 70 feet off the bottom."

"How big is it?" Dianne asked.

"It's about 300 feet long by 30 feet wide at its widest point."

"We should find the animals we're looking for on that ledge," predicted Dianne.

"We're going down slowly. If they're there, I don't want to panic them."

"Also, let's not use our searchlights. Instead, let's use night vision goggles. That way, we won't disturb the natural setting."

"I'll guide us in with sonar while you two look around."

Slowly, Jerry let the submarine drift downward. When he reached the level of the ledge, he very slowly approached it.

"You have to see this!" exclaimed Dianne. "There are octopus-like creatures sleeping all over the place."

"That's not all that's here," stated Trang. "Right there, in the middle of the ledge, is my combustion chamber."

"It's setting on top of a fairly large pile of white rocks with lots of highly reflective crystals in them," commented Dianne. "It looks like your combustion chamber is the centerpiece of some sort of display."

"What's its purpose?" asked Trang. "What I mean is; why would those animals collect those rocks, pile them up like that, and put my combustion chamber on top of the pile?"

"It's the pack rat tendency," commented Jerry.

"I would like to offer another possibility," Dianne said.

"What would that be?" Jerry asked.

"The rocks look like gemstones, and since we haven't seen any on the bottom, they might be rare and difficult to come by. It's possible these creatures look upon them as status symbols. Maybe the male with the biggest pile of decorative rocks gets the most females. This kind of behavior isn't without precedent. Back on Earth, the males in various species do all sorts of things to impress and attract females."

"If you're correct about this species, that would explain why my combustion chamber is so prominently displayed," commented Trang. "It is by far the most highly reflective item they have."

"The biggest animal on the ledge is sleeping right next to it," noted Dianne. "He might be the dominant male, and that rock pile might be his throne."

"If your speculation is correct, he might not take too kindly to us removing the crown jewel from his display," Trang said.

"I'm not sure we need to worry about that," commented Jerry. "I don't think he's big enough to damage this sub."

"It might be dangerous to make that assumption," Dianne warned. "There's quite a bunch of animals on this ledge. We don't know how intelligent they are or if they can communicate and act as a group. What if they all came at us and banged rocks against our hull?"

"Could they do that?" questioned Jerry.

"It looks like they have eight arms or legs or whatever you want to call them. What's interesting is half of those arms have four fingers at the ends, two fingers opposing two fingers. So they can pick things up. The other four arms have jaw-like claws like the crabs. These animals are very well equipped to pick up the crabs and cut them up. And they could pick up rocks and slam them into our sub."

"But how hard could they pound our sub?" Jerry asked. "Have you ever tried to throw a punch when you were underwater? You just simply can't move your arms fast enough to do much damage to an opponent."

"That's a good point, but there are so many animals in this pack that I think we should find a way to recover that combustion chamber without provoking them."

"I agree with her," stated Trang, "and I have an idea how to do that."

"Let's hear it," Jerry said.

"To start with, it looks to me like the grappling claws on your robot arm aren't well suited to picking up my combustion chamber. That means we have to go make something to pick it up with. While we're doing that, let's also make a shiny ornament that's larger and much more impressive than my combustion chamber."

"And use it as a decoy," commented Jerry.

"Right on. We could dangle it a short distance away from this sleeping monarch and make some noise to get his attention. When he sees it, we move away from the ledge. He should follow. Then, we drop it. Hopefully, he'll swim down to the bottom to retrieve it. While he does that, we drop a net around my combustion chamber and haul it to the surface."

"That sounds like a workable plan," stated Dianne, "but we know very little about these animals, so we don't know if they're going to cooperate. For example, the rest of the pack might be on guard duty to protect their display."

"Why would they protect a rock pile?" Jerry asked.

"If it's nothing more than a rock pile, they wouldn't, but that display must have been built for a reason. I don't know for certain what its purpose is, but apparently, it does play a role in their lives."

"Do you have any ideas, other than it being a status symbol for the dominant male?"

"Maybe these animals appreciate the kind of artwork represented by that display. Those rocks weren't just haphazardly piled up. They were carefully arranged into a pyramid."

"Why would they do that?" Jerry asked.

"I don't know, but since that design appeals to them, I think the decoy we build should be shaped like a pyramid. We could even make the angles the same as that one."

"That's a good idea," responded Jerry. "To carry that idea a step farther, let's just build a replica of that display out of shiny metal."

"That should get their attention," commented Trang.

"We'll find out," stated Jerry.

"Do we have everything we need to build it?" asked Dianne. "Or do we need to go up to the Challenger?"

"I think we can improvise something with what we have on the island," replied Jerry. "In fact, it should be easy. We can build a pyramid out of wood, cover it with aluminum foil, and attach a mirror to each side. We can put a few rocks inside it to weight it down."

"I hope it works," commented Trang.

"We'll build a few attention-grabbing backup capabilities into it that we can use if we need to," stated Jerry.

"While you're doing that, I'll make a net to pick up my combustion chamber," volunteered Trang. "All I need is about a hundred feet of rope."

"I think we can scrounge up some rope," responded Jerry. Turning to Dianne, he asked, "Have you seen enough for today? I'd like to get going."

"I would like to spend more time observing these animals. They look like an interesting species."

"When Trang and I leave, you and Moose will have the sub."

"That's good. Let's surface and get you on your way."

"You might even consider spending the night in this area. Trang and I will be back tomorrow morning."

"I'll talk to Moose about that, but it sounds like a good plan."

Twenty-five minutes later, Jerry and Trang were in the cargo shuttle. They took off and headed for Pioneer Island.

TIME: Day 35, 10:00 AM

Jerry and Trang returned to Mystery Lagoon. After bringing the cargo shuttle to a halt, they stepped out onto its left wing and waited for Moose and Dianne, who were approaching with the submarine.

When they arrived, Jerry asked, "How was your night out?"

"I'm happy to say it was pleasant and peaceful," responded Moose. "We weren't threatened by anything. A couple pterodactyls flew over in the moonlight, but they paid no attention to us."

"Over the years, we've camped here occasionally," Trang said. "It was almost always peaceful."

"Why didn't you relocate and live here?" Dianne asked.

"We found security and comfort where we are living and wanted to stay near our shuttle."

"You found 'security and comfort' in the midst of lupusaurs and long-arms?" questioned Dianne.

"Security comes from learning how to deal with known dangers, and our strategies have been effective. But if we can get our shuttle repaired and off the ground, we might move to a better area."

"The first step is to recover your combustion chamber," stated Jerry.

"I'm ready to dive," responded Trang.

"Let's get our stuff."

A few minutes later, Trang and Jerry emerged from the shuttle. Trang was carrying the net he'd made, and Jerry was carrying the pyramid.

Moose looked at Jerry and his pyramid and busted out laughing. "If you put the right decorations on that thing, you might make a Christmas tree out of it," he said.

"You shouldn't be laughing at my artistic creation. I might be sensitive and never try this again."

"That would be a big loss for humanity," responded Moose with a chuckle.

"OK! I've never claimed to be an artist. All I'm trying to do is impress a bunch of animals, especially the head honcho."

"Well, if they're easily dazzled by sparkling glitter, I'm sure that thing will fit the bill."

"We'll soon find out," Jerry said.

A few minutes later, the submarine disappeared beneath the surface with Jerry, Trang, and Dianne onboard. Turning to Dianne, Jerry asked, "Did you and Moose go back down to observe the octopus colony?"

"We've been down twice, yesterday afternoon and this morning."

"Did you see anything that might have a bearing on our present mission?"

"Maybe, but I'm not sure."

"Tell me what you saw."

"Evidently, the big one sitting next to the pyramid is some sort of monarch who gets waited on."

"Why do you think that?"

"This morning, we watched two smaller members of the colony

bring him a crab for his breakfast. The crab was still alive, but its claws had been clipped off."

"I see what you're getting at," stated Jerry. "The implication is that if he's being waited on, he has the ability to communicate with his colony and give orders that are being obeyed. I think we have to assume that he will order his tribe to attack us, if he feels he or his possessions are in jeopardy."

"That's my conclusion," stated Dianne.

"It's difficult to imagine that they could damage this sub enough to put us in danger," commented Trang

"I don't think so either," Jerry said, "but we're going to be cautious and alert anyway."

A few minutes later, Jerry said, "The ledge is directly ahead of us."

"What's your plan?" Dianne asked.

To answer the question, Jerry picked up the glittering pyramid with the submarine's mechanical arm. He extended the arm to its full 25 feet and swung it out to the submarine's left side. He slowly drifted toward the west end of the ledge. "We are going to cruise slowly along the edge of their colony," he said. "I will dangle this thing just above their heads, practically in front of their noses. Then, we'll see what happens."

Cruising only fifteen feet away from the ledge, Jerry dangled his glittering pyramid ten feet in from the edge and just a couple feet above it, almost bumping into some of the animals. "It is getting their attention," he said.

"It sure is," agreed Dianne. "It's almost having an electrifying effect on some of them. It's attracting them like a magnet, and they're starting to follow it."

"It looks like they're actually studying it," stated Trang. "If curiosity is any indication of intelligence, then these animals are quite intelligent."

"That might be," responded Jerry, "but I need to get the attention of the big guy."

"You're almost upon him," Dianne said, "and he is looking."

"Half of his herd is already milling around your monument," noted Trang. "If he senses that his herd is being led away, he has to try to grab that glittering jewel."

Briefly, Jerry set the sparkling pyramid down next to the big guy's homemade pyramid. "Mine is definitely more impressive," Jerry said.

"You need to convince him," stated Dianne.

"If his herd follows you, he'll be convinced," commented Trang.

Jerry lifted the pyramid and headed for the east end of the ledge. "He's following me."

"They all are," stated Dianne. "This is amazing. Why are they so fascinated by that thing?"

"If we knew that, we'd know why they built a pyramid in the first place," responded Jerry.

"The big guy is at the front of the pack," noted Trang.

"And he's reaching for the pyramid," commented Jerry.

"He wants it," Trang said.

"I'm not ready to give it to him just yet," stated Jerry.

"You might not have a choice," Dianne said. "We can't pull away from him. He can swim faster than we can go."

"True enough, but I can tow him away from this area."

"He has used four of his arms to grab it," stated Trang. "How far are you going to pull him?"

"A hundred yards beyond the ledge should do it."

"It doesn't look like he's going to go for that," observed Dianne. "He's let go."

"We're close to the east end of the ledge, so let's just set it down and see what they do."

After parking the pyramid on the ledge, Jerry backed the submarine toward the west. "The big guy is circling it," he said. "It looks like he's trying to decide what to do. Let's hope he's a slow thinker."

It only took a minute to reach the combustion chamber. Jerry quickly dropped the net over it with the mechanical arm and pulled the draw rope tight, closing the net. He lifted the combustion chamber and set it on the forward deck, where it was secured in place by the mechanical arm. Immediately, he put the submarine on a maximum speed course toward the surface.

Jerry beamed sonar pulses toward the ledge. "They're not following us," he said.

"Good!" responded Trang.

Chapter Thirteen

While Jerry and his crew were busy in Mystery Lagoon, Connie and Michelle were entertaining Geniya and Akeyco. They were sitting at an outdoor table in front of the medical lab discussing the cultures of their home planets.

Matthew and Denise interrupted them. "Mom!" Denise exclaimed. "I found a sick squirrel. Can you make it well?"

Connie looked at the limp gray rodent with its long bushy tail hanging lifelessly. "Are you sure it's still alive?" she asked.

"We saw it trying to climb a tree, but it kept falling. It must be alive, because it tried to get away when I caught it."

"How come there's blood on your hand?" Connie asked.

"It tried to bite me when I picked it up."

"It looks like he did bite you."

"He did, but he's so weak, he didn't bite very hard. It's just a little bite. It doesn't even hurt."

Connie took the squirrel and put it on the table. Except for slow, irregular breathing, it did not move.

Taking Denise's hand in hers, Connie looked closely at the bite. "I need to take you to the lab," she said. Turning to Michelle, "Bring the squirrel, but put some gloves on first, and don't let it bite you."

In the lab, Connie squeezed a drop of blood out of Denise's wound and entered it into the blood analysis machine. Connie instructed the machine to look for foreign organisms. She also drew blood from the rodent and put it into the machine.

Connie opened the squirrel's mouth and obtained a saliva specimen. She entered it into the machine. "I hope the germ that made this animal sick isn't in its saliva," she said.

While waiting for the machine to complete its analysis, Connie cleaned and treated her daughter's puncture wound. "That should take care of you for now," she said.

Connie turned to the machine and anxiously looked at the results it was reporting. A deeply worried expression spread across her face. "This isn't good," she said. "The virus is in all three specimens, and it's a nasty looking little bug that's going to be difficult to treat."

"Am I going to get sick?" Denise asked.

"You've been exposed to a bad virus, but I don't know if you're going to get sick."

Turning to Akeyco, Denise said, "I'm not afraid because my mom's a good doctor. If I get sick, she'll make me get well."

"My mother and I are doctors too, and we will help your mother cure you, if you get sick."

"I like you," stated Denise, while giving Akeyco a hug.

Returning Denise's hug, Akeyco said, "I like you too. You are a good girl, and you are brave."

"I am brave, and I am not going to get sick."

"That's a good attitude," responded Akeyco.

Speaking to Matthew, Michelle said, "Why don't you show me where you and Denise found the squirrel."

"Okay," Matthew replied.

"I'm coming along," declared Denise.

The children headed for the door with Michelle following them. "We'll be back soon," Michelle said.

"If you find any sick animals, stay away from them," warned Connie. "I don't know how serious a problem we're dealing with."

"We'll be careful," responded Michelle, "but I do want to look around to see if there are any other sick or dead squirrels there."

"That's a good idea," commented Geniya. "I'm coming with." Turning to Connie, she said, "I would like some gloves and containers, because I might want to bring something back. If my suspicions are correct, I've seen this disease before."

"I don't know if I like the way you said that."

"The disease I suspect is serious, but I think we can cure it. I just need to see some infected animals that are still running around, so I can look for the salient symptoms."

After Geniya stepped out the door, Akeyco said to Connie, "I can fill you in."

"Good! I would like to know what my daughter is in for."

"She might not get sick."

"How will she be affected if she does?"

"This disease attacks the nervous system. The earliest symptoms are disorientation and difficulty in maintaining balance. As the disease progresses, the victim becomes unable to control sustained muscle activity. Something as simple as going for a walk becomes impossible because the nerves the body uses to control muscle activity are damaged by the virus. Finally, the heart muscles shut down because the nerves necessary to their function stop working properly."

"How fast does the disease progress?"

"Ten years ago, one of our people was killed by the disease. Death came a week after he experienced disorientation."

"How old was he?"

"He was my age."

"All of a sudden, you seem very sad. Was this person close to you?"

"He was my twin brother, and we were very close."

"I am truly sorry this tragedy happened in your life. It must have been a difficult time for you and your parents."

"It was a sorrowful time for all of us, especially me. It took me a long time to recover, but some good did come from my brother's death."

"Tell me about that."

"Before he died, I promised him that I would become a doctor and devote my life to keeping people well in our society. I also promised to find a cure for the disease that killed him."

"Did you succeed in that quest?"

"I think so."

"It sounds like you're not certain."

"We don't have extensive lab work backed by large scale testing in the field. All we have are a few successful experiments."

"Tell me what you did."

"I'll start at the beginning. When my brother was ill, we didn't know anything about the disease. We tried to cure him with the antibiotics that we had. But he didn't respond to anything, and we lost him."

"How did you find an effective treatment?"

"Sometimes cures for diseases can be found in nature."

"That's true, but usually, that's a long process of trial and error that can take years."

"We didn't have years, or I should say, we didn't think we had years. We were worried that others in our small group would get sick and die, so we looked for a quicker approach."

"What did you do?"

"To start with, we were reasonably sure that my brother got the disease from a sick gray squirrel. They are numerous where we live. In fact, they've been part of our diet from time to time. My brother shot one with a slingshot. It wasn't quite dead, and it bit him when he picked it up."

"Did he dress it out, cook it, and eat it?"

"Yes!"

"Even though it was sick?"

"We didn't know it was sick."

"How do you know it was the source of your brother's exposure to the disease?"

"Within days of my brother's illness and death, we started finding sick and dying squirrels."

"So you suspected the squirrel that bit your brother was sick; even though, you had no direct evidence?"

"I believe the circumstantial evidence we had was overwhelming."

It seems that way, but you haven't yet told me how you found a cure."

"I'm getting to that. I had to give you some background information first. Like I said, those squirrels are numerous in our area and have been part of our diet. They've always been healthy and robust at reproducing and maintaining their numbers. When they started getting sick, we asked ourselves if anything had changed in their environment to make them susceptible to illness. In 20 years, we'd never seen them be anything other than healthy, so we wanted an explanation."

"Did you find one?"

"Yes. In our area, there is a nut-producing bush that grows on rocky terrain that isn't able to support large trees. These bushes blossom and produce nuts three times a year. The squirrels collect and store them. The nuts are their main source of food, so we call them squirrel nuts."

"What do the nut bushes have to do with the illness?"

"We noticed that the sick squirrels seemed a little underweight, so we investigated the nut bushes. We found them to be diseased and producing stunted nuts inside normal shells. The squirrels were busy chewing into shells that didn't contain much food, so they had to lose weight."

"Why would being slightly underweight cause them to be susceptible to disease?"

"It shouldn't, and that's the point."

"So you suspected that there might be a natural substance in healthy nuts that gave the squirrels what they needed to resist the disease?"

"It seemed like a good possibility, so we checked it out."

"How?"

"We didn't have the sophisticated equipment needed to do a thorough analysis of the nuts to identify the chemicals in them, so we had to use a different approach. With our airplane, we traveled to a different area, and we were able to find a supply of healthy squirrel nuts. We picked a couple bags full and brought them home to feed to sick squirrels. Some were too weak to chew the nuts, so we crushed some of the nuts into paste-like nut butter for them. Five of the seven animals we fed fully recovered."

"That's very convincing for the squirrels, but how do you know that feeding squirrel nuts to my daughter will cure her if she becomes ill?"

"I was accidentally bitten while feeding a sick squirrel, so I ate large quantities of the nuts every day for a week, and I did not get sick."

"But there's no way to know if the nuts kept you from getting sick. You may simply have had a stronger immune system than your brother had."

"That's possible, but if we can find squirrel nut bushes here that are diseased, and if we can find sick squirrels with the same symptoms as when my brother died, then, I think we'd better find some healthy squirrel nuts and get Denise started eating large quantities every day for at least a week. They are, after all, good healthy food. There are no dangerous side effects, so what do you have to lose with this therapy?"

"In view of your brother's tragic death and your avoidance of the disease, that does seem like a prudent approach. But before we start feeding squirrel nuts to Denise, I am going to run some of them through our robot lab. It is a very good piece of equipment and should be able to identify all the chemicals in the nuts. I want to make sure there aren't any toxins. Also, we might find one or more chemicals that would seem to have medicinal properties."

"If so, maybe we can isolate them and make a potent medicine."

"We will pursue all possibilities. Whatever it takes, we are going to keep Denise alive and healthy."

"There is another test you should run."

"What do you have in mind?"

"It would be helpful if we could determine exactly how the squirrels get sick. What is the source of the virus? How does it get into so many squirrels at about the same time?"

"Something tells me you have a theory about that."

"I have often wondered if the same microbe that causes the blight in the nut bushes also causes the squirrels to get sick."

"Why do you think that might be possible?"

"The diseased nut bushes still produce nuts, but they are deformed and very small. However, the squirrels do eat them, and what they're eating might contain the virus that makes them sick. In the process of infecting the nut bushes, the virus might be transformed into a form that is able to infect squirrels."

"But you also think there is a chemical in the nuts that kills the virus and keeps squirrels from getting sick."

"I believe that chemical exists in healthy nuts."

"What you're saying is that the virus that infects the bushes thrives because it prevents the bushes from producing the chemical that would kill the virus. In effect, the virus is creating for itself a safe home inside the nut shells where it can live until the squirrels show up for dinner. Then, it can move on to its animal host."

"I believe that is what's happening."

"But why does the virus need to move on to an animal?"

"It might need to live in an animal to transform itself back into the form that is able to infect the nut bushes," replied Akeyco.

"You're outlining a very complex lifecycle for what is nothing more than a microorganism. It reminds me of butterflies. They lay eggs, which hatch into caterpillars, which metamorphose into butterflies, which lay eggs and repeat the cycle."

"I know I might be sounding farfetched, but I think the virus does have a lifecycle involving changes in form. If we could prove it; then, we could find the best way to interrupt the cycle and eradicate the virus. Unfortunately, our best medical equipment is in our starship on Aphrodite, and I haven't been able to run the tests I need to run to get definite answers."

"I can run the tests, and we'll do that as soon as we find some healthy and diseased nuts."

"Let's join the others and see what exists here."

"What about this squirrel?"

"If it has the disease we've been discussing, it won't live more than a day or two without treatment. It already has irregular heart rhythm."

"If we could cure it, I would have more confidence in treating my daughter."

"Your machine isolated the bug, and you've looked at it. Do you think any of your antibiotics will kill it?"

"The machine said no, so we have to hope that the disease is what you think it is. And we have to find a supply of the nuts you've been talking about."

"Let's go see what my mother has found."

Connie and Akeyco walked toward the northeast corner of Stellar Plateau. Geniya met them and said, "It looks like the disease we're familiar with. All the signs are here. Look at these nut bushes. They are blighted. The only squirrels I've seen were wandering aimlessly in a disoriented state."

"We need to capture them," stated Akeyco. "Then, we need to find some healthy nut bushes."

"Since you're on crutches, you should let us capture the squirrels," responded Michelle.

"I would like to do something to help."

"You've already given us crucial information," stated Connie.

"I would like to do more. Let me have one of your RPVs, and I will search this island for the nuts we need."

"Most of this island is already on video. Your search will be quicker if you start with that. When you find the areas with nut bushes, I'll help you look at them with an RPV."

"That does sound like the fastest way," agreed Akeyco.

"I'll wander around here on the plateau and see if I can find some nut bushes that aren't blighted," Geniya said.

"I'll go with you," stated Michelle.

TIME: Day 35, 2:00 PM

Jerry, Moose, Dianne, and Trang arrived from Mystery Lagoon. Connie briefed them about Denise's exposure to a potentially fatal disease. She finished her briefing with, "So far we haven't located any healthy nuts. For some reason, they've all been hit with blight."

"Have you looked at video from the other islands in this lake?"

267

"We've started, but so far, our search has been fruitless. Somehow, the blight has spread to all the islands."

"It could have been spread by birds or even the wind," commented Dianne.

"We have nearly two months of video from the countryside," stated Jerry. "Have you looked at any of that?"

"Are you referring to the video from the cameras on the sauropod's head?" Connie asked.

"Yes! Those sauropods wander over a lot of real estate. Most of it is open, because they tend to knock down trees that get in their way."

"The nut bushes like open areas," stated Akeyco. "They need lots of sunshine."

"It's going to take a long time to look at all that video," commented Dianne.

"I will put everyone on the project," stated Jerry. "In less than a half-hour, we'll find some healthy nuts. Then, we'll get on the chopper and go harvest them."

"What if we don't find any?" Connie asked.

"Then we go to the Crater Lake area and get some," stated Trang.

"Do you know where some are?" Jerry asked.

"The squirrels are part of our diet. The bushes are where we hunt squirrels."

"Maybe we should fly down there and get some," suggested Dianne.

"I don't think that will be necessary," commented Moose. "I think I know where some are."

"Where?" Jerry asked.

"When I was stranded on the back of a styracosaurus a couple weeks ago, I had ample opportunity to look around. There was a rocky area that had a lot of nut bushes growing in it."

"Are they the kind of nuts we're looking for?" Jerry asked.

"I don't know, but there were gray squirrels scrambling around."

"I think we should fly over there and take a look," suggested Akeyco.

"I know your determination," commented Geniya, "but your broken ankle has not yet healed. You should stay here. I will go along to make sure we get the right kind of nuts."

"Are you ready to go?" Jerry asked Geniya.

"Anytime you are."

"If my wife is going to put herself in danger, I need to be there with a rifle," stated Trang.

"Your marksmanship might get tested," commented Jerry. "We've flirted with death every time we've been over there."

"I can handle a rifle," stated Trang.

"I'd like to come along," Dianne said.

"It looks like I have my crew," stated Jerry. "Let's go."

"I'll grab a couple RPVs," Moose said. "We might need them."

A half-hour later, Jerry and his crew were in the helicopter circling the area where Moose thought they might find some squirrel nuts. Geniya was searching it with binoculars. "I found some," she said.

"Are they healthy?" Jerry asked.

"They look good, but we need to get closer,"

"That might be a problem," commented Trang. "There's a large herd of big dinosaurs there."

"I believe that's the local styracosaurus herd," Moose said.

"Maybe we can scare them away with this chopper," suggested Trang.

"I really don't think so," responded Moose. "They stand their ground against T-Rexes. It's hard to imagine that they would be spooked by this bird, which was designed for quiet operation."

"We'll soon know," commented Jerry, as he headed toward the bushes and the herd.

As Moose predicted, members of the herd glanced at the helicopter only briefly and then went back to whatever they were doing. Some were grazing while others were resting and looked like they were contentedly chewing on something.

Geniya studied the bushes. "It looks like we have a supply of healthy nuts," she said. "It's too bad they are in the midst of a dinosaur herd."

"Let me use the binoculars," requested Moose.

Geniya handed them to Moose. "Circle the herd slowly," he said to Jerry.

Moose focused on one animal after another. Finally, he said, "There's the one I'm looking for."

"Why that one?" Trang asked.

"That's the one I rode for an hour."

"How do you know it's that one? They all look the same."

Moose handed the binoculars to Trang. "Look at his neck shield. Do you see that L-shaped scar?"

"Yes!"

"That's the one I rode."

"He might be the biggest one in the herd," noted Trang.

"He's the herd leader," stated Moose.

"Now that we've found him, what do you plan to do?" Trang asked.

"I am going to approach him from upwind and let him get my scent. If he's not alarmed, I'm going to walk into the herd and pick some nuts."

"Are you crazy?" exclaimed Trang.

"No! I've been there before, and they tolerated my presence. Since they weren't concerned about me then, why would they be now?"

"That sounds good, but I don't like it," stated Dianne. "I'm coming with, so I can cover you."

"I understand your concern, but I have to do this alone. Old L-Scar is familiar with me and my scent. I don't think this is the right time to throw a new scent at him."

"I was with you the last time you approached him. He should know my scent."

"Maybe, but maybe not. As you will recall, he stepped forward one step and flared his nostrils while smelling me. He does have my scent. He might not have yours, and I don't want to confuse him with a new scent. Besides, why risk two lives when it's only necessary to risk one?"

"Why do you have to be so difficult to argue with?"

"I'm just being reasonable."

"That's debatable, but I'll agree with you and cover you from this chopper."

"That, I appreciate."

"Let me have the binoculars," requested Moose.

Trang handed them to Moose, who used them to study the grass as it was hit by light gusts of breeze. "Set me down right over there," he said to Jerry. "That will put me about 40 yards upwind from L-Scar."

A half-minute later, Moose stepped out of the helicopter wearing an empty backpack. Strapped to his waist was a 10.5 mm pistol armed with explosive bullets. He carried his .44-caliber rifle, which was also armed with explosive bullets.

Jerry climbed 100 feet above Moose. Dianne sat in an open door on the helicopter's left side. Her feet rested on a bar just below and outside the door. Supported by a safety belt, she leaned out the door and searched the grass and shrubs around Moose. Her .35-caliber rifle was pointed at the ground. She held it with her trigger finger ready for action. Armed with a .44-caliber rifle, Trang did guard duty from the helicopter's right side.

Slowly, Moose turned completely around, studying his surroundings with a searching gaze. Satisfied that there was no immediate threat, he looked at L-Scar. The animal was peacefully grazing on vegetation that looked like wild pea vines in full bloom.

Moose wore a headband that his communicator was attached to. He had taped the microphone to his chin. A small speaker hung just above his right ear.

"It's time to do what I came here for," stated Moose, as he started walking toward the big dinosaur. "He should remember me. It's only been a couple weeks."

"Be careful," warned Dianne. "That's a very big animal you're approaching."

"It's because of his size that I am not worried about him. What I am worried about are the smaller animals, like the saber tooth that almost killed Connie. Please cover my back."

"You're covered," stated Dianne and Trang in unison.

Moose continued walking toward L-Scar. When he was about ten yards away, he stopped and said, "So far, he's ignoring me. Apparently, he just doesn't see me as any kind of a threat."

"I'm not sure you should make that assumption," responded Dianne.

"I've seen how these animals react to known enemies, and believe me, they do not ignore them. I believe I am safe."

Moose started walking. "I am going to pick some nuts," he said.

Just then, L-Scar lifted his head, looked at Moose, flared his nostrils, and sniffed several times. Then, he stepped toward Moose, who had already stopped walking.

"You're not as safe as you think you are," stated Dianne.

"Don't shoot!" commanded Moose. "I don't believe I am in danger. I think this brute remembers me and just wants to say hello."

Moose stood still and waited while L-Scar approached him. He reached out as far as he could with his right arm. L-Scar stopped, touched his nose to Moose's hand, and sniffed. Satisfied with the scent, the big dinosaur turned to his left and stepped forward a couple yards. This left Moose facing the animal's right shoulder.

L-Scar twitched his shoulder muscles, attracting Moose's attention. Moose immediately spotted the problem. "It looks like you picked up a couple more of those pesky sty-ticks," he said.

The big dinosaur, once again, twitched the muscles under the sty-ticks. "I think you're trying to tell me you want them removed, and you're too big to argue with, so I'd better get busy."

Moose shouldered his rifle and drew his hunting knife. He reached up and slid the knife's edge under the tick. Twisting the knife a bit, he pried the tick's inch-long suction tube out of the dinosaur. The tick dropped to the ground, where Moose stepped on it. Having gorged itself with dinosaur blood to the point of being bloated, the tick popped like a balloon, leaving a splotch of blood on the ground and on the bottom of Moose's boot. A few drops of blood oozed out of the dinosaur's puncture wound.

Moose repeated the process with the other sty-tick. Then, he backed up a couple steps and visually inspected L-Scar's right side. "It looks like that should take care of you for now. Anyway, I have to go pick some nuts. I guess you could come along and stand guard if you want."

Moose backed away from the big dinosaur while warily keeping an eye on him. He had already put his knife back into its sheath and now had his rifle in hand.

L-Scar turned his head to the right and watched Moose turn and walk toward the bushes. The big dinosaur hesitated for a few moments; then, he turned toward Moose and followed him.

"L-Scar is following you!" Dianne exclaimed, sounding very alarmed.

"Don't shoot!" ordered Moose. "He's not going to attack. If he felt threatened by me, I would already be dead."

"Why is he following you?"

"I invited him to."

"There's no way that he understood your invitation."

"How do you know that? We don't know how intelligent these animals are."

"I don't care how smart he is. There's no way that he could understand English."

"That's true, but he might've sensed that I like him and desire his protection. He might be doing nothing more than giving me safe passage into the middle of his herd."

"He might be keeping an eye on you to make sure you're not a threat to the herd."

"If he saw me as a threat, I would not be allowed into the herd."

"So why is he following you?"

"He might be curious. This is only his second encounter with humans, and he obviously remembers the first encounter. He even remembered that I removed sty-ticks from him. I believe he's quite intelligent as far as animals go, so it is reasonable to expect him to be curious."

"You might be right, but it makes me nervous to see him following you so closely."

"Is he doing anything threatening?"

"No, he's just following you."

"Stay alert, but don't shoot unless I'm clearly under attack."

"By then, it might be too late."

Moose looked back over his right shoulder without slowing his pace. "He is kind of close," he commented.

"That's why I'm nervous."

"I know, but if he wanted me dead, he would charge. Right now, he reminds me of a big German shepherd following his master."

"I don't know how you can be so calm with a ten-ton dinosaur barely five yards behind you."

"Call it intuition if you want, but I just don't believe this guy means me any harm."

"What do you think he's going to do when you stop walking and start picking nuts?"

"We'll know in a couple minutes, but it's interesting to note that I've walked by three of his herd members, and they ignored me. Maybe this guy likes me and really is making sure I get safe passage into the herd."

"You just implied that he has emotions and the ability to think."

"Well, maybe he does. I was on his back when he orchestrated the defense against the T-Rex pack. His strategy was well executed, and it was effective."

Moose walked another 30 yards with L-Scar following. Arriving at the first nut bush, he said, "This bush looks healthy."

Moose walked around the bush, so he could see L-Scar while picking nuts. Rifle in hand, he faced the big styracosaurus. "I don't know why you're following me, but I have to pick some nuts. Are you going to behave, or do I have to shoot you?"

L-Scar stopped walking and faced Moose with an inquisitive looking stare in his eyes. "I can't believe this," commented Moose. "It looks like this beast is trying to get to know me."

"It's possible that he might be intelligent enough to see humans as something new in his world," responded Dianne.

"Well, it definitely looks like he's studying me."

"I hope that's all he does."

"Why should he do anything else?"

"He's a wild animal."

"I know, but he has never been taught to fear humans."

"That's true, but I wish he weren't so close to you. He could kill you."

"I know he could, but animals don't necessarily kill just because they can. Back on Earth, animal trainers frequently work with animals that could easily kill them. Despite that possibility, most trainers die of old age."

"I hope you're not planning to train this beast."

"No, but L-Scar seems to be doing more than just tolerating my presence. He seems to be entertained by my presence."

"It does look that way, but I wish you would pick the nuts and get out of there."

"Okay, watch him closely, I am going to lay my rifle down and get busy."

Moose leaned his rifle against a rock and removed the pack from his back. He started picking nuts, and L-Scar watched him.

"These nuts do look healthy," he said.

"To make sure they are, you need to crack a few of them," stated Geniya.

Moose placed a couple nuts on a large rock. He picked up a fist-sized rock and hit them with it. The shells cracked open, exposing the nuts. Moose picked them up and examined them. "These things remind me of hazelnuts," he said, "and they look good. I feel like eating them."

"Wait until we test them," warned Dianne.

"Okay, but I am going to stuff this bag, because they look really good, and they're making me hungry."

"You're always hungry."

"That's because my highly refined sense of taste allows me to appreciate the subtle flavor variations in good food."

"If he were still on Earth, he would probably be a premier judge at gourmet food competitions," stated Jerry, with a bit of laughter.

Moose ignored Jerry's comment and moved from bush to bush, rapidly filling the bag. L-Scar watched him for a while; then, he turned and looked away for a few moments. He returned his gaze to Moose, dropped to his knees, and then down onto his stomach. He blinked his eyes a few times, and then, closed them.

"I guess I wore him out," commented Moose. "He seems to be taking a nap."

"Why don't you finish picking the nuts and get out of there," stated Dianne.

"It seems like I am perfectly safe here," responded Moose. "This big guy wouldn't be sleeping if there were any predators around. Maybe this would be a good time to climb onto his back and go for another ride."

"No way," stated Dianne.

"I was just kidding."

"That's what you told me the last time you got onto his back. Get the nuts and let's get out of here."

"OK! You don't have to be so adamant about it. A guy just can't have any fun around here anymore."

"There are safer places to have fun than on the back of a styracosaurus," responded Dianne.

"I don't know about that. Here in the countryside, L-Scar's back just might be one of the safer places to be."

"You might be right, but I will feel better when you're back onboard."

"My bag is full, so I'm heading for the pickup point."

Moose walked out of the herd without incident. He boarded the waiting helicopter, and a few minutes later, all were back on Pioneer Island.

Dianne and Connie crushed some of the nuts, prepared specimens, and entered them into the automated lab for analysis. Within minutes, the lab reported its findings.

Connie directed the lab's computer to compare the results to the analysis obtained earlier for the diseased nuts and report the differences. The formulas for two complex organic chemicals appeared on the monitor along with the notation that they were present in the healthy nuts. The monitor also displayed an image of a complex microorganism and indicated that it was present in the diseased nuts but not in the healthy nuts.

"It looks like Akeyco's theory is correct," noted Connie.

"That's possible," agreed Dianne, "but if these chemicals are toxic to the virus, I wonder how they kill it."

"It will take some experimentation to find out," responded Connie. "But for right now, the most important thing the lab is telling us is that these nuts are not toxic to humans, and that means we can add them to my daughter's diet. I sure hope they are nature's cure for the virus she's carrying."

"It worked for me," stated Akeyco. "I was bitten. I made the nuts a major part of my diet, and I never got sick. Also, most of the sick squirrels I fed were cured."

"That's all very encouraging," responded Connie.

Chapter Fourteen

TIME: Day 36, 8:30 AM

Jerry, Trang, Mike, and Moose were sitting at an outdoor table in front of the habitation capsule enjoying coffee and tea. "How is Denise this morning?" Trang asked.

"She's still her usual self, full of energy and curious about everything," Jerry replied.

"That indicates the virus hasn't yet had any effect on her."

"My wife did a blood test a short time ago, and the virus count has gone up only a little."

"That's very encouraging," commented Trang.

"It is, but I will feel better when the virus has been eliminated."

"We have four competent doctors working on that problem," stated Trang. "They are a capable team, and they have excellent equipment to work with. They will cure your daughter."

"I hope so, but I can't help worrying about her."

"I understand how you feel; I lost my son to this virus."

"That must have been very difficult for you."

"It was a tough blow. I was heartbroken for a long time, but there wasn't any way I could bring him back."

"That must have been hard on you."

"It was, but unfortunately, there are tragedies in life that we have to accept. We do what we can to prevent them, but when they happen, we must accept them and move on."

"Right now, we have a medical team that is working hard to prevent Denise from becoming a tragedy."

"They will be successful," Trang assured Jerry.

"You bet we will," declared Connie, who had just arrived on the scene. "We're going to run several experiments to find alternate ways to kill the virus, just in case the natural drugs in the nuts fail."

"Let me know if there's anything I can do to help," Jerry said.

"Thanks, there is something we need. Some of the experiments we want to run require the equipment and microgravity on the Challenger. Dianne will perform the tests, but she needs a ride."

"I could take her up," offered Moose.

"I need to go up too," Mike said. "I want to start building my Aphrodite lander." Turning to Moose, he said, "You can join my crew since you're going to be up there anyway."

"Be happy to. It sounds like an interesting project."

"I have a combustion chamber that needs refurbishing," stated Trang. "I've been led to believe that you have an excellent machine shop on your starship."

"We do," responded Jerry, "and I've always enjoyed working in it."

"Sounds like you just volunteered to refurbish the combustion chamber," commented Mike with a broad grin.

"I got the same impression," Trang quickly said.

"I'm not sure how you guys came to that conclusion," reacted Jerry. "The term 'combustion chamber' wasn't mentioned anywhere in my remark."

"Your feigned reluctance doesn't fool me," stated Mike. "You're just as curious about Trang's technology as I am, and I know you want to work on that chamber."

Trang closely observed Jerry's eyes and facial expression. "I can see that Mike is right," he said. "So if you'll help me refurbish it, I'll tell you how it works and answer your questions."

"You got yourself a deal," responded Jerry.

"That was some pretty tough negotiating you did," Mike said to Jerry. "But I'm wondering how you guys are going to install the thing after you've rebuilt it."

"What do you mean?" Jerry asked.

"It's my understanding that you need some special tools that haven't been recovered."

"That's true," replied Jerry, "but I can make the tools if Trang can provide the specs."

"I can do that," Trang said.

"It seems strange that your bottom-dwelling pack rats didn't put the tools on display with the combustion chamber," commented Mike.

"The tools don't shine like the combustion chamber," stated Trang. "They're just a dull metallic gray."

"If that's the case, maybe they never took the tools," responded Mike.

"That is possible," admitted Trang. "When we opened the capsule and saw that the combustion chamber was gone, we assumed that the tools were gone too. There are some moon rocks in the capsule. Maybe the tools are under them."

"We should take a look before we leave," Jerry said. "There's no sense making new tools, if we don't need to."

"I'd like to see the moon rocks," Mike said.

"I'll drive," offered Moose.

"See you guys when you get back," Connie said, as the men stepped into the ATV for the short drive to the south end of the plateau.

"We won't be gone long," responded Jerry. "I want to get Dianne to the Challenger as soon as possible, so she can get started with her experiments."

"She'll be ready when you return."

A few minutes later, Moose parked the ATV next to the capsule. Trang hopped out and eagerly opened it. He reached in and removed a rock. "This doesn't look like a moon rock," he said. "It resembles the rocks in the pack leader's pyramid, and there are several more of them in there."

"Why would they put glittering rocks in the capsule?" Jerry asked.

"I don't know," replied Trang, "but I can speculate. This capsule was a one-of-a-kind thing in their world. It was something to be possessed. Maybe the pack leader uses these sparkling rocks to mark his territory and put some of them in the capsule just to tell others that the capsule belonged to him."

"But what would he do with the capsule?" Jerry asked.

"I don't know. Let's get all the rocks out and see if there's anything special about them." One by one, Trang handed the rocks to Jerry and Mike.

"I wonder where they got them," questioned Mike. "It's unusual that they could find rocks that are all spherical and about six inches in diameter. How could these things form in nature?"

"You're the geologist," commented Moose. "You should be able to figure that out."

"Solving that problem is definitely on my list of things to do."

"I wonder why the bottom dwellers collected them," questioned Jerry.

"Maybe they place value on these rocks," speculated Moose. "To them, they might be jewels."

"Are you implying they were using my capsule as a treasure chest?" Trang asked.

"Why not? It has a door that can be opened and closed, and they have nothing else like it."

"If your speculation is correct, it's possible we stole the crown jewels," commented Trang.

"That's a possibility," agreed Moose.

"Let's see what else they put in there," Trang said, as he returned to removing rocks from the capsule.

A few moments later, he exclaimed, "You're not going to believe this!" For all to see, Trang held up a knife with a shiny metal blade about ten inches long and a plastic handle with jewels set in it.

"Why would your people on Aphrodite send you a knife?" Jerry asked.

"My people did not send me this knife."

Jerry was shocked as the full impact of Trang's statement struck him. "Where did it come from?" he asked.

"I wish I knew," replied Trang.

"Even more important than where the knife came from, I want to know how old it is," stated Jerry. "If it's fairly new, we might have an urgent mystery to solve. If it's an artifact from an ancient civilization, we can take our time investigating its origin."

"I might be able to determine how old it is," stated Mike.

"How?" Jerry asked.

Mike reached for the knife, and Trang handed it to him. While visually inspecting it, Mike said, "I can use the lab equipment on the Challenger to determine precisely what this knife is made out of. If there is a rate of decay for any of the basic elements, I can use that to date the knife. If there is a rate of deterioration for the metal alloy or the plastic handle, I can use that."

"It sounds to me like there are a couple pretty big *ifs* in your dating scenario."

"I know, but I believe I can come up with a fairly accurate estimate of how old this knife is. When we get to the Challenger, I'll put my crew to work building the moon lander; then, I'll tackle the age problem. I might need an hour or two to get you an answer."

"That'll work. Let me look at the knife."

Mike handed it to Jerry. After briefly examining it, he said, "This knife is extremely well made. It looks like some advanced technology went into its manufacture, and that would eliminate people just entering the age of metals."

"That's my feeling too," agreed Mike.

Jerry gripped the knife by its handle. "I would be comfortable using it," he said. "That indicates its owner had hands about the same size and shape as mine."

"I wonder how the octopus colony took the knife away from its owner," questioned Mike.

"Maybe he accidentally dropped it in the lake," responded Trang.

"Or he may have tragically lost his life," commented Moose.

"How do you think that happened?" Jerry asked.

"He could've been fishing a safe distance upriver above the falls. If he got lucky and hooked a big one, he may've been so preoccupied with landing it that he failed to notice that the river was carrying him too close to the falls. When he realized his peril, it was too late."

"Leave it up to Moose to invent a tragedy connected with a fishing story," commented Mike.

"Well, it could've happened that way," insisted Moose.

"The possibility does exist," agreed Jerry. "And that means we need to explore the river above the falls to see if anyone is living up there or if anyone ever has."

"The owner of that knife had to live somewhere around here," stated Moose.

"Let me find out how old it is before we start looking," suggested Mike. "If it's 100,000 years old, we'll have to conduct a different search than if it's less than 50 years old."

"Let's see if there are any other surprises in this capsule," Trang said, as he went back to removing rocks.

A minute later, he said, "I found my tools, and there aren't any moon rocks in there."

"Apparently, the octopus leader got rid of them because they didn't glitter enough," commented Jerry.

"Or he got rid of them because he thought they marked the capsule as someone else's territory," commented Trang.

"Who knows what goes through the minds of those beasts," Moose said.

"If they also live in Clear Lake, that's a question we need to explore," commented Jerry. "But for now, I'm glad we found the tools. We have one less thing to make. Is there anything else in that capsule? If not, let's head for the Challenger."

Trang stuck his upper body into the capsule and looked around. After a few moments, he backed out and said, "It's empty, except for this."

"What's that?" asked Jerry.

"I believe it's a belt buckle with a large emblem."

"That supports my tragedy theory," argued Moose.

"In what way?" Jerry asked.

"If the man had accidentally dropped his knife into the lake, the bottom dwellers would not have the belt buckle, only the knife."

"You're assuming the belt buckle and the knife came from the same individual," responded Jerry.

"That seems like a reasonable assumption," stated Moose.

"I'll take the belt buckle and the knife to the lab," Mike said. "Maybe metallurgical analysis can place both objects in the same society, and maybe I can date them to the same time period."

"I'd like to have that information as soon as you get it," Jerry said.

"We might be able to get some additional information from this emblem," commented Trang. "There is an elaborate diagram here, along with some inscriptions. This could be nothing more than artwork, but it's also possible that there's a story here about the race this came from."

"Let me look at that," requested Mike.

After examining it for a few moments, Mike said, "My wife might be able to help us with this. She seems to have an intuitive talent for reading the messages in this kind of artwork."

"Let's put an image of this in the computer," Jerry said. "Then, she can study it and give us her insight."

"I'll do that when we get back," responded Mike.

"I don't think there's anything more to be gained here," Jerry said, "so let's go pick up Dianne and head for space."

"I am ready," exclaimed Trang. "I haven't been in space in 30 years, and now, I get to visit an alien starship."

"I believe this is the first time we've been referred to as aliens," commented Mike.

"*Alien* is a relative term," responded Trang.

"I know, but each race tends to think of itself as the center of everything and think of others as aliens. I've just never thought of myself as an alien."

"Being in the interstellar exploration business, I've often found that it's beneficial to see myself as the alien. It tends to give me better insight into what members of the other race might be thinking."

"When you two get done philosophizing, maybe we could get going," stated Moose.

Trang and Mike stared at Moose for a few moments; then, Mike said, "If we were talking about food or fishing, he wouldn't be in such a big hurry."

"I think you're probably right," agreed Trang, "but I am eager to see your ship."

A few minutes later, the men were back at the habitation capsule. Mike approached Michelle and silently handed her the belt buckle. It immediately sparked her interest, and she studied it for a few moments. "Where did you get this?" she asked.

"It was in the space capsule, along with this knife."

Michelle examined the knife, but she returned to the belt buckle. "It seems like I've seen something similar to this before," she said.

"Really, how could you? I mean where?"

"Back on Earth."

"Are you serious?"

"Yes, when I was a science reporter, archaeology was one subject that fascinated me. I'd published a few articles on artwork found on walls in caves. That was ten years ago, and I'm searching my memory, but something about this looks familiar."

"Wow!" exclaimed Mike. "This belt buckle may have been brought here by a race that also visited Earth."

"I know," responded Michelle. "This belt buckle might add support to Akeyco's common origin theory."

"How long will it take your memory to come up with something concrete?"

"If I rely only on my memory, it might take a while, but all archaeological knowledge ever gained on Earth is in our computers. So I will enter this image into the computer and ask it to find similar artwork from Earth. We'll see what comes up."

"I'm excited about this," stated Mike.

"I am too," Michelle said, as she and Mike took the emblem to a computer terminal. With a digital camera, they placed the image in the computer. They also took pictures of the knife from several perspectives and entered them into the computer.

"I am going to take these items to the lab on the Challenger and find out what they're made out of and how old they are," Mike said. "Let's compare notes later today."

"Okay," replied Michelle.

"Let's head for space," stated Jerry.

Twenty minutes later, Jerry was seated in the personnel shuttle preparing it for takeoff. As a matter of professional courtesy, Jerry allowed Trang to sit in the copilot's seat.

Jerry fired up the nuclear reactor and fed high-pressure steam through the turbine. Shifting the propeller into gear, he taxied out of South Bay and immediately poured on the steam, bringing the turbine up to full power. The shuttle rapidly accelerated to 45 mph, rose up out of the water, and glided on its hydrofoils. The ease with which the shuttle accomplished this seemed to indicate that it had a mind of its own that was yearning for a speedy return to space. It seemed eager to unleash its immense power and demonstrate its ability to perform its mission.

Wanting to show off his shuttle to Trang, Jerry fired its nuclear thermal rocket at full power, and it came to life with a thundering roar. The immediate 2g acceleration hit everyone hard, pressing them firmly back into their seats. In just a few seconds, Jerry rotated the shuttle into a steep climb.

"We're on our way," Trang exclaimed, jubilantly.

As propellant was depleted, the flight control computer steadily increased acceleration to 3g. Five-and-a-half minutes after taking off, the shuttle arrived in orbit, less than a mile from the Challenger.

Noticing how close they were to the starship, Trang said, "Excellent timing on the takeoff."

"We managed to hit our launch window right to the second," responded Jerry. "Then, our auto-pilot adjusted our acceleration and flight path to bring us into orbit at the right time and place."

"Your starship is an impressive sight."

"We'll be in the hangar in a matter of minutes."

"I am looking forward to a tour of your ship."

"In return, I expect a tour of your ship."

"My ship is crippled. We have to get it off of Aphrodite before I can show you around."

"Mike will deliver to your crew what they need to make temporary repairs and get it back in space. Then, I would like to see it."

"You got it, but it will still be a crippled ship in need of major reconstruction."

"We're here," Jerry said, as he guided the shuttle into the hangar. The hangar door automatically closed, and the hangar was pressurized. In a state of weightlessness, Jerry and his passengers floated out of the shuttle.

"This hangar is where we'll build your Aphrodite lander," Jerry said.

"You can't imagine how thrilled I am with the possibility of getting my starship back into operation."

"With Mike on the job, that's not just a possibility, it's a certainty," stated Jerry.

"I am fortunate that you have such a capable chief engineer."

"Mike is the best in the business," stated Jerry.

"Kon is also very good, and he likes working with Mike."

"With a team like ours, it's just a matter of time, and your starship will be operational."

"When that happens, my people will have a decision to make. Do we stay here? Or do we complete our journey?"

"Where do you need to go to complete your voyage?"

"Back to Proteus."

"How do you think that decision will come down?"

"We've lived here for such a long time that this feels like home."

"It sounds like you want to stay."

"Most of us do."

"What about you?"

"I miss being in space, but this planet has become home."

"You could stay here and just live on your starship part time."

"That requires an operational shuttle."

"Let's grab the combustion chamber and get busy."

A few minutes later, Trang and Jerry arrived in the shop. "What do we have to do to this thing?" Jerry asked.

"First, we're going to give it a thorough cleaning. Second, we're going to check out its electronics. Third, we're going to test its electromagnetic feed lines. Finally, I need a source of charged particles of ordinary matter that I can send through the feed lines to make sure they work. If we're lucky, we won't have to repair anything."

"That's a lot to expect after being underwater for 30 years."

"All electronic components are in sealed compartments."

"So we have to hope nothing sprang a leak."

"This is a very robust piece of equipment, so it's possible no leaks developed."

"Let's get started."

Three hours later, Trang said, "It looks like we got lucky. Everything appears to be in working order. All we have left to do is the final test, but I'm hungry."

"Me too. Let's go eat and run the charged particle test after lunch."

"Good idea!"

When they arrived in the cafeteria, Jerry said, "I feel like eating something spicy."

"I love hot spicy food," Trang said.

"One of my favorite meals is Cajun pizza. You can have a piece of mine. If you like it, we'll share it and cook a second one."

Jerry pulled the pizza out of a freezer and placed it in an oven. "It'll be ready in a few minutes," he said. "During our long voyage, we had a chef on duty much of the time, but now, our menu is more limited."

"Is that true because you aren't talented in the kitchen, or is it true because the basic ingredients are no longer available?"

"Our kitchen is 100 percent functional, and all ingredients are in stock."

"That's a rather round-about way of saying that you're not a talented cook."

"Kitchen talent is Moose's claim to fame, but right now, we're in a weightless condition. That tends to make preparing special dishes rather difficult. We're more or less stuck with dishes that were premade for the weightless situation."

"So how are we going to eat the pizza?"

"It was created for microgravity. The cheese holds it together."

"It smells good. When will it be ready?"

Just then, the oven timer beeped. "Does that answer your question?" Jerry asked.

Trang smiled.

After letting it cool off a bit, Jerry offered Trang a piece. He tasted it and said, "This is delicious. It has a special kind of hot spicy flavor."

"I guess I'd better put another one in the oven."

A short time later, when Trang and Jerry were getting started on the second pizza, Mike arrived. "How is your lunch?" he asked Trang.

"Best I've eaten in a long time. I think I'm starting to acquire a taste for alien food."

Mike grinned at Trang and said, "I think it's going to take a while for me to see myself as an alien, but I could certainly look upon that concoction you're eating as an alien dish."

"It's delicious," stated Trang. "You ought to try it."

"I have, and it's too hot for me. I brought along some of Moose's smoked meat. I'm going to heat up a tube of split pea soup to eat with it."

"Have you learned anything about the knife and belt buckle?" Jerry asked.

"They're old."

"How old?"

"I'm having a hard time determining that with certainty. Depending on what assumptions I make, I'm coming up with an age range of 75,000 to 150,000 years."

"That makes them artifacts and not a pressing problem," commented Jerry.

"That's only true if you assume that the society the owner of the artifacts came from is now extinct," responded Mike.

"Good point, but we haven't seen any evidence of any group living in our area."

"That doesn't mean they're not present," argued Mike. "Before we landed, we looked at the whole planet, and we saw no evidence revealing Trang's people or Zeb or Zonya and her family."

"Zeb was only one person and was living in a cave. Trang's people were also living underground, and we didn't look closely at the area where Zonya is living."

"You just made my point. There could be one or more groups living underground in our area, and they would be hard to spot unless we were specifically looking for cave dwellers or got lucky and caught them out in the open."

"My feeling is that we're alone in our area, but while we're up here, we might as well take a close look at the area around Mystery Lagoon, especially the river valley above Rainbow Falls."

"I'll put some thought into the search and program our instruments to carry it out," stated Mike, as his communicator beeped. "Hello," he answered, "this is Mike."

"Hey Mike, this is Kon. Our situation has taken a turn for the worse."

"What happened?" Mike asked.

"We lost another electrical power unit. It broke down due to lack of maintenance. How far along are you with the lander?"

"We just started building it."

"When do you think it will be ready to land here?"

"In a couple weeks."

"Is there any way to speed that up?"

"How soon do you want it?"

"Can you get it here tomorrow?"

"Are you serious?"

"Yes!"

A very worried expression spread across Trang's face as he listened to his chief engineer talk to Mike. Trang knew that he could lose all of his people on Aphrodite.

"Tell me what the problem is," requested Mike.

"Our electrical power plant is composed of eight units. Six units are now out of operation, because we cannot do the required maintenance. Most of the power from the two operational units is being used to operate the magnetic containment fields for storing our antimatter fuel."

"I see the problem," responded Mike. "If you lose either of those units, your antimatter will explode."

"And we will no longer exist," stated Kon.

"What kind of power units do you have, and what do you need from me to fix them?"

"We use antimatter to generate electricity."

"How do you do that?"

"Power generation is really quite simple. The core of each power unit is a hollow sphere. Antimatter particles and ordinary matter particles are fired into the sphere from different directions. They meet at the center and annihilate each other releasing energy. Most of the energy is in the form of very intense light. This light is converted into electricity by photovoltaic cells lining the inside of the sphere."

"How can such a system require maintenance? It sounds like you have no moving parts."

"There aren't any moving parts in the spheres. The problem is that the photovoltaic cells convert only seventy percent of the energy released in the antimatter combustion into electricity. The rest heats up the sphere, and it must be cooled."

"What kind of cooling system do you have?"

"The walls of the spheres have tubes in them. We use electric motors to pump water through the tubes. The water reaches the boiling point and becomes high-pressure vapor. This flows through a turbine, which runs a generator to produce additional electricity. The vapor condenses back to liquid water and is pumped back through the tubes in the spheres."

"That sounds like a very efficient cooling system," commented Mike. "Instead of dumping the heat as waste, you use it to make additional electricity."

"It's an excellent system. The problem is the electric motors that operate the cooling systems haven't had any maintenance in 30 years. Six of them have broken down. The turbines are also in need of maintenance.

The other maintenance problem we have is the photovoltaic cells. They slowly degrade with use and have to be periodically remanufactured."

"I see what you're getting at," responded Mike. "As the cells degrade, they convert less and less energy to electricity. This leaves more energy to heat the spheres, which puts greater stress on the cooling systems. Electric motors that are wearing out simply can't handle the load."

"That's precisely our problem, and I need your help."

"Exactly what do you need by tomorrow?"

"Actually, I don't know if I have until tomorrow. I need to get one of our power units up and running before I lose one of the two that are still online. If I don't succeed in this, we're history."

"What do you need right now?"

"I need a 100-horsepower electric motor, two if you have them. Also, I need converter units to convert our power to what your motors need to run."

"We don't have any 100-horsepower motors in stock, but we can make them in our shop."

"How long will that take?"

"No more than a few hours. You can transmit the specs to my communicator."

"Hang on a second while I call them up."

A few seconds later, Kon asked, "Are you ready?"

"Go ahead," replied Mike.

"Okay, now that you have the specs, how do you plan to deliver the motors?"

"That's something I'll have to figure out. I'll be back in touch soon."

"Thanks, and don't wait too long."

Mike called Moose, explained the situation, and transmitted the motor specs. "I'll get the project started right away," responded Moose.

Turning to Jerry, Mike said, "We have an emergency on our hands."

"I know," responded Jerry. "I've been listening to you and Kon. This is very serious. We have to find a way to deliver those motors today."

"How are you going to do that?" asked Trang. "Your starship wasn't designed to land on anything, and your shuttles only work in an atmosphere. Aphrodite has no air."

"I can't land my starship on Aphrodite, but I can get close and hover."

"That sounds dangerous," commented Trang. "What if you lose power?"

"Then, we would crash, but I can't think of any reason why we would lose power. This ship's propulsion system is very reliable."

"How close do you propose to go?" asked Mike.

"I would be comfortable hovering as low as 2,000 feet."

"So I have to figure out how to drop the motors 2,000 feet without wrecking them."

"We might be able to do that with one of our ERVs (external repair vehicles)," Jerry said.

"They weren't designed to be used as landers," stated Mike, "but Aphrodite's gravity is only about .1g, so that might work."

"There's something you need to consider," Trang said.

"What?" Jerry asked

"It would be a double tragedy if my people lose a power unit when we are near their base. The resulting antimatter explosion would also incinerate us."

"Does Kon have instruments to monitor the health of those power systems and give us a few minutes warning?"

"All parts of our power units are monitored, so we can be aware of any degradation in performance. Kon should be able to predict the approximate time to failure for various components."

"At full power, we can be 300 miles away in just five minutes. Can Kon assure me that we would have at least that much time?"

"If a cooling system motor fails, the power unit can continue to produce electricity for a few minutes until it overheats and goes into a meltdown."

"You're not giving me definite answers," stated Jerry.

"I wish I had concrete answers for you, but our remaining power units are badly in need of maintenance. As you know, systems that are near the end of their useful life spans can fail at any time."

"That's true, but as I understand it, the expected failure that will shut a unit down is a cooling system motor breakdown, and if that happens, the unit can run until it overheats. But Kon said part of the power is generated by the cooling system. If you lose that power, is the remaining electricity produced by the photovoltaic cells enough to power the antimatter containment fields?"

"Yes!"

"So we would have several minutes to escape the imminent blast?"

"For a cooling system failure, that is correct."

"Once again, you're giving me a qualified answer."

"I have to. I want you to fully understand the risks involved in a rescue attempt."

"I appreciate that. So what's the possibility of a failure in the direct energy conversion unit?"

"Those cells don't fail abruptly; they gradually degrade."

"What about the particle injector guns?"

"Very reliable. We've never had a failure in them."

"If Kon will provide me with a real-time readout of data from the instruments monitoring the health of the cooling system motors, I will accept the risk and attempt a rescue mission."

"Thank you and I agree with your decision. The risk is manageable. I'll have Kon wire a data line to a communicator and transmit the motor monitoring data to us."

Turning to Mike, Jerry asked, "How long will it take your crew to secure everything?"

"Less than ten minutes."

Jerry contacted Dianne and asked, "Where are you at in your microgravity experiments?"

"I am in the middle of growing some complex molecular structures that promise to kill the virus Denise is carrying. The project needs to run a few more hours."

"Is there any way to finish sooner?"

"I could raise the temperature some to speed up the growth rate. I might be able to finish the project in two hours."

"I would like to leave sooner than that. We have a whole group of people on Aphrodite facing certain death if we don't get there on time."

"Your daughter's life is at risk too. She might need the drugs I'm making."

"Hang on a minute, while I call my wife."

A few moments later, Jerry received a response, "Hi, this is Connie. What's up?"

"How is Denise doing?"

"She's not yet showing any symptoms of the disease, but the virus count has gone up slightly since this morning. It seems like the natural drugs in the nuts are slowing the reproductive rate of the virus, but they're not stopping it."

"What if she eats more nuts?"

"She's already eating as many as her digestive system can handle."

"Is there some way to isolate the drugs and give them to Denise without her having to eat the nuts?"

"That's what Dianne is doing. She's growing synthetic forms of the drugs. This would be difficult to do down here, but the microgravity on the Challenger enables the process to move forward. I am hoping to have enough of the drugs by this evening to do an IV."

"What happens if you don't have the drugs?"

"Our daughter could get sick and die, but why won't I have the drugs? Dianne assured me that I would have them by this evening."

"Trang's people on Aphrodite lost a third of their electrical power. If they lose another unit, they will be vaporized. We need to go there as soon as possible."

"You can't leave yet. The acceleration would ruin Dianne's project."

"I know, but there has to be another way."

"Is it possible to move Dianne's project into the personnel shuttle?" Mike asked.

Jerry referred the question to Dianne. "I need the equipment in the medical lab," she replied.

"And your best estimate to finish the job is two hours?"

"I might be done in two hours, but that's assuming I don't run into any problems."

"Let me know if that happens, otherwise, call me when you're finished."

"Will do," replied Dianne.

"We can't leave here for two hours without risking my daughter's life, and the trip to Aphrodite will take two hours, so Kon should have his motors in about four hours."

Mike contacted Kon. "If I get the motors to you in four hours, will that work?"

"I hope so. The problem I have is that our equipment is worn out and can have sudden breakdowns. The unit I lost a short time ago broke down unexpectedly."

"So the truth is that you don't know for sure how much longer the two operational units will last?"

"That's right."

"You have six units that are down, right?

"That's correct."

"Are they all down because of cooling system failure?"

"Yes."

"How long can you run a unit without cooling before it overheats?"

"No more than a few minutes."

"So if you lose one of the operating units, you could run each down unit for perhaps five minutes and buy an additional half-hour."

"I've already considered that, and it should work, but it won't do us any good unless you're almost here with the new motors."

"Is there anything else you can do to buy a little time?"

"We're considering all possibilities, but I hope it doesn't come to that."

"I hope so too. Keep us informed."

"Will do."

Turning to Jerry and Trang, Mike said, "What a tragedy this will be if we don't get those motors finished and delivered on time. I am going to go help my crew, and I will make sure we get them done in less than four hours."

"I appreciate that," stated Trang. "Let me know if I can help."

"That goes for me too," Jerry said.

"I believe I have enough people, but I will call on both of you if I need more help." Mike left and headed for the shop.

"Let's go to the flight deck," Jerry said to Trang. "I want to develop a flight plan that will get us to Aphrodite in the shortest possible time."

"That will involve full power acceleration until we're halfway there, and then, full power deceleration the rest of the way."

"Also, we need the optimum flight path that takes us directly to your base."

"I hope this doesn't come down to a situation where every minute counts."

"I do too, but we need to give ourselves the best chance for success."

"While you're working the flight path problem, I'll monitor the cooling system motors."

Two hours later, Jerry's communicator beeped. It was Dianne. "I have enough serum to treat Denise," she said.

"I'll have Moose fly you home," Jerry replied.

A few minutes later, Moose and Dianne left the hangar in the personnel shuttle. "By tomorrow morning, Denise should be free of the virus," Dianne said to Jerry using her communicator.

"I hope so," stated Jerry.

"Good luck with your rescue mission," she replied.

"Let's head for Aphrodite," stated Jerry, as he pressed the anti-matter engine ignition button. The flight control computer immediately fired the engines, brought them up to full power, and put the Challenger on course for Aphrodite.

"It sure feels good to be back on the flight deck of a starship under full power," commented Trang. "I just wish this flight were under better circumstances."

"That depends on how you look at it," responded Jerry. "We are going to save your people from destruction. It seems to me that those are pretty good circumstances."

"That's true, but I'm worried that we won't get there on time, and that takes the fun out of this flight."

"What's your latest read on the health of the motors?"

"They're running rough, but they're still running."

"Sometimes, well made equipment just seems to find a way to keep going, even when worn out. I believe we're going to get there on time."

"I hope so. It will be a huge load off my mind when we get the new motors installed and running. Have you talked to Mike lately?"

"No, let's get a progress report."

Jerry beeped Mike. "How are you doing with the new motors?"

"One is almost finished. The other one will be done in an hour. When are we going to be at the moon base?"

"In a little under two hours."

"That will give me time to test the motors and load them on one of the ERVs. Also, I'm having some legs attached to the ERV."

"Will the ERV survive the landing?" Jerry asked.

"If you're willing to drop down to 2,000 feet and hover for a few seconds, I believe I can pull off a soft landing for the ERV."

"How are you going to do that?"

"I've gone through the numbers, and if I strip the ERV of nonessential equipment and install an extra fuel tank, I can not only do a soft landing, I can also return the ERV to 2,000 feet."

"How long will it take to make the modifications?"

"The motors and the ERV will be ready when we arrive at Aphrodite."

"If the modified ERV works, do we still need the Aphrodite lander?"

"How comfortable are you with taking the Challenger down to 2,000 feet and hovering there for a while?"

"I don't see any problem doing that. The moon's gravity is so weak; we won't even be using ten percent of our power. We could hover at 2,000 feet all day. How many trips to the surface would the ERV have to make?"

"I will have to get back to you on that. Right now, I need to finish this project."

"Okay, we'll talk later."

An hour and forty-five minutes later, the Challenger dropped below 10,000 feet as it descended toward Aphrodite. Using the starship's optical systems, Jerry had the area below displayed on a large video screen. He zoomed in on Trang's starship. He was amazed at the destruction caused by the meteor impact. "That meteor almost cut your ship in half," he said.

"It wrecked our machine shop, and it destroyed the support structure on one side of our ship."

"So we need to build some beams for that side of the ship to hold it together."

"If you do that, we can get our ship off the ground and back into space. Then, the big job will start."

"Just looking at that damage, I would guess that it will take a year or two to repair your ship and put the shop back in operation."

"You can't imagine how much I appreciate what you're doing. We owe you a great debt for undertaking such a big project."

"Your wife and daughter pointed us in the right direction to save Denise's life. I am grateful for that."

"That didn't take much effort. We still owe you."

"We'll figure something out, but right now, we're approaching 2,000 feet."

When the Challenger came to a complete stop, hovering at 2,000 feet, Mike launched the modified ERV. He let it freefall for 1,000 feet; then, he fired its main engine. Even though it produced only 600 pounds of thrust at full power, it was enough to slow down the modified ERV and bring it to a stop a few feet above Aphrodite. Mike throttled back the rocket, and the ERV settled down to a gentle landing.

"Great landing!" exclaimed Kon through his communicator.

On the Challenger's flight deck; Trang, Jerry, and Mike stared at a large video screen. They watched four people wearing space suits run to the ERV. Due to Aphrodite's low gravity, they ran in great leaping bounds. They quickly opened the ERV and removed the new motors. In the low gravity, the motors were very light, and two of the space-suited individuals easily carried them away.

"All clear," stated Kon.

Mike fired the ERV's main engine, and a minute later, the ERV was onboard the Challenger. "We're ready to go," Mike said.

"How do you always make everything look so easy?" Jerry asked Mike.

"That's part of my job description."

"That sounds like something Kon would say," commented Trang. "I definitely have the right team for getting my starship back in operation."

"Thanks for the compliment," responded Mike, "but we have a tough job that's going to take at least a year."

"For the last 30 years, I've had to deal with the possibility of never getting my ship back. Having it fully functional in a year, or even two years, sounds pretty darn good to me."

"Delivering the motors with the ERV went so smoothly that I think we should skip building the Aphrodite lander," stated Mike. "I believe I can deliver the beams with the ERV."

"How many trips will that take?" Jerry asked.

"Kon needs five 60-foot beams. With the Aphrodite lander, I would've built them in 30-foot sections and delivered them all at the same time. With the ERV, I'll have to build the beams in shorter pieces, and I might have to make as many as ten trips to deliver them."

"How much time for each trip?"

"Let's see, we have refueling, loading, and unloading, plus flight time. I'm going to guess a half-hour per roundtrip."

"So somewhere around five hours should deliver all the beams?"

"I think so."

"Okay, let's skip the Aphrodite lander. How long will it take you to make the beams?"

"On an emergency basis or on a normal schedule?"

"A normal schedule."

"It shouldn't take us more than four or five days."

Mike's communicator beeped. "This is Kon. Thanks for the motors. We have them installed and running. We can breathe a little easier now that the emergency is over, but we're not completely out of danger just yet. We really need to make at least two more units functional."

"What would it take to do that?"

"I have three motors that are repairable. I can fix them if you can build me some key parts."

"Send me the specs."

Kon did as requested. Mike reviewed the specs and said, "I think we can make these parts in about an hour."

"Let's deliver them before we go back to Alcent," Jerry said.

"Okay," responded Mike. "I'll get busy right away."

An hour-and-a-half later, with the parts delivered and the ERV back onboard, the Challenger headed back to Alcent. "I am going to sleep really good tonight," stated Trang.

Chapter Fifteen

TIME: Day 37, 8:00 AM

Trang and Jerry were in the Challenger's cafeteria enjoying breakfast. "Have you talked to your wife this morning?" Trang asked.

"Yes."

"How is Denise doing?"

"She's going to be okay."

"I am happy about that."

"You can't imagine how relieved I am. I was very worried about my little girl."

"You hid it well, but I knew what you were going through."

"Thanks for your patience and understanding yesterday."

"What do you mean?"

"Even though your people on Aphrodite had a life-and-death emergency, you didn't pressure me to go there before completion of Dianne's serum production project."

"I was worried about Denise too. I didn't want her to die the way my son did. I was sure that our medical staff could save her, if given enough time to make full use of your medical lab."

"What makes our medical team so good is that they bring together some unique capabilities from worlds that are light-years apart, but it was the knowledge that you've gained from living here for 30 years that put the team on the right track to save Denise. I appreciate what your wife and daughter did."

"That was quite a turnabout of events."

"What do you mean?"

"If you and your wife hadn't saved my daughter's life, she wouldn't have been here to help save your daughter's life."

"That story has a nice ring to it."

"Helping each other is how life should be lived," stated Trang. "There is a great deal that we can do for each other, and I am very happy that you and your people turned out to be friendly rather than hostile."

"We feel the same way about you."

"I spoke to Kon this morning. He said to extend a heartfelt thank you for the new motors."

"I'm glad we arrived on time."

"Not as glad as they are."

"I can imagine how relieved they must feel. The thought of being incinerated does tend to create a little anxiety."

"They slept pretty good last night," stated Trang.

"After all the tension we worked our way through yesterday, I think we deserve a break. Let's find something relaxing to do."

"What do you have in mind?" Trang asked.

"Not much, I would be content to just be lazy all day."

"That does sound good, but we have to do something. We can't just lie on the beach and stare at the sky all day."

"Why not?" questioned Jerry.

"I need to be doing something."

"Like what?"

"How is the fishing around your island?"

"It's great."

"Let's go catch a few and have an outdoor fish fry."

"That sounds like fun. After breakfast, let's test your combustion chamber, and then, let's go down to the island and do some fishing."

"How do we go down? Both of your shuttles are down there."

"Moose is coming up to work with Mike on the beam building project."

"I had almost given up hope on ever getting my starship back, but now that those girders are under construction, I am so excited that I can hardly wait."

"The waiting game is sometimes a difficult game to play. We need to take your mind off of waiting. How adventuresome are you?"

"What do you mean?"

"I've already been fishing around the island a number of times. I'd like to go someplace new, like saltwater fishing."

"Where?"

"There's a large saltwater bay 100 miles southwest of Pioneer Island. We could haul the submarine over there and do an underwater cruise. After we explore the bay for a while, we could do some fishing."

"That does sound like fun," responded Trang, "but have you forgotten about the knife and belt buckle?"

"No, I just haven't had time to think about them."

"Maybe we should explore the river above Rainbow Falls and see if anything catches our attention. Also, we could do some fishing while we're up there."

"Yeah, we could get lucky and hook a big one. Then, we might be so preoccupied with landing it that we lose track of where we are and end up going over the falls."

"I'm not that adventuresome," stated Trang.

"The best way to explore that area would be to fly in with the chopper and follow the river to its origin."

"Let's do that today and go deep-sea fishing tomorrow," Trang said.

"That's a great idea, but we're not exactly on vacation. We need to install your combustion chamber sometime and get your shuttle off the ground."

"I don't need it until I get my starship back. When we landed on this planet, we weren't expecting to stay 30 years, so we didn't come here prepared to stay that long. What I'm getting at is we're almost out of antimatter fuel. There isn't any fuel in our shuttle. We transferred it to our airplane, and it's almost depleted."

"We could spare enough fuel to get your shuttle operational, but eventually, we're going to run out too."

"Are you saying that you're not able to manufacture antimatter fuel?"

"That's right. We came here on a one-way mission."

"Our technology is the greatest reward we can give you for helping us out of our predicament. We will show you how to easily make antimatter fuel."

"You've already agreed to refuel my starship and give us the age control drug. It seems like I am getting the better end of this deal."

"You've saved my people on Aphrodite, and you're helping me get my starship back. So I believe I am getting the better end of the deal."

"It's a super business deal when both parties are satisfied. Let's go test your combustion chamber, and then, let's go have some fun."

TIME: Day 37, 1:00 PM

Jerry and Trang were in the helicopter flying over Mystery Lagoon. They flew only 300 feet above the water as they approached the 500-foot high falls at the east end of the lagoon.

"What an inspiring sight," commented Jerry.

"It's awesome," stated Trang. "I sure wouldn't want to go over it in a barrel."

"Where did you get that expression?"

"I think it came out of a movie made on Earth. When we passed by Earth several decades ago, we recorded quite a number of your TV channels for a few days."

"I had assumed that's why you speak English so well."

"We learned several languages, but most of what we recorded was in English, so we concentrated on it."

"I'm glad you did. It makes our communication easy."

Jerry climbed until the helicopter was about 50 feet above the falls. "Looking at waterfalls has always had a relaxing, hypnotic effect on me," he said. "Especially, a big one like this. Somehow, it just seems to have a way of drawing my mind into it and away from everything else."

"We are facing the power and beauty of nature wrapped up in a single display. It's hard not to be drawn into it."

"I could hang around here all day, but I think we'd better move on."

"What's your plan for exploring the river?" Trang asked.

"I'd like to take a fairly quick look at it. If anything grabs our attention, we can investigate it on the way back."

"I'll keep my eyes open for a good fishing spot."

"What does a good fishing spot look like? What I mean is you're just looking at water. How can you tell that one patch of water is going to be better for fishing than another patch of water?"

"Finding good fishing spots is a natural talent. You just have to have a nose for smelling them out."

"That sounds like something Moose would say."

"Is he your resident fisherman?"

"He claims he is."

"We'll just have to bring home a catch that outshines his talent."

"That sounds like competition to me."

"Friendly competition."

"That might be, but Moose will take it as a challenge."

302

"I'm ready to go fishing," stated Trang. "Does this thing go any faster?"

"Yes, it does, but don't forget that we came here to look for clues to the origin of the knife and belt buckle."

"Well, so far, all we're seeing is a lazy river wandering through dense forest with an occasional meadow for a break. I think we could go faster and still see this."

"I guess you're right. If we spot anything unusual, we can always slow down and look at it."

Twenty minutes later, Trang and Jerry reached the foothills and started seeing occasional rapids and small waterfalls. As they gained altitude, the thick lowland forest gradually gave way to rocky terrain, thinly populated with trees adapted to the local conditions. Eventually, they came to a large meadow. Near its center, the river ran into a lake about 300 yards wide by 500 yards long.

"That's where we need to go fishing," Trang declared.

"Okay, but first, let's find the origin of this river, and then, we'll come back here and go fishing."

Ten minutes later, Trang said, "I'm starting to see snow in the shady areas."

"You should, we're now at 12,000 feet."

Several minutes later, at 14,700 feet, Jerry and Trang followed the river around a cliff, and dead ahead, they saw a huge white snow field atop a glacier. "We just found the river's origin," stated Trang. "Now, let's go fishing."

"You really do remind me of Moose."

"In what way?"

"Maybe it's your one-track mind that's zeroed in on fishing. We didn't come up here just to go fishing; we came up here to explore this place."

"We've already done that, so let's go fishing."

"I don't think a quick overflight could qualify as exploring."

"You're right, so let's compromise. While I'm fishing, you can explore the area around the lake."

"That's quite a compromise. I do the work, and you have the fun."

"That works for me," Trang said.

"I have a better idea. Let's explore the area first to make sure there's nothing dangerous lurking in the bushes. Then, let's both do some fishing."

"I guess I can live with that much delay, but what do you expect to find hiding in the bushes?"

"I don't know. I just think we should look around before we have fun."

"You are right, of course, but that meadow looked so peaceful when we flew over it that I just didn't sense the presence of danger."

A few minutes later, Trang and Jerry arrived at the meadow. "I am going to circle the lake, so we can look behind every rock and bush," Jerry said.

"The meadow is fairly open, so that shouldn't take long."

Jerry circled the lake at an altitude of only 50 feet. "It looks deserted," he said.

"Let's make one more pass a little farther away from the lake," Trang suggested.

"Okay."

After completing the second circuit, Trang said, "Nothing down there except birds and rodents."

"We'll make one final pass around the area. This time, we'll hug the cliffs."

About halfway around, Trang pointed at the base of the cliff directly ahead and said, "There's a cave behind that bush."

"Is it a dangerous cave?" Jerry asked.

"What do you mean?"

"Will it attack us while we're fishing?"

"What kind of silly question is that?"

"I'm wondering why you're worried about that cave when your desire is to go fishing."

"I'm not worried about it. I just think we should explore it."

"I thought you wanted to go fishing."

"Once again, you seem to have forgotten the knife. Need I remind you that my people and I have lived in caves for a long time. The society the knife came from may have lived in caves. We should be looking for caves and exploring them when we find them."

"Well, if you feel that strongly about it, let's forget about fishing and go cave exploring."

"You're not fooling me. I know you're just as eager to see what's in that cave as I am."

"Well, okay, but before we go in, let's see if there are other caves here."

Jerry continued the flight around the meadow. He and Trang discovered three additional caves.

"You're the cave expert," stated Jerry. "Which one do you want to investigate first?"

"Let's take a look at those two."

"Why those two?"

"They're close enough together, so that they might lead to the same underground cavern. There are advantages to having a front and backdoor. If people lived here long ago, there may have been more activity in these two than in the other two. Consequently, we would be more likely to find artifacts there."

"We'll land a short distance away and fly an RPV into them. I want to make sure there aren't any predators living in there before we go walking in."

"You're assuming the society of the knife owner is no longer around."

"That is my belief, but we don't know that for sure."

Jerry landed the helicopter 60 yards from the pair of caves. "I need you to stand guard while I look inside," Jerry said.

"You got it," responded Trang.

Jerry put on a headset and launched an RPV. He flew it into the right-hand cave of the central pair and hovered. The RPV's cameras automatically adjusted to the lower light level.

"This cave is quite spacious," Jerry said, "and there's an opening in the back wall."

"How high is the ceiling?"

"About ten feet."

"What kind of headroom in the back wall opening?"

"About seven feet."

"What's the opening shaped like?"

"It looks like an arch-top doorway."

"It sounds to me like you're describing a manmade cave."

"It sure looks that way."

"My guess is that the cavern you're describing is an entry room, and the opening in the back wall leads to an underground complex."

"I am going to find out," stated Jerry, as he flew the RPV into the opening, which turned out to be a tunnel. Twenty feet down the tunnel, there was a doorway on the right. Jerry flew the RPV through the doorway and found an empty room. The RPV's instruments sized the room at 20 by 25 feet. The room was deserted. Jerry flew the RPV out of the room and continued down the tunnel. He found four additional rooms before the tunnel ended in a room sized at 30 by 40 feet. In a wall to the left, Jerry found an open, arch-top exit. He flew the RPV through it and found a tunnel with five side rooms measuring 20 by 25 feet. After the last room, the tunnel opened to the outside world through the left-hand cave of the central pair. Satisfied with the initial reconnaissance, Jerry brought the RPV back to the helicopter.

While flying the RPV around the underground complex, Jerry had described in detail everything he had seen. "What do you think?" he asked.

"Based on what you've said, there's no doubt that this cave complex was manmade, and it appears that it has been deserted for a very long time. I think we should go in, look around, and see what we can learn."

"But I thought you wanted to go fishing."

"This is too exciting. We have to go in and explore this complex. We might find something to prove my daughter's common origin theory."

"That would be a major discovery, but I wonder if it's safe to leave our chopper unguarded for a couple hours."

"We haven't seen any large animals up here that could wreck it."

"That's true, but if something small like a pronghorn sheep shows up, and it happens to be a ram, and it decides to use our chopper for head-butting practice, we could end up getting stranded here."

While pointing at the caves, Trang said, "It wouldn't be all bad. We would have a place to live."

"Being a cave dweller, you'd probably feel right at home."

"I would, and I'm sure you could adjust to it."

"I'd really rather not, because we could end up getting stranded here for a long time. Your airplane is almost out of fuel, and this lake is a bit small to operate my shuttles from."

"You're right. We would either have to float down the river or be stranded here. My airplane doesn't even have enough fuel to get here."

"What did you just say about your airplane?"

"I said it doesn't have enough fuel to get here."

"That's what I thought you said."

"I was just stating a fact."

"It's not what you said that got my attention; it's the implication. A few days ago, you sent your airplane home. You and your family stayed behind knowing that they could not come back and get you. That means you stranded yourselves here and put your fate totally in our hands."

"You sound surprised."

"I am. After holding me captive, you turn right around and put yourselves in our hands."

"That is quite a turnabout of events."

"You seem amused by all of this."

"When you think about it in the way that you just put it, it is rather amusing. But in all seriousness, you and I have much in common. We are starship captains, and we do what we have to do. My situation was desperate. In my place, you would've done everything I did."

"That might be true, but just the same, it took a lot of courage to place yourselves in the midst of a group of aliens when you had no way to leave."

"Courage is essential to what you and I do," stated Trang.

For a few moments, Jerry thought about some of the life and death situations he and his people had been through since leaving Earth. Then, he said, "Let's go explore those caves."

"It seems you've decided to leave our chopper unguarded."

"Not completely. What I'm going to do is park an RPV on top that rock over there and aim its cameras at this chopper. I will program it to sound an alarm in my communicator if it sees anything approach. Then, I will quickly put on a headset and take a look."

"That should leave us free to investigate the caves without worrying about a ride home."

A few moments later, Trang and Jerry approached the right-hand cave of the central pair. "Before going into this cavern, I really should have flown the RPV into the other two caves just to make sure that they're all uninhabited," Jerry said.

"I can tell you that without the RPV."

"How?"

"I've lived in the wilderness for a long time, and I've become an expert tracker. All I have to do is study the area in front of each cave, and I can tell you if anything has gone in or out recently."

When they reached the cave farthest to the right, Trang examined the ground in front of it for a couple minutes, looking for a spoor. Finally, he said, "It looks like nothing of consequence has gone in or out of this cave in recent days."

Trang and Jerry walked to the cave farthest to the left. On the way, Trang studied the terrain in front of the two central caves and concluded that nothing of any size had recently gone in or out of them.

When they approached the cave farthest to the left, Trang immediately cocked his rifle and became very alert. He stopped and stood still with his rifle pointing toward the cave. Jerry followed his example. Slowly, Trang began stepping backwards with Jerry following his lead.

When they were 50 yards away, Trang said, "There's a saber tooth in that cave, and there's a pretty good chance there's more than one. Might even be a mated pair with kittens."

"How do you know all of that?"

"I picked up the scent of cat urine. Apparently, there is air flowing through the cave from an opening in the back, because I picked up the scent quite strongly."

"I thought I smelled pine needles and that the scent was coming from those evergreen bushes next to the cave."

"No! That was cat urine you smelled."

"Why do you think there are kittens in there?"

"The only time they mark their dens so strongly is when they have kittens. It's a warning. Only one of them will leave the den at a time. One is always on guard, and either parent will viciously attack anything that gets too close."

"Will they leave us alone when we explore the central complex?"

"That depends."

"On what?"

"On whether or not they're hungry."

"Do you have a way to find that out?" Jerry asked.

"We could go in and ask them."

"Great idea! You lead the way."

"No way! I'm not that crazy."

"Well, it was your idea."

"I know, but I've had some second thoughts, and I believe we need a better plan. How much noise do your RPVs make?"

"Almost none. They were carefully designed for silent flight."

"Let's fly one in there and see what the cats are doing."

A short time later, Jerry said, "This cave has three rooms, and the den is in the room farthest back."

"What are the cats doing?"

"They're sleeping."

"How many adults are there?"

"Only one."

"Which one?"

"It's the female, and she has three kittens piled up against her."

"That means the male is probably out hunting, and since the female is sleeping, we should be able to safely explore the central complex."

"What if the male comes back while we're in the cavern?"

"He won't come back until he makes a kill."

"If he comes back with prey, will he drop it and come in looking for us?"

"I don't believe he would leave his kill unguarded. I think he would deliver it to the den before looking for us."

"That sounds reasonable. Are you sure the female won't leave her kittens unguarded?"

"Yes!"

"That means she won't follow us into the cavern, so let's go cave exploring."

"Before we go in, there's one more thing we need to check out."

"What are you concerned about?" Jerry asked.

"The cave the cats are in might have an underground connection to the complex we want to explore. If that's the case, the female will feel threatened and attack us."

"I haven't seen one, but I'll take another look."

A minute later, Jerry said, "There's a small opening high in the back wall. It looks like the air vent you said might exist. I haven't found anything that looks like a hallway to the main complex."

"So, are you ready to go cave exploring?"

"Yes, but first, I am going to aim one of the helicopter's cameras at the area in front of the two cave entrances and program it to sound an alarm if anything approaches."

"It sounds like we're covered. We have the helicopter watching our backsides, and the RPV watching the helicopter. I'm ready to go in."

Being an experienced cave dweller, Trang led the way. He and

Jerry inspected the entry room. Then, they walked down the hallway to the first side room and explored it. The first thing that caught their attention was a luminescent section of the ceiling. "I wonder how that lamp works," questioned Jerry.

"I don't know, but it sure lights this room with a nice soft glow."

"All the rooms have ceiling lamps."

"Someone sure put a lot of work into building this cave complex," commented Trang. "It's cut out of solid granite. It has a ventilation system, and it has ceiling lamps."

"It also has a rugged sense of permanence about it. But how do the lamps work? If these caves are as old as the knife we found, the lamps should have quit working long ago."

"It sure seems that way. These caves could be as old as 150,000 years."

"How would you design and build a lighting system that would last that long?" Jerry asked.

"To start with, it would have no moving parts, and it would be made out of materials that don't degrade with time."

"Is it possible to make solar cells that last 150,000 years?"

"I don't know, but I doubt it."

"Is it possible to make some kind of electric lamp that would last 150,000 years?"

"Again, I don't know, but I doubt it."

"This lighting system could be non-electric," speculated Jerry. "The glowing ceiling panels might be the bottom ends of skylights. Maybe if we could remove that panel, we would find a tunnel that leads to the top of this cliff or to a south-facing wall."

"You've just described a lighting system that could last 150,000 years. Before we leave, we need to inspect the top and south side of this cliff."

"I agree," stated Jerry. "If this is a skylight, we should be able to find the other end of it."

"It should be obvious."

"The only argument against the skylight theory is that they would only light the caves during the day. What about during the night?"

"You're forgetting that dark nights are rare. We have two suns and two moons."

"That's right," acknowledged Jerry, "and that makes skylights a simple way to put light in these caves most of the time. It's so simple that it's brilliant, and it could even be a very efficient design. If each light carrying tunnel has an internal ceramic mirror finish, very little light would be lost between the entry ends and the ceiling panels."

"That kind of finish would allow the tunnels to have some bends in them without losing much light."

"Our speculation sounds so good that it has to be the way they did it. I'm betting we'll find the proof when we're back outside."

"I think so too."

Jerry and Trang moved from room to room. When they reached the large central room, Trang said, "We've looked at the entry room and four side rooms, and we haven't found any artifacts. It seems certain that this complex was manmade, which means people once lived here, which means there should be artifacts. Why haven't we found anything?"

Mike dated the knife between 75,000 and 150,000 years old. If the knife came from the people that lived here, these caves could be 150,000 years old. What kind of artifacts would last that long?"

"Stone tools are the first things that come to mind," replied Trang.

"But would they've had stone tools? The knife was a product of high technology."

"Good point. This entire cave complex was made by people with technology. Primitive people could not cut caves in granite."

"That means they would not have had stone tools, unless their society was too small to maintain their technology."

"That's a definite possibility," stated Trang, "and it fits into my daughter's common origin theory. If an advanced race from another star planted human colonies on earthlike planets, they would have given them everything they needed to get off to a good start."

"That would include a secure place to live, like these caves."

"And they would've had high-tech tools and equipment," added Trang, "but with a small society, they would not have had the industrial base to maintain their technology."

"It seems like they would've lost their technology after just a few generations, and then, they would've had to make stone tools and weapons, like arrowheads, spearheads, and knives."

"If they made any of those items, where would we find them?" Trang asked.

"It seems like this cavern would be the best place. Outside, they would've been buried long ago by natural processes."

"That's true, but we've already been in six rooms, and we haven't found anything. It's like the rooms were swept clean."

"Maybe the people who lived here moved to a new location and took everything with them," suggested Jerry.

"Why would they leave such a secure home?" Trang asked.

"Maybe they ate everything that lived in this area and had to move or starve."

"That's a possibility, but I wonder where they went and how they lived securely."

"Maybe they didn't live securely," commented Jerry. "As far as we know, they're now extinct. Their move might've led to their demise."

"They could've moved to Mystery Lagoon. The large dinosaurs can't get into that area, and there's ample land around the water. Also, the knife and belt buckle were found in the lagoon."

"I guess that theory is as good as any, but I don't think we're going to figure it out today. So let's look at the rest of these rooms, and then, let's go fishing."

A short time later, Trang and Jerry walked out of the left entrance to the cavern. "I am surprised we didn't find anything in those rooms," stated Jerry.

"I am too, but we believe it's been a long time since they lived here. A lot can happen in 150,000 years."

"We didn't find anything in the caves, but we did find the caves, and that's a huge discovery. We now know without a doubt that people once lived here, and they had the technology to cut a large underground complex out of solid granite."

"Now that we know all of that, we have a couple new mysteries to solve," commented Trang. "Where did they come from, and what happened to them?"

"We might be able to find the answer to the second part of your question, if we could figure out where they went after they left here."

"Unless we get lucky, that's going to be tough to do. If they were planted here by a starship and lived here long enough to lose their technology before moving, it's quite likely they did not have the ability to excavate new caves to live in, so whatever shelters they built could not possibly be around anymore."

"Not necessarily," argued Jerry. "Primitive people could dig caves in sandstone cliffs."

"That's true, so we should look for them and natural caves to explore."

"That's a project for another day," stated Jerry. "It's getting late, so let's catch some fish and go home."

"I'm ready," stated Trang.

"You claim to be the expert at smelling out fishing spots, so how do you want to do this?"

Trang gazed at the lake for a few moments. "We could fish from that rock over there, but I think we'll do better if we take the boat out."

"I would rather fish from the boat than from shore. Being on the water is just more fun."

Jerry and Trang removed the boat and fishing gear from the helicopter and carried it the short distance to the lake. Jerry took the rolled up deflated boat out of its carrying bag and set it down at the water's edge. He pressed the inflation button, and in a matter of seconds, the boat became fully inflated and ready for use. It was big enough for three people.

Jerry pushed the boat into the water. He put the oars in it and took the center seat. Trang loaded the fishing gear, stepped in, and took the rear seat. Jerry rowed the boat toward the middle of the lake. "I wonder what kind of fish are in this lake," he said.

"We'll soon find out," responded Trang, as he cast out a two-inch long lure and began reeling it in with an erratic motion.

"We're only going to find out, if you catch something."

"As far as we know, no one has fished this lake for a very long time, so there should be fish here for the taking."

Trang proved to be right. He received a strike before he had even reeled the lure halfway back to the boat. He played the fish a couple minutes while bringing it in.

"That fish reminds me of the trout I used to catch in mountain streams back on Earth," commented Jerry, "except it's much bigger."

"It looks like it might weigh between two and three pounds," noted Trang.

Jerry cast in the opposite direction and received a strike almost immediately. "Fishing was never this good on Earth," he said.

"Do you have any lakes on Earth that haven't been fished in for 100,000 years?"

"No!"

"That does make a big difference."

When Jerry landed his catch, he said, "It looks just like yours, and it's about the same size."

A half-hour later, Trang and Jerry had 13 fish, all weighing between two and three pounds. "I think this is enough for a fish fry," Jerry said.

"That's good, because we need to leave in a hurry. The male saber tooth is returning with his kill. These cats do know how to swim, so we have to leave, or we'll have to kill the cat, because he will attack."

"How do you know he's coming back?"

"Take a look at all those flying scavengers. They're circling the male hoping to intimidate him into dropping his prey."

"That means he can't attack us, because if he leaves his prey, the scavengers will get it."

"He'll call his mate to guard the prey; then, he'll attack us."

"Let's just get out of here," stated Jerry, as he began rowing toward the helicopter as fast as he could.

When they reached the shore, Trang carried the fish and the fishing tackle. Jerry carried the boat and oars. At the helicopter, Jerry connected a hose to the boat and quickly sucked the air out of it. He rolled it up and shoved it into the chopper. "I'll bag it up later," he said.

Trang had already stowed the fish and tackle. "I'm ready to go," he said.

"Let's wait until the saber tooth gets here. I want to see what it killed."

"If you want to avoid killing the cat, I think we should take off, deploy our pontoons, and land on the lake. These cats can easily exceed 50 mph in a charge, but they can't swim very fast."

"Good idea," agreed Jerry, as he fired up the turbine and lifted off. He flew over the lake, deployed the pontoons, and landed about 40 yards offshore.

The turbine had barely wound down to a stop when Trang spotted the saber tooth. It was upriver working its way along the rough terrain next to the rapids. "It looks like he killed a mountain antelope," Trang said.

Jerry looked at the cat through binoculars. "That antelope looks bigger than the cat," he said. "But he doesn't seem to be having any trouble hauling it home."

"For their size, they are very powerful animals."

"Those vultures are sure aggressive," commented Jerry. "One just hit the cat's rump with its talons."

"That one's living dangerously. It must be an immature young adult."

"I wonder if these vultures ever succeed at intimidating a saber tooth into abandoning its prey."

"I've never seen it happen."

"Some of them are sure trying hard to make him drop it."

"Those are the dumb ones. The smart ones are keeping their distance."

Trang had hardly finished speaking, when the saber tooth dropped his prey, leapt eight feet straight up, and turned completely around in the midst of the leap. He grabbed a diving vulture with his claws, pulled it into his mouth, and crunched. Then, he landed softly on all four feet. With a twist of his neck, he threw the dead vulture on top of a bush. He looked skyward and let out a fierce snarling growl. Calmly, he picked up his family's dinner and resumed his journey.

"Wow! That was fast!" exclaimed Jerry. "That whole thing took only a few seconds."

"It's amazing how deadly effective he was. Dropping the prey, the leap, the twist, the grab; it was all perfectly timed."

"My wife was almost killed by a pair of these cats. She shot one; I shot the other. After watching this one, I can see how truly fortunate we were."

"I'd like to hear about that encounter."

Jerry told Trang the complete story. "We were very lucky," he concluded.

"It sounds like your wife pulled the trigger less than a second before it was too late."

"Her shot was a reflexive reaction. She fired from the hip. There simply wasn't time for her to raise her rifle and take aim."

"Your wife must be very good with guns."

"She's quick and accurate."

"It's fortunate for her that she has that skill."

"Weapons proficiency was part of our survival training, and she excelled with firearms."

"It's kind of ironic that a person skilled at saving lives would also be skilled in the use of guns."

"Why?"

"Doctors save lives; guns take lives."

"Since arriving here, my wife has used both skills to save lives."

"I know, but it just seems ironic that a doctor would be a skilled killer."

"You do have a way of making it sound ironic, but on this planet, it's a matter of survival."

"The cat just spotted us," stated Trang.

"Will he do what you predicted?"

"You can count on it."

At that moment, the saber tooth dropped his prey and let out an ear-shattering scream. "He just sounded the alarm," Trang said.

A few moments later, the female came bounding out of the cave. She quickly looked in all directions before fixing her gaze on the helicopter. Her fur bristled, and she let out a snarling scream.

The male picked up his prey and hauled it toward the den with a sense of urgency. "When he has securely stored his kill, he will join his mate, and they will attack us," Trang predicted.

"Why would they do that? They've never seen a helicopter before. They've never seen people before, and they probably can't see us now. Why are they so agitated when they don't have any previous experience to base it on?"

"It's just their temperament, and they have kittens. Also, they probably consider this meadow to be their territory, and they will attack intruders."

"It's kind of like, 'shoot first and ask questions later'."

"That sums it up."

The male dragged his kill into the cave entrance, then emerged snarling. The female retreated to the cave entrance, where she stood guard. The male charged toward the lake, leapt far out over the water, and hit the water swimming vigorously.

"It won't take him long to get here," stated Trang. "Have you seen enough, or do you want to wait for him?"

"I've learned enough about their behavior for now," responded Jerry, as he fired up the turbine and took off. "Let's see if we can find the outside ends of the skylights."

"That should be easy."

Jerry flew over the river to the south side of the cliff, and then slowly climbed. The slope of the cliff gradually changed from near vertical to about 60 degrees.

"There they are," Trang said, while pointing at the skylights.

"They sure look solid."

"They were definitely built to last."

"And they're low maintenance," added Jerry. "The angle of the transparent covers is steep enough so that debris should not pile up on them and close off the light."

"I'm impressed with the simplicity and the ruggedness of the design," stated Trang.

"I am too, and I'm getting video of all of this, so we can look at it later."

"Good idea."

A few moments later, Jerry said, "Okay, that's done. Now, let's go home and eat some fish."

"I am hungry," stated Trang.

As they left, Trang pointed at the cave complex and said, "I sure wish I knew who built all of that and where they came from."

"If we don't find any more clues than we found today, that's going to be a mystery for a long time."

"If we get lucky and solve the mystery by the time I get my starship in good working order, I will have a big decision to make."

"What do you mean?"

"I will have to consider going to the star these people came from and checking out the planet they lived on."

"That could be very dangerous."

"Why do you think that?"

"If these people had the ability to travel between stars 150,000 years ago, just think what kind of technology they must have by now. By way of comparison, America launched my mission to the stars less than 200 years after the Wright brothers made the first airplane flight. Imagine 150,000 years of technological development compared to 200 years."

"That's beyond my imagination."

"I think it's safe to say that when you arrive at their planet, you would look like a relic out of the stone ages, and you would be totally at their mercy."

"If they still exist as a high-tech society."

"Why do you say that?" Jerry asked.

"Like you said, if they had interstellar travel 150,000 years ago, by now, their technology would have to be awesome beyond imagination. Travel between stars should now be like going for a walk in the park."

"I see what you're getting at. For them, interstellar travel should be so easy that they should be around. We should have seen them."

"I don't know about that. They might not want to be seen, and their awesome technology would allow them to make themselves undetectable."

"So what were you getting at when you said, 'if they still exist'?"

"It's all the work they put into that cave complex. They obviously wanted the human colony they planted here to survive and prosper. It seems like they would've come back here to check on this colony once their technology advanced far enough to make interstellar travel very easy. If they had done that and found that this colony had failed, it seems like they would've started another one and made sure that it had everything it needed to prosper."

"Since that wasn't done, you think that they might've suffered some tragedy."

"It seems reasonable."

"Yes, it does," agreed Jerry, "but there are other possible explanations. For example, by the time interstellar travel became very easy for them, their objectives may've changed. They might simply have no longer been interested in starting colonies on planets that already had an abundance of life. They might've adopted a non-interference policy."

"Definitely a possibility."

"So, if we can figure out where they came from, why do you want to go there?"

"If Akeyco's common origin theory is correct, the planet the cave dwellers came from might be the birthplace of the human species. Wouldn't you like to go there and learn about where we came from?"

"That would be exciting, but my mission is to explore this planet and get a human civilization started here. I don't know why the cave dwellers failed, but I guarantee you that I will not fail."

"If you can avoid a tragic accident and a deadly illness, our age control drug will give you plenty of time to be successful. In fact, you should live for several hundred years. What are you going to do with all that time?"

"It was just a couple days ago that you told me I would have a long life, so I haven't yet had time to think about it, but the possibilities are exciting."

"It's not going to take you very long to see all the opportunities that long life will open up for you."

"You're right, and I am very excited about it, but I have a lot of work to do here before I can even think about leaving on a long interstellar voyage. Besides, I like it here. This is home. Also, there's B-2. Rex and Shannon might need help again. If so, I will have to go there."

"When was the last time you heard from them?"

"Michelle is in touch with them almost every day."

"How are they doing?"

"Rex and his family are fine, and they are hopeful about the future. Those chemical warfare doomsday machines we destroyed have been out of operation for nearly three months now. In another three months, the last of the poisons spewed out by them will have broken down into harmless chemicals, and what little animal life remains on the planet will have a chance to recover."

"That sure was a tragic war they fought."

"It was horrible. If we hadn't come along to destroy those machines, most remaining animal life on the planet would've been killed. It was only a matter of time."

"That's the kind of war that could've destroyed the civilization that sent the cave dwellers here."

"I get the feeling that you're determined to go check it out, if we can figure out where they came from."

"It's the kind of mission that appeals to me, but I would have to think about it for a long time before taking it on."

"That's a problem for the future. I have no doubt that we'll get your starship repaired, but we may never figure out where the cave dwellers came from."

"It will take time, but I think we'll solve the mystery."

A couple minutes later, Jerry landed the helicopter on Pioneer Island. "Let's go fry some fish, build a big campfire, and enjoy the evening."

"Sounds great!"

Chapter Sixteen

TIME: Day 38, Pre-sunrise.

Jerry and Connie woke up early. They went outside to enjoy the double sunrise and the breathtaking views over the lake.

"Early morning is my favorite time of the day," commented Connie. "It's so quiet and peaceful."

"I sometimes wish I had more peace and quiet in my life," stated Jerry.

"You'd get bored with too much of that."

"You're probably right, but I wouldn't mind trying it for a few days."

"That's not likely to happen for a while, so let's just enjoy what we have at the moment."

"Okay, take a look behind you," suggested Jerry, while pointing at the eastern horizon.

Connie turned around and exclaimed, "Wow! That is spectacular. The whole sky is glowing orange, and it's reflecting off the lake."

"We're only a minute or two away from first sunrise."

"That must be Alpha Centauri B. Only its orange color could make the sky look like that."

"You're right. Today, Alpha Centauri B will rise a half-hour ahead of Alpha Centauri A. Less than six months from now, there will be a day when B will rise at the same time that A sets."

"That's going to be an amazing event for us earthlings," commented Connie. "Think about it, for several weeks before and after that day, it's just not going to get dark. We'll have normal days with a Sun-like star traversing the sky, but then, when it should be night, we'll have a dim orange sun in the sky. That's going to be eerie."

"Much of what we have here is strange compared to what we had on Earth, but that's what makes our life so interesting and challenging."

"And enjoyable," added Connie, as the first direct rays of orange light from a rising Alpha Centauri B lit her face with a soft orange glow.

"You look wild as an orange-tinted blond."

"Good! That means I fit right in here on this wild planet."

"You are a perfect fit into my life, no matter where we are."

Connie turned around, embraced her husband, and kissed him warmly. "I love you, and I love it here." She turned back to face Alpha Centauri B. "Take a look at this gorgeous sunrise," she said.

"It is breathtaking," agreed Jerry.

"It's so beautiful here that I wouldn't want to live anywhere else," Connie said, passionately.

"I wouldn't either, but Trang is talking about leaving."

"Why?"

"He's thinking about going on another interstellar voyage."

"He must have some pretty awesome destination in mind if he's willing to leave this planet."

"He does. He wants to investigate what he believes might be the origin of the human species. If we can figure out where the cave dwellers came from, he might go there."

"I think I know," stated Michelle, who just arrived.

"How did you figure that out?" Jerry asked.

"From the artwork on the belt buckle emblem."

"That's a strange looking diagram," commented Jerry. "I couldn't make any sense out of it."

"At first glance, it doesn't make any sense. It just looks like some weird, complicated geometric design, but I played around with it in the computer. I converted it to various 3-d shapes and looked at them from different perspectives. But that didn't get me anywhere, so I went back to the basic diagram and simplified it by removing parts of it. When I removed all the lines and looked at the remaining points against a dark background, I became convinced I was looking at a star chart."

"Where did you go with that idea?" Jerry asked.

"As you know, stars aren't stationary objects, they are in motion. So I asked the computer to consider Sun-like stars in our part of the galaxy and go back in time. I asked it if there was a location from which an observer could have seen the pattern on the emblem."

"What did the computer come up with?" Jerry asked.

"It came up with a match."

"Really!"

"Yes!"

"How far back in time?"

"The best match occurred 123,000 years ago. At that time, an observer on a planet orbiting a Sun-like star located 60 light-years from here could've seen a star pattern matching the diagram on the belt buckle."

"Did the computer put names on the stars in the pattern?" Jerry asked.

"Yes, and what's exciting is the five central stars in the pattern are Alpha Centauri A and B, the Sun, Tau Ceti, and Delta Pavonis."

"Wow!" exclaimed Jerry. "This is another piece of evidence supporting Akeyco's common origin theory."

"And the time period of 123,000 years ago fits quite nicely in the 75,000 to 150,000-year age range my husband came up with for the knife."

"This is exciting," stated Connie. "It seems like it really is probable that humans, Proteans, the people at Tau Ceti, and Zeb's people have a common origin."

"That's right," agreed Michelle. "Our ancestors in the distant past may have come from that star 60 light-years from here. I think we should give it a name and call it the Genesis Star."

"We might be jumping to conclusions too fast," stated Jerry. "That's a fitting name, only if that star really is the birthplace of the human species."

"For the sake of discussion, let's assume that it is for the time being," responded Connie. "We can always change the name later."

"But I thought the first evidence for human life on Earth was found in Africa and dates back about 3,800,000 years," argued Jerry.

"That's true," agreed Michelle, "but Neanderthal Man became extinct. They were replaced by Cro-Magnon Man."

"Maybe Cro-Magnon Man descended from humans planted on Earth by colonizers from the Genesis Star?" suggested Jerry.

"It's certainly possible," responded Michelle. "Even after losing the advanced technology they started with, they would've still been superior to the Neanderthals and could've wiped them out as they expanded around the planet."

"If that's what happened, I wonder why they succeeded on Earth but failed here," questioned Jerry.

"There are lots of ways to fail," commented Connie. "A highly contagious, deadly disease is one way to wipe out an entire population."

"We have to make sure that doesn't happen to us," Jerry said.

"That's my number one responsibility," stated Connie, "and I have lots of high-tech equipment to work with."

"My husband is quite talented at keeping high-tech equipment in good working order," commented Michelle.

"I know," agreed Jerry, "and right now, he's working hard to get Trang's starship off of Aphrodite."

"I talked with him late last night," Michelle said, "and he told me that the beam building project is going faster than expected."

"Trang will like that," stated Jerry, as he picked up his communicator and called Mike. "Good morning Mike! How are you doing?"

"Great!"

"Your wife just told me you might finish the beams sooner than you thought."

"We should be done by tomorrow afternoon. Kon and I decided to make the beams only strong enough to safely get the starship off Aphrodite, rather than build them to original specs."

"Aphrodite's gravity is barely .1g, so that should save a lot of time."

"It's going to take a year or two to fully rebuild the ship, so we thought it made good sense to just get it into space as soon as possible and get started with that. We can strengthen the beams later. Also, the lighter beams will ease the delivery problem. I can easily deliver them in three trips with the modified ERV, instead of the ten I thought it might take."

"Once again, you've turned a seemingly difficult job into an easy one."

"That sounds like a compliment."

"It was."

"Thank you."

"Has Trang been told about the change?"

"I don't think so. You guys were busy all day yesterday and were partying last night, so we decided to tell you this morning."

"You just changed our plans for today. We were planning to go

324

deep sea fishing, but I think we should try to get Trang's shuttle out of the jungle."

"I don't want to be blamed for depriving you of a fishing expedition," commented Mike with a chuckle.

"Don't worry. It won't be canceled, just delayed. If we can get that shuttle out of the jungle by tomorrow afternoon, we can go to Aphrodite the next day."

"I will have the beams ready by then."

"Jerry, old buddy, this is Moose. When you get ready to put the deep-sea fishing trip back on the calendar, I'll be available to go with."

"Are you sure you have the time? I don't want to put any pressure on your schedule."

"Don't worry about my schedule. I'll make the time. Somebody has to show you how to catch the big ones."

"That sure sounds like bragging," stated Mike.

"It sounded like a challenge to me," commented Jerry.

"You guys can take it anyway you want," responded Moose, "but my fishing skills are an undisputed fact of life."

"Jerry! You need to rescue me," stated Mike. "It's getting awfully deep up here, and your starship's recycling systems are on the verge of being overloaded."

"I think there's only one way to deal with this," replied Jerry, "and that's to have a contest. I have a few fishing tricks up my sleeve, and I believe with a little planning, I can catch a bigger fish than Moose."

"You're on," stated Moose. "What will be the prize for this contest?"

"Bragging rights will be good enough for me," stated Jerry.

"You'll have to earn them first," responded Moose.

"No problem."

"We'll see about that."

"Go ahead and make your best plans. I'll let you know when the trip is on, but right now, I have to get Trang out of bed. We have work to do."

TIME: Day 38, 10:30 AM

Jerry landed the cargo shuttle on Crater Lake and brought it to a stop near the lake's center. "The last time I landed here, I got captured by aliens," he said.

"I don't believe that will happen today," responded Trang with a broad grin. "As far as I know, there aren't any aliens living in this area."

"If you're sure about that, I won't worry about it."

"You can trust me on this one."

"Okay, let's go to your shuttle and get the job done."

"That sounds good to me," Trang said.

Jerry opened the cargo shuttle's upper doors and raised the elevator deck to its top position, where it became the helicopter's flight deck. Everyone went to the helicopter and quickly prepared it for flight.

Jerry designated two people to remain on the cargo shuttle to stand guard. Then, he and the remaining people took off and headed toward Trang's shuttle.

Turning to Trang, Jerry asked, "Is there any part of your shuttle that we can't walk on?"

"No, it's all rugged, sturdy structure."

"Good, we'll get started with the cleanup job while you and Jim go pick up your crew."

When the helicopter arrived over Trang's shuttle, Jim brought it to a hover just above the treetops, which put them 200 feet above the shuttle. Jerry and two assistants stepped into the cage hanging on the end of the winch cable. With the controls in his right hand, Jerry pressed the button to begin the descent. "Keep you eyes open and your guns ready," he said, as they dropped slowly and cautiously through the thick green foliage into the dense jungle.

Speaking to Trang through his communicator, Jerry said, "We have lots of trees to cut down before you can fly your shuttle out of here."

"Let's not start that until after I get my crew here. We need extra people on guard. There might be a large lupusaurus pack in this area."

"Their den might be under your shuttle."

"Why do you say that?"

"When we explored your shuttle, it looked to us like the area under it might be a rest area for a large group of animals."

"That could only be a lupusaurus pack. There aren't any other animals in this area that would live there in a large group. Be very alert. They can leap quite high and might be able to get on top the shuttle."

"When the rest of my crew comes down, have them bring along an RPV, so I can look under the shuttle and recon the immediate area."

"Will do," replied Trang.

"We're here," stated Jerry.

Jerry's two crew members stepped out and immediately assumed guard duty, looking for any wildlife that might pose a threat. Jerry stepped out and sent the cage back up to the helicopter.

Shortly thereafter, the cage returned with the other two crew members and some equipment. The cage was returned to the helicopter, and the rest of the equipment was sent down.

With everything unloaded, Jim said, "We're on the way to pick up Trang's crew."

"Try to stay out of trouble while we're gone," Trang said.

"Before we do anything, I'm going to scout the area," Jerry said, "and I am going to look under this shuttle first."

The area under Trang's shuttle was very large, not just because the shuttle was enormous, but also because of its design. It consisted of a big delta wing smoothly blended into its fuselage, rather than a conventional swept wing. The space under the shuttle was cave-like and dark, because dense vegetation walled it in and prevented most light from entering the area.

Jerry circled the shuttle with the RPV and found an opening through the living wall of foliage. He noted that the break in the plant life appeared to be a well used game trail.

After exploring the area under the shuttle for a few minutes, Jerry called Trang and said, "There's no doubt in my mind that your shuttle is a roof over a lair. There are three breaks in the vegetation that make up the walls of this den. All three look like well used game trails."

"Stay alert! The lupusaurs are vicious, intelligent hunters, and they will be back sometime."

Jerry flew the RPV along each of the three game trails. Then, he searched the jungle around the shuttle. "The area seems to be clear," he said to his crew.

Jerry kept two of them on guard duty. The other two fired up high-power debris blowers and began cleaning the shuttle.

Twenty minutes later, Trang arrived with his five-person crew.

They went to work with vine cutters, rakes, shovels, and forks to clear compost and living plant life off the shuttle in areas where the blowers weren't adequate for the job.

"We're fortunate that none of these trees have ever fallen," commented Trang.

"They're still young and healthy," stated Jerry. "They're just not old enough to fall."

"That might be, but we've had some powerful tropical storms, every bit as destructive as any of the hurricanes you saw on Earth. Fortunately, this area escaped the worst of them."

"So, do you think this vehicle is still in flying condition?"

"With a new combustion chamber and some fuel, it will fly."

"Where does the new combustion chamber go?"

"It is the first stage combustor for the antimatter rocket in the aft fuselage."

"How was an engine buried in the fuselage damaged?"

"When we fought the battle with Zeb's colleagues, one of them died under the tail. In his death throes, he emptied his rifle in the fuselage directly above him. Some of the bullets wrecked the combustion chamber."

"How long will it take to change out the chamber?"

"Five or six hours should do it; unless, we run into problems."

"When do you want to start working on it?"

"Right after I give you a quick tour." Trang led the way to a hatch in the fuselage, which he opened with an electronic key.

"This shuttle is much bigger than my cargo shuttle," commented Jerry. "Why is it so big?"

"We followed a different design philosophy than you did. This bird serves a second purpose. When we're in space, it is used for part of our living quarters. Then, when we land on planets, we have furnished apartments for the landing party."

"But you have been living in caves."

"After the battle and the loss of the new combustion chamber, we decided to abandon the shuttle and move to an area better suited to our needs."

Trang led Jerry down the central hallway to the largest apartment, which they entered. "This is one of the rooms Geniya and I lived in during our space travels."

Jerry glanced around the room. His eyes focused on the Star Trek pictures on one wall. "Why the pictures of Captain Kirk, Spock, and Scotty?" he asked.

"My wife and I are Star Trek fans. When we cruised by Earth, one of your TV channels was running a Star Trek marathon. We managed to record sixty-seven episodes. My entire crew became Trekies. That's how we all became so fluent in English."

"The Star Trek series is a classic. Everyone on my crew has seen every episode several times. We have all of them."

"I would like to get the ones we don't have."

"Give me a list of the titles you have, and we'll give you the rest."

"Thanks, I appreciate that."

"By the way, when we explored this shuttle with a little bug, we saw a locked door at the aft end of the cargo bay. What's on the other side of that door?"

"An antimatter-fueled rocket with a primary combustion chamber that is full of bullet holes."

"What's the engine's basic design?"

"In its primary combustion chamber, it uses antimatter to heat water to a high-pressure, high-temperature vapor. To get the most out of a given quantity of water, we employ an extra long nozzle. As the vapor expands down the extended nozzle, it cools off losing energy, so we add energy to the vapor by injecting additional antimatter into it at various points along the nozzle. In effect, the nozzle is an extended secondary combustion chamber."

"I like the concept," responded Jerry. "It reduces the amount of water you need to fly into orbit, which reduces the internal wing space that you need to devote to water tanks. Internal space is at a premium, so that's a big advantage."

"Also, this shuttle's blended wing-body design creates extra internal space. The wing roots are very thick, and the apartments we live in actually extend into the wings about 15 feet. Just beyond them, we've located the antimatter-fueled, air-breathing turbines and the lift fans. From there on out, the wings are water tanks for the main propulsion rocket."

"I can see how the elongated nozzle with extra fuel injection greatly increases the efficiency of your shuttle, but the aft end doesn't seem long enough to house such a nozzle."

"The nozzle is built in three sections that retract for storage."

"That's yet another design efficiency. When we explored this shuttle a few days ago, we had no idea how capable it really is."

"There's more. After takeoff, the lift fans can be disengaged, and the turbines can be used as ordinary jet engines. Since the turbines operate with antimatter fuel, the range is anywhere on the planet, many times over."

"So why did you bring down an airplane?"

"It is small and more practical when we only want to take a few people out and back."

"I am impressed with your design and mission philosophy."

"There's still more. The flight deck on this shuttle can be used to operate my starship. It is a complete backup system. If the starship's flight deck were to become inoperative for whatever reason, a meteor hit, for example, the starship could be operated from this shuttle."

"I am really impressed. Is there still more?"

"That's pretty much it, so let's get the rest of the tools we need and get busy installing that chamber."

TIME: Day 38, 7:00 PM

"This installation took a little longer than I thought," commented Trang, "but this engine is ready to go."

"When do you want to attempt a takeoff?" Jerry asked.

"You sound like you think this bird won't fly."

"Well, it has been stranded here for more than 30 years."

"One leg of our interstellar voyage took almost that long, and this shuttle still performed well when we needed it."

"Okay, let me rephrase the question. When do you want to get this bird out of here?"

"Let's go outside and check our crew's progress."

When they were back out on the wing, Trang slowly turned completely around, looking at his shuttle and the surrounding jungle. "It looks like we're ready to go," he said.

"Are you sure? It looks to me like we need to cut down a few more trees."

"I won't have any trouble lifting out of here. This shuttle has finely tuned controls. It was designed to get into and out of tight spots."

"What's your flight plan?"

"Straight up until we clear the treetops by a couple hundred yards, then, I'll transition to forward flight, cruise to Sandstone Lake, and make a hydrofoil landing."

"Do you have enough fuel to do that?"

"I think so, but it will be close."

"We could go up to the Challenger and get some."

"I don't think that will be necessary. I've worked the numbers several times, and I believe I have enough with a small safety margin. Anyway, the landing approach will be over Crater Lake, so if I run out, I'll just land there."

"I haven't seen your numbers, but I get the feeling that you're cutting it too close. If an unforeseen problem comes up, and you don't even make it to Crater Lake, you could end up crashing in the jungle. Then, you lose your shuttle, and maybe even your life."

"I guess that is a possibility," admitted Trang.

"For the minor inconvenience of a trip to the Challenger, we can pick up enough fuel to get this shuttle into and out of orbit a few times. Just give me back the fuel when we get your starship back into space."

"You got yourself a deal."

"The rest of the deal is that you need to put my crew up for the night. I'm not going back to Pioneer Island tonight. I want to go directly to the Challenger from here."

"Not a problem. My people will show your crew the best in cave dwelling."

"Is it safe to leave my chopper parked in front of your caves for the night? What I mean is; will anything attack it because it carries the human scent?"

"I don't think so, but we can post a couple guards to make sure."

"Well, it looks like we're done for the day. Let's clear out."

TIME: Day 39, 9:00 AM

Jerry and Trang landed on Crater Lake after spending the night on the Challenger. They opened the cargo shuttle's upper doors and moved the elevator deck to its top position. Then, they awaited the arrival of Jim and the helicopter.

"As soon as we install these fuel canisters, we can get my shuttle out of the jungle," exclaimed Trang, enthusiastically.

"It's really amazing when you think about," commented Jerry.

"What is?"

"The fact that there's enough energy available from the antimatter in these two canisters to take your shuttle into and out of orbit several times, and we can easily pick them up and carry them."

"We can carry them, but it's a stretch to say that it's easy. They do weigh a hundred pounds each."

"That's true, but most of that weight is for the tank, the electro-magnets, and the power pack. The antimatter is only a few ounces. Compared to the rockets used in the early days of the space age, it's amazing that so little antimatter can take your shuttle into and out of orbit many times."

"We definitely live in a marvelous age. So why does your heli-copter rely on alcohol fuel?"

"Our antimatter technology isn't as advanced as yours. We can easily make alcohol, but the equipment to make antimatter was impossible to bring along."

"We're going to give you our technology."

"I appreciate that. It won't help my chopper, but I'll be able to refuel my starship."

"There's our ride," commented Trang, while pointing at the still distant helicopter.

A short time later, Trang and Jerry were back on top of Trang's shuttle with three guards. A loud, snarling growl got their attention. A lupusaur had jumped onto a cut-down tree. From there, it had leapt onto the shuttle and screamed out its menacing growl. The nearest guard quickly aimed and fired his rifle, instantly killing the beast.

"They're back!" exclaimed Jerry.

"When I fire up the turbines and turn on the lift fans, it's going to get very windy under this shuttle, and they will have to leave or be blown away."

Two more lupusaurs hopped on the shuttle and were quickly killed by the guards. "Let's get these fuel canisters installed and get out of here," stated Trang.

Again, the rifles boomed. "How many do we have to kill before they get the message?" Jerry asked. "They remind me of piranhas. They just keep coming."

"These animals are the dominant predator in this area, and they're used to getting their way. Around our cliff homes, it took quite a while for them to accept the idea that they had to leave us alone."

"Maybe if we push the bodies off the shuttle, so they can see the results of coming up here, they'll leave us alone."

"It's worth a try," responded Trang.

332

Trang and Jerry headed for the carcasses, and one by one, they dragged them to the edge of the wing and pushed them off. The bodies fell into the brush below with a crashing thud. The guards shot three more in defense of Trang and Jerry.

Jerry and Trang looked down on the dead animals. Living members of the pack were examining them. They pushed them with their noses and rolled them over. Getting no response, they looked up at the humans and growled hideously, but they kept their distance.

"I think they got the message," commented Jerry.

"I don't trust them," stated Trang. "Let's get the fuel canisters installed and take off."

Trang glanced over the left wing's upper surface and spotted the access panel he was looking for. He opened it, reached inside, and pressed a button. A cradle on the bottom of the chamber rose up, and Trang placed one of the fuel canisters on it. He pressed another button and the cradle descended back to the bottom. Support clamps moved in from the sides and locked the canister in place. Finally, a fuel line connected itself to the canister. Trang closed the access panel. "We're done with this one," he said.

"That was too easy," commented Jerry.

"All of our systems are designed for easy operation and maintenance. Let's drop this canister into the other wing."

"Are those lupusaurs ever going to quit howling?"

"It almost sounds like they're mourning their dead," commented Trang.

"I don't know what they're doing, but the shrill tone and the loudness of it are having a bone chilling effect on my spine."

"It is terrifying, but our guards are very good with their rifles."

"Let's get out of here anyway."

Fifteen minutes later, Trang and Jerry were inside the shuttle, seated in the cockpit. Jim had already returned and picked up the guards.

"The time has come," stated Trang, as he turned on the flight control computer, which he instructed to run through a systems check.

Jerry heard equipment coming to life all over the shuttle. After being dormant for thirty years, the shuttle seemed to rejoice at waking up from its long sleep. Green lights were coming on all over a video display as various systems passed their checkout.

"Everything is a go," stated Trang, jubilantly.

"Well, let's find out if this old tub can get off the ground," stated Jerry.

Trang initiated the start sequence for the turbine in the left wing. It came to life with a barely perceptible whine and a muffled roar. "The engine is running well," stated Trang.

"Was there any doubt?" questioned Jerry.

"Let's just say that there was some concern, and I'm now breathing easier."

Trang hit the start sequence for the turbine in the right wing. It also came to life with a barely audible whine and a subdued roar.

"Your sound insulation is effective," commented Jerry. "I can barely hear the engines."

"They're just idling. Believe me; you are going to hear them when they're at full power."

"How long are we going to sit here and idle?"

"These engines haven't been run in a long time. I need to bring them up slowly while I monitor their health."

"Understood."

"Also, I want to give the lupusaurs a chance to escape. A sudden, full-power takeoff would kill or cripple those that are under the shuttle."

"You're showing a lot of concern for vicious killers."

"That may be, but I don't believe in killing when it isn't necessary."

"I don't either."

Trang shifted the lift fans into gear and said, "Even with the fans running at this low power, it should be pretty windy under this shuttle. I'm surprised they're not yet leaving."

"This has been their home for a long time, and they are stubborn animals."

"Well, this is my shuttle, and it's going away," stated Trang, as he brought the turbines up to a higher power setting.

"There's a lot of debris blowing around out there," commented Jerry, while looking out one of the flight deck windows.

"There go the lupusaurs," stated Trang.

"Wow! Are they ever leaving in a big hurry. I didn't know they could run that fast."

"They're not as fast as the saber tooth cats, but they make up for it with teamwork."

"Are we going to sit here and talk all day, or are we going to find out if this thing can still fly?"

"So far, everything looks good. The engines are performing exactly as they should."

"We need to get out of here before we get hit by some of the debris you're blowing around out there."

"You're right. I'm going to assume the engines are totally healthy."

Trang rapidly pushed the throttles to full power. The nearly empty shuttle leapt off the ground and cleared the treetops with a display of agility that seemed out of character for a vehicle its size.

Trang climbed to 3,000 feet before beginning the transition to horizontal flight. Upon reaching 200 mph, he disengaged the lift fans and used his turbines as jet engines to continue accelerating and climbing.

"Man, it feels good to get my shuttle back!" exclaimed Trang, who was acting like a kid with a new toy. "Thanks to you, fuel isn't a problem, so we're going to have some fun before we land."

"What do you have in mind?"

"This shuttle's been grounded for a long time, so I think a thorough test flight is in order."

"That could be dangerous for a vehicle that's been out of action so long."

"What you and I do for a living is dangerous. Our lives are filled with risks."

"That's true, but I try to avoid unnecessary risk."

"Would you feel better if I landed and left you off before I do this test flight?"

"No! I'll stay right here."

"I thought so."

"What kind of test flight are we going to do?"

"We'll climb to 110,000 feet and reach a speed of mach seven. After cruising for several minutes, we'll begin our descent to a landing on Clear Lake. We'll eat lunch with our wives, put some water in the wing tanks, take off, and test the rocket. Then, we'll land on Sandstone Lake."

"That sounds like two test flights."

"The wing tanks are empty, so we have to make a second test flight."

"I hope I live through all of this."

"You have nothing to worry about. This vehicle is designed for absolute safety and reliability."

"If that's true, why do we need to make these test flights?"

"As a responsible captain, I have to check this thing out before I can return it to operational use and put my people at risk."

"That sounds good, but I think you nailed it earlier."

"What do you mean?"

"You said we're going to have some fun, so I suspect that the real reason for these test flights is that you enjoy flying your shuttle and haven't been able to do that in 30 years."

"Well, that might have something to do with it."

"It's got more to do with it than you're admitting."

Trang smiled and didn't say anything.

"What I'm wondering is how are you going to get to mach seven at 110,000 feet with turbojets?"

"They're combined cycle engines. At 80,000 feet and mach 3.5, they will convert to ramjets."

"Now, I'm really impressed with your shuttle. Being able to reach mach seven at 110,000 feet with air-breathing engines greatly reduces the quantity of water required to achieve orbit, and that translates directly to increased payload."

"We had to come up with an efficient propulsion system. It was the only way we could get all the capability and mission flexibility we wanted."

"Maybe we should let our wives know we're coming home for lunch."

Trang called Geniya. "We have our shuttle back," he exclaimed, joyfully.

"Where are you?" she asked.

"About 15 minutes away from Pioneer Island."

"How does it feel to be back in the pilot's seat?"

"My feelings are flying high, right along with the shuttle."

"You sound high. Are you going to make a couple passes over the island, so we can see your new toy in operation?"

"Is that a request?"

"I would love to see a flyover."

"Since you asked, I think we could do that."

"Like you weren't planning to, anyway."

"Well, maybe we were."

"Just don't blow us away with loud acrobatics; we are a nice quiet community."

"OK! We'll take it easy."

"Sounds good."

"Oh, one other thing, Jerry and I are hungry."

"How about a picnic lunch on the beach of South Bay?"

"That will be fun. See you shortly."

Geniya turned to Connie. "We don't have much time to put this lunch together."

"We have more than enough food in the refrigerator for a picnic lunch." Connie grabbed an ice chest and filled it with selected items. She filled a basket with bread, sweet rolls, and fresh fruit. "Let's go," she said, heading for the door with the ice chest.

"That was quick," Geniya remarked, carrying the basket.

"It was easy. Moose has provided us with quite a variety of smoked fish and meat products. They're perfect for a picnic lunch. Plus, there's the salad I made up this morning."

Connie and Geniya stepped into an ATV and headed for South Bay. "Where are the children?" Geniya asked.

"Michelle and Akeyco took them to South Bay, so they could play on the beach and go swimming."

"Good, they can join us for lunch."

"They'll be excited when the shuttle arrives. They don't even know it's on the way."

Connie drove the ATV as fast as safety allowed while Geniya searched the sky. Halfway to South Bay, she spotted the approaching shuttle in the southern sky. "There it is!" she exclaimed, unable to contain her excitement.

Because of the shuttle's size, it appeared closer than it was. By the time it arrived over the island, Connie and Geniya were parked at the south end of the plateau, overlooking South Bay.

At an altitude of 1,500 feet, the shuttle passed directly overhead. It had very little speed and seemed to float effortlessly across the sky. Trang had changed his mind about doing a hydrofoil landing and had engaged the lift fans. He wanted to demonstrate his shuttle's low speed handling characteristics.

"It sure is graceful in flight," stated Geniya. "What a shame that it was stranded on the ground for so many years."

After floating around the area for a few minutes, Trang piloted his shuttle to the south and slowly descended into the water a couple hundred yards outside of South Bay. Deploying the shuttle's marine propeller, he taxied into the bay.

Connie and Geniya rode the elevator from the top of the plateau down to the beach. "This 150-foot descent in an open cage is still a thrilling ride," commented Connie.

"Not to mention the view," noted Geniya. "You sure have a picturesque setting for your home."

"We love it here."

Once on the beach, they put the ice chest and basket on the table and stepped into a boat, which they rowed out to the shuttle. Their husbands were waiting at an open hatch a few feet above the water.

"Thanks for picking us up," Jerry said, while stepping into the boat.

"What's it feel like to fly in a shuttle from Delta Pavonis?" Connie asked.

"Trang has a very well designed vehicle," replied Jerry. "It's fun to fly and it's very capable."

"When will I get to fly in it?"

"We have another test flight to do before we open it up to the public," responded Trang.

"I hope you're not putting my husband at risk."

"No, we just have to check out a few things."

"How did your flight to here go?" Geniya asked.

"Smooth as silk. Everything worked well."

"I can only hope things go so well when we lift our people and starship off of Aphrodite," Geniya said, her anxiety obvious.

Trang's jubilant mood faded. "They've been stuck there for a very long time, and we are now so close to rescuing them. We must remain confident that all will go well."

Turning to Jerry, Trang said, "We owe you a huge debt of gratitude, in addition to what we are going to give you."

"The antimatter production technology and the age control drug have astounding implications for our future. You owe us nothing more. Besides, we would help you with the rescue even if you gave us nothing more than a heartfelt, thank you."

"I like you," stated Trang. "We have much in common. Let's eat and go make another test flight."

"Good idea!" exclaimed Jerry. "I am hungry."

Shortly, everyone was seated at the outdoor table. "When can I go inside Trang's shuttle?" Matthew asked.

"I want to see it too," Denise demanded.

338

"I also would like a guided tour," stated Akeyco.

"Are you saying you've never been in your own shuttle?" Connie asked.

"I was born after my people abandoned it."

Turning to Trang, Geniya said, "I think you need to give us a tour before you leave."

Speaking to Jerry, Trang said, "It looks like our next test flight is going to be delayed for an hour or two."

"Popular demand is hard to resist," responded Jerry.

"Especially, when it comes from a higher authority," commented Trang.

"I thought you were the captain," teased Jerry.

"I am, but I'm a married captain."

"What's that comment supposed to mean?" demanded Geniya.

Enduring Geniya's stare, Trang seemed at a loss for words. He turned to Jerry and asked, "How do I get out of this?"

"I'm afraid you're on your own," replied Jerry with a broad grin.

All eyes were on Trang while he wracked his brain, searching for the right thing to say. Momentarily, it came to him, and he turned to his wife and said, "What I meant is that you have more influence over me than anyone else, because of our warm, loving relationship."

With a smug smile of satisfaction, Geniya said to Connie and Michelle, "I believe he slipped out of that one without even a bruise."

A half-hour later, everyone was finished with lunch, and Trang welcomed them to his shuttle. Matthew was especially curious. Despite his youth, he seemed to grasp the significance of exploring an aircraft/spacecraft that was designed and built by a human species from another star. He questioned everything, wanting to know what it did and how it worked. When the tour was over, Michelle said, "He definitely takes after his father and will probably be a great engineer someday."

"Or a brilliant science reporter like you," Connie said.

"Now that you put it that way, I do see both of us in him."

Jerry's communicator beeped. It was Mike. "We're about an hour away from finishing the beams," he said.

"That's a couple hours sooner than you told me this morning."

"We didn't run into any problems, and we're farther along on the learning curve."

"Your earlier than expected completion makes it possible for us to deliver them yet today."

"That's the way Moose sees it. He's all hop-de-trot to go deep sea fishing tomorrow."

"He wants to lose his bet that soon."

"I'm not going to lose," stated Moose, jumping into the conversation.

"By tomorrow evening, you'll have to eat your words and swallow your pride," responded Jerry.

"Sounds like we're going to Aphrodite yet today," commented Mike.

"If Trang can get us back to my shuttle, we can be up there in a couple hours."

"I can do that," Trang said, obviously excited about the immediate beam delivery.

Everyone left Trang's shuttle, except him and Jerry. They taxied out of South Bay and took off.

"In our haste to get going, you forgot to pump water into the wing tanks, so we could test the rocket," commented Jerry.

"I didn't forget. I'll test it later. Right now, I just want to get those beams to my starship."

"I can understand that."

After an uneventful flight, Trang landed on Sandstone Lake. Jim was waiting with the helicopter and gave Trang and Jerry a ride to the cargo shuttle in Crater Lake.

Jerry immediately began filling the tanks with water. "It's going to be close, but I think we can make our next launch window," he said. "We should be ready to take off in about 15 minutes, and that is our next opportunity."

Jerry beeped Jim. "I'll have Moose bring this shuttle back and give you guys a ride home."

"We don't mind waiting for Moose. We're being graciously entertained by the local cave dwellers."

"That's great," responded Jerry. "Enjoy yourselves."

Forty minutes later, Trang and Jerry were onboard the Challenger. Speaking to Moose, Jerry said, "I need you to take the cargo shuttle down to Crater Lake and give Jim and the boys a ride home."

"Okay."

"Then, I would like you to get the elevator deck out of the shuttle, load the sub, and get everything ready for tomorrow's fishing expedition."

"I can do that, but I'm worried about you."

"How so?"

"It's going to be late when you get back from Aphrodite."

"Why would that worry you?"

"I'm concerned that you won't be a well rested competitor for tomorrow's fishing contest, and I don't want you to whine about lack of sleep when you come in second best."

"I'll get more than enough sleep to beat you. We're only going to Aphrodite and back."

"When do you expect to return?"

"It's going to take a couple hours to get there, a couple hours to off-load the beams and tools, and a couple hours to return. Mike and I will take the personnel shuttle down. It seems like I should be home around midnight."

"I guess you might get enough sleep to be a viable competitor tomorrow."

"I appreciate your concern, but since you're going to get a full night of sleep, I'm wondering what excuse you're going to dream up when you fail to out-fish me?"

"I'm not going to need one."

"We'll see, but right now, you'd better head for the shuttle. We're only a few minutes away from your de-orbit window."

"I'm on the way."

Two hours and twenty minutes later, the Challenger was hovering above Trang's starship. Mike launched the modified ERV to deliver the first load of beams. During the following hour and a half, the ERV made three additional trips, delivering all beams and the tools needed to install them.

"I guess we're ready to depart," Jerry said.

"The ERV needs to make one more trip to the surface," stated Trang.

"We've already sent everything down," responded Jerry.

"Not everything."

"What else do we need to send down?"

"Me," replied Trang.

"You want to ride the ERV down to the surface. It wasn't designed for that. It could be risky."

"I know, but that's my crippled starship down there, and I need to be actively involved in the structural repairs. I want to be at the controls for the takeoff. This is something I need to do."

"I understand," responded Jerry. "You'll need a space suit. We are about the same size, so you can borrow mine."

"I appreciate that."

Jerry put the Challenger on autopilot, so he could leave the pilot's seat. He went to his personal closet, took out his space suit, and helped Trang suit up. "You know the way to the hangar. I'll tell Mike you're on the way."

"Thanks!"

A few minutes later, the modified ERV left the Challenger for one more trip down to Aphrodite. Part way down, Trang called Jerry. "This is fun," he said. "You should try it sometime."

"I will if the need arises."

When the ERV landed, Trang stepped out and joined his long stranded people. The ERV lifted off for its return flight to the Challenger.

"Glad to see you're safely down," stated Jerry. "Let us know if you need anything."

"Will do," replied Trang. "Once again, thanks for everything."

When the ERV was back onboard, the Challenger departed Aphrodite. Jerry called Connie. "We're on our way home," he said. "Warm up the bed for me."

"That sounds promising," she replied.

Chapter Seventeen

TIME: Day 40, 10:30 AM

Jerry landed the cargo shuttle in the middle of the large saltwater bay located 100 miles southwest of Pioneer Island. The bay was approximately 20 miles wide by 80 miles long and connected to the ocean by an inlet 20 miles across.

"We're not in the ocean," commented Jerry, "but this bay is big, and it is filled with saltwater."

"It should give us a taste of deep sea fishing," stated Moose, who was sitting in the copilot's seat.

"Before we do any fishing, we need to take the sub down and look around for a while," stated Jerry.

"I know," responded Moose. "My wife's been talking about this all morning."

"That's understandable. She's a biologist on her first visit to an alien sea."

"Well, I'm not a biologist, but I'm excited about being here too. Who knows what kind of dangerous animals we might run into."

"If that's the kind of excitement you're looking for, you could end up with a lot more than you want."

"What do you mean?"

"During Earth's dinosaur age, there were some giant predators living in the seas that looked like they came right out of a nightmare."

"That's true," agreed Moose, "but we don't know if similar monsters live here."

"Let's get in the sub and go find out."

A few minutes later, the little submarine dropped clear of the shuttle and headed for the depths. Jerry, Connie, Moose, and Dianne were onboard. Mike and Michelle volunteered to stay with the shuttle.

"What are we going to do while they're gone?" Michelle asked.

"We're going to be busy," replied Mike.

"Okay, why are you grinning?"

"Have you been listening to Moose and Jerry lately?"

"Are you referring to all their macho talk about catching big fish?"

"Precisely."

"What does that have to do with us?"

Mike continued to grin at his wife until her face lit up, and she said, "I get the feeling you've been quietly planning to outdo them."

"It does sound like fun, doesn't it? Imagine this, when they come back, one of them will be all talk about how he won their contest. When that talk has run its course, I'll say, guess what I did today. Then, when I have their attention, I'll quietly display my catch for them to feast their eyes on."

"How do you plan to do this?"

"I have a theory I am going to test. Then, we'll see what happens."

"Would you mind explaining that?"

"My theory is that you can find any kind of fish here that exists on Earth."

"How does that help you?"

"I am going after a different kind of fish than they're after. What I will try to catch might not exist here, but I believe that it or something similar does."

"What are you hoping to catch?"

"Back on Earth, there are bottom fish that grow quite large. For example, freshwater sturgeon can grow to several hundred pounds."

"But this is saltwater."

"This planet might have a saltwater version of Earth's freshwater sturgeon. If not, maybe I'll catch something similar to Earth's halibut. They are bottom dwelling saltwater fish and can grow to well over 100 pounds."

"What do you think Moose and Jerry are trying to catch?"

"They're going after a migratory fish that grows larger than Earth's king salmon. In fact, the one that Moose caught in Clear Lake a couple weeks ago did weigh just over 100 pounds."

"How do you know that's what they're after?"

"Moose made two new lures that are enlarged, altered versions of the one he used to catch the hundred-pounder."

"What about Jerry?"

"Last night, on the way back from Aphrodite, he was hard at work in the shop. He put his imagination into making a couple lures that are distinctly different from Moose's. He proudly showed them to me and explained why they're better than Moose's original that worked so well."

"So what's your strategy?"

"I have another theory."

"Which is?"

"It seems reasonable to assume that big fish living on or near the bottom would feed on smaller fish living down there. So the first thing I'm going to do is bottom fish for something small. Then, I'm going to use it for bait."

"I think you have too many theories that have to hold up for you to be successful."

"You might be right, but I'm going to give it a shot."

"Well, maybe you'll get lucky."

"I admit it. There is an element of luck in fishing, but I am going to put myself in a position where I can get lucky."

Meanwhile, the submarine was cruising at a depth of 90 feet, near the center of the bay. "How deep is it here?" Connie asked.

"About 200 feet," replied Jerry.

"I came here to study marine life," Dianne said. "Does the sonar show anything nearby?"

"There's a group of large creatures near the surface a half-mile to the left, and there's a huge animal a mile directly ahead. It appears to be heading toward a large school of fish that is a quarter-mile ahead and 45 degrees to the right."

"I think we should go there and see what happens when the giant arrives," commented Dianne.

"How big is it?" asked Connie.

Jerry put the question to the computer, and it sent out sonar signals at many different frequencies to size the animal. Then, it displayed a sketch on the video screen with numbers on it.

"It looks like we just discovered Alcent's version of Earth's extinct elasmosaurus," commented Dianne.

"And this one's about 90 feet long," stated Jerry.

"I think we should stay away from it," warned Connie. "It's huge!"

"I don't believe it can hurt us," responded Jerry.

"Why do you think that?" Connie asked, sounding worried.

"To start with, this sub is very rugged. It is able to withstand the immense pressure at a depth of 5000 feet."

"But look at the size of that animal," argued Connie. "It's a monster!"

"That's true, but half of its length is made up by its long, snake-like neck. Another 15 feet goes to its tail. That leaves about 30 feet for its body, which means that its body is smaller than our sub. And the four flippers attached to the body are for swimming and just don't have the heavy bony structure needed to be a threat to our sub."

"But it's hideous," argued Connie. "It's right out of a nightmare, and I don't want to get close to it."

"It might look hideous," agreed Dianne, "but Jerry's right. Getting close to it should not put us in serious danger."

"Why are you so sure about that?"

"Look at this sketch," advised Dianne. "This animal just simply isn't equipped to damage our sub. It is very well equipped to do what it does best, and that's to catch and eat fish."

"It looks like we're going to arrive at the school of fish at the same time it does," commented Jerry, while viewing the sonar display.

"It appears that the fish aren't yet aware of the approaching hunter," noted Moose. "They're just nonchalantly milling around."

"Safety in numbers is one of the benefits fish receive from forming large schools," stated Dianne. "There are several thousand fish in this school. Even if the elasmosaurus eats quite a few of them, the survival odds for each individual fish are still very good."

"We're here," announced Jerry, as the submarine slipped into the school.

"This is amazing," exclaimed Connie. "There are fish everywhere. I've never seen so many at the same time."

"They don't appear to be concerned about us," commented Dianne. "Other than getting out of our way, they seem to be ignoring us."

"Apparently, they don't see us as an enemy," noted Jerry.

"Look at their size," exclaimed Moose. "They all look over a hundred pounds. I'd sure like to troll one of my new lures through them."

"You'd do better with one of mine," commented Jerry.

"I can't believe this," exclaimed Connie. "We're steadily approaching a sea monster, and you guys are talking about fishing.

346

Has it occurred to either of you that fishing this bay could be dangerous? The monster could use its long neck and wide open jaws to strike like a giant snake and grab one of you while you're fishing."

"That's a possibility we'll have to guard against," acknowledged Jerry.

"The fish are getting frenzied in their movements," commented Dianne.

"The elasmosaurus is less than 100 yards away," noted Jerry, "and it's coming on fast."

"There it is!" exclaimed Connie. "It's coming right at us!"

At the last instant, the beast veered to the right. Its long, snake-like neck was coiled. Suddenly, the coiled neck straightened out, snapping the beast's head forward with unbelievable speed. Wide open jaws snapped shut, crushing a doomed fish in a vice-like grip. The beast released the dead fish, turned it around, and swallowed it headfirst.

Immediately, the elasmosaurus used its long neck to strike again. This time, it missed. Twice more, it missed. A fourth strike was successful, and it repeated the killing and eating process. Then, as quickly as the attack began, the beast retreated in the direction from which it came.

"I hope that thing never comes to Clear Lake," stated Connie.

"I hope so too," agreed Jerry. "A swimmer encountering it would have no chance."

"We need to install a sonar warning system in the river at the south end of Clear Lake," recommended Moose.

"We also need to install one around our island," stated Connie. "Our children love to play in the water."

"We have to warn Mike and Michelle," Dianne said. "They might be sunbathing on top the shuttle. An elasmosaurus could easily grab one of them."

"Mike installed a sonar system in the shuttle's cargo bay," Jerry said. "He deployed it before he launched this sub, and he has it programmed to sound a warning if anything of consequence approaches."

"Even so, we should tell him what we've just seen," Dianne insisted.

Jerry called Mike and described in detail the experience they had just been through. "It sounds like your cruise is keeping you awake despite your shortage of sleep last night," commented Mike.

"It's definitely doing that," responded Jerry.

"Where are you going now?"

"There's a group of large creatures a half-mile north of us. We're going to check them out."

"Be careful. You don't know what you're getting into."

"We are inside a very sturdy vessel."

"I know, but be careful anyway."

"You can count on that. Talk to you later."

Turning to Michelle, Mike said, "Wow! What an adventure they're having."

"They're not as exposed to danger as we are. Maybe we should go back inside."

"I don't think that's necessary, because our sonar will warn us. Besides, I need to catch my bait, so I can get down to some serious fishing."

"You sure put a lot of trust in your sonar."

"It's very reliable, and it does have performance monitoring software. If there's any malfunction, it will let us know. So just relax and enjoy yourself."

"You relax! I'm going to keep a nervous finger on the trigger, just in case."

"Thanks dear. That leaves me free to concentrate on catching some bait."

"How much concentration does it take to dangle your fishhook along the bottom?" teased Michelle.

"It's not just a fishhook; it's a carefully designed lure."

"All that just to catch bait."

"Fishing is more than just luck. It requires planning and talent."

"You're starting to sound like Moose."

"You'll talk a different tune, after you see the results my strategy gets."

"Now you really sound like Moose."

Just then, Mike's fishing rod bent sharply. "I don't know what I've hooked, but it's definitely bigger than bait," Mike exclaimed.

"Are you going to be able to land it with that light-weight, 'bait-catching' tackle you're using?"

"I don't know, but I'm going to try."

"You're going to be busy for a while."

"No doubt about that. Keep your eyes open for trouble."

"Don't worry! You still have a guard with a nervous trigger finger."

"Good! I have to concentrate on this, because I've hooked something heavy, and it's going to take time and patience to bring it up from the bottom with this tackle."

"You can do it. You always find a way to make the difficult look easy."

Meanwhile, on the submarine, Jerry said, "We're getting close."

"I wonder what kind of animals they are," questioned Moose.

"We'll soon know," responded Jerry.

"The sonar generated images indicate they are similar to Earth's extinct ichthyosaurus," commented Dianne.

"Are they dangerous?" Connie asked.

"They're fish eaters," replied Dianne. "I don't know if they would attack people in the water."

A couple minutes later, the submarine arrived in their midst. "They look big enough to be a threat to swimmers," noted Connie.

"Are you going swimming?" Jerry asked Connie.

"No!" She instantly replied.

"When you mentioned swimmers, I didn't know what you had in mind," Jerry teased.

"I wasn't suggesting that we go swimming."

"These creatures might be friendly," commented Dianne.

"I don't want to find out," stated Connie.

"I think they might be among the more intelligent members of the animal kingdom," commented Dianne.

"Why?" Connie asked.

"Look at them. Two are snuggled up against our hull. They appear to be studying us with an avid curiosity."

As Dianne finished speaking, the creatures that were pressing against the hull on either side moved away and were replaced by two others. "These two are just as curious as the last two," commented Dianne.

Jerry glanced back and fourth between the two animals and said, "I sense intelligence when I look into their eyes."

"I do too," agreed Connie, "and this is kind of spooky."

"What do you mean?" Jerry asked.

"Have you ever wondered what it would be like to be in a cage and studied by an intelligent species?"

"No, I haven't, but I see what you mean."

Once again, the animals moved away and were replaced by two others. "They are taking turns observing us," noted Dianne. "I wonder if they're discussing us."

Moose turned up the sound from the exterior microphones. "There is a lot of chatter going on out there," he said.

"Yes, but is that normal chatter or are they discussing us?" Dianne asked.

"If I had to put some money on the line, I would bet that they are discussing us," commented Jerry. "Since they've never seen anything like us, they might be trying to figure out what we are and if we're a threat to them."

"What if they decide we are?" questioned Connie.

"I don't know how they could reach that conclusion," replied Jerry.

"But what if they do?"

"I don't see any way they could hurt us inside this sub. They're only 12 to 15 feet long. They're just not big enough to damage this boat."

"I don't think we have to worry about them even trying," commented Dianne.

"Why do you think that?" Connie asked.

"Take a really good look at them, open your mind, and tell me what you sense."

Connie did as directed. "I feel the presence of fun-loving creatures," she said.

"I do too," Dianne said. "In many ways, these animals remind me of dolphins, but they seem smarter than dolphins."

"Dolphins are fun-loving and intelligent enough to be trained to do some amazing things," commented Connie.

"Would you like to train a couple of these creatures?" Jerry asked.

"No thanks," Connie replied. "I am content to just study them from the safety of this boat."

"But we could learn much more about them with some direct human interaction," argued Jerry.

"You sound serious. Sometimes, I can't tell if you really are serious or if you're just pulling my leg."

Jerry grinned and said, "That might be, but in this case, you can't deny that we could learn more by interacting with them than we can learn by just observing them."

"That's true, but what can we do that won't be dangerous?"

"I would like to surface and walk around on deck."

"That sounds dangerous. What do you hope to learn that justifies the risk?"

"To start with, I don't believe there would be much risk."

"I don't know about that. I believe these animals are fast enough to leap completely out of the water, which means they could knock you off the deck and into the water. Then, you would be at their mercy."

"With the deck rails deployed, it would be difficult for them to knock me off the deck."

"I can tell that you've already decided to do this."

"You know me so well."

Jerry brought the submarine to the surface and deployed the deck rails. The ichthyosaurs stayed with the boat, taking turns pressing against the hull and looking inside.

"They sure are curious," stated Jerry. "I wonder what they're going to do when they see me climb out of here."

Jerry made eye contact with each of the ichthyosaurs looking through the hull; then, he quickly climbed up the ladder, through the hatch, and onto the upper deck. The two ichthyosaurs surfaced on either side of the boat and swam with their heads out of the water. After gazing inquisitively at Jerry for a few seconds, they dropped their heads back into the water and made some chattering sounds.

What happened next really got Jerry's attention. All around the boat, ichthyosaurs surfaced and swam with their heads out of the water. They stared at Jerry and made barking, squawking sounds to each other.

Moose joined Jerry and said, "We seem to be surrounded by creatures from the Mesozoic era, and they sure are noisy."

"They're talking about us with lots of enthusiasm," stated Dianne, who had just climbed on deck.

"I wish I could understand their language," Jerry said.

"There's more to language than understanding individual sounds," commented Dianne.

"What are you getting at?" questioned Jerry.

"When you listen to the overall tone, what's your impression?"

"It sounds like the chatter you hear at a party where people are having fun."

"That's the feeling I get, which indicates they might be enjoying our presence."

"Why would they enjoy having us around?"

"I don't know for certain, but intelligence and curiosity frequently go hand-in-hand. We are a puzzle for them to solve, and they seem to be engaged in enthusiastic speculation."

"Whatever it is they're saying, their temperament is a dramatic contrast to that of the lupusaurs," noted Jerry. "Every contact any of us have ever had with them has resulted in them attacking."

"How do you know these animals aren't planning to attack?" asked Connie, who was now on deck.

"I don't know that for sure, but they look like well fed fish eaters who enjoy life and avoid combat."

"How do they avoid combat when they share this bay with elasmosaurs?" Connie asked.

"I believe this pod could kill an elasmosaurus."

Connie looked at the ichthyosaurs. "Their jaws are lined with what look like shark teeth," she said.

"Now picture in your mind what would happen if an elasmosaurus grabbed one of these guys."

"The rest of the pod would probably attack and chew its long neck to shreds."

"What a bloody mess that would be," commented Dianne.

"It's a bloody mess that the elasmosaurus could not possibly survive," stated Jerry. "If they have any brains at all, it seems like they would stay away from ichthyosaurus pods and avoid provoking mass attack."

"I agree with that," stated Dianne. "These ichthyosaurs might have the fun-loving nature of dolphins, but they don't have the blunt snouts that dolphins have. Their elongated, teeth-lined jaws just have to be awesome weapons. I sure wouldn't want one of them coming after me."

"How long are we going to hang around here?" Moose asked. "I'm ready to go fishing."

"We might have to wait until they leave us," commented Jerry. "This boat isn't fast enough to outrun them, and we're not going to get close to fish when we're surrounded by ichthyosaurs."

"Okay, let me rephrase the question, how long are they going to hang around us?"

"I don't know, but they don't look like they're in any hurry to leave."

"So how are we going to shake them?"

"We have to figure out something, because I am ready to give you some fishing lessons."

"We'll see who gets the lessons," retorted Moose.

"Before you guys get all jacked around by your fishing egos, there is an experiment I want to conduct," stated Dianne.

"What do you have in mind?" Jerry asked.

"Intelligent, playful animals will sometimes mimic human behavior."

"And you think these guys might fit into that mold?"

"I want to find out by presenting them with a simple task. I brought along a brightly colored beach ball, hoping to meet this kind of animal."

Dianne dropped into the submarine and came back with the ball, which was red, white, and blue, and 12 inches in diameter. It was tightly inflated and made out of tough, heavy-duty plastic. "I want you and Moose to get on opposite ends of the deck and throw the ball back and forth. Also, I want you to jump up and down a bit and gleefully act like you're having a blast."

The men did as requested. "You have their attention," Dianne said. "In fact, there's one over there who just isn't taking his eyes off the ball. Try throwing it at him."

Jerry tossed the ball toward the ichthyosaur. It rose partly out of the water and batted the ball back to Jerry with a quick head movement.

"He passed the test," declared Dianne.

"What do you want to try next?" Jerry asked.

"Throw it a few yards in front of him."

Jerry aimed the ball five yards in front of the ichthyosaur. Its eyes followed the ball's flight as it swam to meet it. The animal's timing was perfect. He arrived when the ball did and batted it back to Jerry.

"He's good," commented Dianne.

"Considering that he's never done this before, it is an amazing performance."

"That's true, but these animals have to be quick and accurate with their head movements. That's how they catch fish."

"What do you want to try next?"

"If we could get them to bat the ball around among themselves, we could leave while they're preoccupied."

Jerry threw the ball at a different animal, but it batted it back to him. Jerry pointed at the first animal, which was expectantly watching him. While holding the ball out, he pointed at it, then at the second animal.

"Now, they're both looking at you with eager anticipation," noted Dianne, "and they seem to understand."

Jerry passed the ball to the first animal, who batted it to the second animal, who batted it back to Jerry. "How is your experiment going so far?" he asked Dianne.

"They've convinced me that they're intelligent and playful."

"I believe they're also friendly, but I'm not yet ready to dive in and go swimming with them."

Dianne and Jerry continued the experiment, bringing additional animals into the game. Eventually, Dianne said, "I think we've learned all we can for the time being, so let's leave and let them keep the ball."

"How do you plan to do that?" Jerry asked. "Every time we toss it to them, they bat it right back."

"Let's just leave it on deck and dive. I'm sure they'll pick it up and continue the game until they tire of it."

"It would be interesting to see what they do with us out of the picture."

"Great idea," responded Dianne.

Jerry went below, returned with an RPV, programmed it to keep an eye on the ball, and launched it. "Okay, everyone below, we're going to dive," he said.

Jerry passed the ball one more time, and when it came back, he placed it on deck and went below. Immediately, he put the submarine into a dive.

Back on the shuttle, Mike's arms were aching painfully, but his long struggle with the fish was coming to a conclusion. He had succeeded in bringing it to the surface.

"That sure is a strange looking fish," commented Michelle.

"It resembles Earth's freshwater sturgeon, and it looks like it might weigh 200 pounds or more."

"And you're going to use that fish for bait," teased Michelle.

"No way! It's heading for the cooler, if we manage to land it."

"How are we going to do that? It's huge!"

"I wasn't expecting anything this big, so I'm missing an important piece of gear. I need you to go to my locker and get my gaff."

"What's a gaff?"

"It's a pole about six feet long with a steel hook on one end."

"Is it safe to leave you here without a guard?"

"The sonar hasn't sounded an alarm, and I don't see any pterodactyls."

"I'll be right back." Michelle ran into the shuttle and quickly returned with the gaff.

"I need to move this fish around the wingtip to the outboard trailing edge, where I will be closer to the water."

"That shouldn't be difficult. He looks exhausted."

"I am too."

Mike walked along the wing's leading edge and patiently guided the fish to the wingtip, then around it to the trailing edge. He handed the fishing pole to Michelle. "Keep the pole bent like this to maintain tension in the line," he said.

"Got it, but I don't see how you're going to lift that huge fish out of the water."

"As tired as I am, I don't think I can, so I'm going to deflect that aileron down into the water and use it as a ramp."

Mike turned on his wrist computer, accessed the shuttle's flight controls, and deflected the aileron. He picked up the gaff and hooked the fish behind its lower jaw. Using pure determination, Mike found the strength to drag the heavy fish up the aileron and onto the wing. He pulled the weakly struggling fish well away from the water. He drew his hunting knife, and with his weight behind the thrust, he jammed the knife through the fish's skull and into its brain. The fish quivered for a few seconds, then lay still.

Mike sat down next to the fish and relaxed his aching, exhausted muscles. "It only took an hour, but I've got my fish. If it's anything like Earth's sturgeon, we have some delicious seafood dishes to look forward to."

"And I have a husband who is going to have stiff, sore muscles for a few days."

"That's okay. I plan to spend them being lazy on the island.

Maybe I'll fire up Moose's smokehouse and see what kind of smoke-cured fish I can come up with."

"I'm sure he'll be more than ready to offer helpful advice."

"He is very talented at making smoke-cured foods, so I will listen."

"I know you're tired, but there is a pair of pterodactyls approaching from the south. We should get this fish out of sight, in case they're hungry."

"You're right, no sense in tempting them."

Mike rose to his feet and hooked the gaff into the fish's lower jaw. Slowly, he dragged it to an open door in the shuttle's fuselage. "This fish might weigh 250 pounds," he said.

After putting the fish away, Mike pulled a hose out of the shuttle, turned on a pump, and washed the blood and fish slime off the wing. When the job was finished, he said, "I am going to relax and enjoy the balmy sea air and sunshine for a while."

"I'll trust your sonar and join you, but I'm keeping my rifle handy. The pterodactyls have disappeared, but there may be others in the area."

"You worry too much."

"I see that you're wearing your pistol, and it's probably armed with explosive bullets."

"Well, we do live on an alien planet that we're still learning about."

"It might be an alien planet, but I love it here. It's so primitive and pristine."

"I love it here too."

Meanwhile, on the submarine, Jerry said, "We're a half-mile away, and they haven't followed us."

"Let's surface and see what they're doing," Dianne said.

When the submarine's radio antenna was above water, Dianne tuned in to the RPV's signal. Wearing a video headset, she watched the ichthyosaurs. "They're having a party with their new toy," she said.

Speaking to Connie, Jerry said, "And you didn't think we could train them."

"I'm not sure we did," Connie replied. "It's obvious that they're fun-loving, and I suspect that they might be intelligent enough to invent their own games for the toy we gave them."

"It looks to me like they've done exactly that," Dianne said.

"They've formed two groups of four with open water between them, and they're batting the ball back and forth. The rest of the animals appear to be spectators."

"That was quick," commented Jerry. "I wonder what level they're able to think on."

"I don't know," responded Dianne, "but I would like to check in on them occasionally and present them with additional toys to see what they do."

"How will we find this pod in this large bay?" Jerry asked.

"If they hang onto that ball, we'll find them. It has three radio transmitters built into it."

"I thought you said that it's a beach ball."

"It is, but I had Mike build some special capabilities into it."

"So, what if we come back in a few days and find the ball but no ichthyosaurs?"

"That would tell us something about them."

"I don't mean to interrupt your discussion," Moose said, "but the fish are only 200 yards away, and I'm ready to catch a couple."

"I think I'll let you do that before I put my line in the water," responded Jerry. "I want to see what I have to beat."

"It doesn't matter when you get your line wet. You're not going to out-fish me anyway."

"So far, you haven't shown me anything except talk."

"Stay tuned and you'll see the results of real talent."

"Is it my imagination, or is it really getting windy out here?"

Moose ignored Jerry's comment and selected one of his new lures. "This one should do the job," he said. "If not, I have a never-fail backup. Give me a speed of about three mph."

Moose dropped his new lure into the water and watched its action. "You might want to look at this," he said to Jerry. "This is how a real lure works."

Jerry looked at the ten-inch-long, triple-jointed lure. Each of its four sections moved with a jerky, exaggerated motion. "It looks like a fish with a spastic nervous condition that's struggling to swim," he said.

"It's intended to look like easy prey," Moose said. "Now that you've seen it, you're probably worried about the outcome of our contest."

"I haven't seen it catch anything yet."

"You will," stated Moose as he glanced at his wrist sonar monitor. "The fish are about 40 feet down, so I have to add some weight."

Moose added a one-ounce sinker, cast the lure out, and fed out additional line. He glanced at his wrist monitor. "My lure should enter the school in a few seconds," he said.

"What if they aren't hungry?" Jerry asked.

"There are thousands of fish down there. Some of them are bound to be hungry."

Moose's fishing rod bent sharply. "What did I just tell you?" he said.

Jerry stopped the motor and let the boat drift. Moose was using heavy-duty tackle and was prepared for a large fish. Even so, the struggle between man and fish was well fought and continued for quite some time.

Suddenly, the sonar system sounded an urgent alarm. Connie, who had been watching the monitor inside the submarine, quickly climbed on deck with her rifle in hand. "A huge creature is zooming up from the bottom!" she yelled.

She had hardly finished speaking, when the head and long neck of an elasmosaurus broke the surface only 40 yards away. The beast had Moose's fish in its mouth. Whipping its head upward, it pulled line off Moose's reel at a furious pace. Then, it spotted the submarine and its crew and glared at them with savage ferocity.

It only took the elasmosaurus a few seconds to decide what it wanted to do. Crunching down on Moose's fish, it bit a huge chunk out of its mid-section. In one quick gulp, the beast swallowed the chunk of fish in its mouth, while the tail and head fell into the water.

Immediately, the elasmosaurus coiled its long neck back against its body and lunged toward the humans. With quick tail and flipper strokes, it reached incredible speed surprisingly fast. Its neck uncoiled, driving its head forward with the speed of a striking rattlesnake.

Connie saw the wide-open, teeth-filled mouth coming right at her. Instantly, she pointed and fired from the hip. The explosive bullet struck the beast's neck where it joined the body, and the bullet exploded between two vertebrae, nearly severing the neck.

The monster's head missed Connie by inches and hung over the deck rail behind her, while the long neck draped across the deck and shook vigorously with convulsing muscle spasms. Even though the animal was mortally wounded, its heart was still working, and it pumped gush after gush of blood out of the open wound with each beat, rapidly coloring the water crimson red.

"We have to get out of here!" yelled Jerry. "With all that blood, there's bound to be a feeding frenzy here real soon."

"We have to get this long neck off our boat!" Connie shouted.

"It's too heavy to lift," exclaimed Jerry. "We have to dive out from under it."

Not wanting to lose his prized new lure, Moose had already frantically reeled it in. He looked at the fish head the lure was hooked into. "Not much left of this fish," he said, while holding it up.

Jerry glanced at it briefly and exclaimed, "We can study your trophy later. Right now, I need everyone inside."

Suddenly, the water came alive with dozens of predators savagely attacking the mortally wounded elasmosaurus. The shark-like creatures aggressively competed for mouthfuls of flesh.

"That was quick," stated Jerry. "Where did they come from? How did they get here so fast?"

"I don't know," exclaimed Dianne, "but they're still coming, and they're getting bigger."

"Let's get out of here," shouted Connie. "We're in the middle of a shark feeding frenzy, and we're too close to the water." A ten-foot shark leapt out of the water and tore a chunk out of the elasmosaurus neck only a couple feet in front of Connie's face. She reflexively jumped back.

Two seconds later, Connie was inside the submarine. Dianne and Moose were right behind her. Jerry dropped through the hatch and closed it. He immediately put the submarine into a shallow dive, but he kept it close to the action. "Now, we can watch in safety," he said.

Turning to Connie, he said, "That was close. Thanks for being so quick with your rifle."

"You guys were so preoccupied with your fishing that you just threw all caution to the wind."

"That's not exactly true," countered Jerry. "We were relying on the sonar to warn us of approaching danger, and it did sound the alert."

"It only gave us a few seconds, and that might not have been enough, if I hadn't been glued to the sonar screen."

"Okay, I was taken by surprise. I expected more than just a few seconds warning. Where did that thing come from that it got here so quickly?"

"Apparently, it was lying on the bottom," Dianne speculated. "Playing dead on the bottom might be one of its hunting strategies."

"That makes as much sense as anything," commented Jerry. "The frantic struggle of the fish Moose caught most likely grabbed its attention."

"It did select that fish to attack," stated Connie.

"It robbed me of a prize winning catch," stated Moose.

"Instead of complaining, you should be happy that you're still alive," commented Dianne.

"I am, but we face the possibility of death every day, and I'm not going to quit having fun because of that. I am just going to be more careful."

"I am glad to hear that," responded Dianne.

"I did manage to save my magnificent new lure. Once these sharks have stripped this carcass clean, they'll be well fed. And the local elasmosaurus is out of the picture, so I should be able to safely put my new lure back in the water."

"I will beat whatever you catch," stated Jerry.

"I can't believe this," exclaimed Connie. "After what just happened, you guys are going to go ahead with your egomania fishing contest."

"Why not?" questioned Jerry. "Moose's reasoning is sound, and we did come here for adventure."

It only took the sharks a few minutes to reduce the elasmosaurus down to its skeleton, which sunk. One by one, the sharks swam off in different directions, and small fish and sea birds cleaned up the scraps. Slowly, the water cleared as the spilled blood steadily diffused into an ever larger volume of water. In less than a half-hour, the sea around the submarine looked normal. Except for the skeleton lying on the bottom, the once mighty elasmosaurus had disappeared.

"Let's go fishing," Jerry said, as he brought the submarine back to the surface.

"I'm ready," stated Moose.

"Maybe this time, you could land a complete fish, instead of just its head."

"How exciting would that be? What I mean is whatever happens today, you're not likely to come up with a fishing story that tops mine."

"I hope you're right about that."

As it turned out, Moose was correct. During the next hour, he and Jerry each landed two fish without incident. They were migratory fish similar to Earth's king salmon.

Who won the contest? Well, Moose claimed victory for catching the biggest fish, 117 pounds. But Jerry also claimed victory, because his two fish had a combined weight of 195 pounds; whereas, Moose's two fish totaled 181 pounds.

When the submarine returned to the shuttle, the adventurers were warmly greeted by Mike and Michelle. Immediately after the greetings, Mike turned to Moose and said, "I heard you successfully landed a fish head today. That must have required tremendous talent."

"You're keying in on the wrong part of the story," Moose protested.

"What do you mean?"

"While it's true that I only landed a fish head, the story is far bigger than that. I actually had a monster on the line, and I challenge you to come up with a fishing story that tops that."

"I can't. You definitely have all the honors when it comes to monsters."

"It was huge and staring right at me."

"That must have been terrifying."

"It was, but Connie saved the day with a quick shot. After the sharks cleaned up the mess and things got back to normal, I tapped into my vast reservoir of fishing talent and won the contest."

"How much did the winning fish weigh?"

"One hundred seventeen pounds," Moose proudly proclaimed.

"How many did you catch?"

"Two."

"And together, they weighed how much?"

"One hundred eighty one pounds."

"It seems like a man with your talent should be able to beat that with just one fish."

"Maybe you and I should have a contest. Then, you could show me how it's done."

"That sounds like a good idea," responded Mike.

"Okay, but I don't want to hear any whining when you go down in defeat."

"I'll prepare myself for that, but in the meantime, I need your help for a little project I have planned for tomorrow."

"Sure, what do you need?"

"I caught a small fish today, and I need some tips on how to smoke it."

"No problem. I have some big fish to smoke tomorrow, anyway, so I could slip a small one into the process. What did you catch?"

"I have it stored in the forward cargo hold. Let's go look at it."

Mike let Moose lead the way. When he entered the cargo hold and spotted Mike's fish, he exclaimed, "Wow! What's that?"

"That's just a little something I picked up while you and Jerry were jawboning each other about some fishing contest."

"It looks like a sturgeon, and it's huge. How did you catch that?"

"Well, you know how it is. Prize-wining talent just always seems to find the big ones. How much did you say your contest wining fish weighs?"

"Not as much as this one," Moose grumbled.

"That almost sounded like whining."

"It wasn't whining; it was envy. How could you keep so quiet about catching something so big?"

"I didn't want to bother you and Jerry when you were busy with your contest."

"Baloney! You knew you had us beat and wanted to get maximum mileage out of trouncing us, so you waited until now to lay it on me."

Mike grinned smugly and said, "Judging from your reaction, I would say I succeeded."

"You won this one, but your record catch will not stand. I will beat it."

"I'm sure you will, but until that happens, I'll just have to sit back and savor the flavor of my victory. Speaking of flavor, I would appreciate your help in smoking some of this. When it comes to food preparation, your capability is top-notch."

"At least, I'm getting due respect for some of my talent. But you'll have to tell me how you caught this fish if you want me to help you cure it."

"I can do that."

"I don't want you leaving out any of the details."

"You can count on that."

A few minutes later, the cargo shuttle lifted off, and Jerry put it on course for Pioneer Island. "I trust everyone had enough fun for one day," he said.

"I'm ready for a few days of peace and quiet," responded Connie.

"I'll help you with that," offered Jerry.

Chapter Eighteen

TIME: Day 41, 3:00 PM

Moose, Mike, and Jerry were home relaxing in the shade of a large tree, waiting for the smoke curing process to run its course. "The fish should be almost done," commented Mike.

"It won't be done until the master chef determines that it has reached perfection," asserted Moose.

"Maybe it's time for the master to taste some of it and even seek out a second opinion," suggested Jerry.

"I could certainly nibble on some and give out an opinion," volunteered Mike.

"I believe it's a bit too soon," noted Moose, "but if you guys insist, we'll try it."

Turning to Jerry, Mike laughed and said, "It sounds like he wants us to believe that he's going to taste freshly smoked fish only because we're forcing him to."

"And right after that, he's going to tell us about his finely tuned sense of taste and how it enables him to create and appreciate the ultimate in gourmet food."

"You guys can snicker all you want, but my creations are appreciated by one and all."

"I'm ready to sample this creation," stated Mike. "Especially, since I caught the big one."

"I will beat your record," declared Moose, "so enjoy it while you can."

"Right now, I'd just like to enjoy a small piece of it."

"OK! But I don't think it's ready yet," stated Moose, as he reached into the smokehouse with prongs and removed a piece of sturgeon and a piece of salmon. He cut them up and the taste test was on.

"It must be done," stated Mike. "This sturgeon is delicious."

"It is good," agreed Jerry, "but I like the salmon better."

"Once again, the master has come through," commented Moose, "but that's no surprise."

"He is a constant bundle of humility," stated Jerry.

While munching on the fish, Mike said, "In this case, he deserves a standing ovation. This is a delicacy."

"Thank you," responded Moose.

Speaking to Mike, Jerry asked, "Have you heard anything from Kon about the structure repair?"

"No, but I am curious about how they're doing."

Jerry reached for his communicator. "I'll give Trang a call," he said, as he entered the number.

"Hello, this is Trang."

"Hi, this is Jerry. How are you doing with the new beams?"

"We have four installed, and we're almost done with the fifth."

"You're making great progress."

"Our engineers did a terrific job setting this up, and the weak gravity on this moon makes the girders easy to handle."

"When will you be ready to lift off?"

"We're shooting for tomorrow morning."

"Are you going to need anything from us?"

After a few seconds of silence, Trang said, "I don't think so."

"Your hesitation tells me that you're concerned about something."

"I was just running through a mental checklist of possible problems."

"Did you come up with any showstoppers?"

"I don't think so."

"That's not a definite answer. You're worried about something."

"You're right. I am, and I should be. This ship has been out of action for a long time, and anything could happen."

"Is there anything specific that we can help you with?"

"Nothing I can put my finger on."

"I'll accept that for now, but I want to know what's going through your mind."

"Have you ever read about the lives of test pilots and the uncertainty they face when taking up an experimental aircraft that's loaded with new technology?"

"Yes, I have."

"My starship was almost cut in half by a meteorite, and it has been grounded for 30 years."

"So now you feel like a test pilot."

"I don't have untested new technology, but because of extensive damage and time, I do face uncertainty on takeoff. However, I don't believe there's anything you can do for us. We've already done a successful checkout of all crucial systems, including a test of the main engines."

"It sounds like you have everything under control, and you're certainly not going to put any kind of burden on your engines getting off Aphrodite."

"Twelve percent of available power will get us out of here. In fact, I'm not going above 15 percent. In effect, we will be limping our way home."

"I'm guessing you'll be here the day after tomorrow."

"If all goes well, I'll drop in for lunch in two days."

"Lunch?"

"Why do you question that?"

"I'm not questioning your arrival time. It just seems like lunch doesn't fit the occasion. We should be having an all-day party to celebrate the rescue of your people and the return of your starship."

"Great idea! I've waited 30 years for this, and I will definitely be in a fired up mood and ready to let it all out."

"So you do have a wild side."

"I've been accused of that."

"Okay, it's a deal. Day after tomorrow, we'll party all day."

"That's a party I don't want to be late for, so I need to get off the phone and get back to work."

"Let us know if you need anything."

"Will do."

"How big is this party going to be?" asked Moose.

"I think it's safe to assume that all of Trang's people will want to come," replied Jerry.

"The people living on Aphrodite might not be able to come," commented Mike. "They've been living with gravity less than one-tenth g for a very long time, and their bodies might be so weak that they can never return to one g."

"You might be right," stated Jerry. "I'd like to discuss that with Geniya."

"She's on the beach with our wives and children," Mike said.

"They might enjoy eating some of this smoked fish," commented Jerry. "Let's pack some in a basket and join them."

Twenty minutes later, the men stepped off the elevator onto the sandy beach of South Bay. Seeing her father, Denise came running out of the water and across the sand. She grabbed Jerry's left hand and started pulling him toward the water. "Come swimming with me," she pleaded.

"Don't you want to see what's in this basket?"

"I want to take you swimming."

"First, you have to look in the basket," stated Jerry, while setting it on the picnic table.

Denise opened the basket and looked at the smoked fish for about two seconds before she selected a piece and started eating. "This is good," she said.

"Eat as much as you like; then, we'll go swimming."

"How did you know I was hungry?"

"You're always hungry. You are a growing girl, and you are supposed to be hungry."

"Moose makes good fish, and I love it."

"The master chef strikes again," declared Moose.

While everyone feasted on the freshly smoked fish, Jerry asked Geniya, "What is the physical condition of your people on Aphrodite?"

"They've adjusted to the low gravity."

"Does that mean they cannot come here?"

"We hope to bring them here eventually, but they will have to undergo an extended period of rehabilitation first."

"How are you going to do that?"

"We're going to create a controlled artificial gravity environment for them and gradually bring them back to one g."

"I know of only one way you can do that, and you only have two vehicles you can use."

"Unfortunately, you are right. Our shuttle and starship will be tied up for 60 to 90 days. But this is unavoidable. We simply have to restore our people's physical ability to live at one g, so we are going to join our shuttle and starship together with a long tether. We'll spin the combination and use the resulting centrifugal force to subject our people to an ever increasing artificial gravity."

"Your starship is far more massive than your shuttle, so there won't be much artificial gravity produced on it, which means that your people will be living on your shuttle."

"That's correct. We'll start them out at one-tenth g and gradually bring them up to one g."

"And you think it will take 60 to 90 days to rehabilitate them?"

"That's just a guess. We don't have any experience with undoing the effects of living in a one-tenth g environment for 30 years. All we can do is closely monitor their progress and proceed accordingly."

"Dad! I'm done eating. Let's go swimming," Denise insisted.

"I'm coming too," declared Matthew. Then, he turned to his father and said, "I'll race you into the water." Mike was sitting, so Matthew got a head start and won the race.

Once in the water, Matthew said, "Dad, pick me up and throw me, so I can dive." Mike did as requested, and Denise thought it looked like fun, so Jerry had to pick her up and throw her into a dive.

"They're sure having fun," commented Michelle.

"The children love their fathers," stated Connie. "I wish there were more time for them to be together."

"That would be nice, but our husbands actually do quite well, considering all the things that have happened since we arrived here."

"I guess you're right," agreed Connie. "I just wish there were more time for days like today."

Michelle's communicator beeped. It was Zeb. "How is everything on Pioneer Island?" he asked.

"We're having a little picnic on the beach."

"Sounds like fun. I wish we could join you."

"I could talk to Jerry about picking up you and your family. I believe today is out of the question, but tomorrow morning might work."

"If he wants to do that, it will be interesting."

"What do you mean?"

"My children and grandchildren have never been in space. It will be interesting for me to watch them react when they see this planet from hundreds of miles up."

"It will definitely be a fascinating experience for them."

"Why don't you talk to Jerry and get back to me."

"You got it."

TIME: Day 42, 8:15 AM

Jerry's communicator rang out its early morning chimes. He answered it and received an immediate reply. "Good morning! This is Trang. I just wanted to let you know that we're ready to lift off."

"I hope everything goes well for you."

"It should. We just finished another checkout of crucial systems, and everything is working well."

"You only have one more test to run, and that's the most important one."

"We've installed a video camera on a nearby hilltop, so you can watch us. If we're struck by tragedy, you'll know what happened."

"You've done your homework, and I expect to see you here tomorrow."

"The next few minutes will tell the story. You should have video now."

Jerry turned on a large, wall-mounted video screen. "I see your ship," he said.

"Okay, we're ready for the final test."

Jerry watched the crippled starship's main engines ignite and slowly power up. After just a few seconds, the starship seemed to float up off the ground. It slowly gained speed and altitude. "I believe they're going to make it," Jerry said to Connie, who was sitting at the breakfast table with him.

"We should've had Geniya and Akeyco here to watch this with us," responded Connie.

"Don't worry, they're watching."

As time ticked away, the camera continued tracking the starship as it steadily climbed away from Aphrodite. Connie and Jerry watched its progress until it was only a small speck on the video screen.

Once again, Jerry's communicator chimed. It was Trang. "All systems are functioning normally," he said.

"Thanks for the update."

"Man, it feels good to have my starship back, crippled though it is."

"It will take time, but we will restore it."

"Thanks, and I'm ready for that party you're planning for tomorrow."

"Zeb and his family will be here too."

"Good, I want to meet them."

370

"I have to go pick them up this morning."

"Okay, have a great day."

"He sure sounded happy," noted Connie.

"If I were in his shoes, I would be sitting on cloud nine right now."

"I have to go talk to Geniya and Akeyco. I don't want to miss out on what they must be feeling."

"I should get going to Zonya's Island. I have to pick up some people who are eager to come here. Some of them have never been in space, so it's going to be fun to watch their reactions."

"Enjoy yourself."

"You can count on that." Jerry gave Connie a goodbye kiss and said, "See you later."

TIME: Day 42, 11:00 AM

Mike, Michelle, and Jerry flew the cargo shuttle to Crater Lake. Then, Mike and Michelle went to Zonya's Island with the helicopter, picked up Zeb and his family, and returned to the shuttle. While Mike and Jerry prepared the helicopter for stowage inside the cargo bay, Michelle gave Zeb and his family a tour of the spacious shuttle. Zeb's granddaughter, Tara, and grandson, Joeby, were stunned by its size.

"This bird is really big," exclaimed Tara.

"How can something so big fly?" Joeby asked.

"It has a powerful rocket engine," Zeb replied.

"How does a rocket work?" Joeby asked.

"When we get to Pioneer Island, I will make a toy rocket for you and show you how it works."

"Is it scary to go into space?" asked Tara.

"I'm not afraid," exclaimed Joeby. "The Earth people go there all the time. They have a starship."

"Will we see their starship?" Tara asked.

"Not today," replied Zeb, "but next time there's a shuttle going to the starship, I'll ask if we can go along."

"Is the starship bigger than this shuttle?" Joeby asked.

"It is many times bigger."

"How did the Earth people get it into space?" Tara asked.

"They built it in space and used shuttles like this one to carry up the pieces."

"The Earth people must be really smart to do all that," commented Joeby. "Will they teach us to be smart too?"

"What do you want to learn?" asked Zeb.

"I want to learn how to do the things the Earth people do," stated Joeby.

"I do too," declared Tara.

"Maybe we should live on Pioneer Island with them," suggested Zeb. "Then, we can ask them to share their knowledge with us."

"Will they let us live with them?" asked Tara.

"I believe so."

"Is Pioneer Island better than our island?" asked Joeby.

"It is bigger and safer."

"I want to live there," Tara said.

"Me too," declared Joeby.

"You will soon see the island," commented Michelle. "I need to get you seated, because we're going to take off pretty soon."

Tara and Joeby were given window seats in the cargo shuttle's small passenger section. Their parents, Ron-Y and Ricki, were given the other two window seats. Zeb sat next to Joeby, and Zonya sat next to Tara.

Meanwhile, Mike and Jerry completed securing the helicopter to the elevator deck. They lowered it into the shuttle and closed the upper cargo bay doors. Then, they walked into the passenger compartment. "We're ready to go," Jerry said, as he looked at the eager, but apprehensive, faces of his young passengers. However, being seasoned space travelers, Zeb and Zonya looked like relaxed professional astronauts.

While casually glancing at the younger passengers, Mike said, "I'm not sure who is the most wary of this, the children or their parents."

"Let's take off before they worry themselves to death," stated Jerry.

"They might look worried," commented Michelle, "but they are ready to go. You have to understand that this is a giant step for them. They're going from a primitive life directly into the space age."

"That is a giant leap forward," agreed Jerry. "Let's hit them with it, so their stomachs can settle down."

"You guys are the pilots," stated Michelle. "I am the stewardess."

"Since you're the only one who understands their language, that's good," commented Mike.

Jerry and Mike stepped into the cockpit. Michelle stood in front of her passengers and said, "Please make sure your seatbelts are fastened. We'll be taking off in a few moments."

Michelle sat down next to Ricki and said, "Don't be nervous. Just relax and enjoy this."

A muffled whine was heard as the turbine came to life. Slowly, the shuttle started moving under the thrust of its marine propeller. Then, Jerry brought the turbine to full power, and the shuttle accelerated rapidly. It quickly reached 45 mph and rose up out of the water and rode on its hydrofoils. Tara and Joeby pressed their faces to the windows, fascinated by the speed with which the water was rushing by. Then, the powerful NTR roared into action and the resulting acceleration pressed everyone back into their seats. In a matter of seconds, the shuttle lifted off and pitched into a full power climb away from Crater Lake.

The children's emotions were overwhelmed by what was happening. They lost their voices and stared in silent, awestruck fascination at the lake and surrounding jungle, which were swiftly receding. The rapidly accelerating shuttle passed through widely scattered cumulus clouds and swiftly climbed into the stratosphere. It continued climbing and gaining speed. Soon, it was above the atmosphere and in the stark blackness of space.

Tara found her voice. "Why is the sky so dark?" she asked.

"We are above the air that you breathe," replied Zonya. "This planet has the kind of air that makes the sky blue."

"I see stars," exclaimed Joeby.

"In the vacuum of space, you can always see stars," explained Zeb.

The shuttle continued its climb. Jerry decided to follow a high altitude ballistic flight path, rather than, a low level flight path. He wanted to gain an altitude of several hundred miles, so the children could clearly see that they lived on a spherically shaped planet.

Eventually, the shuttle reached the required speed, and Jerry shut down the NTR. Suddenly, it was very quiet in the passenger compartment, and everyone was weightless. "What happened?" Tara asked.

Michelle released her seatbelt and floated into the middle of the compartment. "We will be weightless for at least 15 minutes," she said. "So you may release your seatbelts and drift around for a while."

Tara hesitated. She seemed unsure as to whether this was a good idea. However, Joeby was more adventuresome. Michelle's smile was all the assurance he needed. He left his seat with a bit too much energy, and with nothing to grab onto, shot straight across the compartment, headfirst. He threw out his hands and used his arms to come to a stop, but he put too much effort into the landing and found himself propelled back toward his seat. Zeb caught his grandson and laughed at his first experience with weightlessness.

Joeby laughed too and exclaimed, "This is fun!"

Emboldened by her brother's experience, Tara decided to try it too. Learning from her brother, she left her seat gently and floated slowly toward Michelle. "This is weird," Tara said, "but I like it. Is this how it is on your starship?"

"It's like this now, but during our long voyage, we made artificial gravity."

"I want to visit your starship, so I can float around."

"Someday soon, we'll take you there, but now, you should look out the window at your home."

Tara did as directed. "Where is my home? It isn't flat anymore. It has turned into a round ball."

"It always has been a round ball, but it is so big that it just seems flat when you are down there."

Tara stared out the window, silently struggling to understand the concept that her home wasn't flat, but that she was actually living on a large ball moving through space. For an eight-year old child, this was a huge new perspective on her world and would take time to grasp. "Is Earth a big round ball?" she asked.

"Yes, and it's about the same size as this planet."

Tara turned to her grandmother and asked, "Is the planet you and Zeb came from a big round ball?"

"Yes," replied Zonya, "and it's also about the same size as this one."

"Are all planets round?"

"Yes, but they're not all good places to live. Some are very cold, and others are very hot."

"I like our planet," declared Tara. "It's a good place to live."

Ricki and Ron-Y were glued to the windows while listening to the ongoing discussion. They were determined to soak up an appreciation of their new perception of the planet they lived on. However, when the discussion wound down, they felt a need to experiment with zero-gravity, so they released their seatbelts and floated around the passenger compartment.

The shuttle passed through the peak of its trajectory and began its descent. Minute by minute, time marched forward. Eventually, Mike's voice came through the intercom. "It's time for everyone to be seated. We're only moments away from entering the upper atmosphere."

The shuttle made a steep descent through the atmosphere and leveled off at 3000 feet, before beginning a more moderate gliding descent to a landing on Clear Lake. After cruising into South Bay, Jerry entered the passenger compartment and said, "Welcome to Pioneer Island."

Jerry opened a door in the side of the shuttle and threw out a neatly packaged boat, which self-inflated when it hit the water. He waved at Connie, Denise, and Matthew, who were standing on the beach. Then, he turned to his passengers and said, "Everyone in the boat."

Matthew and Denise weren't about to wait for the boat to come in. They hit the water running and swam toward the shuttle. Already wearing shorts, Mike and Jerry kicked off their shoes, pulled off their shirts, and dove in to meet their children. Being good swimmers, Tara and Joeby didn't want to miss out on the fun, so they followed Mike and Jerry's example.

Zeb turned to Michelle and said, "My ankle's still in a cast. I have to ride the boat."

Facing Zonya, Zeb asked, "What's your excuse?"

"I'm not wearing my swimsuit."

"Your shorts and halter top will do just fine. Why don't you dive in and join our grandchildren."

Zonya was hesitant. She was now in the home of the Earth people and hadn't been introduced to anyone. She felt reserved and wasn't quite sure she should jump in and be rambunctious like the people already in the water, who were yelling and engaged in some sort of playful water fight. When she saw Connie run into the water to join the fray, she needed no additional encouragement. These Earth people have a strange way to welcome visitors, Zonya thought, as she dove in. Ricki jumped in right behind her. Ron-Y helped Zeb into the boat and then dove in too.

Michelle stepped into the boat. "I'll row you ashore," she said.

"I can do that. The only problem I'll have will be getting out of this boat without getting my cast wet, but I can wait for help. I think you should dive in and join the fun."

"I guess my shorts and halter top are perfectly good swimwear."

"You look great, jump in."

Fifteen minutes later, Moose and Dianne came down the elevator carrying a picnic lunch. They put everything on the table and yelled, "Lots of delicious food here in case anyone is hungry."

Moose helped Zeb out of the boat, and he sat down at the outdoor table. The swimmers made their way to the food. Michelle was first and introduced the newcomers to Moose and Dianne.

Midway through lunch, Tara turned to Zeb and said, "The Earth people are fun, and their food is delicious. I want to stay. Will they let us live here?"

Zeb looked into Michelle's eyes, and she passed the question along to Jerry. "Tell Tara they can live here as long as they want," he said.

Speaking directly to Tara, Michelle said, "After lunch, I will show you around your new home."

Tara's eyes opened wide, and a bright beaming smile lit up her face, "We can stay!" she exclaimed, unable to contain her enthusiasm.

"Mom, can I give her and Joeby a ride in our elevator?" Matthew asked.

"I will have to come with you, because they don't understand our language and you don't understand theirs."

"If they're going to live here, I will teach them our language, and they can teach me theirs."

"That's a good idea," responded Michelle.

"I want to help teach them," stated Denise. "It will be fun."

"We might have to invent some word games for them to play," commented Connie.

"Let's see how they do on their own first," suggested Michelle. "I want to find out how imaginative they'll be with this language problem. I'm betting they will cope with it very well."

"Okay, you and I can work with their parents and grandparents. We'll find out who makes the most progress, the children or the adults."

"This will be an interesting competition, but we have a head start, because Zeb already knows quite a bit of English."

"To be fair, the competition will just measure the progress of Tara and Joeby compared to Ricki and Ron-Y."

"I believe we just found the word game you suggested," stated Michelle.

"I see what you mean," responded Connie.

Michelle turned to Matthew and Denise. "We're going to play a word game," she said. "Both of you are going to teach Tara and Joeby. Connie and I are going to teach Ricki and Ron-Y. If you kids learn to converse in English before us adults; then, you win."

"What will the prize be?" Matthew asked.

"I haven't thought of that yet. What do you think it should be?"

"If we win, I want to drive the ATV all the way around the island and take Denise, Tara, and Joeby along."

"You're too young to drive. You might have an accident, and somebody will get hurt."

"I'll be careful, and Dad can come along."

"It's too dangerous. I'll be worried."

"But Mom, Dad can help me drive."

"I'll have to talk to him about that. If he says yes, you can drive around the island."

"That's a deal," Matthew said. "Now, let's go ride the elevator."

"Okay," replied Michelle.

Not wasting any time with the word game challenge, Matthew went to Tara and Joeby and attempted to explain to them with a combination of gestures and words that he wanted them to ride the elevator with him and Denise to the plateau. His enthusiasm proved irresistible. Tara and Joeby left the table and followed him and Denise. "Come along," he said to Michelle.

"It looks like we have some capable contestants," Connie said to Michelle.

"I believe you're right, so I want you to make some progress for our side by explaining to the adults where we're going and get them to come to the plateau with you."

"It's going to be tough to beat that performance your son put on."

"I've seen you communicate with King and Queen. Surely, you can communicate with Ricki and Ron-Y."

"Of course, I can. I was only recognizing that our children are going to be tough contestants if they're able to maintain their enthusiasm."

"It's up to us to make sure that they do. After all, we do want them to win."

"You're right about that. See you on the plateau."

When Michelle arrived at the elevator, the children were already onboard. Tara and Joeby appeared apprehensive, but Denise and Matthew weren't showing any fear, so they couldn't either. They wanted to do whatever the Earth children did. It was a simple matter of peer pressure.

Michelle turned on the elevator and the open air cage began its ascent. The elevator was sturdy and safe, but the cage was hanging on the end of a rope that was being reeled in by a winch on top the cliff. Even though the cage was stabilized by guide ropes, it still had some side motion and made creaking noises. Matthew and Denise had ridden the elevator many times and had learned to ignore the noises and extraneous motions, but Tara and Joeby seemed nervous about every creak and wiggle.

The elevator steadily ascended the face of the 150-foot cliff. Matthew and Denise looked down at the activity on the beach. It was obvious that they enjoyed height and the views that came with it.

When they reached the cliff top, Matthew immediately became a tour guide. He wasn't at all concerned that Tara and Joeby didn't understand him; he would teach them words later. For now, he just wanted to show them his world. He pointed at a distant island toward the south and said, "Zeb lived there until we found him." Pointing at Western Island, he said, "King and Queen live there." Pointing at the distant shoreline and mountains to the east, he said, "Giant dinosaurs live over there." Pointing northeast, he said, "Mystery Lagoon is far away over there. It has huge waterfalls, and we found Akeyco near the falls. She was hurt, but we saved her." Pointing at the tents and small temporary houses on the plateau, Matthew said, "We live here, and you can live here with us."

Tara and Joeby soaked up the picturesque views that existed in every direction. They were most amazed by the huge body of water that surrounded Pioneer Island. It was in dramatic contrast to the small river that surrounded Zonya's Island. "Lupusaurs could never come here," Joeby said to his sister.

"We will be safe here," agreed Tara.

TIME: Day 43, 8:30 AM

Jerry's communicator rang. It was Trang. "We're here," he said, jubilantly.

"Where is 'here'?" Jerry asked.

"We've just entered a 250-mile high orbit around Alcent."

"It sounds like your journey from Aphrodite was uneventful."

"It was, and I'm happy to say that my starship is functional, even though, it is badly crippled."

"I'm glad you had a safe trip."

"Are we still on for the party?"

"You bet."

"What time does it start?"

"Whenever you get here."

"How many are you prepared to entertain?"

"All of you are welcome to come."

"Good! All of my people want to come. They are a happy bunch right now."

"When do you expect to arrive?"

"I will be docking with my shuttle in less than an hour. A couple hours after that, we'll be there."

"It seems like that schedule doesn't give you enough time to pick up your people."

"They're already on the shuttle. They came up here to see this starship and visit with their colleagues who have been stranded on Aphrodite."

"I can understand that."

"What does the lunchtime menu look like? Should we eat before we get there, or should we show up hungry?"

"You should show up starving. We've built a large barbecue pit on the beach. We have plenty of fresh steak and fish, plus a variety smoked meats and fish. Also, we have all the side dishes."

"You're making me hungry."

"Good!"

"See you later."

"We'll be there."

TIME: Day 43, 11:45 AM

Nearly everyone was on the beach of South Bay preparing for the day's festivities. However, Geniya, Akeyco, Connie, and Jerry were on the plateau overlooking the beach. They wanted to see the arrival of the shuttle from the cliff top.

Suddenly, a sonic boom jolted everyone's senses. High in the northwestern sky, Jerry spotted a glint of sparkling light. He focused on it with binoculars and resolved the shape of Trang's shuttle as it banked into a tight, diving, 180-degree turn. Flying south over the eastern half of Clear Lake, it quickly lost altitude until Trang leveled off and headed for Pioneer Island. He landed on hydrofoils south of the island and cruised into South Bay.

"It's time to show Trang my new toy," Jerry said.

"You aren't really going to do this, are you?" Connie asked.

"Why not?"

"What if you don't make it all the way to his shuttle?"

"Then, I'll get wet."

Jerry picked up his newly assembled hang glider. He waited until a door opened in the fuselage of Trang's shuttle and Trang and several others stepped out onto the wing. Jerry ran to the edge of the cliff, jumped off, and yelled, "Let the party begin!"

He glided over the beach, then, over the water on his way to Trang's shuttle. He did his best to pilot the glider as perfectly as possible. He did not want to land in the water. Jerry's piloting skills paid off. He landed on the outboard part of the wing Trang and his people were standing on. Facing the new arrivals, Jerry said, "Welcome to Pioneer Island."

"I thought we were the ones dropping in for a party," exclaimed Trang with a boisterous laugh. "You never told me you had a hang glider."

"It's been here for a few days. I just haven't had time to assemble it, but since we're having a party, I put it together this morning. I thought we could have some fun with it."

"It's obvious that you enjoyed your leap of faith."

"Yeah, I did. It was wild, and now that I've shown you how it's done, it's your turn."

"What kind of scheme is that? I just got my starship back, and now, you want me to jump off a cliff."

"It's not exactly how you're making it sound. Besides, it seems like it was just yesterday that you told me you have a wild side."

"That's true, but I wasn't expecting this when I said that."

"Does that mean you're getting too old for the thrill of jumping off a cliff?"

"OK! I'll do it. Then, I'll be ready to check out all that food you told me about."

"Several minutes later, Jerry and Trang were on top the cliff. "This thing is easy to fly," Jerry said. "Just hang onto it like this and control it by shifting your weight around."

"Looks simple enough," replied Trang.

"You are a pilot, so flight control is in your blood, but do you have the guts to jump?"

"What choice do I have after watching you? I'll never live this down if I don't go for it."

"You're right about that."

Trang took a deep breath, ran, and jumped. He controlled the hang glider like an old pro and landed on the wing of his shuttle. Some of his people were still on the wing waiting for the boat to return. Trang looked at them and said, "Who wants to be next?"

A young woman stepped forward and said, "I'll jump. It looks like fun."

A few minutes later, Trang was on the beach filling a plate with food. He sat down next to Jerry. "What other surprises do you have for me?"

"That's the only one, and you'll have to admit that it was a thrilling ride."

"Yeah, it's not everyday that I have the opportunity to jump off a cliff."

"Here comes another jumper, one of your people. I predict that glider will be in use all day."

"I hope we don't kill anybody with that thing," stated Trang.

"It's very forgiving. I don't know how you could screw up with it."

"We'll trust them to stay alive and have fun."

"There won't be any problems."

"You were right about this food," commented Trang. "It's delicious. I believe I'll gain some weight today."

"That's what supposed to happen at parties," stated Geniya, who just arrived with a food tray. Behind her were Connie and Akeyco.

"Whose idea was this party?" Akeyco asked.

"I think it just sort of happened," replied Jerry.

"Spontaneous parties are the best kind," commented Connie.

"I'm glad it happened," Akeyco said. "Our people and your people are getting acquainted in a fun-filled setting."

Connie looked around. "They're not having any problem finding ways to entertain themselves."

"That should be easy," Geniya said. "They could easily spend all day discussing our home planets."

"We're in the early stages of blending our cultures together," stated Connie, "and this party is perfect for that."

"Don't forget the unique cultural background of Zeb and Zonya," added Michelle, who had just arrived.

"Each of our cultures has something special to offer," stated Akeyco. "We can create a strong society with a bright future if we unite and share our special strengths."

"Unique cultural strengths are important," noted Jerry, "but physical assets are also important. If we form one society, we will own two starships, three space shuttles, an airplane with global range, a submarine, and a helicopter. That's an awesome collection of high-tech equipment for a society with a population under 100."

"That equipment gives us strength and capability far beyond our numbers," stated Trang. "There is no doubt about it; we must unite and go into the future together."

"I have two people with me who want to form a special union," Michelle announced.

"And who would they be?" Connie asked, while smiling at Zeb and Zonya.

"You guessed it," responded Michelle. "They want to get married."

"When?" Jerry asked.

"Today," Michelle replied.

"That was quick. It seems they just met only a few days ago," Jerry teased.

Michelle translated Jerry's comment to Zeb and Zonya. After thinking about it for a few moments, Zonya said, "Tell Jerry that when he brought us back together, our romance was as exquisite as a bottle of fine wine that had been aged for 30 years."

Michelle did as requested, and Jerry said, "I don't believe a properly aged bottle of fine wine should be kept waiting, so let's get them married. What kind of ceremony do they want?"

"Since I am the only one who understands their language, they want me to conduct the ceremony, and they want the two starship captains and their wives to sign on as witnesses. Also, Ron-Y and Ricki will be witnesses."

"Before we do this, I need to go to my shuttle," Trang said. "I have something that is fitting for this occasion."

Jerry turned on the loudspeakers he had set up for the party and announced, "In 20 minutes, we are going to have a wedding ceremony for Zeb and Zonya right here on the beach. You are all invited to attend. Come as you are."

Everyone came, and the wedding took place under a blue sky contrasted by a few fluffy white cumulus clouds. A gentle breeze rustled through the trees in the forest, which complimented the soft splashing sound of the surf. Against this background, a chorus of cheerful songbirds preoccupied with the mating season provided appropriate music. At the conclusion of the ceremony, Zeb kissed the bride. And of course, some of the women shed tears, as seems to be the case at many weddings.

Trang picked up a bag behind him, pulled out a bottle, and handed it to Zonya. "I've been saving this for a special occasion," he said. "It is a bottle of fine wine from Proteus. It is 150 years old."

Michelle translated Trang's remarks to Zeb and Zonya. Realizing the extra special nature of the gift, tears came to Zonya's eyes. "Tell Trang thank you," she said.

Michelle did as requested. Then, Zonya continued, "Today is a very special occasion deserving of the opening of this treasure. We are celebrating the union of three cultures. I propose that Zeb, Trang, and Jerry share the first wine from this bottle in a toast to our union."

Michelle translated while Zonya poured three small glasses of wine. The men raised them high. "To a bright future for all of us," Jerry said. Then, the men sipped the wine in unison.

"I propose the second toast for our wedding couple," stated Trang.

Zonya handed the bottle to Trang, who poured two small glasses of wine for Zeb and Zonya. They joined hands and used their other hands to hold the glasses high. "May your love last forever," Trang said, "and may you find strength, security, and freedom in our new society."

Zeb and Zonya sipped on their wine and thanked Trang for the special wish. Everyone cheered for the wedding couple, whose union added a romantic touch to the birth of a new nation springing from different planets, a nation truly formed from an interstellar melting pot.

Book Review

Thank you for reading *Alcent Adventures*. I hope that you enjoyed it. This is my second book, and it is important to me to find out what you think of it. Please take a few minutes to answer the following questions:

Did you enjoy the story? _____ Why? _____

_____

_____

_____

_____

What did you like the most about the story? _____

_____

_____

_____

_____

If you could change one or two things in the story, what would you change?

_____

_____

_____

_____

I am currently writing a sequel. If you could have two or three things happen in the sequel, what would they be? _____

_____

_____

_____

_____

Would you like to be notified when the sequel is available for purchase? _____

If so, please print your name, address and phone number:

_____

_____

_____

_____

Thank you for completing this book review. Please send it to:

Daniel L. Pekarek
Alcent Adventures
P.O. Box 23781
Federal Way, Washington 98093-0781

DL Pekarek @ aol.Com